Passion Working Overtime

Marcus's body trembled when she sighed and leaned against his chest. Not that he needed much encouragement. He planted firm kisses along her jawline that led to her mouth, which he took greedily. With both arms wrapped around her, Marcus answered her sighs with a moan. Office sounds right outside his door faded away. The ticking from the brass clock on his desk seemed to slow down. After a deliciously long time they parted.

"I think we just broke about five company rules," Nicole said, her eyes still closed. Seconds later, she opened them and smiled.

Marcus felt as if he'd been turned upside down, held by his ankles, and given a hard shake. He took a deep breath and tried to step away. Nicole held on tight.

"You're the boss," he murmured, still captivated by the bad-girl gleam in her eyes, and bent his face lower for another kiss . . .

Also by Lynn Emery

GOTTA GET NEXT TO YOU
TELL ME SOMETHING GOOD
ALL I WANT IS FOREVER

LYNN EMERY

Kiss Lonely Goodbye

HarperTorch
An Imprint of HarperCollins*Publishers*

HARPERTORCH
An Imprint of HarperCollins*Publishers*
10 East 53rd Street
New York, New York 10022-5299

Copyright © 2003 by Margaret Hubbard
ISBN: 0-06-008929-6

First HarperTorch paperback printing: August 2003

HarperCollins ®, HarperTorch™, and ❦™ are trademarks of Harper-Collins Publishers Inc.

Printed in the United States of America

Visit HarperTorch on the World Wide Web at www.harpercollins.com

10 9 8 7 6 5 4 3 2 1

one

"We shall all greatly miss our dear brother. He left behind loving family and a host of friends."

"You're at the wrong funeral, Rev," Nicole muttered. She slid to the left to avoid a jab from her mother's elbow.

She gazed at her least favorite great-uncle, the late Hosea Summers. Dressed in a thousand-dollar black pinstriped suit, he lay in a fancy, gunmetal gray slate coffin with real brass trim.

In accordance with his wishes, the family had brought Uncle Hosea home to Lafayette Parish for his final rest. Nicole's mother and father had arranged the services at Sacred Heart Catholic Church. Uncle Hosea had always said he didn't want to be buried in Houston, Texas. He mostly got what he wanted. Great Uncle Hosea's pet name for Nicole had been "That smart-mouthed rug rat." He'd rattle off the words in that gruff steel pad voice that made her want to kick his shins. Which she did regularly from age three to fifteen. Enough was enough. She caught Reverend Paine's eye, then tapped her wristwatch.

Reverend Paine stammered, then rumbled on a few seconds longer and ended with a prayer. The organist did her job with a mournful version of "Nearer My God to Thee." The large extended Summers family filed by to pay their last respects with dutifully serious expressions.

At six feet two, Stanton Summers was still a commanding physical presence despite his sixty years. Nicole had inherited his stature and her mother's temperament. Nicole's father was the only mourner who seemed genuinely touched. He stood at the casket, while the rest filed by with only cursory glances. Nicole joined him. She tried to work up some bit of sentimentality, failed, and gave a mental shrug.

"Come on, Daddy." Nicole tugged at his arm.

"Unc was a pain in the ass most of the time, but he was a hell of a businessman. He would have been pleased with the turnout," Stanton said as he looked around.

"Yeah, he could insult everyone at once," Nicole joked. She followed his gaze at their colorful assortment of relatives. "Maybe I should carry on his legacy. I know exactly what he'd say about Aunt Cora's latest husband. Then there's Cousin Elton. He—"

"Behave, Nikki," Stanton broke in with a frown. "Anyway, Uncle Hosea lived and died the way he wanted."

"Slumped over a thick financial report. The king was in his counting house, counting out his money," Nicole said, repeating an old nursery rhyme her great-grandfather sang to her as a toddler.

"Hell of a businessman," Stanton repeated, missing the sarcasm of Nicole's response.

A couple came up to offer condolences just then. While they talked to her father, Nicole's attention wandered. Slowly the large room had filled with people from the service. Many had come in late only to make an appearance. A tall man with wide shoulders walked in a side door behind a woman with twin five-year-old boys. His steel gray suit molded to his well-developed body like only fine silk-blend fabric could. The newcomer had skin the color of mink, expressive cocoa brown eyes, and a full mouth that could inspire hot fantasies. He wore a solemn expression in keeping with the occasion and still looked absolutely drop-dead sexy.

"All the good ones are taken," Nicole said, low.

"What?" Stanton stopped talking to the couple and glanced at her.

"Who is that?" Nicole nodded toward the man.

"Emelda Ourso and her boys," Stanton replied. "Jeff must be parking the car." He turned back and resumed his conversation.

Nicole tugged at his arm to get his attention. "Isn't the guy standing there her husband?"

Her father followed her gaze. "No. You remember Jeff. He went to school with your sister."

"Please tell me he's not my cousin."

"Jeff?" Stanton blinked at her.

"No, *him*." Nicole jerked her head again at the handsome man.

"He looks familiar, but he's not a relative." Stanton's attention was diverted when two more people came up and started talking to him.

"Hmm, now there's good news," she said.

Nicole stole glances at the man from time to time. He moved with the grace of a trained athlete. She watched him sign the guest book provided by Robertson's Funeral Directors. His broad nose gave him a royal look, like Nicole's notion of a Nubian prince. While she mused at her own girlhood dream, he lifted his fine face and gazed straight at her. After a formal, polite smile, her prince moved on.

"Thanks for coming." Stanton shook hands with the two men and accepted a peck on the cheek from a woman. When they left, he turned back to Nicole. "How are you holding up, sugar?"

"Better now," she murmured, still watching the man.

Her prince walked through the door leading back into the sanctuary of the church. She was considering following him when her father's voice brought her up short.

"Life goes on. Uncle Hosea really cared about the family."

"Okay, I'll take your word for it."

"His own children were a big disappointment." Stanton bit off further comment when the subjects of his assessment walked in.

"Maybe they won't notice us." Nicole took an intense interest in the tips of her shoes. Her cousins Jolene and Russell Summers marched toward them.

"Hello, Uncle Stanton," Russell said. "Terrible day."

"Yes, I'll miss Daddy so much." His sister gave a delicate sniff.

"Hmm." Nicole eyed them both. Her father put a warning hand on her arm.

"If there's anything I can do to help with the company, let me know," Stanton said in an earnest tone.

"Thanks, Uncle Stanton. I'll call you if necessary. Of course, I know the business inside out."

Nicole pursed her lips to suppress a wisecrack. Jolene and Russell would probably drink a toast with expensive champagne to celebrate later on. They'd clashed with their irascible father for years over money. Russell had wanted control of the business, something Uncle Hosea had said would happen over his dead body. Well, Russell's wish had finally come true.

The pretense around Nicole was wearing thin. Nicole

glanced around for her prince. He provided the only source of pleasant distraction, yet he seemed to have vanished. Nicole's brother, Terrell, strolled up. At thirty-seven, he was a handsome copy of her father.

"These little meatballs are tasty." Terrell polished off three speared on a long toothpick. He patted his mouth with a napkin.

"Glad somebody is having a good time," Nicole said with a sour expression.

Terrell smiled as he finished chewing. He took a drink from his glass of ginger ale. "Might as well. Uncle Hosea wasn't sentimental. He'd appreciate us having only the best food at his funeral."

Nicole's grandmother and Stanton's mother, Lillian Mayveaux Summers, wore a dark blue suit with gold tone buttons. A matching hat with a half veil along the front and soft feathers wrapped around the rim completed the ensemble. At seventy-six she walked slowly but without faltering.

"What in heaven's name is going on? Francine is rolling out a large television. This is hardly the time to watch soap operas." Mother Lillian huffed in irritation.

Francine, one of seven lawyers in the family, wore a tight-lipped expression. She directed one of her three teenage sons pushing a thirty-two-inch set into the room. Nicole went to her.

"What's up?" she asked her older cousin.

"You heard the expression about stuff hitting the fan?" Francine whispered. "Well, stand back, 'cause you're about to get a big splatter."

"Me?"

"You better believe it. Excuse me everyone." Francine waited until the murmur of voices died down. "Uncle Hosea left instructions with an attorney, Phil Waserstein, to deliver this tape to me along with his last will. Naturally the latter is only to be shared with family affected. He did want this tape played now."

"Now? This is disgraceful!" Mother Lillian frowned at her great-niece. "Francine, I should think you'd know better."

"Grandmother, as a lawyer it's my legal and ethical duty to comply with legal instructions." Francine pressed a button on the remote.

Russell pushed his way through a knot of people. "I have his will."

"Another will? That's impossible," Jolene spluttered, her eyes glittering with outrage.

"I think the tape will explain everything. Here we go," Francine muttered as an aside to Nicole.

The tape came on with music from a vintage Miles Davis recording. The music faded away. Uncle Hosea sat in his favorite leather chair. He was in his library at home. Wearing a relaxed expression, Uncle Hosea nodded once and crossed his legs. Every silver hair in place, he was dressed in one of his favorite thousand-dollar black silk suits.

"Hello, there. I hope you're eating well and enjoying my funeral. Isn't technology wonderful? I feel like we're right in the same room. Well, maybe we are. I could be standing right next to you, Lillian."

Mother Lillian jumped but recovered quickly. "I never liked my brother-in-law's sense of humor."

"Still can't take a joke, I see." Uncle Hosea gave a gruff laugh. His expression turned serious. "Now to business. I won't bore you with the details of my last will and testament. That I preferred putting on paper, all nice and ironclad, Russell and Jolene."

"This is humiliating." Jolene bristled when Francine waved at her to be quiet.

Uncle Hosea folded his hands in his lap. "For my dear children and business competitors, the good news is I'm dead. I left a hefty estate behind. I sold off my insurance agency, most of the real estate holdings, and a few other odds and ends for a healthy profit." Uncle Hosea grinned widely.

"The bad news is my children won't get as much as they hoped for and my competitors won't get off so easy. Don't worry, Russell and Jolene. You'll be very comfortable. No doubt you still won't be satisfied. Tough! Thank God I won't be around to hear your whining. As for my security firm, I'm leaving it in the hands of someone with as much guts and killer instinct as I have—or had, I should say. Go get 'em, Nicole. Have fun, kids."

Uncle Hosea lifted a heavy tumbler of amber liquid and drank deeply. After a sigh, he reached over and picked up a long cigar. He lit it and puffed smoke rings.

"Ain't this the life?" He laughed heartily. "Goodbye, everyone. It's been a real pleasure getting on your nerves all these years."

He gave a jaunty wave as the picture faded and the tape ended. There was stunned silence for several minutes. Mother Lillian spoke first.

"He wasn't supposed to drink or smoke." She scowled at the screen. Several relatives giggled, then stopped when she glared at them.

"Uncle Hosea was a proud man who had always been active. He couldn't stand the thought of ending his days feeble and dependent on others," Stanton put in. "That's why he traveled and enjoyed himself in the last two years."

"You mean he made a fool of himself with women half his age," Mother Lillian put in. "Disgusting!"

Uncle Hosea had always preferred much younger women. Jolene and Russell were in their late thirties. Their mother, one of Uncle Hosea's three ex-wives, had been thirty years younger than him when they married.

"Mother, please. This isn't the place for such talk." Stanton shot a look of censure at her. His mother puckered her lips in annoyance but said nothing more. "Uncle Hosea chose the way he wanted to live."

"We all know how much he liked control," Nicole said. She crossed her arms. "What's this got to do with me?"

"Nothing. Russell and I are his only legal heirs," Jolene said in brisk voice.

"Not according to the last will," Francine replied.

"Are you saying he's leaving money to Nicole?" Russell's eyes narrowed to slits.

"We'll meet later, but Nicole is now an heir." Francine wore a frown that said she fervently wanted to be anywhere else.

"How much?" Jolene said, cutting to the chase.

"Not here—" Francine raised a hand.

"How much?" Jolene repeated with a glare.

Francine sighed deeply. "I don't think we should talk about it now." She glanced around.

Nicole leaned close to her. "Obviously the old—"

"Ahem!" Reverend Paine's brows drew together as he gazed at her.

She started over. "Obviously Uncle Hosea meant for us to discuss it now. He wouldn't have sent this little bombshell from the great beyond otherwise."

"Let's go somewhere a little more private." Francine looked at the minister.

"This way." Reverend Paine led them to smaller rooms used for Bible study and Sunday school classes.

Jolene and Russell marched ahead of them all. Terrell followed with Stanton, Analine, and Mother Lillian. No one sat down in the blue folding chairs arranged in a circle. For several minutes there was only a lot of angry staring and tense silence. Francine finally joined them.

"Sorry, I had to make sure I got the tape. Reverend Paine and our cousin Darcus will take care of greeting people."

"Fine, fine." Russell waved at her with impatience. "What is going on?"

"The bottom line is your dad left the Summers Security, LLC to . . ." Francine took a deep breath and squared her shoulders as though bracing for a strong wind. "Nicole."

"What!" Stanton and Terrell yelled in unison.

"That's ridiculous!" Nicole's mother sat down hard and fanned her face.

"No way. I'm not taking over a group of crossing guards! Forget it." Nicole shook her head until her shoulder-length hair bounced.

"You sure can forget it!" Russell said. "My father isn't going to get away with this. I put up with his bad temper and disrespect for years. I poured my blood into that company."

"He included provisions that exclude almost all of your inheritance if you fight the will," Francine replied.

"We're his children!" Jolene snapped.

"He executed the will in Louisiana. A parent has the right to leave his assets to whomever he chooses," Francine said. "I've explained it to you at least five times already. So will his attorney Phil Waserstein."

"Russ, do something!" Jolene shouted in frustration.

"There's no point talking to them. They're going to gang up on us. Let's get out of here."

Stanton blocked the door. "Wait, Russ. Be reasonable. We can work something out."

"Uh, Uncle Stanton, we're talking about a business with net sales of over ten million last year," Francine said.

"Yeah, and twenty full-time employees, thirty more contract and part-time workers and a lot of headaches," Terrell added.

Nicole shook her head again. "No thanks. I've got my own career."

"Oh, please!" Analine burst out. "I wouldn't call strolling into your father's office whenever you please a career."

"You're right of course, Nikki. It's unreasonable to think you could run a company," Stanton added.

Nicole ground her back teeth. "I didn't say I couldn't do it, just that I didn't want to."

"There must be a way out of the will." Terrell turned to Francine. "Nicole doesn't have management skills."

"Russell will need help, too," Stanton said to his son. "Ahem, Uncle Hosea mentioned a few problems."

"I know." Terrell nodded and glanced at Russell.

"I did *not* poorly manage Summers Security. This is something you people set up!" Russell shouted as he waved his hands in the air.

"I don't care about Uncle Hosea's will. I don't want to run a security business. It's boring." Nicole crossed her arms.

Francine put a hand on her shoulder. "You have to take over for at least a year."

"Impossible," Stanton said promptly.

"No way," her older brother agreed.

Nicole tapped the toe of her Ann Klein black leather pump. "Listen you two, I'm not exactly an idiot."

"But you know as well as we do that becoming CEO is out of the question," her father replied with a firm shake of his head.

"Hosea must have been senile," her mother said.

"Which means the will is invalid," Jolene said, leaping on her comment with eyes ablaze.

"There is a doctor's statement included that your father

was mentally sound despite his poor physical health." Francine pursed her lips when Jolene scowled at her.

"I inherited it legally," Nicole tossed back. "Not that I want it." She looked at Francine. "I'll talk to that lawyer and find a way out."

"Summers Security will be sold and people will lose jobs if you refuse to become the CEO," she answered.

"Over my dead body she will." Jolene flung open the door and stomped out of the room. Russell gave them one last hostile frown before he followed her.

"That alone might make me change my mind," Nicole retorted. She looked at Francine. "You're serious? I have to take over Summers Security?"

"If you don't, it will be broken up into units and sold off piece by piece." Francine sat down with a weary sigh. "God, this has been a day."

"Help me find a way out of this mess." Nicole sank into a chair next to her.

"In a year you can sell it off if you like. Apparently Uncle Hosea wanted you to try it for at least that long." Francine took a long envelope with the company logo on it from the pocket of her suit jacket. "He left you this. You're to get with his vice president and read it."

Nicole pulled back as though Francine was trying to hand her a snake. She stared at the envelope with a grimace. "The only meeting I'm going to have is with a consultant who'll tell me how to unload this thing."

"Don't be hasty," Stanton said. "We should discuss the ramifications Francine has pointed out."

"There might be a bright side to this situation." Analine wore a thoughtful expression.

"She means you'll meet eligible men," Terrell mumbled aside to Nicole.

Analine raised an eyebrow at them both. "And what's wrong with marriage?"

"A two-for-one bonus, sis. You get a new career and more chances to find a husband." Terrell winked at her.

"Very funny." Nicole jabbed him with an elbow. She turned to Francine. "Frannie, help!"

"Excuse me." A deep voice came from the open doorway.

Nicole looked up at six feet four inches of delicious man. Up close he was more than handsome. Tight dark curls the color of deep coffee covered his head like loops of soft wool. He had the neck and shoulders of a linebacker and the slim waistline of a runner. She backed up to get a better look. Head to toe he was one sweet package.

"I think you're my new boss." He stuck out a hand with long fingers. "Marcus Reed. I'm vice president and operations manager at Summers Security."

She took his hand and felt a shock of heat when it closed around hers. A slow smile spread across her face. Finally some good news that was *genuinely* good.

"Nicole Summers Benoit, proud new owner of a business," she purred.

two

_N_icole stared around the boardroom. The atmosphere reeked of thinly veiled hostility. All six of the top management staff sat around the large oval table. Russell didn't bother to hide how he felt. His lips seemed sealed in a permanent sneer. The others wore impassive expressions, but Nicole wasn't fooled. For thirty minutes she'd gotten terse answers to most of her questions. They gave up information in the most concise, unhelpful servings possible.

As for Marcus Reed, she'd gone from considering when to ask him out after she'd sold the business to plotting devious ways to hurt him, _bad_. His smiling condescension was communicated with such finesse that she almost admired the technique. Almost . . . Nicole rocked back in the huge blood-red leather captain's chair at the head of the table.

"Thank you all for your reports on the status of Summers Security." Nicole wore a relaxed smile as she looked around at them. "You've been quite helpful. I've learned _a lot_ this morning in a short time."

"I'm sure you've realized that Summers Security is more

than security guards at church socials." Russell gazed at her with a tight smile. "Our unit on computer forensics, which has only been in place for one month, is maybe a year away from profitability. And we—"

"The software could use improvement," Nicole cut in smoothly. "I worked on security applications in my father's business." The truth was Nicole had sat in on meetings about the application, mostly not paying attention to the bone-dry details.

Marcus swiveled his chair slightly until he faced her. "We have the third-generation upgrade developed by Millennium Technologies. The program you're talking about doesn't capture as much data from cache files."

"I see." Nicole didn't really see.

"Also, our security officers are scheduled using a computer program. Of course you've read that in the report. Do you suggest we use a split-shift model or continue with rotations currently being used?" Marcus tapped on the keyboard of the laptop computer in front of him. Colorful charts and bar graphs appeared on the white screen facing them at the opposite end of the room.

Eight pairs of eyes looked at her without glancing at the screen. They all knew what he was talking about. Nicole didn't have a clue, but she did know one thing. She was the boss and she'd had enough.

"Obviously I'm going to have to learn the business from the ground up. Not to worry. I'm a quick study. To that end I'll expect this list of additional reports on my desk by the end of business tomorrow." Her smile warmed up again at the shocked expressions on their faces. She handed a stack of papers with her list to Russell.

"Pass them around, please," Nicole said in her best you're-here-to-do-my-bidding tone. "You'll find additional instructions. Fortunately, my father gave me a crash course in what to ask, and what answers to expect." Nicole stood and smoothed down the red jacket that matched her skirt. "Thank you. I believe that's all for now."

"I can't have my staff tied up," Russell blurted out. "We're providing security to the minor league football play-offs for the next two weeks."

"As Marcus so helpfully pointed out, security is planned weeks ahead with your wonderful computer program." Nicole glanced around at the table with one eyebrow raised. "You have prepared for such an intricate event I hope?"

"Of course," Marcus said. "Jacinta and Andre have it under control."

He nodded to the dark-haired Latino woman to his left and the young black man seated across from him. Both looked to be fresh from college. From the staff files Nicole had skimmed, she knew both were twenty-somethings with MBA degrees from Ivy League schools.

"Very reassuring. Tomorrow by end of business," she said firmly.

Nicole let her expression reinforce the fact that the meeting was indeed over. The staff cast furtive glances toward Marcus for guidance. He looked straight ahead as though he didn't notice. Seconds later they filed out one by one. Russell alone did not get up from his seat. Instead he sat at the other end of the table with a sour expression. Marcus was near the door when Nicole spoke up.

"One moment please," Nicole said.

Marcus's dark eyes registered surprise for only a second. He nodded and came back. "Of course."

Russel watched their exchange with a sneer. "You have no idea how to run any business, much less Summers Security."

Nicole's father and Uncle Lionel came through the side door from Uncle Hosea's large executive suite. Stanton frowned at Russell. "Young man, you know better than to criticize a member of this family in front of employees!" his basso voice rumbled ominously.

"My father should have appointed *me* CEO when he learned how sick he was." Russell could not keep the whine from his voice.

Uncle Lionel grunted. "Fat chance."

"Lionel, please." Stanton shook his head.

"Oh, give me a break, Stan." Uncle Lionel waved a hand and sat down. "Our business is out in the streets since that video played at the funeral."

"He's got a point, Daddy." Nicole shrugged. "Besides, Uncle Hosea apparently trusted Marcus."

"We worked closely together." Marcus managed to sound respectful and modest without seeming obsequious.

Nicole felt a shiver up her spine. Marcus Reed had style. His smile could melt the polar ice cap. She gazed at the way his shoulders filled out the light brown suit jacket he wore. Too bad his charm covered a snake. Her ex-husband had cured her of an appetite for candy-coated serpents. Marcus was another version of Jack Benoit. That thought alone brought her sharply back to reality.

Russell turned his animosity toward Marcus. "Marcus has been an *employee* for seven years."

"Marcus helped your father build this company into a national presence," Uncle Lionel said mildly. He gazed at Russell through narrowed eyes. "You, on the other hand, made a few missteps."

"That's enough for now," Stanton cut in. "Marcus, I'll get right to the point. I hope you're not entertaining other offers."

"No, sir. I can honestly say I'm not seriously considering a move at this time. Though I've been approached by the district manager at Pinkerton."

Stanton nodded with a sober expression. He glanced at Nicole as a signal. "Have you two talked?"

She cleared her throat. "Only briefly. We had a few urgent decisions to make this morning. Then it was time for the first management team meeting."

Nicole didn't glance at Marcus as she spoke. She imagined him wearing a placid smile in full knowledge that the "we" she spoke of mainly meant him. Still, she intended to remedy that situation fast. No pretty boy know-it-all was going to keep the upper hand on her.

"Let's sit down then." Stanton waved a hand at the conference table, and they took seats. He looked at Nicole again to take the lead.

"We know you could move on to a choice job in the industry with no problem," she began. "However, we'd like you to sign an agreement not to leave for at least six months. Your expertise and knowledge of this company in particular is invaluable in a transition. Summers Security and the employees need you."

The words raked her throat raw, but Nicole's delivery was flawless. Marcus had shown himself to be an inflexible, misogynistic, condescending smart-ass. She'd play the game for now, though.

"Frankly, my daughter needs all the help she can get," Stanton said. "I'll be here two days a week to support her as well. But of course I've got my own company to run."

Uncle Lionel leaned forward. "Naturally we'll compensate you."

"Thank you, that's very generous." Marcus turned to

Nicole. "The late Mr. Summers and I worked hand in hand. More important than money is knowing the new boss has confidence in me."

"As I said, we realize that one asset of this company is its staff. You've done so much to build up the customer base and infrastructure." Nicole smiled at him with effort.

"So you want me to stay?" Marcus pushed.

Nicole wanted to swipe the smarmy set to his full lips right off his face. He wanted her to crawl, to admit she couldn't handle Summers Security without him. *Be damned if I will, you cocky chump!*

"I want what's best for the firm right now. With your skills and knowledge, of course I want you. To stay on, I mean," Nicole added and blushed. She glanced away from the glint of amusement in his arresting eyes. His mouth twitched a fraction, but he continued to wear a professional demeanor.

"I care about the people who work here and the customers we serve. I'll stay for at least six months," Marcus said.

"Excellent!" Stanton beamed and rubbed his hands together.

Uncle Lionel clapped a hand on his shoulder. "Knew we could count on you, son."

"Just a minute." Russell stood. "You talk about the future of this company as if I'm not in the room. May I remind you that I'm vice president of development. My father founded this company. I intend to run it once this absurd will is invalidated. I—"

"Shut up, Russ," Uncle Lionel rumbled. "You're vice president of exactly nothing. Hosea had sense enough not to put you in charge of anything you could damage."

"The important thing is to pull together as a family, not just think of ourselves individually," Stanton replied.

"Nice speech, Uncle Stanton. If we're going to pull together, then why won't Nicole resign and give the business to me as its rightful owner?" Russell wore a scornful smile, and he leaned on the table with both fists. "I'll tell you why. She's holding this company ransom hoping I'll pay her extortion money. Well, you can forget it!"

"Russ, don't be an ass," Uncle Lionel barked. "Sit down and listen to reason."

"Under Texas law there can only be one person responsible for the license of a security agency. They call that person the manager," Russell said. He stuck out his chest. "Nicole doesn't qualify because she doesn't have three years' experience in the security business. Which means I'll be the manager."

"Everybody can kiss their jobs goodbye." Uncle Lionel shook his head slowly.

"Lionel, please! You're not helping," Stanton admonished.

"Excuse me," Marcus said. "Mr. Summers designated me as manager six months before he got sick. So, there's no problem with the license."

Nicole didn't like the sound of that. She made a mental note to study the state licensing regulations. "Good. Now Russell doesn't have to lose sleep over our license."

"I'm just as qualified to be manager," Russell protested.

"Don't worry, Russ. We'll let you blow the guards' new whistles if you're good," Uncle Lionel shot back.

"Have fun, Uncle Lionel. Just don't think you can push me until I quit. Nicole won't take my company that easily." Russell cast a final defiant glance at them all, then walked out.

Stanton sighed. "You see what we're up against?" he said to Marcus.

"Yes, sir." Marcus folded his hands on top of the table.

If he was amused or disturbed, he didn't let it show in his expression. Nicole studied him a few moments. She wondered what wheels were turning in his attractive head. Marcus Reed wasn't just a pretty face. He knew his own value. If he had any doubts about his position at Summers Security, they'd just put those to rest. What would he do next? She gazed at his neat fingernails, the long, tapered fingers and smooth skin on the back of his hands. His arms filled out the sleeves of his suit nicely. Her gaze went up his chest to his face again. Nice package, he seemed to be an all starch and straightlaced overachiever on the way up. Yet Nicole suspected once out of that suit he could turn into a sleek, sensual creature. The image of his naked flesh set off a flash fire in her body.

"I said, do you agree?" Uncle Lionel said loudly.

"Nicole, focus. I know this is overwhelming for your first day in the office," her father added.

She blinked and realized the three men were staring at her hard. "Sorry. Long day and it's just barely lunchtime." Nicole gave them a forced, weak smile.

She shook off the effects of a budding, and quite forbidden, fantasy involving her employee. He'd probably slap her with a sexual harassment lawsuit, especially if he could have glimpsed the naughty pictures in her head. She gave herself a solid mental shake, then concentrated on the discussion.

"As Russell pointed out, we've started a digital forensic unit. Also, Mr. Summers and I had planned to submit bids on federal contracts related to homeland security measures," Marcus said.

"But can you handle that kind of work?" Uncle Lionel frowned at him.

"Some of it will involve training security personnel at airports. Myself and two staff have spent the last three months getting trained in that specialized area."

Marcus pressed a button on the laptop computer. Moments

later Uncle Hosea's secretary, who was now Nicole's secretary, knocked and came in with four printed copies.

"Here you are, Marcus." Catherine Lawson, know as Cat around the office, gave him a warm smile. She glanced at Nicole with frank curiosity.

"Thanks. Here you'll see what we had in mind."

Nicole smiled at her. "Thank you, Cat. I'll meet with you later."

"Sure. Can I get you anything, Ms. Summers?"

"I'm good," Nicole said. The woman nodded and left.

"Nicole." Her father raised one thick eyebrow at her. "Looks sound to me. What do you think, Lionel?"

"Don't need to tell me this was *your* idea, Marcus. Excellent the way you look ahead." Uncle Lionel nodded in approval.

"Thank you, sir." Marcus straightened his tie and sat back in his chair.

"I agree. I'll study this and the reports I asked for. In fact, do you have a more detailed version?" Nicole asked as she looked at him.

Marcus glanced down at the keyboard without touching it. His dark brows drew together just a fraction, the only hint he was irritated. Nicole pressed her lips together to suppress her glee.

"I have an outline of items to include in bid documents, but—"

"Include it with the other reports. End of business tomorrow as I said." Nicole turned to her father and uncle. "Why don't we have lunch? I'm in the mood for fresh shrimp salad."

Stanton let a beat pass as he gazed at her. "Yes, why don't we? Marcus will join us."

"Great idea," Uncle Lionel chimed in before Nicole could

speak. He stood. "I'm hungry. I'll call right now and get a small room set aside at Brennan's." He went to the other end of the room and picked up the phone on a long side table against the wall.

Marcus wore a serene expression. "I'm free, as a matter of fact."

"Good. We'll meet in the lobby in thirty minutes," Stanton said.

"Yes, sir." Marcus made a few nimble keystrokes on the laptop, then made a graceful exit.

"The bum!" Nicole burst out the instant the heavy door whisked shut behind him. "He spent the morning undermining my authority."

"How, specifically?" Stanton asked.

"Well, he—" Nicole raised a hand. She searched for words. Seconds went by while her father drummed his fingers on the table. "It was just his attitude. You know what I mean. Talking down to me while he's got this kiss-ass smile on his face."

"A certain amount of tension is to be expected under the circumstances. None of the management staff know what kind of changes to expect." Stanton sat forward. "You've got to establish credibility with your staff. They've probably heard you're not too thrilled to be their new boss."

"Speaking of which, any news on how I can get out of here?" Nicole muttered.

"The will is ironclad. Now stop whining," her father commanded.

Nicole indulged in a few more seconds of pouting before she sat up straight and grinned. "I've got at least six months to show Mr. Wise-Ass Marcus Reed who he's dealing with."

"Nicole," her father's voice grumbled low, his usual warning sound.

Nicole laughed and waved both hands in the air. "Just kidding around, Daddy." She grew serious again. "I don't want to see anybody unemployed or a Summers family business go down in flames. I'll take care of business."

"Good, girl." Stanton's scowl relaxed into a paternal smile of affection. He kissed her forehead. "I knew I could count on my cute little honey-bunny."

"Please don't call me that in front of anybody!" Nicole shook her head hard. "I've got enough of a hurdle getting respect. They all think I'm a pampered Black American Princess as it is."

Her father grunted. "They're right. Not that I can't take some of the blame for indulging you all these years."

Uncle Lionel came back rubbing his hands together. "It's all set. Stanton, we've got a few minutes to make that call to Washington, D.C. to the lobbyist."

"Right. We pooled resources with other minority business owners to hire a top lobbying firm. Separate, we could never afford their hefty fees."

"Okay. Stay and use the phone here. I'll meet with my secretary." Nicole retrieved the phone and hooked it to a jack set in the conference table.

"See you in a little while, baby." Stanton hit the speaker button as he spoke, his mind already on his own business.

Nicole waved goodbye to them and retreated through the door directly into her office. Once the door closed, her shoulders slumped. Getting through her first morning as head of Summers Security had taken a toll. She massaged the back of her neck and rolled her arms in a circle to loosen up. The view from her window was less than wonderful. She stared at parking lots and traffic on the street below. The five-floor office building sat in downtown Houston miles from Uncle Hosea's expensive home in River Oaks. With a sigh, she went to the small wet bar in the eastern corner of the office and got a bottle of spring water. As she glanced around, Nicole started planning how to redecorate.

Russell came through the door without knocking. His eyes narrowed to slits. "Who postponed the meeting with Federated Food Stores?"

"You must know I did or you wouldn't be in my office, Russ." Nicole sat back in her chair and stared at him.

"I'm handling that account. You've probably jeopardized a very lucrative contract." Russell took a few steps closer and folded his arms across his chest. "You don't know much about this field. I think you should let me handle things for a while."

"Really?" Nicole spoke in an even tone.

"I'm going to help you out. We can meet once or twice a week and I'll keep you informed of what's going on. In fact, I can even have Cat e-mail reports to you if you don't want to come into the office. I know you didn't want this place dumped on you."

"You'd do that for me?" Nicole said with a wide-eyed expression. "I don't know what to say."

Russell shrugged and spread his arms. "It makes sense. I can run the business for the next year."

"Interesting proposition. You'd be the boss, but as a service to unburden me," Nicole added quickly.

"Exactly." Russell smiled at her. He strolled over to the coffeepot nearby and poured himself a cup. "You want to get back to your, er, career."

"I appreciate the offer." Nicole rocked the leather chair gently as she gazed at him.

Russell looked around the office as though it were his already. "No problem. We're family."

She picked up her pen and started to write. "But no thanks.

I rescheduled the meeting with Federated Food Stores for next Wednesday. That way I'll have more time to look over their needs assessment."

"I'll pick up the pieces when you're tired of playing boss." He strode out and shut the door with a solid bump.

Nicole's father and Uncle Lionel came in through the side door. Stanton sighed. "You look odd sitting at Uncle Hosea's desk, Nikki."

"Ready for lunch? I sure am!" Uncle Lionel patted his stomach.

"Ready as I'll ever be. I'll tell you both one thing, Marcus Reed is due for an attitude adjustment. He's subtly undermining my authority." Nicole took her Fendi handbag from the desk drawer.

"From what I could see Marcus has been nothing but helpful." Stanton looked at his brother.

Uncle Lionel shrugged. "It's tough having a woman in charge, especially when she doesn't know beans. Sorry, Nikki, but that's the truth."

"He'll have to get over himself." Nicole went to the door when the two men stood to let her go first.

"Now, Nicole Marie, don't start anything. You need him." Stanton shook a finger at her.

"Since I had this place dumped on me I intend to be in charge, starting with this lunch. I'm in charge, so get used to it." Nicole lifted her nose in the air when she spotted Marcus waiting by Cat's desk.

Her father and uncle exchanged a glance. "Lord help us!" they said in unison.

three

Lunch went better than Nicole expected. By the time they'd ordered coffee and dessert, she knew more about Marcus. Nicole tried not to let her interest show as Marcus talked more about himself. He stayed away from his personal life and concentrated more on his work history. She wondered just who were the women in his life. Looking at him, Nicole doubted he'd lived the life of a monk. His handsome face and fine body would draw women like crazy, she mused. He'd sure caught her eye at the funeral. In fact, Marcus Reed seemed capable of stirring up female hormones everywhere he went. At least two women in the restaurant besides the waitress had practically done cartwheels to get his attention. Mr. Wonder Charm must be waiting for her to roll over like a little poodle. As if sensing the defensive move, Marcus looked at her and turned on a dazzling smile. Nicole mentally readjusted her anti-lover-boy suit of armor.

"I'd be happy to spend more time with Ms. Benoit," he said.

"What?" Nicole blinked in confusion. She stared at her father.

"I said you two will need to work hand in hand over the next few months." Stanton looked at her hard. "You okay?"

"Fine." Nicole recovered and smiled. "I intend to have weekly meetings with the management staff and bimonthly company meetings with all employees."

"I think Mr. Summers means you and I meeting alone." Marcus assumed a casual pose as he took a sip from his glass.

Nicole thought he'd put emphasis on the word "alone," yet when she looked at him he seemed all business. "Yes, well, of course."

"With your guidance, I'm sure Summers Security can at least hold ground. I'm sure Nicole will follow your lead," Stanton said.

"Only sensible approach she can take, considering," Uncle Lionel put in.

"I don't know about providing security services. At least I didn't until two weeks ago," Nicole admitted.

"I'm sure you'll be up to speed soon enough." Marcus nodded at her.

"I intend to be up to speed by the end of the week," Nicole said with a cool smile.

"That's Summers blood talking. Meet the challenge." Uncle Lionel winked at her.

Nicole saw Marcus stiffen. "You'll notice my uncle has his feet firmly planted in the nineteenth century," she joked to avoid another tense moment.

"Huh?" Uncle Lionel's thick brows pulled together to give his broad face a confused expression.

"Eat, Lionel," Stanton said with a sigh.

"Excellent food. Hmmm." Uncle Lionel promptly forgot the subject. He savored another mouthful of cheesecake.

Once they finished eating, Uncle Lionel paid the bill, and

they went back to the office. Cat waved a thick wad of messages when they entered the foyer outside Nicole's office.

"Most important ones are on the top," Cat said.

"Wonderful." Nicole took them from her.

"Welcome to the world of being in charge," Uncle Lionel said.

"Marcus, pleasure getting to know you better." Stanton shook hands with him.

"Same here," Uncle Lionel rumbled. He glanced at the large round digital clock on the wall above Cat's desk. "We better shake a leg, Stan."

"Right. We have a meeting in Lafayette this evening." Stanton turned to Nicole. "Bye, baby. Marcus."

"Goodbye, sir." Marcus nodded to both men.

Nicole felt like a small child being left by her father on the first day of school. "Daddy, wait."

"Call me anytime. Though I'm sure with Marcus by your side you won't need me as much."

"I intend to be right here for her, sir." Marcus smiled at her father.

"Stan, we really have to leave. We're cutting it close as it is." Uncle Lionel waved goodbye and headed for the door.

Stanton kissed Nicole on her cheek. "One benefit is I get to kiss the boss and she can't fire me," he teased.

"That is a nice perk." Marcus glanced at Nicole. His smile widened when she blushed.

"Why do I feel like I've just been patted on the head like a puppy?" Nicole wisecracked.

"Marcus, for you." Cat held out the receiver of her phone.

When he walked away, Stanton pulled Nicole aside. "He's your best ally. Russell is sure to be a bit of a problem."

"A bit of a problem? That's a *bit* of an understatement," she retorted.

"Even more reason to build a solid relationship with Marcus. He's not only good at what he does, but he seems genuinely loyal to the company."

"Yes, Daddy. I hear you loud and clear." Nicole pushed down her natural inclination to rebel. "He's not the knight in shining armor you think. He resents the hell out of having me as his boss."

"Then win him over. You can turn on the charm when necessary. Well, if ever there was a time, it's *now*. Like my father used to say—"

"The best way to win a fight is to make friends with your opponent. Or at least let him think so until the right moment, then pow!" Nicole grinned. Grandfather Alcee had been a crafty guy, a nicer version of his brother Hosea.

"So, maybe you've heard that one a few times." Stanton chuckled. His expression turned serious again. "I'll call you in a few days."

"Yes, sir." Nicole gave him a mock salute.

"And control your mouth," he tossed back and wagged a forefinger at her nose. "Remember, you need these folks as much as they need *you*."

"I got it." Nicole pressed her lips together.

Stanton held up one palm. "I hear your mother starting to ooze out. I'll say no more."

"I really do appreciate the advice, sweetie." Nicole gave him a quick hug.

Uncle Lionel stuck his head in the door, a cell phone pressed to his ear. "Stan, come on."

"Bye, darlin'." Stanton waved to Cat and Marcus, and they waved back. He looked at Nicole again. "Don't forget what I said."

"Goodbye," Nicole said in a clipped tone. Stanton only laughed again as he left. "Watch my mouth. Funny."

Marcus hung up the phone and walked over to her. "Maybe I should return some of those messages. That way you'll have a chance to get your office organized and decorated."

"I'm not quite ready to hang frilly pink curtains," Nicole replied, then clamped her mouth shut again. Her father's warning reverberated in her head like a fire bell.

"Sorry, I didn't mean to—"

"It's okay," Nicole broke in.

"The first day running a company you didn't expect to inherit must be tough. I just wanted to take one more worry off your hands," Marcus replied smoothly, no hint that he was offended.

Nicole gazed at him, feeling skeptical that he was sincere. Still, she had to give him credit for being poised. She'd be just as slick.

"You're right, of course. But I have to dive in sometime. Might as well start now. Thanks for the offer." Nicole flashed her best smile. "I'll call if I need you. How's that?"

Marcus gazed at her for several seconds, then cleared his throat and looked away. "Sounds fine. I'll be in my office the rest of the afternoon." He turned to leave.

"Marcus?" Nicole said in a silken tone.

He froze, then turned slowly. "Yes?"

"Make up a list of clients I can visit this week. Three or four of the top contracts. The personal touch will inspire confidence," Nicole said.

"Uh, good idea, Ms. Benoit." He blinked rapidly.

"Call me Nicole. I know Uncle Hosea was a stickler for formality, but I'm not him." Nicole gleefully watched him shift his weight from one foot to the other.

"Sure." Marcus hurried off as though late for a meeting.

"Lesson number two in who's the boss." Nicole grinned and went into her office. "I'll have the phone attached to my ear for the rest of today," she said to Cat.

Cat looked at the door where Marcus had stood, then at Nicole, with both her auburn-dyed eyebrows raised. *"Yes, ma'am."*

Marcus slapped his hands together as he looked up at the wall. "Man, do I need this workout."

"Rough day, huh? I knew something was up when you called me." Shaun, his boyhood pal from the Fifth Ward, stood beside him adjusting his gloves.

They were about to tackle their favorite sport, indoor rock climbing. There were only a few other climbers at Texas Rock Gym. Marcus had called Shaun's cell phone earlier that day and arranged for them to meet. Shaun would anchor the rope while Marcus scaled walls studded with hand and toe holds. Then Shaun would take his turn with Marcus below. Marcus had made a case for being first—forget their traditional coin toss. He needed to release the tension in his muscles after the last two days.

"Brother, I couldn't wait until Friday," Marcus muttered. "A midweek climb will help me make it to the weekend."

"That answers at least one of my questions about your new boss," Shaun joked. His grin widened when Marcus let out a grunt. "A nut buster, right?"

"She's got a mouth on her for sure." Marcus frowned at the memory of Nicole issuing instructions.

"Naturally, they all do," Shaun retorted.

"Judging from the way he was whispering to her, I'd say Daddy told his little princess to try tact instead of a club. We'll see how long that act can last."

"A battle of the wills. Wish I could witness the first few rounds." Shaun chuckled.

"She can turn on that slinky voice and bats her long eyelashes until forever. I'm not going to be her lapdog!" Marcus scowled at the wall as though ready to punish it in Nicole's place.

"Good-looking, huh?" Shaun adjusted his waist harness in preparation.

"I guess."

"If she's that fine, going to the office might not be so bad after all." Shaun wiggled his eyebrows.

"I came here to relax and leave that soap opera behind for a while." Marcus paid even more attention to his harness.

"The Young and the Clueless. Stay tuned for our next episode. Is the brother in trouble? Will the lovely new boss—"

"Maybe I'll wrap this rope around your neck instead." Marcus's eyes narrowed to slits.

"Message received. Let's rock," Shaun quipped.

Marcus groaned at the oft-repeated pun. "For a young guy you sure can come up with some dusty jokes."

Shaun shrugged off the sour response with another laugh. Marcus attacked the wall as though he were conquering Mount Everest. Foot by foot he ascended. Still part of his mind was on a set of walnut brown eyes. Nicole Benoit was both what he had expected and a surprise rolled into a lovely body. She could certainly be a "nut buster," to borrow Shaun's colorful description. Nicole was one tough cookie. Her father had made it clear she was daddy's darling with his presence. Yet Marcus felt fairly sure Nicole had an iron will, most likely the result of getting her way. Typical profile, he mused as he continued his climb. He had little doubt Nicole was spoiled rotten and had a nasty temper when crossed. She'd given him a glimpse of both traits her first day in the office.

Still she could turn sweet when it suited her purpose. The memory of the way she said his name, all satiny and alluring, came back to him. She rolled the first syllable out with a hint of a Creole accent. Marcus mused on her heritage. Old man Summers had told him about the family's roots. Her thick, shoulder-length hair was brown with red highlights. She had a figure that could bring dead men back to life, especially when she walked. But that voice. He'd stopped dead in his tracks at the sound, so stunned at how it had flowed toward him. Only moments before she'd seemed the typical sarcastic sister. When he'd turned around, the sight of her voluptuous lips curved up in a smile had sent a shiver down his back. When an image of her shapely legs clicked on, Marcus sucked in a deep breath and let it out.

"Fake," he said to himself, and grit his teeth.

"Hey! If you're getting tired, give a brother his turn," Shaun shouted.

"No way!" Marcus yelled back without looking down.

Instead he looked up at his goal. Marcus kept going until he reached the top, the way he'd handled his career. The same way he'd rise once he walked away with most of Summers Security, as planned. Anticipation of that day made him feel a lot better. The pure physical exertion made his muscles tingle. His prescription had worked. All the kinks were gone. With a grunt of satisfaction he started down. He got to about two feet from the bottom and dropped to the padded floor.

"Damn, that felt good." Marcus wiped sweat from his face and neck. He drank deeply from the water bottle he carried.

"Well, I didn't have a bad day. I'm not going up so high. I want to get that steak." Shaun rolled his shoulders.

"Me, too. You know what? This day wasn't so bad after all."

"You had some kinda religious experience up there?"

"Nope, just cleared my head. Up you go." Marcus gave Shaun a fraternal slap on the shoulder.

four

Nicole glanced at him sideways. Marcus was so all business. Ramrod straight in the driver's seat, he seemed determined not to look at her. They were in one of the three company Dodge Durango SUVs on their way to Johnson Technologies, a midsized telecommunications firm. He'd given her a complete report in a flat voice. While he'd talked, Nicole had wondered just what it was about her that made him so uptight. If they were going to be a team, she'd have to figure out how to put him at ease. Maybe a little music would help. She turned on the radio. Hip-hop music jumped out of the speakers with a driving thud that shook the vehicle.

"Damn!" Nicole blurted out as she fumbled to find the volume control.

"I'll get it," Marcus yelled over a stream of street poetry.

"I think I've got it," she shouted back.

Just as she found the knob and turned the sound down, his hand closed over hers. They jerked away at the same time, and somehow her hand ended up in his. Marcus let go first without looking at her. Nicole still felt the heat from his touch. She'd been surprised by the roughness of his skin.

"You've been working construction or something? You didn't get those hands from pushing papers around all day," Nicole said.

"I enjoy rock climbing. I also play a little guitar to relax." Marcus cleared his throat as though the words had come out against his will.

"Interesting." Nicole updated her mental file on him.

"LeRoi won't be in, but his daughter will meet with us." Marcus steered the Durango to the exit lane and they drove down the ramp.

"Okay." Nicole nodded. "Rock climbing, huh? Kind of risky."

"Not if you're careful and get the right training. Mostly I do indoor to keep in shape." Marcus cleared his throat. "Ellen Johnson mostly runs the company these days anyway. LeRoi is semiretired."

"I read a profile of her in *Black Enterprise*. So, what do you play?"

"Excuse me?" Marcus glanced at her briefly, then back at the traffic. He looked baffled by her question.

"On the guitar."

"Blues and old school R&B." He checked traffic before making a right turn. "Ellen really kept the company going, even managed to turn a profit while most telecom companies went under. She restructured. For two years now their survival hasn't depended on tech companies."

"Most dot coms tanked when the new economy got old." Nicole glanced around at the scenery as she spoke casually.

"You've done your homework." Marcus glanced at her as though surprised and impressed in equal measure.

"Nah, I heard that on CNN once when I was channel surfing trying to find the shopping network," she said with a laugh.

"I see."

"That was a joke."

"Okay." Marcus wore a brief, tight smile and drove on in silence.

Gees, lighten up, man! Nicole was piqued at his humorless disapproval. She pushed down the urge to goad him even more. Her father's advice echoed in her head. Still, he was her employee. He should at least meet her halfway. Okay, she thought. Tackle the subject of her being the boss head on.

"Listen, I appreciate how unsettling this whole change has been for you." Nicole sat erect and wore her best professional demeanor to match his all-business mode. "I know a little more about the security business now, but I definitely want us to work as a team."

"Of course."

Nicole ground her teeth. His tone was lifeless, no defiance but no enthusiasm either. She tried again. "I realize you're used to being pretty much in charge and working on your own. You probably think the last thing you need is some woman who knows doodly-squat about security telling you what to do."

"I've worked with a lot of different people, Ms. Benoit."

"Call me Nicole, Marcus," she corrected.

He paused a beat. "Okay, Nicole."

"Tell the truth—why haven't you blanketed the world with your resume?" She raised one eyebrow at him.

"How do you know I haven't?" he tossed back.

"Because you promised us at least six months, and you're a man who does what he says he's going to do."

Marcus turned into the parking lot of Johnson Technologies. He parked the Durango but didn't turn off the engine. His hands still rested on the steering wheel as he turned to her.

"I could still be lining up my next job," he said with an impassive expression on his handsome face.

"I intend to win you over long before six months go by." Nicole lifted her chin confidently.

"Really? Money doesn't mean everything."

Nicole heard a trace of contempt in his tone, but she decided to ignore it. She held his gaze without batting an eyelash. "Most people say that until they hear the right dollar amount."

"I'm not most people. There are other aspects of a job that I value more."

"Such as?"

"I need to work in an atmosphere that encourages creativity and autonomy, to name two."

"Don't pack up just yet. I'm willing to give you what you need." Nicole beamed at him.

Marcus gazed at her without smiling back. "You've got your late uncle's iron will."

"Just let me counter any offers you might get in the next six months. Deal?" Nicole stuck out her hand.

He took her hand for only a moment, then let go quickly. "Deal. Now we'd better get going. Ellen's waiting, and she's more of a stickler for being on time than I am."

"Yes, sir," Nicole said crisply. She pretended not to notice the sharp look he threw her way.

Two hours later and they were heading back. Marcus talked more business during the ride to the office, but questions on a very different topic, his personal life, bounced around Nicole's head.

She thought she'd done a good job of paying attention as

he'd talked. Once they were back in Nicole's office and the door was closed, Marcus stared at her as though waiting.

"So do you think we should move ahead?" Marcus stood with one hand in a pocket.

"What?" Nicole gazed back at him.

"I'm afraid I may have dumped too much information on you at once. I'm sorry." He tilted his head to one side.

Nicole looked him straight in the eye. "Yes, you can meet with Genesis Software about the new security task program."

"You told me that ten minutes ago. I asked if I should go ahead with hiring staff for the branch office in Lake Charles."

His serene demeanor only served to increase her annoyance, with herself as much as with him. Nicole spun around and marched to her desk.

"Your report doesn't include a budget for that branch office. I'll make a decision when I get complete information." She looked at her Citizen wristwatch. "Have it on my desk within the hour."

"I included a rough estimate of the total operating cost, but I'll break it down to the last paper clip if that's what you want."

Nicole crossed her arms. "You've got a problem with details?"

He studied her as the wall clock ticked off the seconds. Nicole was acutely aware that she was being sized up. His expression seemed to shout that she didn't measure up to some standard he had. Marcus Reed was a proud man who'd pulled himself up out of the 'hood. To him she must seem like a spoiled dilettante with the power to make his life difficult, at least for a few months.

"Regretting that promise to stay on? I know what an ordeal change can be for some people."

"You'll find I'm very adaptable, Nicole," he answered, his voice even deeper than normal. "I'm not going anywhere."

The challenge in his brusque response sent a thrill up her spine. Nicole nodded once and sat down. She picked up a letter Cat had left on her desk. "Good. I'll give you a call after I look at that budget breakdown. Paper clips and all," she said as she scanned the page.

"Done."

Nicole glanced up just as he whirled around and strode out the door. Her eyes narrowed to slits. "I'm going to have fun training you, Mister," she murmured.

Two hours later Nicole sat across from Russell. Instead of summoning him, Nicole had agreed to meet with Russell in his corner office. She was giving diplomacy one last attempt. With more of her mother in her than she cared to admit, reining in her impatience proved to be a constant battle. Nicole tried to follow her father's example in dealing with her cousin. Stanton was respected for his business sense and his ability to build alliances under the most demanding circumstances, yet even the most forbearing saint would have cracked under the situation Nicole now found herself in.

"Russell, we've gone over the reasons I don't agree with your plan three times. I'm not going to change my mind," Nicole said through clenched teeth.

"If we want to win over the Fortune 500 companies, Nicole, we have to go state of the art," Russell insisted. "We could double or even triple our profit. Using pupil scanners at ATM machines would put us miles ahead of our competitors."

Nicole counted to ten. "Russell, not one of the banks you contacted is interested. *Not one.*"

"That's because you won't let me put together a full video

presentation and buy the prototype. Brandon assures me this is new millennium technology."

"Unproven technology. Your frat brother has a reputation for losing other people's money," she retorted.

"Who didn't suffer losses when the bull market ended?" Russell waved a hand. "We can't stop moving forward because of one downturn."

"We discussed this in a meeting. Marcus and I agreed that these new devices seem promising, but—"

"You and Marcus," Russell cut in. "Every time I try to take this company to a higher level one of you blocks me."

"*But*," Nicole pressed on louder to get his attention, "those machines are too expensive. Your pal wants us to beta test the things and pay big money in the process."

"Brandon might convince his people to lease us the V-Protex for six months. I could set up a test site at the Pink Isle riverboat casino in Lake Charles. First Federal has an ATM machine installed there." Russell sat forward eagerly.

Nicole gave a short laugh. "Russell, think about what you just said. I'm not going to pay for Brandon's field test." Those were Marcus's words, actually. Nicole wouldn't have known the difference.

"Cooperative deals are made all the time, Nicole. Maybe a few more years' experience in the corporate world would help you understand the way business is done."

That was it! Nicole stood and looked down at him. "Work on equipping the new branch office."

"Buying staples, ink pens, and notepads can be done by your secretary," he snapped.

"Cat doesn't have time," Nicole lobbed back. "Ordering staples, ink pens, and notepads is your forte."

"I'm going to enjoy watching you crash and burn," he replied in a flat tone.

"Are you going to do your job or not?" Nicole stared back at him with a frown. "You can move on anytime."

Russell picked up the receiver of his phone and pressed a button. "Bring me the office supply catalogues," he said to his secretary, then slammed it down again. He gave Nicole a defiant smile that stretched his facial muscles to the limit. "I'm going to be right here, *cousin*."

Nicole drew in a deep breath, counted to ten, and let it out. "Look, this constant fighting is a waste of energy for both of us. Together we can really take Summers Security to the top."

"Running a company can be scary, huh? All those sharp employees watching you. A dozen decisions to make each day." Russell crossed his arms. "No thanks. I'll stick to ordering supplies for now."

Nicole spun around. "Fine," she muttered as she walked out.

Russell's secretary, a tall brunette named Amber, eyed Nicole with interest as she strode past. "Uh, you won't need that coffee after all, Ms. Benoit?"

"No, but a huge dose of aspirin would be nice," Nicole tossed over her shoulder without breaking her stride.

Cat was standing in the hallway leading to Nicole's office. She took one look at her boss's expression and hastily took two steps out of her way.

"I'll get you a cool glass of orange juice. It's good for high blood pressure."

Nicole glanced at her with a frown. "Is that a joke?"

"No, no. I'm really into natural healing. You should drink herbal tea instead of coffee. Going caffeine free is much better for your nerves."

"Uh-uh." Nicole went straight to the refrigerator in her office and got a cola. She picked up a napkin from the table nearby.

"I'll stock up on juice. You've got a lot more meetings with Russell coming, you know," Cat said in a controlled voice.

"More cola. I'll get my own headache pills," Nicole mumbled and sat down hard. She glanced up to see her brother standing in the door.

He crossed the space between them and kissed the top of Nicole's head. "Poor little sis. I stopped by to see how you're doing."

"Guess," she said with a grimace. "I just finished another delightful discussion with Russell. Murder is still illegal, right?"

"I'm pretty sure," Terrell said and laughed. "I'll check on the possibility of justifiable homicide as a defense." He perched on the edge of her desk.

"Please do." Nicole took another sip from the can of cola, then put it down. She rocked back in the chair.

"Here's another plan—fire his obnoxious butt." Terrell pursed his lips. The expression made him look even more like a younger version of their father.

"I can't. Uncle Hosea might have had a low opinion of him, but the will specifies that he hold some kind of position in the company. He'd be a fool to damage the company. He'd take money out of his own pocket. If for no other reason, he'll be careful," Nicole said.

"Nikki, Russell *is* a fool." Terrell slid off the desk. He went to a leather chair and sat down.

"I've got my eye on him. He's pathetically predictable, lucky for me." Nicole waved a hand in the air. "What brings you to Houston?"

"Dad is thinking of setting up an office here. He's hinting I should run it. I think he wants someone in the family to be here for you."

Nicole clapped her hands together. "Praises on high!"

Terrell held up a palm like a school crossing guard. "Hold on. You know how much I love living in Lafayette. Besides, I'm not sure we even need an office in Houston."

She seemed not to hear him. "Now if we can convince the rest of the family to pack up, life would be perfect." Nicole grinned at him.

"Does that include Mama?" Terrell laughed again when her grin melted away.

"Good point. How Daddy deals with her has always been a mystery to me," she quipped.

Terrell's expression became serious. "Yeah, she pushes him to the limit sometimes. But he's not always in the right either."

Nicole picked up the can of cola. "Which is why I'm happily single and planning to stay that way."

He brightened again. "Not me. I want to juggle Little League coaching and dance recitals."

"Have a ball. One marriage cured me of that affliction."

"Let it go, Nikki. The guy wasn't all bad." Terrell wore a lopsided smile at the sour look she gave him. "C'mon. You were crazy about him all through high school and college."

Nicole grunted. "Three years of hell. The last seven have been wonderfully drama free, and I mean to keep it that way."

"Isn't your bio clock ticking?" Terrell's eyebrows formed twin arcs over his dark eyes.

"I don't know what all the fuss is about turning thirty. Last month was a snap." Nicole snapped her fingers as a kind of proof. "Had a ball with my girls and kept on kicking."

"You go, girl. On to thirty-five," Terrell quipped.

"Shut up," she tossed back.

"No new man?"

"I'm dating." Nicole stuck out her chin when he stared at her hard. "I've got a company to run."

"You gave Marcus the eye the first time you saw him."

"I'm his boss so he's off limits. Not to mention he's got a serious chip on his shoulder about me being the boss." Nicole tapped out a tune with the ink pen in her hand.

"In other words, *he's* all business. I know you, little sister."

"Terrell," Nicole glowered a warning at him.

"Bye, sis. I see you don't need my help." Terrell blew a kiss at her. He turned to find Marcus standing in front of him. "Hi, Marcus. Good seeing you again."

"Same here." Marcus blinked at him in obvious confusion.

Terrell gave him a good-humored grin. "Terrell Summers, Nicole's brother. We met at the funeral."

"Right. Sorry. I met so many members of the family that day." Marcus shook his hand and smiled back.

"Our family really turns out for a good funeral," Terrell joked. He glanced from Marcus to Nicole. "You two make a good team."

"Goodbye, Terrell." Nicole wore a stiff smile.

Terrell turned his back to Marcus and winked. "Y'all have a real nice day."

All Nicole could do was seethe as he left. Terrell gave Cat a cheerful goodbye and went out. Nicole glanced back to find Marcus staring at her. He raised a dark green folder in his hand.

"I was coming to give you the budget. If you're busy, I'll come back."

Nicole gazed at the smooth brown skin on the back of his hand instead of at the folder. His long fingers seemed to suggest he was good with hands. Her gaze traveled up his well-built arm to the broad shoulders filling out the cream-colored dress shirt. Chemistry? Try explosive, judging by the way her body zinged and pinged when he looked into her eyes. Distance was in order right about now, she thought with apprehension.

"I'll look over it and, uh, get back to you." Nicole reached out for it. She moved back when Marcus took a step forward.

"Something wrong?" he said quietly, still gazing at her intently.

"Nothing. Everything is just fine."

As he came closer, Nicole stiffened her spine mentally. His cologne cracked through her effort to think of him as her employee. She tried to identify the fragrance. The hint of citrus mixed with a musky undertone tickled her nose in a pleasant way.

"I included a three-year projection as well. We might want to reconsider the whole idea. On page ten . . ." He opened the folder and stood close to her.

His body heat seemed to snake out and wrap around her. "I've got a few calls to make," Nicole said as she escaped to the other side of her desk. "Leave it. I promise to read every bit and call you."

Marcus looked at her for a second, then nodded. "Sure. Talk to you later?"

Nicole felt another zing at the promise in that question. Damn! Everything the man did seemed to send her mind on the most unbusinesslike path. Ruffled, she picked up her phone.

"Yes, yes. I'll go over the report and get back to you. Thanks," she replied.

His expression tightened at the seeming curt brush off. Without another word, he turned around and left. The door shut behind him with a solid thump. Two minutes later, Cat went in.

"This isn't your day, huh?" she said, and jerked her head in the direction Marcus had just gone. "You butt heads with Marcus, too?"

"No, of course not." Nicole put the telephone receiver down. "Did he say something?"

"Not Marcus. He's the original strong silent type. Once you two get to know each other, I'm sure you'll click."

"Uh-huh. You've got something for me, I see." Nicole gestured to the stack of files in Cat's hand.

They spent two hours poring over client feedback surveys, contracts and government forms the company had to fill out. All the while Nicole kept hearing the words "You'll click" in the back of her mind. The scent of citrus and musk seemed to linger in the air.

five

Nicole glanced around the lobby of Caldwell Protection Agency. She admired the tasteful, elegant décor. Tall plants were arranged in terra-cotta pots all around, giving the place a tropical look. When she'd discovered that Marcus had a conflicting meeting, she'd insisted on coming alone. Grateful for a break from fighting his magnetism, Nicole had insisted that he not change his schedule. Despite getting lost twice, she'd made it only fifteen minutes late. A short, shapely woman in a navy pinstriped skirt and white blouse spoke to the receptionist briefly, then walked toward Nicole.

"Ms. Benoit, I'm Kelli Caldwell." She stuck out her hand and gave Nicole a firm handshake.

"Nicole, please. Good meeting you, Kelli."

"My office is right this way. I've got coffee, glazed donuts, and soda. I say early morning meetings require good fuel to make them productive." Kelli walked rapidly as she spoke. She waved away two staffers. "Later, guys. I promise."

Nicole almost skipped to keep up. "Seems like you've got enough energy already."

"I like to keep moving." Kelli rounded a corner that led directly to an open door. "Here we go."

"Good." Nicole took a deep breath and let it out. "I was afraid we'd take a jog while we talked."

Kelli laughed. "Have a seat, Nicole. I'll serve you a nice cool glass of anything to make up for that little fifty-yard dash."

"A *real* cola would be nice." Nicole sank into a tan leather chair facing Kelli's desk.

Kelli glanced at her sharply. "I assume you mean with the bad stuff, sugar and caffeine?"

"I know, I know. You don't put poison in your body." Nicole waved a hand. "Give me whatever you've got."

"Don't tell my loving husband who works out five times a week and is into organic foods, but . . ." Kelli opened a small refrigerator in a corner of her office and held up a six-pack of cola.

"Kelli, you're my new best friend." Nicole grinned at her.

The two women exchanged small talk. Nicole warmed instantly to her. Although obviously fit and youthful, Kelli was a good ten years older than Nicole. Kelli popped the top off two cans, poured the contents in paper cups, and sat next to Nicole. She raised her cup in a toast.

"Hey, us women in the biz have to stick together. Welcome to the male-dominated world of security, darlin'."

Nicole tapped her cup against Kelli's as she laughed. "That bad, huh?" She took a sip.

"I've been in this business for eleven years. Most of the guys are polite, but condescending. That's an improvement since the old days." Kelli made a face and took a swallow of cola.

"Wonderful. I'm so looking forward to networking in this town."

"Luckily you've got Marcus. A little stern, but he's good people under that starched exterior." Kelli nodded.

"Right." Nicole considered what else was underneath those tasty outer layers. Before her thoughts could gather the wrong kind of steam, she pushed them away.

"Don't tell me Marcus is giving you a hard time. I'd be so surprised. He's never treated the rest of us women like some of the old boys." Kelli turned to Nicole with interest in her hazel eyes.

"No, no. But it's hard on all the staff adjusting to a new boss." Nicole covered her expression by raising the cup to her mouth and drinking again.

"So true. Employee drama, the worst kind of trouble for any business owner. But I've got good news." Kelli beamed at her.

"Kelli, those words give me chills. The last time I heard them was from beyond the grave." Nicole gave a shudder.

"What?"

"My uncle left a video will in addition to the paper version. That's how he told me I was the proud new CEO of Summers Security," Nicole replied.

Kelli howled with laughter, her head thrown back. Cola sloshed onto the blue carpet in the process. She finally recovered enough to put the cup down on her desk. Still laughing, Kelli got a napkin and dabbed at the pool of soda near her chair.

"Sorry. Please don't be offended, but that Hosea was a real SOB. Lord, but I wish I'd been there to see it." Kelli sat down again.

"Trust me, you're not the only person who held that opinion of him." Nicole leaned back in her chair. "How long did you know him?"

"Sixteen years. I didn't join my husband in the business

until he decided to go full-time with it. Jamar worked as a security guard for fifteen years with Pinkerton." Kelli frowned. "The first time I attended a trade show with him, he introduced me to Hosea."

"And?"

"Hosea took one look at me and said, 'Little lady, you shouldn't have to worry about anything more serious than the grocery list.'" Kelli shook her head. "I told him to stuff his head up his you-know-what in a roundabout way. He got the message."

"Bet he didn't like being told off."

"Actually we got to be buddies later. Hosea liked people who gave as good as they got. He didn't like doormats and was impatient with underachievers." Kelli lifted a shoulder. "That's why he and Marcus hit it off."

"Uncle Hosea had a lot of trust in him, for sure."

"His trust was justified. He's one of the best in this business. Anyway, I was about to tell you about a networking group you'll really like. There are four of us women in the security business in and around Houston. We meet for lunch every third Wednesday of the month. Now we'll be five strong. What do you say?"

"I say my third Wednesday lunches are all booked from now on!" Nicole smiled at her.

"Good for you. Let me give you my card. Call me anytime to ask questions, bounce ideas off me, or just to whine." Kelli went to her desk. She took a business card from a holder on it. "Whining into a sympathetic ear can be therapeutic," she quipped.

Nicole was touched by her gesture. Although she'd never admit it to anyone but her father, the last three weeks had been scary and full of tension. Her throat tightened unexpectedly with emotion. She took the card and stared at it.

"Thanks, Kelli. This is the most welcome I've felt in this town since I got here."

Something in Nicole's voice must have given her away. Kelli came back and sat in the chair next to her again. "Listen, don't let it get you down, especially not on yourself. *Call me*. I mean it."

"I will." Nicole inhaled deeply and let it out. With the release of air went some of the strain of feeling alone.

"Good." Kelli patted Nicole's shoulder.

"Knock, knock." A thirty-something man with a boyish grin stuck his head in the door. "Didn't mean to interrupt, but—"

"Yes you did," Kelli cut in. She smiled at the man with affection. "But you're forgiven as usual. Nicole, this is my husband, Jamar."

Jamar came all the way into the room with a wide smile and his hand outstretched. "Nice meeting you. Look forward to seeing you at the Black Chamber of Commerce meetings."

"Here we go, girl. He's recruiting again," Kelli said in a stage whisper.

"Ignore her," Jamar said. "We're a viable organization helping Black entrepreneurs get a leg up in a tough business environment."

"Sounds like something I need." Nicole shook his hand.

"Excellent. Give me your card and I'll send you more information. I'll send you to our website."

"Here you go." Nicole took one of her cards from the sterling silver case in her purse. "My e-mail address is on there."

"Good deal. Well, ladies, I'll order us lunch from the Health Nut Deli. How about a taco?"

"I could go for one of—" Nicole began.

"Thanks, sweetness, but I'm treating Nicole to a lunch out with our group," Kelli broke in.

"Oh, okay. Well, have fun. I'll be in touch, Nicole."

"Great." Nicole waved to him.

"Eat healthy." Jamar gave his wife a look that seemed to hold a message.

"Bye, babe." Kelli waved him out the door. She went to her desk and retrieved her purse.

"So we're having lunch with the others?" Nicole stood.

"I just made that up. Those tacos are made with soy burgers, soy cheese, and soy taco shells with organic lettuce. You don't even want to know what the sauce is made from!" Kelli shook her shoulders and groaned.

Nicole laughed as she followed her out. To save time they went to a small restaurant not far from Kelli's office. Kelli kept Nicole entertained for the next hour and a half over their grilled chicken salads.

"Honey, you haven't lived until you've gathered evidence for a custody battle over who gets the pythons." Kelli rolled her eyes. "A word of advice, stay away from people who seem a little intense over their pets."

"I'll remember that." Nicole laughed. "I've learned a lot in the last couple of hours listening to you. I really appreciate it."

"Must be tough stepping into Hosea's shoes. At least I had Jamar for support before me and the other ladies got together." Kelli wore a sympathetic expression.

Nicole pushed her salad aside and frowned. "Kelli, I've just *got* to qualify with the state licensing commission so I can be the manager of Summers Security. Until I do the employees will never really consider me the boss. But I've got so much to learn about alarm systems, Texas law, courier services—"

"Slow down, Nicole." Kelli patted her on the arm like a big sister. "My pals and I put together study materials for the licensing exam. I'll e-mail the whole packet to you as an attachment when I get back to my office."

"Don't be alarmed if I hug your neck and sob with gratitude." Nicole laughed as she shook her head. She picked up her fork and dug into her neglected salad. "Suddenly I've got my appetite back."

The next morning Nicole felt a lot better when she arrived at the office. With Kelli's encouragement, she felt a bit more confident. Not even going to work before nine in the morning bothered her.

Cat stood when Nicole walked in. The grim expression on her face dampened Nicole's bright mood. Nicole marched to Cat's desk with a sigh of resignation.

"Now what," Nicole said.

"The licensing commission called. They've had complaints about the guard uniforms. Marcus is out visiting three clients. I sent the call to Russell, since he orders supplies. His new secretary says he can't be disturbed." Cat cleared her throat.

"What happened to the old secretary? She wasn't that 'old.' The woman had only been on the job three months."

"Russell wasn't satisfied with her performance." Cat's eyebrows went up to her hairline. "I'll let him explain it to you."

"I'll deal with that later. Now tell me about the commission." Nicole's bright mood was now completely gone.

"This makes three complaints in the last eight months."

"The uniforms," Nicole repeated. She went to her office with Cat on her heels.

"Yes, it seems the patches that identify them as security guards keep falling off."

Nicole dropped her purse on the credenza behind her desk. "So Russell is in a meeting with staff?"

"No." Cat pursed her lips.

"With a client then." Nicole sorted through messages on her desk.

"Uh-uh. He just got back."

Cat's tone made Nicole look up. "Okay. I'll just give him a call." She punched in his three-digit extension. The fast busy signal indicated he'd punched the Do Not Disturb button.

"Here is the guy's name and number down at the division." Cat held out the phone message memo slip to her.

"Fine. I'll call."

Cat nodded and left. Nicole knew the importance of dealing with the issue as much from what Cat didn't say as from what she did. Under Texas licensing laws for security, uniforms had to clearly identify security employees as guards. She called, only to find out there were other problems. Russell had promised to call the commission back three times.

"Yes, Mr. Frey. I understand. I'll take care of it today. Thanks." Nicole put down the phone and went toward Russell's office. "I'll be in with Russell."

"Good luck," Cat muttered.

"Luck won't have a damn thing to do with it," Nicole tossed back as she kept walking.

Russell's new secretary, a petite woman with her braids pulled back into a bun, jumped to her feet. "Mr. Summers is very busy, ma'am. I can call you when he's free."

"We haven't met. I'm Nicole Benoit, CEO and Russell's boss," Nicole said. "And you are?"

The young woman's eyes widened. "Oh, Denise Sims. I-I've only been here one day."

"It's okay. Welcome to Summers Security." Nicole waved a hand as she went to the closed door to Russell's office. When it opened, she stood aside.

"I'll check the online site and see if that limited-edition

print is still available. Maybe I'll have good news for you tonight. Dinner at seven?" Russell walked beside a tall, leggy
woman with curly auburn hair. His right hand rested on her
waist.

"I can't wait to add another print to my Biggers collection.
You're so thoughtful," the woman purred. She turned to face
Russell.

"You've been so helpful to me. It's the least I can do," Russell said, his voice deepening as he gazed into her eyes.

"Hello," Nicole said in a dry tone. She glanced at Russell,
then the woman.

Russell blinked and seemed to notice Nicole for the first
time. His dreamy expression evaporated into one of annoyance. "Nicole."

His lady friend flashed a megawatt smile at Nicole.
"Nicole, it's a pleasure to finally meet you. Aliyah Manning."
She stuck out a perfectly manicured hand with square
French-tipped fingernails.

Nicole shook it. The cool surface of Aliyah's skin made
Nicole think she'd touched a small reptile. She let go after a
second. "Nice meeting you, too."

"Russell has told me so much about the family. I feel like I
know you already." Aliyah wore the enthusiastic expression
of a salesperson.

"Really?" Nicole smiled back at her, then looked to Russell for an explanation. "How nice."

"Aliyah is a special, talented lady." Russell stood closer to
her. "She's got a great head for business."

"I just let you bounce ideas off me. He's giving me way
more credit than I deserve," Aliyah said to Nicole.

Nicole glanced at the woman from head to toe. Aliyah
wore a short royal blue skirt and white blouse. Her long,
shapely legs probably turned male heads everywhere she

went. Her hair was pulled back into a thick braid that hung down her back about four inches. *I'll bet he's bouncing more than ideas with you, honey.*

"I'm just telling the truth." Russell grinned at her as though they were alone.

Aliyah lifted a shoulder in a humble gesture. She turned to Nicole. "I'm so sorry to keep Russell from important business. I'll get out of the way and let him keep running one of the most successful Black businesses in the Southwest."

"Certainly. The rest of us will try to help him in our own small way." Nicole beamed at her.

Aliyah's ingratiating smile slipped a notch, but she recovered quickly. "I hope we can get together for lunch sometime. Bye now."

"Goodbye." Nicole continued to gaze at her with a fixed smile on her face.

Russell shot a cold look at Nicole. He turned on the warmth again when he faced Aliyah. "I'll call you later."

"I look forward to it." Aliyah fluttered her eyelashes at him. She ignored Denise as she walked out.

Russell shot a chilly glance at Nicole seconds after Aliyah disappeared down the hall. "Is there something you need?"

"Yes, an explanation. Your office will do." Nicole went ahead of him. She turned just as Russell closed the door. "The licensing commission called. Since you were in an 'important meeting' with Aliyah, Cat put him through to me."

"Frey is an obsessive-compulsive bureaucrat." Russell strolled past her and sat down at his desk. "The uniforms are fine. Only one or two guards had a problem, and it's been fixed."

"The company you use doesn't have that great a track record. I checked with a few people in the business. The fabric and workmanship are shoddy. I mean, the patches keep falling off." Nicole spoke in a patient tone, as though talking to a child.

"I saved us a lot of money. It doesn't make sense to get fancy clothes for lower-rung employees." Russell sifted through papers as he spoke.

Nicole held onto her temper. "Russell, our guard license could be on the line over name patches. Spend the extra three dollars per outfit and change."

"Even my father allowed me to make decisions on supplies," Russell said. "I've spoken with Vickers Uniform and they've assured me—"

"Not good enough. Frey may be nitpicking, but he's right. Change to another company. I talked to Andre, and he suggests Cole's Guard Supplies."

"You discussed this with a subordinate behind my back?" Russell said in a flat tone. His eyes narrowed to slits as he tilted his cobalt blue leather captain's chair back. "That's unacceptable. Father specified in the will that I have an important role in this company. My attorney says that includes making management decisions."

"Good, then I'll make you vice president in charge of kitchen, bathroom, and janitorial supplies. You can exercise your managerial judgment on toilet tissue!" Nicole tossed back. She spun around and yanked the door open.

"You can't demote me!" Russell called out. When Nicole kept going, he stormed after her down the hall. "I'll call my attorney."

"You'll be a vice president. You wanted management power, have at it." Nicole rounded a corner, with Russell in pursuit.

"I'm not going to stand for this bull, Nicole. Not even Uncle Stanton will back you up when I tell him." Russell grabbed her arm as they stood in front of the elevators.

"Good, tell him. In the meantime start brushing up on the fine points of brooms and mops." Nicole pulled free of his grasp.

They stared at each other without moving. Nicole weighed the pleasure of feeling her fingers tighten around Russell's neck against doing jail time. She'd decided that stepping over his unconscious body was worth it when the elevators whisked open. Marcus and a stocky man with wispy blond hair stepped out.

"We're fully committed to—" Marcus broke off when he saw Nicole and Russell. He cleared his throat.

Nicole blinked back from the edge of assault. She forced a smile that hurt as Russell let go of her arm. "We'll talk about the uniforms later. Hello."

"Mr. Kleinpeter, this is our new CEO, Nicole Benoit, and Russell Summers, vice president of development." Marcus glanced a warning at them. "Mr. Kleinpeter is impressed with our coordination. I was just telling him teamwork makes the difference."

"Of course it does. Even when we disagree, the exchange of ideas results in a better outcome," Nicole said smoothly. She shook hands with Kleinpeter. "I'm glad you came by. Why don't we go to my office."

"Of course." Mr. Kleinpeter grinned, pleased at the invitation. "I know how busy a boss can be, though."

"You're the reason we work so hard. We'll have something cool to drink. I'm still getting used to how humid Houston can be in the summer." Nicole favored him with her best smile.

"A glass of cold soda would be nice." Mr. Kleinpeter followed her happily.

Nicole kept up a stream of conversation with him for the

next fifteen minutes. She even managed to forget about making Russell's face turn blue. By the time she'd turned him over to Marcus again, Nicole had calmed down. A timid knock on her door interrupted the progress she was making plowing through state licensing regulations.

"Yeah," Nicole answered.

Cat came in with a wary expression. "Uh, I finished these letters for you."

"Thanks." Nicole took them from her. "I'll proof them later."

"You okay?"

Nicole breathed in and out once. "I will be. I'm getting tired of fighting battles." She rested her head against the chair back.

"I hear ya." Cat closed the door. "Guys have a hard time taking instructions from women, even when they know we're smarter. In fact, that just makes it worse."

"Then they'll have to get over their caveman thinking." Nicole rubbed her eyes. "I think they purposely make this print tiny to torture folks."

"Take a break. You can't learn it all in one hour." Cat went to the refrigerator and got out a bottle of apple juice. She put it down in front of Nicole. "Kick back and knock down a cold one."

"Thanks," Nicole said with a laugh. "Maybe I'll do just that."

"Marcus is different. He's got integrity and works hard. I know he seems a little . . ."

"Stiff is the word you're reaching for, Cat," Nicole quipped.

"He's got a big heart underneath that starched surface. Loosen him up. You can do it." Cat nodded slowly.

"Umm, we'll see." Nicole wondered just what it would take to make the "man of steel" unbend.

Marcus knocked, then opened the door. "I thought maybe we could talk."

"I was about to leave. I'll finish updating the database of industry contacts." Cat gave Nicole a pointed look. "You'll work on that project we talked about, right?"

Nicole squinted and waved her toward the door. "It's under consideration."

When Cat closed the door behind her, Marcus walked in and folded his frame into the chair across from Nicole. "What project?"

"Getting some files organized. So, let's talk," she said, deflecting him from the subject.

Curiosity flickered in his dark eyes, but he nodded. "You and Russell."

"My dear cousin." Nicole frowned.

"Being confrontational with Russell isn't the way to go. Believe me, I had my share of disputes with him the first year I worked here." Marcus smoothed down his silk tie. "I found out that giving him a sense of importance goes a long way."

"Really?" Nicole said dryly.

"Taking even the limited responsibility he now has will make things worse."

"I'll think about it." Nicole pressed her lips together as she stared at him steadily. She'd had her fill of men treating her like a dense kid who needed her nose wiped.

Marcus seemed not to notice. "He'll probably continue to question your authority and decisions," he added with a lift of one shoulder.

"Thanks for giving me the benefit of your experience." Nicole picked up her ink pen and made notes.

"Right." Marcus smiled and stood. "I'll let you get back to your project."

"Yes." Nicole counted to ten as an aid to hold her tongue. Her father had no idea how badly she was being tested by these two men.

"By the way, the Reuben contract is up for renewal. Might be a problem with it." Marcus delivered the news casually.

"Summers Security has provided security to his three jewelry stores since forever." Nicole felt a thudding headache coming on.

"Yeah. Old Mr. Reuben was one of your uncle's first customers." Marcus stood. "I'll let you know what happens."

"Okay. What about Mr. Kleinpeter and his dry cleaning stores?" Nicole asked.

"He was noncommittal. Funny, but I was sure he was ready to hire us."

"And you think it's my fault because I didn't control that scene with Russell." Nicole clenched her teeth.

"I'm just saying consider a different approach with him in the future." Marcus gave a crisp nod and walked toward the door.

Nicole simmered as she watched him. What galled her even more was the fact that she couldn't think of a comeback. Marcus seemed intent on pointing out her shortcomings. Indeed, Nicole was beginning to wonder if she was in over her head. The pile of regulations and study materials on her desk seemed to mock her. How could she learn it all, adjust to a new city away from her friends, and deal with resentful staff? The thudding behind her left eye spread to her temples. She rubbed her forehead.

"I'll be in my office if you need me."

She glanced up to find Marcus staring at her. He blinked.

For a second Nicole imagined she saw a glimmer of empathy in his eyes. The glimmer, or whatever it was, died quickly, and the cool regard returned. Nicole took her hand down, sat straight, and smiled.

"Let's meet before you get back to Mr. Reuben. I want specifics on why he's unhappy." Nicole dismissed him by returning to the reports on her desk.

"Yes, *ma'am.*"

When the door closed behind him, Nicole's brave posture wilted. The employees whose jobs she had decided to save didn't want her here, it seemed. Uncle Hosea's will included a clause that specified she had to prove she was competent or lose the business. Nicole hadn't cared about the company at first. She'd proven Uncle Hosea wrong before, and his challenge from the grave had pressed her buttons. Yet doubts crowded her attempts to be strong.

"What the hell am I doing here?" she muttered.

As though to answer her question, the phone rang. Nicole picked it up and went back to being a businesswoman. She would leave Summers Security on her own terms. So, the employees had just better get over themselves, especially Marcus Reed.

Six

Marcus smiled to himself as he headed to his office. He'd stepped off the elevator and into a battle zone. Nicole and Russell mixed like fire and gunpowder. One was sure to set off the other. All Marcus had to do was sit back. The way he saw it, he was in a win-win position. He could pick up the pieces either way. If Nicole stayed in charge, business would probably suffer because she really didn't know what she was doing. If Russell successfully challenged the will, there was no doubt Summers Security would go downhill fast. Then he would start his own company with Summers Security customers. He was sitting under a plum tree just waiting for the ripe fruit to fall in his lap. Perfect, he mused. Marcus waved to his secretary, Shelly, and went into his office.

As he sorted through mail, a disturbing image pricked at him. Nicole. Her lovely golden brown eyes had been clouded by apprehension. She must feel isolated, thrown into a situation she hadn't asked for or totally understood. Marcus took hold of himself. He blocked more pictures of her smile, the way Nicole's hair swung when she shook her head stubbornly.

"I don't like sharp-tongued, spoiled sorority girls," he reminded himself. He concentrated on that image to get rid of any lingering effects from her striking eyes.

"Marcus, we should discuss the future of this company," Russell said as he barged in without knocking.

Shelly came in seconds later. She shot a sideways glance at Russell. "Don't forget your appointment with Mrs. Petersen."

"It's okay. She cancelled," Marcus said. He suppressed a smile when his secretary rolled her eyes to the ceiling and left. "What's up, Russell?"

"We've had our differences, but I think we both agree that Nicole should not be CEO." Russell took a seat.

"Your father's decision was certainly unexpected," Marcus said in a bland tone.

"That's an understatement." Russell crossed one long leg over the other. "I think we should do something."

"You're already doing something, contesting the will." Marcus rocked his leather chair back gently.

"Yes, but in the short term I think we should present a united front. She's not qualified to run this company. My father had a lot of confidence in you. So much so that you were given quite a bit of responsibility." Russell's mouth turned down.

"He could be difficult." Marcus studied the younger version of Hosea. Russell had his father's nose, eyes, and stubbornness. Unfortunately he didn't have his father's brains or business acumen.

"I always thought his becoming a father rather late in life had something to do with it. After all, he was almost fifty when I was born."

"Maybe so." Marcus waited for him to go on.

Russell's brows drew together. "Father was a hard man to

please. He was even harder on his own children, especially me as his only son. But that's beside the point. One of us should have been named CEO."

"Russell, you think that *you* should have been left the business," Marcus replied.

"I've never made that a secret," Russell said with a sniff. "But at least if you had been left the business I wouldn't worry about some incompetent destroying what *we* built."

Marcus fought the urge to laugh. Russell hadn't built anything more than a pile of debt on the company balance sheets. Instead he cleared his throat. "Well, I—"

"We need to take action before Nicole damages Summers Security beyond repair." Russell leaned forward with a grave expression.

"The will is quite clear, as even your attorney has pointed out by now," Marcus replied. "Nicole is to run the business."

"You know how father loved putting the devil in details. There are certain conditions." Russell wore a sly half-smile.

"Really?" Marcus didn't have to pretend interest. He propped both elbows on his desk.

"If she's proven incompetent, an executive committee must remove her and appoint a new CEO." Russell sat back with a satisfied expression. "I say we put new contracts on hold for six months. The company won't show a profit and she'll be held responsible. Most of the family is nervous about her anyway."

Marcus was sure Russell wasn't telling him the whole truth. Not that it mattered. "Nicole signed one yesterday, and the other two are on her desk."

"You should have checked with me first!" Russell complained. "We've got to stick together."

"I wouldn't have agreed to put off three important accounts. I worked hard to get them, and my reputation is on

the line." Marcus relaxed back in his chair. He wasn't surprised that Russell's scheme had holes in it.

Russell stood and looked down at him with distaste. "I
would have made you chief operating officer, Marcus. Taking her side is a big mistake."

"I'm here to do a job for Summers Security, not to get in
the middle of your dispute over Mr. Summers's estate." Marcus opened a folder on his desk. "I realize you're angry, but I
can't help you."

"Fine. Just don't be surprised when I end up with the company." Russell walked out.

Once he was gone, Marcus sat back in deep thought. Now
he had a hint about how Russell and Jolene planned to attack
Nicole. Marcus wondered how he could get a look at the will.
A knock on his office door interrupted his thoughts.

"Come in," he said and wondered if he'd get anything
more done today.

Shelly rushed in. "Mr. Phoung is shouting on line five. I
can't make sense of anything he says."

Nicole came in behind her. "Sorry to interrupt, but—"

"Just a minute. I'd better take this call. An unhappy client
is on the phone." Marcus held up one palm and picked up the
receiver with his other hand.

"Unhappy ain't the half of it," Shelly whispered to Nicole.
She retreated, pulling the door shut as she left.

Nicole sat down. "Who is it?"

"David Phoung runs three midsized grocery stores in
some rough neighborhoods. We installed cameras for him.
One of our guards reviews the tapes twice a week," Marcus
explained quickly, then punched the button for line five. "Hi,
David."

Then all he could do was listen and take notes. Marcus had
a hard time breaking in on the near hysterical stream of

words from the Vietnamese national. Mr. Phoung even lapsed into his native language as he sputtered in outrage.

"I can assure you we'll get to the bottom of this and find out what happened. Of course we'll cooperate with the police. Tell you what, I'll be over there in a few minutes." Marcus spoke in an even tone to reassure him. "Right. Goodbye."

"What happened?" Nicole sprang from her chair when Marcus stood.

"Mr. Phoung found that one of the cameras had been turned off. He's lost about two thousand dollars' worth of merchandise that he knows of so far. He's screaming that our employee was in on the theft." Marcus grabbed his jacket from a small closet in his office.

"Oh crap," Nicole blurted out.

"Come on." Marcus waved a hand impatiently.

"No, uh, I'm sure you can deal with it." Nicole backed up.

"Customers should know that the boss is willing to get her hands dirty. Shelly, we're on our way to the Pak-Sav-N-Go on Almeda," Marcus replied as he pulled Nicole along.

Shelly handed Nicole a small steno pad and ink pen. "Okay. Here, you might need these."

"Thanks," Nicole said and hurried after Marcus.

During the drive over Nicole listened intently as Marcus gave her background on the Phoung contract. He had to admit he was impressed with her questions. Russell had underestimated her. Maybe he had as well.

"So, basically we did a security survey at his stores." Nicole jotted notes.

"Right. Andre did the final report and I reviewed it. We recommended he change the layout. The aisles are angled with large mirrors positioned on the walls."

"And we installed the cameras."

"Like I said, we've got a security guard who reviews the

tapes. A determined thief will find a way to steal even with the best system." Marcus muttered a curse when a red light caught them.

"Take it easy. Spreading us all over the pavement won't help," Nicole said as she darted a glance at him.

"Relax, I haven't killed a passenger in a whole month," he deadpanned.

"I feel better," Nicole quipped. She frowned. "Phoung didn't implement all of your recommendations."

"Right," Marcus said and looked at her in surprise.

"In between getting my nails done and shopping I managed to actually read the files." Nicole didn't look back at him but kept writing.

Marcus looked ahead just as the light changed. He drove on. "Phoung went with a cheaper camera model than we suggested. After three robberies, the police told him those pictures weren't helpful at all. Too fuzzy."

Ten minutes later they arrived at a large store. The offices were on the third floor above it. Marcus opened the door for Nicole. She strode in with confidence, her head up. This woman acts like she's used to being in charge, he mused. Fine, she could do the talking. Her chance to deal with the crisis appeared within seconds. Tameka Grant, their employee, stormed toward them in her olive green uniform. She walked right past Nicole to Marcus.

Tameka stabbed a forefinger in Marcus's chest. "I've been tryin' to keep cool, but if he calls me a shoplifter one more time—"

"Take it easy, Tameka. Let us handle this," Nicole said before he could speak. She blinked when the husky woman glared at her.

"All I'm sayin' is he better watch his mouth. I been in security for six years and ain't nobody ever accused me of nothin'."

"I understand you're upset," Nicole said in a calm but firm tone. "If he doesn't have any evidence . . ."

Tameka turned sharply to face Nicole. "You tryin' to say I'm a suspect or somethin'?" she said loudly.

"Tameka, Ms. Benoit is—" Marcus began but stopped when Nicole raised a palm.

"I can handle this," Nicole said in a tight voice.

Marcus cleared his throat and stepped back. He decided not to go far in case Nicole needed to be rescued. Tameka glowered at her with both hands on her wide hips. Marcus shook his head mentally. The sorority girl was about to learn a hard lesson.

"I don't know who you are or who you think I am, but lemme get you straight." Tameka waved her finger in the air under Nicole's nose.

Nicole looked the angry woman in the eye. "As CEO of this company I expect all of our employees to stand up under pressure. We'll back you all the way, but making a scene isn't going to help."

"Say what?" Tameka looked at Marcus.

"She's your new boss," he said with a nod.

"I don't have to take this mess," Tameka grumbled with less heat.

"Fine. Turn in your equipment. We're going to investigate no matter what," Nicole replied.

"Well, I just don't think it's right the way he talked to me," Tameka grumbled. Still, she lowered her hand.

"Take a few days off," Nicole added when Tameka's hand came up again. "Jesse will be in touch with you."

"Yeah, all right. I need to give my nerves a rest." Tameka

glared at three store employees who stood watching the scene, then she stomped out of the store.

Marcus nodded to a door marked Employees Only. "This way. That was a smooth move, boss lady. I had to suspend her pending the results of an internal investigation anyway."

"I know. I've been reading company policy and the state regs." Nicole fell in step beside him as they went down a hallway.

"When did you have time to get your nails done?" Marcus punched the button to summon the elevator.

Nicole glanced at her fingernails with a frown. "I haven't lately, damn it. Another reason I don't feel like putting up with back talk from anybody these days."

"Life is so hard," Marcus murmured. They got on the elevator.

She shot a heated glance at him but said nothing. They rode up to the third floor in silence. When they got off the elevator, a wiry man hurried down the long hall toward them. David Phoung wore a starched white Tommy Hilfiger shirt tucked into khaki pants. He stood a good two inches shorter than Nicole. Still, the size of his temper made up for his small stature. He started shouting when he was still fifteen feet away.

"I want something done!" he blurted out. "That woman, your employee." Mr. Phoung pointed at them. "She's responsible!"

"I'm getting real tired of fingers in my face," Nicole whispered. Nevertheless, her expression remained composed. "Hello, Mr. Phoung. I'm Nicole Benoit, the—"

"I want something done, Mr. Reed. I can't stay in business losing valuable merchandise. My assistant manager tells me there may have been thefts for at least three months." Mr.

Phoung's words came out rapid fire. He took a deep breath and put both hands on his slender hips. "Well?"

"What kind of inventory controls do you have in place? Have you questioned your employees?" Nicole assumed an air of quiet efficiency. She took the notepad from a pocket in her green blazer.

"Well, I-I don't know." Mr. Phoung blinked at her behind his black frame eyeglasses.

Another man, slightly taller than Mr. Phoung, emerged from an office nearby. "Excuse me. I'm Phan Tran, Mr. Phoung's assistant. I deal with the managers of all three stores."

"Hello. We'll need as much information as you can give. Right, Marcus?" Nicole glanced at him.

Marcus nodded. "Right. Hi, Phan. Why don't we pull up data on inventory reports and employee background checks."

Nicole turned to Mr. Phoung again. "You've called the police?"

"Of course I called the police. I've been robbed!" Mr. Phoung took a deep breath in preparation for another rant.

"Then it's even more important to give them details quickly. The faster they can start their investigation the better."

Marcus admired the cool way she talked the agitated man down. She neatly maneuvered him down the hall to his office. Marcus spent the next hour with Tran gathering printouts. Nicole came back twice to ask Marcus questions she couldn't answer for Mr. Phoung. Then they both spent another thirty minutes with Mr. Phoung. By the time they walked out the door, Nicole had a pad filled with notes.

Marcus opened the doors to the Dodge Durango with the remote. Nicole put on her sunglasses, took off her jacket, and tossed it onto the backseat. Marcus gazed at the white fitted dress shirt that molded to her breasts. Her curvaceous body dressed up the business outfit she wore. The crisp blouse was tucked into the green skirt, which wasn't short. Still, her long, lovely legs made what would have been a prim look on another woman into a spine-tingling distraction. Marcus felt a chill run up his arms despite the hot sunlight that bounced off the pavement.

"I'll drive," Nicole said. She frowned when Marcus hesitated. "What?"

"Nothing. It's just . . ." He mentally shook himself.

Nicole walked past him to the driver's side and got in. She held out her hand for the keys. "Don't make a crack about women drivers. I'm not in the mood."

"I wasn't going to," Marcus replied mildly. "We always drove Mr. Summers, that's all. Boss's privilege."

"Well, I like to drive. My uncle was too proud to admit he'd gotten too old to brave this wild Houston traffic. Besides, you've got more experience with security procedures than I do. You want to make phone calls even before we get to the office. Right?" Nicole gazed at him with an unreadable expression behind the dark glasses.

"Yes," he admitted.

"Then it's safer. I don't want us whizzing through red lights because you're concentrating on missing jelly beans." She pulled the driver's seat closer to the controls to accommodate her height.

Marcus laughed in spite of the situation. He handed her the keys and climbed into the passenger side. "You've got a point. And I don't mind being driven by a woman at all," he said as he fastened his seat belt.

"I'll just bet you don't," she tossed back.

He glanced at her sharply. Nicole shifted into reverse and deftly wheeled the SUV out of the parking lot. Marcus took the slim cell phone from his inner pocket. "That didn't come out the way I intended."

"Yeah, well, the truth has a way of sliding out." Nicole checked traffic, then turned left onto FM 60. She grinned but continued to look ahead at the road.

Marcus decided to let that one pass. He made a series of phone calls, one of them to a buddy who worked in the burglary division of the Houston police force. By the time they would arrive at the office, he would have two of the staff on an internal investigation.

"I want to look over every bit of information you get as soon as you get it," Nicole said as she hit the brake. "I'd like us to solve this crime before the police. Our name is on the line." Nicole scowled, but it wasn't the traffic that worried her.

"Tameka has her faults, but lifting merchandise doesn't sound like her." Marcus stretched out his legs. "Of course you never know."

"I'd like to review her personnel file. Let's see if she's had any conflicts with Jesse or Mr. Phoung's staff," Nicole said. Jesse hired, trained, and supervised the security guards.

"The answer is yes and yes. Tameka has an attitude problem," Marcus replied.

"For real," Nicole retorted.

"She's had minor problems at two other sites but does a good job otherwise. No allegations of theft, though," he added when she looked at him.

"Maybe she didn't have an opportunity. Where was she before?" Nicole said.

"She worked at Wisdom Ministries for eight months."

"You know where each guard works? Impressive." Nicole glanced at him and back at the street.

"I'd like to take the compliment, but Jesse told me when I called the office."

"You still deserve it for pulling together information so fast." Nicole nodded.

"Just doing my job." Marcus felt a flush of pleasure despite his words.

"No, it's more than a job with you, even though you're not thrilled to have me for a boss." Nicole turned to him after she braked at a red light.

"Like I said, change is always tough," he said cautiously.

She only nodded again. The light turned green, and she drove on without saying more. Nicole had seemed to seek some kind of reassurance from him. Marcus suddenly wanted to see her eyes behind the dark glasses. Why? She was a Summers, and that should have been all he needed to know. In fact, she was more dangerous than the old man had ever been. That body, those eyes, and that voice could lead most men astray.

Marcus risked another look at her as Nicole adjusted the rearview mirror. He studied her profile. She lifted her chin and checked her lipstick. The bronze color was a perfect blend for her smooth complexion. When she pressed her lips together, Marcus blinked hard and looked away. The space between them didn't seem wide enough. Marcus pressed his shoulder against the door as though trying to increase the inches.

"Wisdom Ministries. Isn't that Pastor Ike's church? Yeah, that televangelist who claims he's got the power of healing in his hands. He was busted last April with an expensive hooker in his limo," Nicole said, answering her own question. "He was laying hands on her all right."

"Uh, yes, he founded Wisdom Ministries," Marcus replied as he shifted in his seat.

When Nicole turned the air conditioner up his mind turned to the fragrance she wore. The scent seemed to wrap itself around him. A blend of something sweet and piquant, it reminded him of every caution he'd ever heard about Louisiana women. His grandfather had told tales of Creole women who could cloud a man's mind with voodoo. Marcus imagined Nicole seated in front of a vanity mirror dabbing perfume on her neck, then between her breasts. Without thinking he reached over and turned the fan on high. He jerked his hand back when he brushed against her sleeve.

"I think—" Nicole broke off and glanced at him. Her dark brows drew together over the rim of her sunglasses. "Marcus, what is wrong with you?"

Nothing a shower of ice wouldn't cure. "I'm okay. Man, this traffic is horrible."

Nicole gazed at him a second longer before she looked ahead again. "This crazy traffic is just one of the reasons I don't want to live here." She turned into the parking garage of the office building that housed the company.

"Houston isn't all that bad," Marcus said. "The city has all kinds of cultural events and recreational opportunities."

"So, you think I should stick around?" Nicole parked the vehicle on the fourth level in a reserved space marked Summers Security.

"I was just saying, you know," Marcus stammered. He unbuckled his seat belt and got out of the vehicle to cover his confusion.

"I'm going to move into Uncle Hosea's house, another reason for Russell to hate me. But he did leave that to me, too." Nicole pressed a button on the keyless remote. The horn beeped once to signal that the Durango's alarm system was armed.

"Nice address."

Marcus had been to several company parties at the spacious home in River Oaks. The house sat on a corner lot and boasted over three thousand feet of living area, a pool with a spa, and a fireplace, among other things.

"*Big* address. At least I've a housekeeper, if she doesn't quit on me, that is." Nicole led the way into the garage elevator and punched the button for their floor.

"Rosaria is a gem. She could handle the most difficult task just to please her employer."

"Even me, huh?" Nicole didn't look at him.

"I meant your late uncle. You're a sweetheart compared to Hosea Summers. I, uh . . ."

Marcus found himself in deep water. He felt a rush of gratitude when the elevator stopped and the doors whisked open. He was about to make a hasty retreat to safety when her sexy voice stopped him cold.

"Could you come to my office, please?" She headed off without waiting for an answer.

"Let me make a few calls first. I might have more news on the Phoung situation." Marcus backed up a few steps.

"I won't keep you long. In fact, make the calls from my desk." Nicole waved him to follow.

Marcus hesitated. When Nicole glanced over her shoulder with one eyebrow raised, he followed.

"Was it bad?" Cat's eyes were wide. She handed Nicole a stack of phone messages.

"Bad enough," Nicole replied. She took the blue slips of paper without even slowing down. "Marcus and I shouldn't be disturbed unless it's an emergency."

"Yes, ma'am." Cat stared at him with curiosity as he went by her desk. "I made sure you've got plenty of cola, chips, and sandwich fixings. Just in case you work late again."

"You're more precious than gold," Nicole quipped. Cat smiled with pleasure in response.

"You two have become close." Marcus closed the door to Nicole's office.

"Thank heavens not everyone around here loathes me." Nicole dropped the notepad on her desk.

"Not true. It's just—"

"I know, change is difficult," she cut him off. "Now I have to deal with a customer who thinks our employee is a thief." Nicole rolled her shoulders with a grimace.

Marcus watched her closely. Lines of worry marred her lovely forehead. He had a crazy desire to be the one who could smooth them away. "It's easier for an employer to blame outside staff, especially when most of his employees are relatives or family friends."

"Good point. Still, that's a good reason not to suspect them. They've all got a stake in the bottom line." Nicole massaged her neck.

"Relatives can't always be trusted." Marcus couldn't take his eyes off the way she kneaded her flesh. He imagined the sensation of warm satin beneath his fingers instead.

Nicole closed her eyes for a second, then looked at him. "Tell me about it. I've been dealing with mine since I walked through the front door."

"Inheriting a business under these circumstances does pose a challenge." Marcus tried to keep his distance mentally, to see her as the opposition. Yet he couldn't look away from her arresting eyes.

Nicole sighed and sat down heavily. "Challenge is an understatement. I want to do right by the employees. At first I just wanted to dump the whole headache."

"Mr. Summers made that impossible." Marcus heard the note of sympathy in his voice. *Keep your head, man.* His resolve weakened when she sighed softly again and rested her head on the chair.

She shook her head. "Yeah, he did. I feel stuck, and I'm sure y'all consider yourselves stuck with me. Right, Marcus?"

His pulse picked up at the way she said his name. "It's not that bad, Nicole. Sure the staff is a little resistant—"

"You included," she broke in.

"Okay, I've had my moments. But no matter what you might think, we really care about this company. They will come around." Marcus sat down in one of the chairs facing her.

"You will?" She gazed at him steadily.

"I have a lot of sweat invested in this place." Marcus side-stepped the real question in her eyes. He looked away to break the spell of the beautiful lady in distress. "Sometimes it's good to get away."

"Is that an invitation?"

"Excuse me?" Marcus blinked at her.

"Don't panic, I only meant a business lunch." Nicole wore a crooked smile.

"Oh, right. Maybe another day—"

"Never mind, you've got a full day ahead." Nicole patted his arm as though consoling a small child.

"Yes, well." Marcus blinked rapidly and scrambled to figure out just when he'd stepped off a cliff.

"I'll call you later. Okay?" Nicole got busy at her desk. She didn't look at him.

"Yes, later." Marcus felt like a man who had just lost ground in a chess match.

Nicole glanced at him. "And another thing, loosen up. You're sitting over there like you've got a steel rod up your you-know-what."

Marcus wished he could laugh at the joke. The trouble was the joke was on him. Getting loose with her was the last thing he needed.

seven

Two days later Marcus made a valiant attempt to loosen up. At Nicole's suggestion they'd taken off for lunch to talk business and work out at the Taking Shape Gym. Nicole suppressed a smile. Marcus played the gentleman as they ran around the inside track. His long legs would have easily carried him far ahead of her. Yet they were side by side for each of the five laps. They alternated cardio exercise with resistance training. He did chest compression. Three women did a double take in unison when he strolled into the weight room, picked up a set of dumbbells, and did arm curls. She couldn't blame them for gawking. Nicole stared as well, becoming the fourth member of the Marcus Reed Admiration Society.

Marcus had skin like smooth cinnamon candy. The muscles of his biceps rippled with each movement. His broad chest formed a nice line that tapered down to his narrow waist. The royal blue running shorts molded to his body. Topped by a white Old Navy T-shirt, he looked like every woman's fantasy personal trainer. Her own exercise forgotten, Nicole leaned against a weight lift bench and enjoyed the show. Too bad he was Mister tight-butt-chip-on-my-shoulder. Still what a nice butt, and tight was a perfect description, she mused. Marcus realized she was looking at him and stopped his set.

"You're supposed to use the equipment, not lean on it." He jerked his head toward the machinery.

Nicole blushed. "Ahem, right."

Real smooth, girl. Nicole spent the next fifteen minutes working her chest and upper arms. She poured her concentration in the repetitive movements to block out the vision of Marcus lifting weights. Much as she tried, there was no ignoring how he attracted circling females. One smitten lady in particular inspired an unpleasant itch of irritation. Tall and blond, the woman made sure she was in his line of vision. She tossed her long blond ponytail when Marcus looked her way.

"Try to be a little more obvious, honey," Nicole groused under her breath.

"Hi, I'm Heather." The woman flashed her even white teeth at him.

"Heather," Nicole muttered.

"Hi, Heather. Marcus."

He smiled at her briefly, then turned his attention to stacking weights in preparation to perform a set of bench presses. Nicole snorted as she let go of the weight bar she'd been lifting. The twenty-pound metal disc clanged into place. Marcus glanced at her sharply, one eyebrow raised.

"You okay?" he asked.

"Man, those things are heavier than I thought."

"Be careful you don't strain yourself."

Nicole glanced at Heather, now busy doing warm-up stretches. "You, too."

Marcus merely smiled and continued his workout. Nicole

got on a treadmill against a wall across from him. The trim blond strolled over the moment Marcus sat up. Nicole watched Heather go through her best flirting paces. Marcus nodded and smiled. From time to time he glanced across at Nicole, who waved and grinned. Finally he managed to make a graceful exit. Heather watched him walk over to Nicole, a hungry gleam in her green eyes.

"I think you've left behind a shattered dream," Nicole said. Then she flicked her fingertips at Heather with a grin. The woman flashed a silent challenging smile back at her.

"You've got a devilish streak, Ms. Benoit." Marcus wiped his face with the end of the towel over his left shoulder.

"That girl would happily push me down a deep hole to get at you."

"I doubt getting rid of you is easy," he tossed back with a laugh.

"Remember that, Mr. Reed," Nicole blurted out. She blushed when he looked at her with interest.

"I assume we're talking strictly business?"

Nicole would have happily climbed into a hole at that moment. What in the world had made her say such a thing? A tiny voice answered with "His fine body, what else?" She punched the treadmill off and hopped down. To buy time, Nicole covered her face with a towel and pretended to wipe away perspiration.

"Look at the time. We'd better go." Nicole headed for the ladies' dressing room before he could probe further.

Showered and back in business attire, they ate in the club restaurant. After a quick lunch of tuna salad sandwiches and fruit juice they headed to the office. Thankfully Marcus's cell phone rang twice on the ride back.

"Tameka did what?" Marcus scowled as he looked through

the windshield. "Yeah, we'll deal with it. We're only ten minutes away. Okay." He tapped the button to end the call.

"What's happened now?" Nicole pulled up to a red light and stopped.

"Tameka's lawyer has already called the office." Marcus drummed his fingers on the armrest between them.

"Well, well. She didn't waste any time. We haven't accused her of anything yet." Nicole joined him in scowling at the world.

"I've got more good news. Mr. Phoung's lawyer called, too. He says we should pay for the missing stock."

Nicole let out a long whistle. "Oh-oh."

"Each contract says we can't guarantee there will be no loss by theft or other criminal acts or acts of God. Phoung is testing us," Marcus replied.

"So far there is no proof our employee is responsible. Therefore there is no basis for a lawsuit," Nicole said.

"The lawyer's mind is already working." Marcus glanced at her.

"Are you sure Tameka wouldn't help herself to the merchandise?" Nicole wheeled the small SUV expertly around a corner.

"I'm going to test every possible theory," Marcus said in a firm tone. "But I sure hope my first thought about Tameka is the right one. She's a single mother with no one to help."

"Then let's clear her of any suspicion fast. I don't want her kids to suffer," Nicole said.

They arrived back at the office only to be met by more drama. Cat and Russell were waiting when they stepped off the elevator. Both started talking at once. Russell glared at Cat, and she pressed her lips together.

"I could have handled these issues if I'd known you two

were going on an extended lunch," Russell snipped. He glanced from Nicole to Marcus.

"We have to eat, too, Russell." Nicole knew she sounded defensive. Several employees pretended to look busy, but they were obviously drinking in every word.

"Let's go in Nicole's office," Marcus said in a voice of authority. He marched on without waiting for anyone to respond. Once there, he held the door until everyone was inside, then shut it.

"Russell, so help me if you make one more scene in front of my employees—" Nicole shook a finger at his nose.

"*Your* employees?" Russell cut in.

Marcus took Nicole by the arm and led her a few feet away from Russell. "Let's keep calm."

"I should be CEO and everyone knows it," Russell said in a calm tone. "But we'll let our attorneys sort it out."

"Wait! I'm getting a psychic message from Uncle Hosea. He's saying 'When pigs fly,' " Nicole shot back.

"Nicole, remember we just worked off tension," Marcus mumbled.

"Let her make clever jokes. We know the truth." Russell looked at Marcus with a smirk.

Nicole's eyes narrowed to slits as she turned to Marcus. He looked at Russell instead of returning her gaze.

"What's going on?" Marcus asked evenly.

"The silent alarm went off at Best Deal Liquor Store. Andre is talking to the police now. I think they had a burglary, but I haven't had a chance to talk to him," Cat said in a rush before Russell could speak.

"One of the guards got sick at the Delia Fine Gallery's grand opening reception. So, her salon filled with priceless African-American art has no protection. Another didn't show up for his shift at a gospel concert across town," Russell said with a sneer. "If I had the proper authority I could have resolved these issues."

"Jesse called in two people who are on their way to the job sites." Cat cut her eyes at Russell in disapproval. "Everything is okay."

"I'd hardly call four disasters within the first three weeks *she* takes over 'okay.'" Russell crossed his arms and gazed at Nicole.

"You're fired," Nicole said.

"You can't fire him," Marcus mumbled aside to her.

"I know." Nicole exhaled slowly. "But it still felt so damn good saying it."

"I'll be in my office. Pick up the pieces the best you can. Section B, clause six should kick in anytime now. Can't wait to see you explain everything to Francine and the family." Russell strolled out whistling.

Cat sorted through Nicole's phone messages quickly. "You know, I might be able to handle some of these. Y'all need to talk." She cast a look of sympathy at Nicole as she left.

"Ahh!" Nicole searched for something to throw. She spotted a coffee mug with the company logo and picked it up.

Marcus grabbed her arm. "Breaking things won't help."

Another man might have been doubled over in pain by now for making such a mistake. Instead Nicole stared into brown eyes that seemed to pull her into them. She could feel his breath on her left cheek like a whispery kiss. The sensation raised the hairs on her neck. Stiff, self-important, and passive aggressive he might be, but she wanted him. And in an instant she decided to have him, every inch of his fine candy-coated tan body. So began another legendary Nicole Summers Benoit campaign to get what she wanted. She relaxed her arm slightly and let it drop until it rested against his flat stomach. A coy smile would be too obvious. Marcus wasn't the type to fall for the obvious. Still, the way he held onto her and didn't move away said a lot. Best to appeal to his sense of professional decorum. *No drama, Nicole.*

"You're right," she said quietly. "My inner spoiled brat keeps fighting to get out. I'm okay now, thanks."

He blinked as though surprised at her response. Then he let go of her and took a step back. "I didn't count on being referee as part of my new job description," he said gruffly as he put more distance between them.

"I apologize. Dealing with Russell and getting used to the business has me stressed to the limit. Still, that's no excuse." Nicole sat down at her desk.

Marcus smoothed down the front of his suit and cleared his throat. "What did Russell mean about Section B, clause six?"

"The will states in that portion that if I don't meet certain conditions, Summers Security will convert to a Subchapter C Corporation and a board of directors will be appointed. They will then decide who will be CEO."

"Why would Russell and his sister want that? They're listed as owners with the business being a Limited Liability Company." Marcus put one hand in his pocket.

"Silent partners with no clout."

"True. So, they'll take their chances that the family will decide he should be in charge."

"Like you said, getting rid of me isn't easy," Nicole wore a half-smile.

"Plan B in the works?"

She glanced up. He seemed to be evaluating her. *Careful. Play is one thing, business is a whole other game.* Nicole put on a relaxed smile. "I'm working on it."

Marcus lifted a shoulder. "Good luck then. If it's okay with you, I'll call our lawyer about Tameka and Phoung."

"Fine. Just let me know what he says before you leave." Nicole opened a folder.

"I'll probably be working late." He started for the door.

"So will I," she replied.

Nicole felt his gaze on her, but she pretended to read the report in the folder. For a few seconds he seemed to debate whether to say more. Instead he kept going. When the door shut softly, Nicole smiled to herself.

"That's gotta be worth bonus points." She leaned back in her chair. "Two challenges. Uncle Hosea, you old rascal, you knew I'd get sucked in, didn't you?"

Marcus closed the door to his office and sat down at his desk. He rocked in his chair for several minutes, then turned it around until he faced the window. Traffic snaked along the streets below. Nicole was a problem in a way he hadn't bargained on. Her fragrance lingered, leaving him with the aura of a fresh gulf breeze. He shook his head to clear it and reestablish his first impression of her. Still, she seemed to be working hard to do more than play the part of CEO. Maybe he needed to revise his assessment. A knock on his door broke into his thoughts. Russell walked in seconds later.

"Sure, come on in," Marcus said in a tone dry enough to give anyone the hint.

"I figured you'd want to talk." Russell sat down. "I think you see now we can help each other."

Marcus sighed. "I don't know what you mean."

"Nicole might as well pack her Gucci handbag once _we_ team up." Russell smiled.

"For the last time—"

"You don't like her being in charge any more than I do."

"Change is difficult," Marcus said, repeating his now vague stock phrase.

Russell perched on the edge of Marcus's desk. He wore a half-smile. "She needs us and we don't need her. A perfect setup."

"Setup?"

"I mean for her to take a fall. All we have to do is give the situation a little push and, bam! We're in charge." Russell winked at him.

Russell's chummy act should have been amusing. Instead Marcus felt his annoyance turning to anger. "You could try working with Nicole."

"You've seen what she's like," Russell complained. "Completely unreasonable. I've tried, but Nicole won't listen."

"Imagine that, she wouldn't agree to step down and give you the CEO job," Marcus said in a dull tone.

"Exactly," Russell said, missing the point. "Never mind all my experience and expertise in this business." His mouth twisted until his thin face looked fierce.

"From what I can see Nicole is taking her job seriously."

"Humph! I can't afford to let Summers Security go down while she gets on-the-job training." Russell's frown melted into a smarmy grin. "I'll even admit that you've got a few organization skills I lack. I'm more of a big picture person."

"Uh-huh." Marcus was growing weary of this conversation.

"We'd complement each other. I'll also admit that I should have seen this before now. I guess a crisis forces us all to think more clearly." Russell nodded.

"Uh-huh."

"Nicole is a sharp-tongued witch. I know the employees would throw a party if we got rid of her. She's a real—"

"Give her a chance," Marcus cut in, not trusting what might happen if he let Russell go on.

Russell stood and smoothed down his designer dress shirt. "Don't make a decision right now. Take some time and think it over. You'll see I'm right, bro."

"I don't have to think it over, *bro.* I told Nicole's father I'd do my best for at least six months."

"You don't owe them a thing. But we've worked together for almost seven years now." Russell lifted his chin.

"Yes, we have." Marcus lifted an eyebrow at him.

"Er, I've already said we had our issues. I'm willing to put all that aside now."

"How generous. My answer is the same." Marcus picked up his ink pen and started to write. "Goodbye, Russell."

"You can't just dismiss me as though I'm the janitor!" Russell snapped.

"Keep pushing Nicole's buttons and you might end up carrying a mop around here." Marcus looked at him. "The lady can do some damage when she's mad."

"Okay, I'll take over without your help." Russell strode out and slammed the door behind him.

"What the hell are you thinking?" Marcus sat back in his chair to consider his reaction. As if to help him answer his question, Nicole came in without knocking.

"I like you more all the time, Marcus Reed." She grinned at him.

Pleasure spread up his spine like warm massage oil. Marcus smiled back at her. "Oh?"

Nicole closed the door behind her. "You've been giving me the chilly treatment, don't waste time denying it."

"Okay," Marcus replied warily and wondered where she was headed.

"And if you recite that 'change is difficult' crap once more, I'll scream," she added and made a sour face.

Marcus felt heat licking at him. Nicole looked even more

beautiful pouting and threatening a tantrum. "I wouldn't want that. So, what have I done to redeem your opinion of me?"

"I saw Russell stomp out of here. You pissed him off big time. Please, please, please tell me the details." Nicole rubbed her hands together.

"Come on, as our leader you should be fussing at us about not being a team." Marcus pressed his lips together.

"You're right." Then she looked at him hard, with an impish gleam in her lovely eyes. "A tiny hint, that's all."

Marcus laughed out loud in spite of his efforts to keep a stoic face. "Nicole, you're too much."

Nicole tilted her head back and laughed with him. Musical and full, the sound came from deep in her throat. Marcus shivered. Her neck seemed to invite him to press his lips against it. Before he realized it, Marcus was out of his chair and around the desk. He stood over her and put one hand on her elbow. Nicole's laugh bubbled up and then away like sparkling wine.

"You see? We've got a lot more in common than you thought," she said softly, a smile tugging at the corners of her full mouth.

He couldn't look away even though his streetwise instincts sensed danger. "Do we?"

"Um-hum. We both see right through Russell. We also both want the best for Summers Security and we're willing to work hard to get it."

Nicole moved closer to him until her face was less than an inch from his. Marcus could hear himself breathing hard. His gaze traveled along the heart-shaped line of her face, taking in every captivating curve. Tasteful gold hoop earrings hung from her delicate earlobes. Being so near to her made him realize she had the most beautiful tawny eyes he'd ever seen in his life. His small voice of reason fell silent, and he kissed her. Not a light, delicate brush, either.

Marcus started by nipping her earlobe. His body trembled when she sighed and leaned against his chest. Not that he needed much encouragement. He planted firm kisses along her jawline, leading to her mouth, which he took greedily. With both arms wrapped around her, Marcus answered her sighs with a moan. Office sounds right outside his door faded away. The ticking from the brass clock on his desk seemed to slow down. After a deliciously long time, they parted.

"I think we just broke about five company rules," Nicole said, her eyes still closed. Seconds later, she opened them and smiled.

Marcus felt as though he'd been turned upside down, held by his ankles and given a hard shake. He took a deep breath and tried to step away. Nicole held on tight.

"You're the boss," he murmured, still captivated by the bad-girl gleam in her eyes. "Maybe we should discuss the incident over a glass of wine later." He bent his face lower for another kiss.

Nicole patted his chest with one palm and pushed away. She smoothed down the red silk shell she wore and brushed the front of her navy skirt. "I agree. As the top managers of this firm we should take swift action."

"Otherwise things might get out of hand," he said. Desire to touch her again beat inside him like an African drum.

She backed toward the door with a seductive half-smile. "Entirely possible. I have an early dinner meeting. Come over to my house at about eight-thirty. Rosaria will let you in if I'm running a bit late."

I've lost my mind. "I'll be there," Marcus replied.

"Great."

Nicole waved bye-bye with a flirtatious flip of the wrist. The simple gesture set off more trembling in his body. Marcus took another deep breath to recover. He glanced at his wristwatch. Less than six hours to pull himself together. Somehow he had to ignore the spell she cast and not react like a sex-starved fifteen year old.

"What a challenge," he mumbled, staring at the door.

Nicole's older sister, Helena, and her cousin Francine were waiting for her when she walked into Clyde's. The elegant restaurant not only served some of the best steaks in town but their private wine cellar was superb, as well. Helena waved to get her attention, and Nicole joined them.

"Hello, baby sister." Helena's alto voice, so like their mother's, got the attention of several males close by. At age thirty-four, Helena had a Ph.D. in chemistry and was a top executive with the Mobile/Exxon Corporation.

"Hi, and don't call me 'baby sister' for the umpteenth time." Nicole pecked her quickly on the cheek. "What's up, Francine?"

"Hi, cuz. You're looking remarkably relaxed for a woman on the verge of ruin," Francine said, straight to the point as always.

A waitress came over as soon as Nicole sat down and took her order for a glass of iced tea. When she left, Nicole smiled at them. "I'm holding it together."

"Uncle Lionel says Russell is being a real jerk." Francine sipped from her glass of wine.

"And how is that different from his usual behavior?" Nicole quipped. Still, the strain must have shown in her voice.

Helena leaned both elbows on the table. "Let's face facts. They would feel more comfortable with a male family member in charge."

"With the obvious exception of Russell," Francine added quickly.

"Which is the real reason Daddy is trying to talk Terrell into moving here. I know, and it doesn't matter. I intend to stay in charge." Nicole broke off when the waitress came back.

"You're joking. Tell me she's joking." Helena looked at Francine.

"I thought being the boss at Summers Security was the last thing you wanted. What changed your mind?" Francine pushed aside her wineglass.

"Because a lot of people seem to think that A, I can't do the job, and B, that I'm a spoiled lightweight who can't hang when the going gets tough." Nicole's eyes narrowed. "Including Marcus."

"Marcus?" Helena looked from Nicole to Francine.

"Nicole's second in command. He's not just hardworking but he's shrewd, too," Francine said. "He's also gorgeous."

"Oh, my. No wonder she's turned into Miss Nine-to-Five." Helena glanced back to Nicole with a frown.

"Two grown women devolving into junior high gossips. Not a pretty picture." Nicole waved a hand at them.

"Unfair as it might be, people could talk about you two. Don't give Russell or anyone else ammunition," Helena replied.

"Right. No late nights working alone together in the office." Francine scowled. "We've all had to fight the nasty assumption that we used sex to get ahead, even in the new millennium."

"Results count. If I take the company to a whole new level no one will care about idle talk. Besides, men sleep with their employees all the time and no one questions their competence." She lifted a shoulder and sipped from her glass.

"Have you heard the phrase 'double standard'?" Francine said. She broke off when the waiter approached and took their order.

"In other words, you've got to be extra careful about appearances, especially with Marcus Reed. He might even use it against you." Helena nodded and looked at Francine.

"Excellent point." Francine tapped the side of her glass with the tip of one pale pink acrylic fingernail.

"Marcus wouldn't stab me in the back," Nicole said too quickly. Both women glanced at her with speculation. "He's the straight arrow type, comes at you face to face. Unlike Russell. He's becoming more of a problem every day."

"He's the crown prince of jerkdom. All the senior family members know it. Uncle Hosea didn't exactly keep quiet about his shortcomings." Francine shook her head slowly.

"Oh God, yes," Helena added. "For once I agreed with Uncle Hosea. Russ was an obnoxious little boy."

Nicole said a silent prayer of thanks to Russell. For once his bad behavior had proved useful. As Helena went on to list his misdeeds, Nicole realized that both women seemed to have forgotten her stupid slip. She and Marcus would have to be careful, at least for now.

"I hope the food comes soon," Francine said after glancing at her sterling silver watch. "I'm exhausted."

"Between us we had four meetings today. At least mine were at the same office." Helena gave her cousin a look of sympathy.

"A deposition on one end of town and discovery motions at the other end. I really hate driving around Houston." Francine waved to the passing waitress and got her to take their orders.

"You volunteered to drive, so don't blame me." Helena pointed at her, then looked at Nicole. "Since I had meetings at our Houston office and Francine's embroiled in a lawsuit in two states, we decided to carpool," she explained.

"You're driving next time," Francine grumbled and drank the last of her wine.

The three women talked business. Helena played the big sister as always, giving lots of advice. Nicole knew better than to complain. Her sister had ten years of management experience. By the time their food came they were laughing about family and hometown gossip.

"Y'all just reminded me why I'm so homesick. Not that Houston is as bad as I thought it would be." Nicole patted her lips with a linen napkin.

"Who are you kidding? I've seen Uncle Hosea's house, Nicole." Francine waved her fork with a plump mushroom on the end of it.

"Uncle Hosea was loud, bad-tempered, and mean as a pit bull. But the man had good taste. Well, he was a Summers, after all." Helena flipped her hand in the air.

"Excuse me, your superiority complex is showing," Nicole laughed.

"There's nothing wrong with family pride," her older sister said, sounding even more like their mother.

Francine exchanged an amused glance with Nicole. "So, are we going to hang out tonight, ladies?"

"Right, we can crash at Nicole's palatial palace." Helena grinned at her.

"Uh, I thought y'all were leaving for home right after dinner." Nicole's stomach tightened in panic.

"Life is too short to rush around. We might as well enjoy a relaxed evening." Francine massaged her neck. "I can't wait to get out of these panty hose."

Helena studied Nicole for several minutes. "Francine, I think Nicole has plans for tonight."

"I'm thinking of you two. Francine has meetings tomorrow and you need to write a report for your boss, Helena," Nicole added.

"Isn't Nicole so thoughtful, Francine? She's making sure

we don't forget why we need to leave town." Helena's expertly arched eyebrows lifted.

"Uh-huh, or get a hotel room tonight," Francine quipped.

"No, no. I can change my plans." Nicole squinted at the prospect of passing up her first chance at Marcus.

"Gee, we'd hate to interfere with your date." Helena leaned forward. "Tell us all about him."

"He's someone I met recently. No big deal. I'll just call him and reschedule." Nicole took the napkin from her lap, picked up her purse, and stood.

Helena's eyebrows went up even further. "Francine, she doesn't want us to hear."

"I'm going to the ladies' room, if you don't mind," Nicole said low.

"Good excuse," Francine shot back.

Nicole kept going as though she didn't hear their twittering at her expense. She passed the rest room and kept going to the foyer as she dialed Marcus's number on her cell phone. He picked up on the second ring. He was gracious in understanding her need to reschedule. In fact, he was a bit too accepting, in her view.

"Damn!" Nicole muttered as she punched the Off button. This was no way to begin her campaign to conquer a handsome player. Still, she managed a smile by the time she got back to the table.

"Listen, little sister, we just talked it over, and we insist that you keep that date," Helena said as Nicole sat down.

"Yeah, we're happy you've got a love life. That should deflect any unwarranted conjecture about you and Marcus," Francine added. "In fact, I reserved a suite at the Marriott Courtyard Hotel."

"So, call . . ." Helena rested both elbows on the table. "I'm sorry, what was his name again?"

"Nice try." Nicole put away her cell phone. "Cancel the suite. We're going to enjoy my huge flat screen television tonight. Uncle Hosea has a fabulous video collection."

"Are you sure?" Francine exchanged a glance with Helena.

"It's settled. Now I say we get dessert to go. I'll fix coffee, and we can indulge while we watch movies." Nicole waved for the check. Maybe this was a sign that snuggling with Marcus was a bad idea anyway.

eight

Marcus hit the button of his cell phone. He tossed the shirt he was holding back into the closet and went into the living room. So much for choosing the right look. Irritated with himself for being irritated, he plopped onto his sofa and grabbed the television remote.

"Sounded like an excuse to me."

Maybe the lady got cold feet. Then he had a second, less appealing thought as TV channels whizzed by. Another man. Nicole was beautiful, smart, and not the type to swoon over any male. Not that Marcus was being egotistical, but since his days as a popular football player in high school attracting females hadn't been a problem. For most of his life he'd merely had to show up and ladies indicated their interest. Sometimes their attention could be a real pain. For that reason, and the fact that he just wasn't on fire for romance, Marcus had taken a break from the mating dance. He'd been content for the last couple of months, until Nicole had blown into his life like a Louisiana hurricane. He tossed the remote aside after settling on an action movie. The sound was muffled so he could think.

"Wonder who?" he said and rubbed his jaw.

She couldn't have had much time to mix and mingle, not with the hours she'd been putting in. Marcus got up for a glass of imported beer. While in the kitchen he grabbed a bowl of mixed nuts. He munched, poured, and thought some more. Nicole had a lot of guts to go with her smart mouth, he mused. Remembering the way her eyes would sparkle after she would make a tart comment, he smiled. *Fact is, man, you like it.* With a sigh he padded back into the living room of his condo. He sat down with the bowl in his lap and put the mug of beer within easy reach. Only a few days ago he'd found such an evening to be a treat. Instead the muscled movie hero was getting on his nerves. For some insane reason he kept wondering what kind of man she might be with tonight. When his cordless phone rang, he snatched it up.

"Come out to play, old man," Shaun quipped into his ear. "Can't believe you're home alone on a Friday night."

"Me either," he grumbled back.

"Hey, I've got a cure for the solitary blues. I'll swing by with two lovely ladies and—"

"No," Marcus cut him off. The idea left him cold.

"Listen to your partner, man. I'm into quality. This girl I'm dating, Lisa, has a friend."

"I said no."

Shaun hissed into the receiver. "Look, she's the right temperature. The girl's on fire and she's almost done. Now you and me could—"

"We must have a bad connection, 'cause you didn't hear me say no twice," Marcus said louder.

"What's up with you?" Shaun's voice went deeper with concern.

"I'm watching a movie," Marcus replied mildly.

"That's not what I mean and you know it. Okay, I'm coming over." Shaun hung up.

Marcus thought about calling him back, but the truth was he could use the company. He blotted out thoughts of Nicole and tried to get interested in the movie. The overly muscled hero tossed bad guys around like toothpicks. Cars blew up. Buildings burned. All in the cause of truth and justice. Even a buxom brunette in a wet T-shirt didn't register on Marcus's radar. His thoughts kept making a U-turn back to Nicole. When the chimes sounded, he unlocked the door and headed for the kitchen for another beer without looking back. He heard the door shut again with a thud.

"Nuts on the table," Marcus said over his shoulder.

"Thanks, but I prefer popcorn."

He spun around to find Nicole dressed in jeans and a ruby red v-neck cotton shirt. She wore open-toe denim sandals that displayed her crimson toenails perfectly. Her hair was pulled back, but only loosely, with tendrils trailing to her shoulders. The picture was completed with large shiny silver hoop earrings, a bangle bracelet on one arm, a silver watch on the other, and rings on the middle finger of each hand. He knew all this quickly because his gaze swept her from head to toe. Nicole smiled at him. In fear that he might be drooling, Marcus wiped his mouth.

"I thought you had plans," he said.

"My sister and cousin made other plans." Nicole shrugged. "So, here I am."

"This is a real surprise. I was expecting someone else." *Stop babbling, fool!*

Her smile wavered. "Sorry. I shouldn't have presumed you wouldn't make other plans of your own."

"No, no. Not a date. My buddy Shaun is coming over."

Marcus blinked rapidly at the realization. Damn! Shaun would find her here.

"Maybe I'd better leave." Nicole turned to go just as the chimes rang again. "Oh-oh."

Marcus grabbed her arm and started toward the bedroom. "This way. I mean, don't you think it would be better if—"

"Yes. This complication we don't need." She scurried down the hallway, then stopped. "Hey, this is kinda exciting. I've never had to sneak around with a guy before."

Marcus laughed out loud, then stifled it. "Stop being a little brat and go!" he whispered.

"Say, man, this isn't funny," Shaun called through the door.

"I was in the bathroom," Marcus yelled back and waved at her to keep going. Her soft giggle as she closed the bedroom door sent electricity zigzagging up his spine.

"Finally," Shaun complained when Marcus let him in. "Good thing I wasn't being pursued by bloodthirsty muggers."

Marcus yawned. "I'm whipped. Truth is, I plan to be asleep well before the midnight hour. How are ya?"

"Worried about my slick partner." Shaun's thick black brows pulled into one line.

"Thanks, Mama, but I don't need to be tucked in," Marcus cracked.

"Ha-ha." Shaun strolled in and sat down on the sofa. "We're overdue for a serious talk. I'm truly concerned." He nodded for Marcus to sit, too.

Marcus suppressed a groan of frustration. He sat on the edge of the large chair facing Shaun. "I'm okay. Like I said, just tired from working overtime."

"Which is what I'm talking about." Shaun waved his arms in a circle. "We've been through a lot, right?"

"No trips down memory lane, please." Marcus glanced toward the bedroom. "We'll be here all night."

"Just listen. You're working to make somebody else rich. Now I say—"

"I've heard it before," Marcus cut him off quickly. "Now you listen, I've had a long week and I don't want to hear another lecture."

Shaun put both hands on his hips. "What's up with you? I mean, I understand you left the old neighborhood behind. But it looks like you're trying to kick your old friend to the curb, too."

"I appreciate your concern. I really do." Marcus put a hand under Shaun's elbow and lifted him up.

"Yeah, well I don't feel appreciated."

"Let's get together Sunday for a run through the park. Breakfast is on me. How's that sound?" Marcus patted his shoulder.

"Like you're trying to get rid of me," Shaun retorted.

"Don't get paranoid on me. You sound like some of my old girlfriends." Marcus laughed while he turned the big man around and pointed him toward the door.

Shaun walked ahead of him. "There's something going on and you best believe I'll find out about it."

"Yeah, yeah. I'll see you Sunday." Marcus kept a firm hand on his shoulder.

"Ah-ha! The first clue." Shaun veered away and snatched up a small blue object. "You got a woman in here."

Marcus stared at the denim-and-leather purse Shaun waved in the air. He took a deep breath. "So, the last thing I need is company. Right?"

"Right, right." Shaun turned the purse over in his hands. He read the gold initials engraved on the fastener holding the purse closed. "NSB."

"Shaun, it's time to go," Marcus said through clenched teeth.

"Who—" Shaun looked up at Marcus. "Your boss lady!"

"Say it a little louder, I think somebody in California didn't hear you." Marcus yanked him farther away from the hall leading to his bedroom.

"Oh man, you're my hero. I'm getting out of your way, master player. We'll talk Sunday." Shaun's hazel eyes sparkled with excitement.

"Shaun, listen to me. I'm not—"

"Sunday, and don't leave out a thing!" Shaun winked at him, then hustled out.

Marcus raked his fingers through his hair in exasperation. He'd have to straighten Shaun out later. "Damn!"

"Hey, it's a nice color scheme in here, but I would like to come out sometime this year!" Nicole called.

"Sorry, uh, he's gone." Marcus tried to regain his balance.

"I know. What's his name again?" Nicole strolled out. She glanced around the living room.

"Shaun Jackson, we grew up together." Marcus rubbed his sweaty palms on his jeans. "You want something?"

She looked at him, a twinkle in her eyes. "Yes."

Feeling like a kid on his first date, Marcus swallowed hard. The message in her gaze sent heat through his groin. "I meant to drink."

"Diet cola, decaf if you've got it." Nicole sat down on his sofa as though she owned it. She crossed her legs and smiled up at him.

"I'll check."

Marcus went to the kitchen. In the few minutes it took him to get glasses and a tray, he regained his equilibrium. In his time he'd handled plenty of good-looking women who'd wanted to own him. Nicole was just the latest version, he told himself. Sure her eyes were a brown he hadn't seen before. Hints of burnished gold gleamed bright when she laughed.

Then there was the way her mouth curved up at one end when she smiled. Or the way she walked with her shoulders back and head up, like a queen who stepped right off the painted walls of an Egyptian pyramid.

He grabbed a paper towel and dabbed sweat from his forehead. Okay, so maybe she's above average. Still no reason to stumble around like a moron. Marcus took a cleansing deep breath, arranged the tray, and walked out of the kitchen. By the time he arrived in the living room, he was wearing an easy smile. *Keep cool. She showed up here for a reason. You're in control.*

"I didn't have decaf cola, so I brought you a Sprite instead. Hope that's okay." Marcus put the tray on the cocktail table.

"I like Sprite, thanks." Nicole helped herself to a handful of nuts. "These are good. Sorry I chased your friend away. I should have called first."

Marcus sat down across from her and grabbed nuts from the bowl. The lady was used to having her way. He'd have to do something about that. "Yes, you should have."

"Well, you sort of implied I was rude to break our—What was it exactly?" Nicole gazed back at him calmly.

Damned if he didn't find the lady intriguing. Marcus couldn't take his eyes off the silken brown skin of her upper arms. When she raised the glass to her lips, Marcus felt a sharp thirst no soft drink would satisfy. He rubbed his mouth and watched her throat work.

What was going on with him? He had a strict rule. Any woman who showed up on his doorstep unannounced would have been gone by now, no exceptions. Yet here he was serving her like she had an engraved invitation. She lowered the glass and gazed at him. Any thought of tossing her out went up in smoke.

"You tell me," he replied softly.

Nicole blinked rapidly as though stumped for an answer. She looked away and lifted a shoulder. "I'm not sure yet."

She put her glass on the table and stood. Marcus watched her as she walked to his entertainment system. Nicole ran her fingers over his collection of vintage vinyl records from the fifties, sixties, and seventies. Marcus smiled at her bid for a chance to recover.

"Like my collection?" After grabbing a few nuts from the bowl, he walked over to join her. "My grandmother gave me those."

"You're a Buddy Guy fan? Me, too!" Nicole picked up a CD and read the cover copy. "I would have guessed you were strictly hip-hop-generation vibe."

"I see. You know I grew up in the Fifth Ward. I'm from the ghetto, therefore I love rap music," Marcus said.

Nicole had the decency to blush. "*No.* That's not what I meant at all." She avoided his gaze and fingered the rack of compact discs.

Marcus gazed at her without speaking for several seconds. He popped a few pecans into his mouth and chewed slowly. As the silence stretched, she fidgeted. Marcus enjoyed seeing her squirm. She looked even more delectable, if that was possible. Obviously it was, he mused.

"So, what did you mean?" he finally said.

She appeared engrossed in the rack of compact discs on the shelf. "Nothing really. I happen to like hip-hop myself."

"Cool. Even the rich can get down and jam with the community," Marcus teased. He crossed his arms and gazed at her, head to one side.

To her credit, Nicole rallied. She went back to the sofa and sat down. "Thank you, mister Def Comedy Jam."

Marcus laughed. Nicole wore a Drop Dead message in her

eyes when she looked back at him. "Okay, let's play nice. No social commentary," he offered.

"Agreed." Nicole's full lips curved up at one corner as she held out her right hand. "Shake on it."

His smile froze. Her fingers were tapered and tipped by bright red fingernails. He could easily understand why a man would bend and kiss such an offering. His pulse raced as he walked to her. Each step that brought him closer seemed to be in slow motion. Marcus felt a flood of desire when his large hand closed over her slender one. Nicole stood up as though he'd lifted her from the sofa. Maybe he had. Or maybe he'd willed Nicole nearer by the sheer force of his hunger for her.

Nicole closed the distance between them until their bodies touched. Marcus lowered his head, she lifted her mouth. He pulled her tightly against him. Her tongue teased his, the tip flickering along his bottom lip. Needing her filled his mind until there was no room for anything else, second thoughts included. His legs felt like rubber, so he eased her down onto the sofa again. They lay prone, exploring, testing and tasting each other. They kissed forever, or so it seemed. And still it wasn't long enough. He moaned deep in his throat as she pulled away.

"My, oh, my." Nicole took a deep breath. She put a hand on his chest, then gazed into his eyes. "Maybe I'd better go."

"No," he answered. Funny, no warning sirens screamed in his ears after the word slipped out.

"Okay." She drew his mouth back to hers.

They kissed more, deeper, and their hands roamed until both started to push aside clothing and probe. In concert they lifted her shirt up and over her head. Marcus pressed his lips against her neck. He traced a line of kisses down to the tempting mounds of her breasts that showed above red lace. Her sigh was the perfect encouragement. His tongue lapped at her brown sugar skin. Music and bells tinkled in the background like a magical sound track to their lovemaking.

"Phone," she mumbled.

Marcus continued to kiss her body. His fingers tugged at the bra cup that prevented more joy. "Hmm?"

"Your phone is ringing," Nicole said louder and wiggled free. "Better answer it. Could be important." She brushed stray tendrils of hair back into place.

"Voice mail was invented for moments like these." He reached for her.

"We need a reality break anyway." Nicole inched further away.

He snatched up the cordless phone. "Yeah," he barked. "Sorry, Jesse. What's up? Okay, I'll meet you tomorrow morning. Bye."

"Was that Jesse from the office?"

Marcus turned back to her and scowled. Nicole had her shirt back on and tucked into her jeans. "The security system we installed at an art gallery went off. False alarm. Jesse checked it out."

"I remember. Why are you going in tomorrow?"

"Procedure. We always do a complete system run when something like this happens. Probably nothing." Marcus wanted to put aside talk of business.

Nicole wore a serious expression. "Funny how stuff keeps happening."

"Motion sensors can be tricky. If I'm not mistaken, that system is an older model. They're not precise. A spider might have tripped the thing." Marcus gazed at her. "It's really not worth worrying about."

"But think about it. Maybe we need to do a real complete performance audit."

"We can talk about it, sure." Marcus leaned toward her, one arm stretched along the sofa back. "Tomorrow."

"Right." Nicole stood abruptly. "I'll meet y'all at the office."

"Hey! What about . . ." Marcus spread his arms out.

Nicole smiled. "Considering the circumstances, going slow is advised."

"You mean, I'm hired help." Marcus tilted his head back and stared at her through narrowed lids.

"Marcus, you're hardly what I would call hired help." Nicole brushed invisible dust from the front of her shirt. "Besides, we should consider all the possible ramifications. We have to think of more than our hormones."

Her words splashed over Marcus like cold water. The lady wanted to calculate exactly what an affair with him might cost her. Worse still, she was absolutely right. He should have been thinking along those same lines. Instead he'd tumbled headlong into lust. Nicole hadn't lost sight of the gulf between them. In her world his education, achievements, or even money couldn't change the obvious. He didn't have the right family tree.

"I see your point. Sorry, I'm usually more cautious and practical. I shouldn't have presumed." Marcus stood. He picked up her purse and handed it to her.

"We both kind of got caught up in the moment." Nicole took it.

"Apparently the moment is over." Marcus turned away from her. "I'll see you in the morning."

She caught his arm. "I've got a lot to prove, Marcus. At first being forced to take over Summers Security was a nuisance. I was sure Daddy or Francine would find a loophole and I'd get out of it. Then being CEO seemed like a fun challenge. But now . . . I'm ready to grow up and have something of my own."

Marcus turned slowly to face her as she spoke. Nicole stared at him. He read the plea for understanding and support in her magnetic, sultry eyes. Without hesitating, he placed a hand over hers.

"Well, we'd better get to the business of running Summers Security then. Right, boss lady?" he said quietly.

They gazed at each other in silence for several charged moments. When Nicole broke contact first, he instantly missed her touch. Marcus attempted to get a firm grip on his common sense. Nicole seemed to do the same. She cleared her throat and took a step away from him.

"Right. My first and only dictate to you is to never, ever call me boss lady again." Nicole wore a lopsided grin, her hands stuck in the pockets of her jeans.

Marcus grinned back. "I'll try to remember. See you around nine tomorrow morning?"

"Sounds good." Nicole shifted her weight from one foot to the other. "Well, good night."

"Good night." Marcus decided not to move. They looked at each other.

"Oh, what the hell!" Nicole marched over, planted a firm kiss on his lips, and then went to the door.

Stunned into a warm daze that felt so good, Marcus kept his eyes closed and savored her flavor. The soft bump of the door closing snapped him back to reality. He stood rooted to the carpet for another ten minutes, trying to sort through what had happened between them.

The next day Nicole glanced at the dashboard digital clock. She nudged her car up another five miles above the speed limit on Interstate 45. "Can't keep Mr. Reed waiting," she murmured and passed a slow-moving, late-model Buick.

Smiling to herself, she turned up the volume on her compact disc player. The song, a driving beat with provocative lyrics sung by Jill Scott, put her in the right mood to think about last night. Marcus had lit a fire in her that had burned hot for hours afterward. Nicole congratulated herself once more on having had the strength to leave his condo. Yet a tiny prickle of worry kept tugging around the edges of her mind. Who was the hunter and who was the prey? The sensation of his full lips against hers had driven out thoughts of conquest and being in control. She'd have to keep her head on right from now on, she reminded herself.

Nicole arrived at the office twenty minutes past nine despite her efforts to be on time. She parked in her reserved space, turned on the car alarm, and caught the elevator. When she got to her suite, she saw a note on her office door. Marcus's bold signature in black ink spread almost the width of the small sheet of notepaper.

" 'We're in my office. Started without you,' " she read. "Oh, boy. I've been reprimanded already."

She went inside her office and grabbed her favorite leather-covered notepad. Then she went down the hall. Marcus and Jesse were deep in discussion when she pushed open the half-open door. They were seated at the small round table in a corner of Marcus's office.

"Morning. Sorry I'm late. Catch me up." Nicole tossed her purse onto a chair and sat down.

"Good morning," Marcus said in a much too formal tone. He didn't smile or give any sign they were more than boss and employee.

"Let me get you some coffee, ma'am." Jesse Cooper, thirty-seven and every inch the Southern gentleman, dipped his head to her. Though he wasn't much older than them, he had the demeanor of a seasoned wise man.

"No, sit. I'll serve myself. And bless whoever brewed a pot." She smiled at him.

"That would be me," Marcus said.

When she glanced back at him, he appeared absorbed in a spreadsheet. His stiff posture bothered her. Sure, they couldn't be lovey-dovey in front of Jesse, but he didn't have to act like he had ice in his bikini briefs. Suddenly annoyed, Nicole pursed her lips. Still, she'd play along. He would pay later, she decided. *I've got the moves to melt you, brother.* Cheered by the thought, her steps bounced when she walked over to rejoin them. She took a sip from the mug.

"Okay, now I can think." She beamed at both men.

Jesse smiled back at her as though pleased at the attention. "I'm like that myself in the morning."

Marcus continued to wear his white-collar corporate expression. "Here's what we've got. Several security guards seem to be trouble, Tameka being only one example."

"We don't know she did anything wrong." Nicole put the coffee mug down on the table.

"No, and the police don't have a lead on the missing merchandise," Marcus replied.

"I can't get her to return my phone calls." Jesse rubbed his jaw. "I was just telling Marcus that Officer Blanchard, the policeman on the case, says she's acting strange."

"So, maybe she knows something." Nicole nodded to the papers in front of Marcus. "What's that?"

"A report on the guards we've hired." Marcus pushed it toward her. "I like to keep a record of employee performance. No-shows, customer complaints, and general information. I include their strengths and compliments from customers, too."

"Hmm. Of the ninety-six guards we hired, fifteen women

came through the Welfare to Work program." Nicole glanced down the columns with names next to them. "Lots of absences."

"They have usual stuff for single mothers, sick kids or they can't get a baby-sitter. Sometimes there's the occasional boyfriend problem," Jesse said.

"Typical drama for those folks." Nicole shook her head.

"*Those folks* don't have nannies and housekeepers to take up the slack," Marcus said with a bland expression.

Nicole glanced up at him sharply. "I understand they have special challenges."

"Yes, they sure do," he replied.

"I didn't mean to imply a negative generalization." Nicole wondered at the sudden tension between them.

Jesse glanced from Marcus to Nicole and cleared his throat loudly. "Uh, sometimes they get somebody to cover before they call in."

"Maybe we can arrange for a corporate discount at a day-care agency. We can offer it to all of the employees." Nicole made notes. "I'll check on it."

"Hey, that would be great. We've got single fathers, too. I'm taking care of two grandbabies myself." Jesse's head bobbed with enthusiasm.

"Might as well take away one more pressure, right?" Nicole continued to write. "Now the alarm that went off."

"I checked it out. Couldn't find anything. I'll bet it was an insect or something." Jesse pulled a tattered notepad from his shirt pocket. "I suggested the customer put in a new system. We do it for free, but the monitoring rate increases. She agreed."

"Good work. We could clean up with a little creativity. Buy some big spiders and get all our customers to upgrade," Nicole said, careful to keep a straight face.

"Now you're thinking like Mr. Summers," Jesse joked with a grin.

"Ouch!" Nicole wore a mock frown.

Marcus seemed not to notice their lighthearted exchange. He stared at the screen of his laptop. "Do we have a bigger problem?" he mumbled and hit another key.

"Not from what I can tell," Jesse said, serious once more. "Tameka really has disappointed me. I gave her a chance. Maybe she knows more about what happened at Mr. Phoung's store, but I'm hoping she doesn't."

"What exactly went missing?" Nicole looked at Marcus.

"Six cases of cigarettes, ten cases of beer, forty-five bottles of liquor, and five cases of cheese puffs. A few odds and ends of other merchandise, too." Marcus tapped more keys as he spoke. "Total value close to seven thousand dollars."

"Somebody is having one hell of a party." Nicole shook her head.

"If Tameka did it she had help. And whoever took the stuff didn't break in to get it." Jesse craned his neck to read the list on the computer screen.

"Yeah, she'd need a truck and strong hands to help load the stuff." Nicole rested both elbows on the table. "Well, it's up to the police."

"We've got an even bigger problem if our customers start to think we can't provide adequate protection," Marcus said.

"I don't know what else we can do, though." Nicole looked at him.

"Find Tameka and get her to take a polygraph. Do another background check on her. We haven't done one since the annual back in—" Marcus broke off. His fingers flew across the keys. "November of last year."

"A lot can happen in seven months." Nicole looked at

Jesse. "You know her better than us, Jesse. What do you think?"

The older man's brow furrowed as he considered his answer. "I hate to say it, but something just isn't right."

"Check her credit report. See if there's anything strange," Marcus said with a frown.

"I'll do it Monday." Jesse wore a grave expression as he nodded. "In the meantime, I'm gonna make the rounds of a few nervous customers. Calm the waters, so to speak."

"Good idea, Jesse." Nicole sat back against her chair. "Maybe I should help you."

"Well, uh . . ." Jesse rubbed his jaw.

"Better let him deal with it for now, Nicole," Marcus put in. "He's got a relationship with them, for one thing. A call from you might seem like we're in a panic."

"Which could imply we know the problems go deep." Nicole considered his words. "Okay, for now. But if we have more problems, they're going to want to hear from the top."

"I agree," Marcus replied.

"And I for one will be in a panic," she added with a grimace.

Jesse stood. "Don't you worry, ma'am. I say you're doing a darn good job so far." He gave her a thumbs-up sign before he walked out.

"Thanks for the encouragement," she called after him and sighed.

"That was a nice idea about the day care." Marcus didn't look at her. Instead he typed rapidly, his fingers moving across the keys.

"One of the companies I worked for briefly had day care as a perk." Nicole lifted a shoulder. "At least I got something from that job."

"Briefly?" Marcus glanced at her curiously for a second before looking at the computer screen again.

"Too regimented. I moved on. Wish we had some donuts or something." Nicole got up for more coffee.

"Greasy, sticky fried donuts?" Marcus kept typing.

"Hmm, hmm good," Nicole answered with a sigh.

"I'll remember next time. So, you were a corporate lady."

"For a minute. Daddy got me into his college buddy's law firm as a paralegal. Sleazy white-collar criminals and getting rich kids out of trouble." Nicole rolled her eyes. "Give me a plain old thief any day."

"You decided to attend law school and defend the poor?" Marcus stopped typing finally.

Nicole laughed. "You kidding? Being a public defender wouldn't keep me in shoes."

"So much for defending the downtrodden," Marcus said with a lift of one eyebrow.

"There is nothing inherently noble about being poor," she replied with a lift of her chin. "Rich or poor, people have choices."

"I agree. Here we go." Marcus hit a key, then stood. He went to a laser jet printer near his desk.

"What's this?" Nicole followed him.

"A preliminary corrective action plan for David Phoung." Marcus handed her the first sheet as more printed out.

Nicole put the coffee mug down and leaned against his desk. She read each page as he handed her new ones. "Good. I hope it will satisfy Mr. Phoung."

"The only thing that will make him happy is someone going to jail." Marcus rubbed his forehead. "At least his insurance will pay for the loss."

"He didn't want to file a claim, though—his rates will go

up. And he's already in a high-risk area." Nicole continued reading. "I'm going to keep a close eye on these incidents, for lack of a better description."

"Me, too." Marcus took the rough draft from her. "I'll be here a little while longer. Don't let me spoil your Saturday. I'm sure you've got some shopping to do." He went around his desk and sat down.

Nicole stared at him. The olive green cotton knit shirt made his brown skin look warm and inviting. Shopping wasn't on her mind at the moment. "How long are you going to be?"

"Not sure," he said without looking up. "Don't worry. I'm on salary, so this isn't overtime pay." A faint smile played across his full mouth.

"If you were, it would be money well spent." Nicole sat on the edge of his desk.

Marcus looked at her. "Thanks. Why don't we get some breakfast later?"

Nicole felt giddy with pleasure. "I'll go to my office and get a few things done. Monday morning shouldn't seem so hectic that way."

An hour later they sat across from each other over coffee and bagels. Nicole listened as he talked shop. Watching him, Nicole began to realize that her feelings for him went beyond a desire to conquer. *I'm getting in over my head, and I like it.*

nine

Marcus rocked back and forth in his chair. His mind wandered again despite the fact that he had at least twenty-five unread e-mail messages. One of them was from Detective Dayna Tyler. They'd met at a crime prevention conference, dated briefly, and decided to be friends—at least Marcus had decided. She'd taken it well, though.

Dayna wanted to bring him up to speed on the investigation. A detective in the Houston police fraud unit, she'd taken over from the uniforms trying to find out who had stolen Mr. Phoung's merchandise. Much as Marcus tried to focus, Nicole kept messing with his concentration.

The night she'd shown up at his apartment and their Saturday morning breakfast kept repeating in his head. All he had to do was breathe deeply with his eyes closed, and he could smell her delicate floral perfume. If the room was quiet enough, he could hear her melodic laughter.

Marcus shook his head and opened his eyes to the cold, hard truth. He was being played. He knew it, she knew. *Snap out of it, fool.* With rock-hard determination he continued to scroll through his morning e-mail.

Just as Nicole had predicted, Monday didn't seem as frantic as usual. Jesse had succeeded in reassuring their customers. All except Mr. Phoung. That would take more doing. Marcus heaved a sigh just as his secretary came in without knocking. Her already large black eyes were even bigger.

"'Scuse me, Marcus, but a Detective Dayna Tyler is here," Shelly whispered.

"If you whisper she'll think you're guilty of something," Marcus whispered back.

"Oh, no!" Shelly put a hand to her chest.

"I'm kidding," Marcus said quickly and smiled at her. He stood and walked to the door. "Dayna, you've got my secretary nervous."

The statuesque detective grinned as she strolled forward. She wore a crisp, sky blue linen jacket and a matching shirt that was neatly tucked into navy blue slacks. "Didn't mean to scare anybody. Morning, Marcus."

Shelly let out a sigh of relief. "I'll get fresh coffee."

"Not for me, thanks." Dayna smiled at her. "I don't eat donuts either." She slapped her hands on both hips. "Can't afford that old cop stereotype. I could go for some fruit juice, though."

"Yes, ma'am." Shelly lifted her hand as though she were about to salute, froze, then left with an embarrassed smile.

Marcus laughed. "She's in the Army Reserve. Guess it's force of habit."

"I served two years in the army myself. God, I loved being a military police officer." Dayna took a seat.

"So, why did you leave?" Marcus sat down behind his desk again.

"About the time I was going to sign up again, my mom got sick. After she died, Dad needed me."

"Serving the public."

Dayna nodded once and took a PDA from her jacket pocket. "Mr. Phoung started out calm, but when he talked about how much money he'd lost smoke came out of his ears," she joked.

"I can't blame him. Smart businesspeople keep track of every penny," Marcus replied.

"At first the uniforms thought they'd wait for some thug entrepreneur to set up shop. Maybe on a street corner or an abandoned storefront. Hasn't happened."

"They moved the stuff to another city maybe?" Marcus said.

"I don't think it's even in the country. I'd say Mr. Phoung's merchandise is winging its way to Latin America or Jamaica."

"Unlikely some kid from the 'hood made that happen, or a paid security guard working on her own," Marcus said.

Dayna pressed a small button on the PDA. "Mr. Phoung owns a total of six stores. He's got very nice inventory software. Somebody's been cracking into it big time. High-speed Internet access has its dangers."

"They got through his firewall?" Marcus said, referring to the security application to block hackers.

"He didn't keep his firewall updated. Didn't you guys advise him to?"

"I'll double-check. But you know, I'm not sure we even knew about or considered his Internet service." Marcus picked up the phone. "Nicole should hear this, too."

"Nice-looking sister, I hear," Dayna said. She glanced up at him with a question in her green eyes. "Y'all getting any work done around here?"

"Gossip isn't worthy of you, Detective." Marcus ignored her smirk and called Nicole to tell her about his conversation with Dayna. "She's on her way," he said to Dayna when he hung up with Nicole. "Let me call Andre, our computer whiz kid."

Five minutes later Nicole and Andre were seated around the table in his office. Marcus didn't miss the way the two women sized each other up. Nicole gave Dayna what appeared to be a fashion police once-over. For her part, Dayna studied Nicole from head to toe as though memorizing her features for a lineup. Marcus was equal parts amused and intrigued by the workings of these two sharp female minds. He gave Nicole and Andre a brief summary of what he and Dayna had discussed before they arrived.

"Detective Tyler doesn't think Mr. Phoung is the victim of a simple theft." Marcus glanced at Dayna to proceed.

"Mr. Phoung's inventory cache files have been cracked. I think stock has been disappearing for some time." Dayna consulted her notes. "Not sure how far back it goes."

Andre, a fresh-faced twenty-four-year-old with ebony skin, sat forward with an eager expression. "We didn't do any kind of computer security consulting for him. I checked."

"Mr. Phoung has been a client for over twenty years. Back then Mr. Summers had three security guards and Mr. Phoung had one store," Marcus explained.

"We only recently began offering computer and Internet security consults, right?" Nicole looked from Andre to Marcus.

"Less than two years," Andre spoke up. "I started not long after that."

"When I realized we didn't know enough about computers," Marcus added with a slight smile. "Andre is working on his master's degree in engineering."

"Actually it's mechanical engineering, with a concentration on computer systems. I started writing my own programs in middle school." Andre wore a boyish grin.

Dayna turned a penetrating gaze on him. "Interesting. Lots of kids enjoy hacking. You one of them?"

"No, no. I just did science projects, I swear." Andre looked nervously at Marcus.

"I don't think turning my employees into suspects is justified," Nicole said, a razor edge to her voice.

"Until we find out what's going on, I'm going to pursue all avenues," Dayna replied in a measured tone.

"Which is her job," Marcus put in. He leaned forward as a kind of buffer between the two women. "And exactly what we need. That said, I checked Andre out thoroughly."

"I didn't accuse him of anything. But Andre might be able to help us track down the cracker if he's so good," Dayna said.

"Sure I'll help." Andre's eyes gleamed. "Man, working to crack an international theft ring and—"

"Whoa," Marcus cut in to head off his youthful zeal. "Don't go off on that tangent yet, Shaft." He gave Andre a pat on the shoulder like a big brother.

"Definitely. It's only a *theory*." Nicole flipped a page of her leather-encased notepad. "I'd bet on a simple explanation— someone seized a chance to sell the goods for drug money."

"You think?" Andre looked let down.

"That kind of volume wouldn't go unnoticed for long. Somebody on the street would talk." Dayna leaned back in her chair. "No addict would bide his time before selling the merchandise for drugs."

"Yeah," Andre said, his expression bright again. "That kind of hack might be simple or something really wicked. When do we start?" He rubbed his hands in anticipation.

"Officer Lela Denton knows all the truly geeky stuff about computers. I'll have her give you a call." Dayna looked at Marcus with a serious expression. "Since we're not sure who is responsible, Lela has to be with him."

"We'll cooperate fully," Marcus said quickly before Nicole spoke.

"Uh-huh." Dayna looked at Nicole briefly. She stood up and smiled at Marcus. "Why don't you give me a call?"

"Sure. I'll keep in touch to coordinate Andre's schedule and give you any files you might need." Marcus stuck out his hand in a brisk, professional manner.

Dayna closed her fingers around it slowly and smiled at him. "We want to get this thing cleared fast."

"Definitely. I called David Phoung, by the way." Marcus walked Dayna out and came back a few minutes later.

Marcus gave Andre instructions. "Meet with me after lunch. I want a status report on your other projects, since you'll have to put them on hold for awhile."

"Done." Andre popped up and scurried off.

Nicole tapped the end of her ink pen on the table. "She's pretty full of herself."

"Detective Tyler is our friend, remember? She's going to help us reassure the client we're not incompetent or thieves." Marcus glanced at her.

"Yeah, right after she's through fingerprinting us all and making us take polygraph exams." Nicole's full lips pursed, making them even more inviting.

He looked away to block the images forming in his head. "Arguing with the police is never a good idea, Nicole. Especially when we're not sure who is responsible yet."

"Are you saying you suspect one of our employees?" She gazed at him with a deep frown.

"I'm saying Dayna has a point. We can't rule out any possibility. But no, I don't think Andre is the hacker," Marcus replied evenly.

"I noticed you didn't mention Tameka." Nicole's eyes narrowed. "Maybe that attitude is because she's covering something up."

"Jesse's instincts have a creepy way of nailing problems, almost like he's psychic. Her behavior bothers me more than a little."

"But you didn't mention it to Detective Tyler." Nicole mimicked Shannon's officious mannerisms when she said her name.

Marcus laughed. "I'll let Dayna do her job without any preconceived notions. So, what was up with *your* attitude?"

"I don't know what you're talking about." Nicole stood and tugged at her soft pink silk shirt. She smoothed down the front of her dove gray skirt. "I've got a ton of work to do. Talk to you later."

"Right, later."

He watched the sexy sway of her hips as she walked away. Marcus felt a stab of desire at the sight. Nicole had been jealous. The idea sent his pulse rate up a notch. He seriously considered calling Shaun to cancel lunch at their favorite restaurant. As though conjured up by the thought, he heard Shaun's deep voice introducing himself to Nicole.

"It's a pleasure to meet you, Nicole. Congratulations on becoming one of the youngest and, if you don't mind my saying, most attractive new mover in this cow town."

Shaun sauntered into Marcus's office a few seconds later, a wide grin on his face. Marcus stood with both arms crossed.

"Give it up," Marcus said.

Shaun spread out his arms and affected an ingenuous smile. "What?"

"Nicole isn't easily fooled. Don't even try it."

"I was totally sincere. The lady is fine!" Shaun closed the door. He shook his head and gave an exaggerated sigh.

"Not every woman is a candidate for your hit list. You're here early. I've still got things to do." Marcus went behind his desk and sat down.

"Eleven forty-five isn't all that early." Shaun took a seat. "And don't get mad with me because she didn't fall for *your* flattery." His grin widened when Marcus shot a heated look his way.

"You're buying lunch for that one," Marcus tossed back.

"Fair enough." Shaun laughed. "Back to your boss. Nicole is hot. If you're not planning to go for it—"

"Stay away from Nicole," Marcus cut him off short.

Shaun studied Marcus with his head to one side for several seconds. "Wow, never thought I'd see the day when a lady could come between us."

Marcus let out a slow breath and willed the tension in his neck to go away. He smiled at Shaun. "I've got my own plans. The last thing I need is you messing with her head. At least not until *after* I'm gone."

"Gotcha, brother." Shaun's expression relaxed into a smile again. "You had me scared for about a minute. Thought you had fallen in love or something."

"I'm hungry." Marcus stood and went to a small closet to get his jacket.

"There's a ten-ounce steak out there with my name on it." Shaun slapped his large hands together. "Let's go."

"I don't know how you can eat that stuff and get through the day."

"I spent the first fourteen years of my life poor as hell. I deserve the good life," Shaun said fervently. "Money means nothing if you don't spend it well."

"On you of course." Marcus shook his head.

"Who else?" Shaun gave a short, cynical laugh. "Women? Nothing beyond a few expenses up front for the chase."

"That sums up the Shaun Jackson mating strategy perfectly," Marcus replied.

"Yeah, you're right." Shaun clapped a hand on Marcus's shoulder, and they walked out together.

Marcus was surprised at the kernel of disgust in his belly. He'd never been bothered by Shaun's ways before. Still, the idea of Shaun playing his game on Nicole set Marcus's teeth on edge. When Nicole came down the hall, Marcus had an irrational urge to block the path to Shaun. While he was trying to diagnose what malady had affected his brain, Shaun affected a winning smile that oozed sincerity.

"Lunchtime at last. I'm sure even beautiful tycoons have to take a break sometime." Shaun put one hand in the pocket of his custom-tailored suit pants.

"Hmm." Nicole's expression remained neutral. She turned to Marcus. "I've gone over the final report on our Lake Charles office. Can we meet this afternoon?"

"I've got that meeting with Andre after lunch and two site visits," Marcus replied.

"Maybe in the morning?" Nicole seemed not to notice the way Shaun examined her from head to toe.

"I'll be in around eight."

"Too early." Nicole wore a slight frown.

"I know what you mean," Shaun interjected smoothly. "I do my best work in the evenings."

"Interesting," Nicole said in a deadpan tone. "What about around five today?"

Marcus shot an annoyed sideways glance at Shaun. "Okay. We'd better get a move on. I've got a lot to do this afternoon."

"If you need to cancel, no problem. Nicole, have you been to This Is It? The best soul food in town." Shaun smacked his lips.

"No, I—"

"Of course, I realize you're not used to cafeteria-style dining. But believe me, it's more than worth it." Shaun walked over to Nicole and put a hand under her elbow. He was poised to guide her toward the elevator.

Nicole lifted her arm and stepped away in one graceful motion. "Thanks, but I have plans. My lunch is on the way."

"You'll get indigestion eating in the office. A nice relaxing meal with pleasant company makes work go better." Shaun waved a forefinger in the air.

"Maybe another time," Nicole said with a restrained smile.

"I'll hold you to that promise." Shaun beamed back as though they had a firm date.

"See you later, Marcus." Nicole walked off.

Marcus faced Shaun. "You're having memory problems?"

"I was going to use the proven Shaun Jackson method of extracting information for you, my man." He spread his hands out.

"Yeah, sure you were." Marcus scowled at him.

"Of course, if she means more to you, just say so. I won't even do a little harmless flirting." Shaun's playful expression sharpened into one of appraisal as he looked at Marcus.

"Nothing you do with women is ever harmless," Marcus shot back with a smile. "Now I'm hungry enough for a steak. Can we go now?"

"Okay, okay." Shaun punched the elevator button.

"You just have to see this cute little shop, Russ. It's adorable," a female voice trilled.

Marcus groaned inwardly when Russell and his girlfriend appeared around a corner. Russell had a possessive arm around Aliyah's waist. He seemed totally entranced by her.

"Well, well. Look at this," Shaun whispered.

"I say we let them have the next ride down," Marcus mumbled with his back to the couple.

"No way. I wouldn't miss this for the world," Shaun replied.

Aliyah's high-pitched titter broke off when she looked at Shaun. Her eyes widened, then she clutched her purse. "Darn! I left my pocket organizer on your desk. Let's go back and get it."

"Are you sure? I think you picked it up," Russell replied.

"No, I didn't," Aliyah insisted. She pulled Russell's arm.

Russell noticed Marcus and Shaun for the first time. His contented smile dissolved. "Marcus."

"Russell," Marcus replied. "Hello, Aliyah."

"Hi." She gave him a brief smile.

Shaun strode over to Russell with one hand out. "Hi. You might not remember me, but Marcus introduced us some months ago."

"No, I don't actually." Russell gave Shaun a brief handshake.

Shaun seemed not to notice his barely disguised disdain. "It was only a minute. Hi, Ms. . . . ?"

She gingerly touched the tips of her fingers to his palm, then drew back. "Hello. Aliyah Manning."

"Right, Ms. Manning. Say, why don't we all go out for lunch?" Shaun said.

"No!" Aliyah blurted out with such force that all three men blinked in surprise. "I'm afraid we've made plans," she finished, her voice lower.

"Yes, we have. Sorry," Russell put in.

"Maybe another time then," Shaun called out merrily. He grinned at Aliyah when she glanced back at them over her shoulder. Russell gave him a vague smile.

Marcus merely nodded to Russell and Aliyah as they turned and went back to Russell's office. "You want to tell me what just happened?"

"I love my life, man. Every day is an adventure," Shaun murmured. He stared at the retreating couple.

"Okay."

Marcus studied Shaun, then followed his gaze in time to see Russell's back disappear around a corner. He was silent for another beat until the realization hit him.

"Let's go. *Now!*" Marcus grabbed Shaun's arm and yanked him toward the open elevator doors.

Shaun pried Marcus's fingers from his sleeve. "This suit costs nine hundred dollars. Don't handle me up like I'm wearing discount clothes."

There were three people on the elevator, so Marcus let go without protest. He glanced at his friend several times as they rode down to the parking garage level. Shaun continued to smooth out invisible wrinkles on his jacket sleeves. Two riders got off on the next floor. Once they got to the parking garage and the remaining passenger started off in the opposite direction, Marcus grabbed Shaun's arm again.

"Tell me Aliyah isn't an old girlfriend. Please, man. I'm begging you!"

"It's a small, small world. You know?"

"Damn!" Marcus swung both arms out in exasperation. "How long ago?"

"I don't kiss and tell."

"Like hell you don't," Marcus snarled. "This is important,

Shaun. You know I've got a big investment here, and if you're—"

"Chill, all right? Look, we broke up a while ago."

"What does 'a while ago' mean exactly?" Marcus insisted.

"A few weeks, no, months ago," Shaun said hastily when Marcus muttered a curse word. "You need to relax, brother. All that nine-to-five living has you wound up."

"Russell has been dating the woman for six months, Shaun." Marcus glared at him. "Is Aliyah her real name?"

Shaun let out a short laugh. "Man, if you could hear yourself right now. Talk about paranoid."

"We came off the same street corner and learned the same player rules. What's the profile?" Marcus stood with his legs apart and his arms folded.

"Let's get some food. My mind can't work on an empty stomach." Shaun gave him a playful tap on the shoulder and strode off.

Marcus had little choice but to follow him. Shaun insisted on driving. They traveled down St. Jacinto in minutes. Though bright sunshine beamed down on Shaun's pearl gray Lexus, the dual-control air-conditioning kept them cool. Shaun hummed along with a hip-hop tune on the FM radio station. He expertly wheeled the luxury car around corners.

"Well?" Marcus demanded. He turned down the volume just as a burst of expletive-filled lyrics started.

Shaun sighed like a parent whose patience was being tested. "Okay, okay. So, we had this little thang. No hearts and flowers, know what I mean? Just mutual physical fireworks."

"I never thought you were a couple," Marcus retorted. "Not your style."

"Hey, I'm gonna find a wifey one of these old days. Soon as I find the right girl." Shaun gunned through a caution light.

"Ms. Right is a lady with a big bank account and some

kind of investments, blue chips and real estate preferably," Marcus deadpanned.

"Say, you know her? Hook me up," Shaun wisecracked. He pulled up to Pappadeaux restaurant on South Loop W.

"I want answers, Shaun." Marcus frowned at him.

"Let's have a beer and some fine Creole food. We both know you've got a taste for Louisiana delicacies these days."

Shaun barked with laughter when Marcus's frown turned murderous. He got out of the car, adjusted his designer sunglasses, and strolled toward the entrance. Once more Marcus found himself trailing after Shaun with no answers and a shorter fuse. Conversation was impossible as they waited in the crowded foyer for a table. Twenty minutes later, they were seated with menus.

"What looks good to you today, dude? Get anything you want."

"You're testing this friendship, *again*," Marcus said through clenched teeth.

A pretty blond waitress came over. "Hi, I'm Jennifer. What can I get you?"

In seconds she was giggling and leaning over them both, her ample bosom close to their faces. For his part, Shaun participated in the wink-and-smile sport. Shaun enjoyed the attention, but his sights were much higher than a working-class lady. Jennifer bounced off with one last perky grin for Shaun. As though he'd forgotten her in seconds, Shaun's gaze scanned the room. He smiled and nodded at a pretty Black woman seated nearby. Marcus shook his head once.

"What's the deal with you and Aliyah Manning, Shaun?" Marcus said. He pointed at him. "Remember, I've heard all of your lies at least twice."

"Hey, everybody wants to get ahead. I can't blame a sista for that."

"She's a player, too." Marcus groaned beneath his breath.

"Looks like my girl is heading for a real soft landing. I'd say she's got Russell's head spinning." Shaun chuckled low in his throat.

"Russell does everything but sit up and beg when she so much as raises her little finger."

Marcus cut off his next comment when Jennifer approached. He had to wait through another round of flirting before he could continue. Meanwhile the woman Shaun had smiled at tried to catch his eye. She didn't seem to care about the man seated next to her. Jennifer noticed her and blocked the woman's view, finally leaving their beers on the table as she and the woman exchanged stony looks. All this drama over lunch he didn't need, Marcus grumbled to himself.

"Tell me the worst about this lady," Marcus said.

Shaun leaned both elbows on the table. "Russell is a grown man. Don't try to rescue him. Besides, he won't believe you and not just because he hates your guts."

"She's that good?" Marcus already knew the answer by the leer that spread across Shaun's face.

"He doesn't stand a chance. Start picking out the suit you're gonna wear to their wedding." Shaun lifted his glass of beer in a mock toast. "To the happy couple."

"I don't believe all she wants is happy ever after." Marcus stared at Shaun hard.

"Why not? Russell's got money and status. I'd say she's struck gold."

Marcus leaned forward and lowered his voice. "Listen to me good, Shaun. You better be telling me everything you know or I'll—"

"Why should you care if she marries old Russ and then cleans him out?" Shaun grinned and slapped Marcus on the shoulder. "Think about it."

"I still don't like it."

"You'll get yours, Aliyah will get hers, and you'll both be happy. Right?" Shaun glanced past him. "Here's our food. Stop worrying, it's bad for your digestion."

"Yeah, right."

Marcus thought about this latest wild card and frowned. He paid token attention to Shaun's good-natured chatter as they ate. Now he had two women to worry about. Heat moved up his spine when he remembered the taste and feel of Nicole. Shaun was right about one thing. He should let Russell handle his own business. Dealing with his unexpected and uncontrollable attraction to Nicole would be Marcus's biggest obstacle.

ten

Nicole tried to concentrate on Jesse's report. Russell didn't help, the way he kept fidgeting in his seat. She knew he was looking for an opening to attack any decision she might make. Sitting next to Marcus didn't help either. Not that he did anything purposely to distract her. Still, he seemed to radiate a vibe that made her think of that night at his apartment. Jesse's voice tugged her back to the meeting. They were all sitting around the wide oval table in the office conference room.

"So, last week things went pretty good. I switched some schedules around. The guys and ladies seem to like the changes. I haven't had any problems with guards not show-ing up." Jesse dropped the single sheet of paper he held and rapped the knuckles of his right hand on the conference table. "Knock on wood."

"Amen," Andre added with a grin.

"Excellent, Jesse." Nicole smiled at him, then grew seri-ous. "Now about the Phoung account and the case of the missing groceries. The police are checking out a list of store employees that have been fired in the last year or so. Also, David Phoung was a little careless with warehouse keys."

"Nicole found out that Mr. Phoung's brother-in-law wasn't very conscientious about retrieving keys from fired staff," Marcus added. He glanced at her sideways. "Good detective work."

"Thanks. I just spent time chatting with his current employees. Most of the top assistants are his relatives, as you all know." She looked around as heads nodded. "His ever helpful but not too smart niece gave out the security code too freely."

"Well, that's it, then. He can't blame us," Andre said.

Marketing director Imani nodded with vigor. Petite and stylish, her natural hair was cut boyishly short, making her look even younger. "For real. I like it."

"Now your spin won't be such a challenge, huh?" Jacinta's black eyes flashed humor.

"Spin is everything, chica," Imani flipped back with a grin.

"Tameka's butt is saved once again. She has a way of landing on her feet." Jesse laughed as the others agreed.

Nicole smiled as they traded jokes. She didn't interrupt for several minutes. They all needed the release. The past week had been tense for everyone. Though they had all worked together, she still felt like a kid with her nose pressed against the window. Imani and Jacinta were good friends outside the office. Jesse acted the role of the kindly uncle to the rest of the young staff. All of them had the easy working relationship of several years as a team. Nicole felt a stab of envy at inside jokes being lobbed across the conference table.

Russell cleared his throat loudly. "So, I'm assuming we're all through with *business*?"

"No, not quite," Nicole replied.

"Good. I'd just like to say one thing about the recent wave of difficulties—"

"Excuse me, but we covered the issues and the actions taken to address them," Nicole said in a controlled voice.

"What about the damage to our credibility with customers?" Russell glanced around at the others. "I don't think they're likely to simply forget. Any perceived weakness in our procedures can have a devastating effect."

"We've all done our best to demonstrate that we can act quickly and effectively when problems occur. As someone pretty new to Summers Security and to this business in general, I'd say you folks have done a damn good job." Nicole looked around at the employees. Several were nodding.

"Thanks, Nicole." Imani smiled at her.

"Me, too. It was even worth being a suspect for about a minute," Andre joked.

"The last few weeks have been a trial for all of us. Probably more for me, since I came here knowing exactly zero about the security biz," Nicole said with a laugh.

The rest of the staff—with two exceptions—joined in. Marcus wore a blank expression, his hands folded on top of the conference table. Russell wore a sardonic half-smile to show what he thought of her. Nicole ignored them both, for now.

"So, lunch is on me. Party on." Nicole raised a palm when they started clapping their hands with glee.

"You're kidding! You're spending company money to feed everyone?" Russell's eyes widened.

"Naturally I get to deduct the entire meal. Business lunch, right?" Nicole lifted a shoulder.

"Hey, you're not your uncle Hosea's niece for nothing," Imani said with a sassy wink.

"Imani!" Jacinta's mouth formed a large circle. The others looked a little uneasy.

Nicole laughed. "Relax. I knew my uncle very well, thank you. Now what are you in the mood for today?"

A spirited debate broke out. After ten minutes they were still arguing passionately between Mexican and Italian. Marcus scribbled notes as though oblivious to the merriment around him. Russell blew out a noisy breath in disapproval. No one seemed to notice when he finally left in a huff. Nicole tapped the keys of the laptop in the conference room. She saved comments about the meeting into her database, exited the program, and shut down the computer.

"Excuse me," she said in an attempt to get their attention. "Hey!"

"Yeah, boss?" Jacinta waved at the others to be quiet.

"It's only ten o'clock. We're not going to spend two hours arguing. Either you decide or I will." Nicole arched her eyebrows at them.

"Chinese," a chorus of voices said, mixed with one groan.

"I never get to choose!" Jacinta complained and stamped a foot.

"That's 'cause we had Lebanese five times in a row when we let you order lunch," Andre said and rolled his eyes.

"Yeah, I'm still tasting garlic," Imani quipped.

Jacinta protested, and the staff continued their friendly debate as they filed out of the conference room. Nicole smiled as she watched them. Then she glanced at Marcus. He seemed engrossed in his own neat handwriting.

"Those guys are great, huh?" Nicole gathered her own reports, pen, and notepad with deliberation.

"Yes, they are," Marcus said. He put the cap on his Cross ink pen and stood.

"Uh, you're eating in with the rest of us?" Nicole said quickly.

"I've got a lot of work still." Marcus nodded to her.

"Wait," she blurted out. "That compliment included you. So, I'd really like you to join us."

He gazed at her for several moments, then looked away. "I'll try."

"Uh, we've got an issue to settle. About that night in your apartment, I'm sorry—"

"I apologize—" Marcus spoke at the same time.

"No, it was my fault for showing up at your place and—" Nicole started.

"Not a good idea," Marcus said.

"I know, I know." Nicole sighed.

"Look, I shouldn't have gotten so touchy-feely. You're my boss and I was way out of line." Marcus let out a long breath, as though relieved.

"No, no, this awkward situation between us is my fault. I got carried away and you know." Nicole's voice trailed off.

"Do I?" he said in a soft voice. Marcus sat back down again.

"Okay, here's the deal. We're a man and woman working closely together," Nicole began, then stopped, searching for a way to go on.

"I follow you so far."

She pretended to be irritated with a bogus frown. "Mr. Comedy Central. Anyway, you and me, bad business. Working friends is a better idea."

"Umm." Marcus put a finger under his bottom lip and gazed at her steadily.

"Umm what?"

Marcus sat back and stretched out one leg in a waiting posture. "Nothing. Go ahead with your logic."

"We're both stressed out. Being in close quarters and sharing tough times can—" Nicole searched for the right phrase.

"Make us think we're right for each other when we're not?" Marcus tilted his head to one side.

"Now that's a good way of putting it. I've got to concentrate on Summers Security, no distractions."

No matter how tempting the distraction is, Nicole could have added. Marcus seemed intent on proving the point. Dressed in navy slacks and a crisp, white, long-sleeved shirt, he looked like a handsome grad student. The cotton fabric did nothing to hide the fact that he worked out. His body looked powerful even in repose. Nicole felt a wistful sigh building and stifled it. Still, her plan to conquer him had kept her awake nights from guilt. When the stuff had hit the fan, with complaints and problems coming hard and fast, Marcus had been there to support her. He deserved her respect, and she had decided to grow up, right?

"This is no time to play."

"Oh, I see. You were going to play me." Marcus chuckled deep in his throat. "You've got me mixed up with someone else. I don't get played so easy."

"No, I didn't mean—"

"For the truth to slip out. Don't worry, Nicole. I think I can handle you." Marcus stood and looked down on her.

"I didn't mean to imply that I took you for a fool." She floundered, wondering just how she'd ended up with a Via Spiga pump planted firmly in her mouth.

"Good, because I was almost offended," he teased. "Just forget it. If anything else comes up I'll be in my office. Unless of course working close to me gets you all upset."

"Cut it out," Nicole said through clenched teeth. "We could try to establish a happy medium. Let's shoot for something between seriously annoying one another and playing tongue hockey."

"What do you suggest?" Marcus wore an unruffled half-smile. He tucked his notepad under one arm.

"We'll talk about it later, when I'm not feeling the need to choke you." Nicole whirled around and went to her office. She turned to slam the door between the two rooms.

Marcus caught it with one hand. "You were trying to be nice about our 'awkward' situation and I got smart. Sorry. You're right of course."

She eyed him for several moments. Suspicion blossomed at the quick turnaround, yet Nicole decided to play along. "Am I?"

He nodded. "We don't want to complicate what's already a perfect setup for major drama. I'll just have to forget you're such an attractive lady, that's all."

Excellent move, Mr. Reed. Nicole let a slow smile spread across her face. "Then we understand each other."

"We sure do. I'll get back to business now, boss lady." Marcus saluted her, then left the conference room.

Nicole closed the door with a quiet thump. She went to her desk, sat down, and proceeded to examine just what had happened between them.

The next day Marcus and Russell were in Nicole's office to discuss several company projects. Marcus behaved as though they'd never touched or discussed the pros and cons of a relationship. Much as she hated it, Nicole couldn't get either his touch or their discussion out of her mind. She knew he meant to get her attention by ignoring the undercurrent between them. His tactic was quite effective, too. Nicole mentally kicked herself. He'd outmaneuvered her. A galling development she intended to change.

"If we're still going to have a Louisiana office, then Lake Charles is a better choice," Marcus said. "Lafayette doesn't have enough business to justify the expense. New Orleans is saturated. Plus neither city has a strong enough economy."

"I made the same point a year ago. I should go to Lake Charles and set up the office," Russell said in a petulant voice.

His whining tone yanked Nicole back to the issue at hand. For the fourth time Russell made her sorry that she had invited him to give his input. Russell and Jolene had complained to the family that Nicole was being autocratic. Their scheming had led to a conference call from Stanton and Uncle Lionel. They'd advised her on how to neutralize them. Since then she'd made an effort to include Russell in more management decisions.

"The answer is no," Nicole said, her tone short.

"You're not being reasonable. My father's will, flawed as it is, does specify that I'm to have some say-so in the direction this company takes." Russell's lips stretched in a tight line.

"You can't sign a lease or enter into any contracts. It doesn't make sense to send you." Nicole frowned back at him.

"You could make me an officer of this company. If I were appointed chief financial officer I could make expenditures, with your final approval," Russell added in a grudging tone.

"You could, but I won't, so forget it. I spent a lot of time in Lake Charles when the riverboat casinos opened." Nicole read over a page of the report Marcus had prepared.

"Gambling problem?" Russell's eyes glittered with malevolent curiosity.

"Daddy did construction work in Lake Charles. I went with him every week to meetings." Nicole ignored his dig.

"You're scared the family will realize I'm more competent than you to run this company. So you won't give me any responsibility. Nice try, but it won't work."

"Do you ever get tired of being an asshole?" Nicole glared at him. "Let me tell you one thing—"

Russell turned to Marcus. "She has the temperament of a pit bull and the mouth of a rap singer. *This* is who runs the top security firm in the Southwest."

"Hold it. Russell has a point." Marcus spread out his arms like a boxing referee urging two fighters back to their corners.

"What? I can't believe you." Nicole turned her heated gaze to Marcus.

"Mr. Summers did make it clear that Russell wasn't to be completely cut out of decision making. On the other hand, Nicole knows the area and has contacts in Lake Charles."

"Hardly a convincing argument. I'm more than capable of making business contacts." Russell stuck his chin out.

"I suggest this, Nicole knows the area and I'm the manager under our license. We'll set up appointments and go to Lake Charles for the day," Marcus went on calmly.

"So, you're siding with her." Russell's eyes narrowed.

"And we'll leave Russell in charge, with the staff reporting to him. Since we're expanding, it makes sense. Nicole, we're going to be out of the office more." Marcus looked at Nicole.

"I'm so grateful, considering this company was started by my father," Russell grumbled.

"Leave Russell in charge," Nicole repeated the words in an undertone. She shook her head slowly. "I don't know."

"I have experience in setting up an office, hiring staff, and getting things in place. We both need to go. Besides, the staff is pretty independent."

"Well . . ." Nicole pursed her lips.

"Work with me on this," Marcus said in a firm tone.

"Fine, okay." Nicole forced the words out.

Russell stood. "At least Marcus is finally using common sense." He walked out with his leather portfolio tucked under an arm.

"You're welcome," Nicole called after him with a grimace.

She turned on Marcus. "What is this you and I going to Lake Charles business?"

Marcus sat back with a smile. "You nervous about being alone with me for that long?"

Nicole felt a flash of annoyance. Yet she was determined not to give him the satisfaction of knowing he was getting on her last good nerve. Instead she forced a smile. "Of course not. All business. I'll make some phone calls and let you know."

"Good. I'll get Imani's marketing survey and make some calls to prospective customers. Shelly has information on commercial real estate companies." Marcus did indeed assume a brisk, professional manner.

Her annoyance deepened at his offhand attitude after pushing her buttons. "Fine," she clipped and tapped the keyboard of her desktop computer.

"Excellent start to our new collaboration," Marcus said.

The blazing look Nicole shot at him was wasted. All she saw was his broad back going out the door. With heroic self-restraint she held her tongue, until the door closed.

"Smart-assed, conceited chump," she muttered and threw an ink pen.

Cat came in and ducked just in time for it to clatter against the frame. She closed the door behind her. "Hmm, I just got back from a coffee break. Let me guess. You had a meeting with Russell."

"And Marcus," Nicole spat. "Those two are really asking for it."

"Look at it this way, you're the one in charge no matter how they kick."

Nicole willed her jaws to relax. She breathed in and out deeply three times. Then she rested her head against the leather of her chair. "You're right. It's about time they find out just how in charge this lady can be."

"That's what I'm talkin' 'bout," Cat quipped with a mischievous grin. "Show 'em who they're dealing with as only a sister can. Now I've got these for you to sign."

They went through payroll checks and other details that needed the CEO's approval. Cat talked about minor office management issues. Nicole nodded, signed, and offered a few comments. Still, her thoughts were on what promised to be a long two-hour trip with Marcus seated next to her.

"You are listening to me, right?" Cat eyed her.

"Of course." Nicole signed the last paycheck and handed Cat the pile of papers. "I know a wonderful restaurant on the lake," she murmured.

"Huh?" Cat gave her a puzzled look.

"Nothing, just planning to be in charge." Nicole gave a short laugh and rocked her chair gently. "Yeah, we'll see who starts running scared."

"Okay, I'm officially out of this conversation. What did I miss?" Cat put one hand on her hip.

Nicole laughed again. "Nothing, Cat. As usual you were two steps ahead of me. I'm going to put Russell and Marcus on notice. No drama, but they will get the message."

"Firm, but fair," Cat smiled and left.

"Firm, yes. No promises on being fair." Nicole smiled as she turned her attention to the work on her desk.

Three days later Marcus drove the company Dodge Durango along Interstate 10 toward Louisiana. He made it a point not to glance at Nicole. She seemed strangely relaxed, and it disconcerted him. He'd been a lot more comfortable when she'd been the one off balance. Nicole seemed unaware he was trying to figure her out. She tapped a foot to the music coming from the radio and flipped another page of the trade magazine on private security.

"I'm guessing you haven't been to Louisiana often," she said without looking at him.

"A grand total of two times, both with Mr. Summers. We met with two clients and came back. I was lucky we stopped for lunch someplace." He edged the Durango up to seventy-five. The scenery whipped by.

"Now it's three." Nicole nodded at the sign welcoming them to Louisiana. "I promise not to rush. If we get through early enough we can have dinner someplace nice. Preferably close to the lake."

"Sounds good."

Marcus risked a quick look at her. Nicole seemed absorbed by an article on preventing identity theft. He shifted in his seat. Static crackled from the speakers as they went out of range of the radio station. Before he could react, Nicole found another one. In seconds a driving zydeco rhythm surrounded them. A male vocalist sang in a husky basso timbre. The Creole French lyrics sounded both exotic and provocative. She hummed along.

"What is he saying?" he asked.

Nicole didn't answer immediately. After listening for several minutes she smiled. "I can only catch a few words. He's begging this woman named Thérèse to be his lover, but she's not having it. He's trying to convince her they belong together. He tells her that the man she's chasing won't satisfy her."

"You caught more than a few words," Marcus said.

"It's an old song. My grandparents still live in a small town called Loreauville. They taught me a few things. M a parle kreyòle ye a trape li osi, to kòne."

Her voice dipped into a throaty quality that sent a jolt of power up his spine. "Yeah, whatever you said," he murmured.

When she laughed the electricity snapped elsewhere in his anatomy. The sound tapped into a place inside him that Marcus didn't know existed. For the first time his unease turned to apprehension. This woman was reaching too deep for comfort. Then she glanced at him with an enigmatic smile that played across her alluring, full mouth. His apprehension evaporated in an instant. In its place was desire. She seemed to offer him a chance to taste something wild, like a moonlit night on the banks of a bayou. He looked ahead at the highway to counter her effect on his senses. His imagination spun out of control and she hadn't even touched him. Marcus cleared his throat.

"I said 'When I speak Creole they will catch it too, you know.'"

"Okay." He wondered if there was any truth to those legends about voodoo love spells.

"My mother's parents are fluent, but most of the younger generations don't speak Creole French at all. In the past five years I've made it my hobby to learn. Louisiana Creole French is one of the most endangered languages around," Nicole said with a serious expression.

"I didn't realize."

"Not many people know about it. It's different from Cajun French in some ways, but mostly the words and phrasing are the same." Nicole seemed to warm to the subject.

"Fascinating subject, Creole culture, I mean." Marcus found this side of her intriguing.

Nicole's eyes lit up. "How much do you know?"

"Very little. My father's great-grandmother came from somewhere called LaFourche. Is that right?" He glanced at her.

"LaFourche Parish. Mais yeah, chere! You've got Creole in your veins." Nicole grinned back.

Marcus shook his head. "Maybe. I don't know anything else. My father didn't hang around long, and his family didn't keep in touch."

"Your parents divorced, huh? Tough."

"They were never married. My old man wasn't big on responsibility." Marcus wondered why he was sharing such details with her. He rarely talked about his dysfunctional family background.

"Too bad. Do you ever see him?" Nicole turned in her seat. Her interest seemed genuine, caring even.

"Nah, I got tired of visiting him in prison. He always wants money." Marcus clamped his back teeth together.

"I'm really sorry," she said softly.

"Don't be. I hardly know the man." Marcus forced a lighter tone to his voice. "My coach in high school did more for me. We still keep in touch."

"That's great." Nicole continued to study him.

"I'm going to pick up some zydeco CDs. Any recommendations?" He wanted to get off the subject of his family.

"Try on some Buckwheat Zydeco to start. Speak of the devil, as my Tante Marie used to say. That's him." Nicole turned up the radio. A new song blared out.

They talked about the music, food, and culture of south Louisiana. Marcus found himself more interested than he realized. His connection to his father's family had always been tenuous at best. As Nicole went on with vivid descriptions of summers spent in rural Creole country, the hint of a Creole accent came through.

"Here I was thinking you were a big-city girl." Marcus smiled.

"I am really. Once I got to be a know-it-all teenager, hanging out with poules and kochons wasn't too cool."

"Translate again please," Marcus said.

"Chickens and pigs." Nicole laughed hard. "My great-grandparents inherited a farm. Passed down from the French slave master they kind of blackmailed."

"Sounds like you've got some high-class skeletons in your closet." Marcus looked at her.

"Don't tell my mother I mentioned it. She and my aunts like to give a different version of the family tree." Nicole wore an impish grin.

"Cleaned it up I suppose."

"You betcha."

"But you found out the family secret."

"My great-grandmother got a little senile in her golden years. I'd listen to her stories. Mama and Grandmamma had no idea what an education I got." Nicole wiggled her eyebrows like a little girl who'd gotten away with being bad.

"You'll have to tell me some of them," Marcus said and gazed at her.

"Name the time and place," she replied, then blinked rapidly, as though bewildered. They exchanged a glance, then both became self-conscious.

"Anyway, about these potential customers." Marcus was eager to get back on safer ground, at least for him.

"Right. Let's go over these profiles you put together." Nicole looked away from him.

For the rest of the ride they studiously avoided any kind of personal disclosure. Marcus felt a mixture of relief and disappointment in a strange way. He hadn't felt so mixed up around a female since first discovering girls as a thirteen-year-old. Forced to cope, Marcus did his best to concentrate on the meetings ahead. Nicole seemed to recover much more quickly, a tiny blow to his male ego that he did his best to mentally shrug off. By the time they entered Calcasieu Parish, Marcus felt drained. Not a good sign, since he would make the presentations to two major companies. Nicole's voice jerked him out of his reverie.

"Ready?" She stuffed a thick file into her soft leather Dooney & Bourke briefcase.

"I've read and reread at least three sources on both Daigre and Sons Construction and Ellender Real Estate."

Marcus knew the companies on paper. Unfortunately his mind kept skipping back to her smile, the scent of her skin, her eyes. He took a deep breath and let it out. "Yeah, I'm ready." He damn well would be even if it killed him.

"Good, because I'm nervous. Man, it feels good being able to confess. Thanks for being supportive in spite of the circumstances." Nicole glanced at him.

"You're welcome." Marcus didn't risk returning her gaze. An unfamiliar feeling crawled over his skin like a small insect. Guilt.

eleven

"Those meetings went so well it's downright scary. We're hot!" Nicole clapped her hands together and grinned. Then she started the Durango. Marcus had agreed she should drive, since she knew the city.

It had been one o'clock in the afternoon when they'd finished their meeting with Ellender Real Estate. A medium-sized business specializing in large commercial properties, the vice president had grilled them for well over two hours. The gruff man had finally hired them.

"You charmed his socks off. Some technique, Ms. Benoit." Marcus made notes as he spoke. "I was sure he'd say no."

Nicole wove in and out of traffic skillfully. "He's really a softie inside, kinda like my uncle Alton. He'd done his homework, too. The man is no fool."

"You had him purring like a big tame cat by the time we left." Marcus finally stopped writing. He put his pen in an inside pocket of his coat and closed the portfolio. "I'd say you've had lots of practice getting your way with men."

"Scared?" Nicole went around a line of cars backed up behind someone trying to make a left turn.

"Of you or your driving?" Marcus wisecracked.

"Take your pick, Mr. Big Stuff."

"Neither."

She laughed. "Yeah, you'd have to say that to prove you're a big strong guy."

Marcus surprised her by laughing too. He seemed to relax for the first time since they'd left Houston. Nicole felt like they had crossed another boundary in their relationship. She felt less and less like he was an object of conquest, much to her chagrin. Liking him too much had not been in her plan. But the fire that had reached down to the soles of her feet when they'd kissed had not been in her plan either. Beyond that mind-bending experience was the magnetism he seemed to exert on her senses. There was no denying it, she enjoyed his wry sense of humor and respected his intelligence. They drove on in a companionable silence.

"So, where is this place that puts eating anywhere else to shame?"

"Mr. D's On The Bayou, best seafood around. In my humble opinion." Nicole turned down Common Street and pulled into the restaurant parking lot. "Here we go. You're going to thank me all the way back to Houston."

"We'll see."

Nicole couldn't see his eyes behind the dark sunglasses. Still, she was sure there was a teasing twinkle in them. She walked beside him, very conscious of his tall, imposing figure. Female gazes slid sideways whenever they passed by. *Yeah, girls. He's with me.* Once seated, Marcus took her recommendations on what to order. They laughed and talked during the meal, about business and the city's history.

"Dessert?" The pretty, dark-eyed Cajun waitress beamed at them both.

"No indeed. I'm two seconds away from bursting open." Nicole patted her lips with the white cotton napkin.

"Nothing for me either." Marcus reached inside his pocket and took out his credit card.

"No, I'll get the check," Nicole said as she put a restraining hand on his arm.

"Tradition." Marcus dropped the card into the small tray with the bill. "Anyway, it's the company account."

"My hero," Nicole teased.

"I thought you'd appreciate my enlightened approach. Women don't want to be taken care of or rescued these days." Marcus sipped from the tall glass of iced tea.

"Why in the world would I insult a wealthy dude whose main joy is buying me anything I want?" Nicole said with a grin.

"You intend to follow the family custom of marrying rich?" Marcus put the glass down and gazed at her.

Something in his eyes tugged at Nicole's insides. "That was a joke. I'm not *that* superficial."

"Oh," he said blandly.

"Besides, my ex-husband cured me of rich chumps," she joked. Still, he must have seen past her attempt at humor.

"Hurt that bad." He tilted his head to one side.

"Not even money could make it worth it." Nicole made a sour face and drank more diet cola.

"How long were you married?"

"Four hellish years if you count the year we were separated." She raised her glass in a salute. "I don't care what people say, thank the Lord for divorce lawyers."

"I'm guessing you two don't speak."

"Your guessing is on target, my friend. Those made-for-television movies lie. It's not easy to hire hit men." Nicole gave a short graveyard laugh.

"I'm sorry he mistreated you," Marcus said in a quiet tone. He looked away when she gazed into his eyes.

"Maybe we should change the subject. This is a celebration." Nicole drained her glass of cola.

"Right." He tugged at his jacket lapel as though putting on his business persona again.

After another quick run through their presentation, they left the restaurant. Neither said much during the ride to their last meeting of the day. For three hours they met with two astute businessmen. They sat in the large, yet functional, office of Joe Daigre. His oldest son, Damien, sat to his father's right at the round cherry wood table in a corner of Joe's office. Marcus watched Nicole work. She demonstrated that she'd done her homework.

Joe Daigre's thick eyebrows formed a line. "We'll study your proposal and get back to you."

"I travel to Houston quite frequently. Maybe we can get together," Damien said directly to Nicole.

Marcus nodded to him. "Sounds great. We can schedule something right now."

"I'll give you my card," Nicole said smoothly.

They wrapped up the meeting a few moments later. They walked out with Joe Daigre beside Marcus. Damien and Nicole followed them down the hall.

"Have a safe drive back to Houston." Damien's copper eyes glittered when he glanced at Nicole.

He strolled off, one hand in his custom silk blend dress pants pocket. The muscles in Marcus's jaw rippled. He opened the door for Nicole and followed her to the Durango. Neither spoke for thirty minutes as Nicole drove them out of the city. She glanced at Marcus several times. He seemed more interested in checking e-mail on his cell phone. Then he turned his attention to the contents of his briefcase.

"I think the meeting went well. The father doesn't like dealing with women when it comes to business, though. But toward the end I chipped away at the old rock." Nicole spoke in a lighthearted tone.

"Good."

"He knows my family. That always helps." Nicole pressed the accelerator and activated the cruise control.

"I wouldn't know. Never had connections, family or otherwise." Marcus rattled a hand full of papers.

"Don't try to tell me nobody ever gave you help."

"After I worked my butt off." Marcus made notes in the margins of a page.

"There you go. Connections." Nicole lifted a shoulder.

"Based on ability, not my last name." Marcus looked at her, then went back to his notes.

"Well, excuse me for being born a Summers. But the fact remains that you have connections. Admit it." Nicole grinned at him.

"If you say so."

More silence. Nicole decided to try again. "You made an impression on the old dude, Joe I mean. Another connection."

"You definitely impressed his son. He did everything but kiss the back of your hand." Marcus pressed the ink pen harder as he wrote in short, stabbing motions.

"He poured on the charm. All part of business. Damien is as tough as his father, just has a different style." Nicole felt his vibe in waves. "You okay over there?"

"Sure."

Nicole glanced at the papers balanced on his knee. "Don't see how you're going to be able to read your own handwriting. And just what do you mean?"

"The guy was making a play for you." Marcus stopped writing. "Don't tell me you didn't notice."

"Oh, I noticed big time." Nicole laughed.

Marcus didn't crack a smile. He rattled the papers louder as he shoved them into his briefcase and took out a folder. "Right."

"My goodness, he disapproves!" Nicole glanced at him, then at the highway again. "I couldn't exactly shoot him down."

"Whatever."

"C'mon, he didn't do anything overtly offensive."

"If you say so." Marcus pursed his lips as though pressing back more words.

"Okay, what," Nicole said finally after ten seconds of the silent treatment.

"Forget it. Since you didn't seem to mind anyway."

"The guy just did a little exploratory flirting. I deflected it. End of story. We'll get his account because he knows we're good."

"I'm just saying we don't need to sacrifice our image or principles to get him to sign up," Marcus muttered. More paper rustled, but quieter.

"I know what this is about, Marcus. Okay, I'm used to having a certain amount of privilege based on my family name. And yes, I don't exactly protest if a guy likes the way I look and that smoothes the way. However, I do have some pride."

"I didn't mean—"

"Damien Daigre will talk to you from now on. He'll get the message."

Marcus didn't answer immediately. He lowered the folder he held and studied her for a time. "Okay."

"Okay." Nicole stared ahead at the gray pavement.

Remarkably, she wasn't angry. In fact, in the last few weeks she'd examined herself more than she ever had before.

Nicole wanted to prove she could take Summers Security to an entirely new definition of success. She wanted the company to be a top performer.

"You've really done a lot of hard work these last few weeks," he said finally, as though he'd read her thoughts.

"Yes, I have. Like I said before, this isn't a game to me anymore. Besides, I'd like to rub Russell's nose in it when I succeed."

Unexpectedly Marcus laughed deep in his throat. The sensuous sound wrapped around her body. Nicole's breathing kicked up several notches.

"You haven't changed completely from those old ways."

"Sorry, I'll try harder." Nicole smiled without looking at him.

"Not necessary, at least not for me," Marcus said.

His tone sent a serious shiver up her spine. "Thanks. I didn't think you cared," she replied.

"Russell deserves a little payback. So do I, come to think of it. Those first few days I—"

"Was less than thrilled," she finished for him. "I know. But we're beyond that now, so let's forget it. Deal?"

"You got it, boss lady." Marcus wore an impish expression.

"You had to go and mess up our new relationship." Nicole gave a theatrical sigh.

He laughed again. "Okay, okay. No more 'boss lady' digs."

The rest of the ride flowed along like a pleasant outing. Marcus relaxed again. Little by little she was chipping away at the Stone Prince. The man admired a serious approach to business. Nicole felt like she belonged at Summers Security. His acceptance of her made the real difference.

The next morning Nicole hummed a tune as she pushed through the double doors leading to the Summers Security office suite. She waved to Imani and Jacinta as they rounded a corner.

"How is everything?" she said in a cheery tone.

"Great, peachy." Jacinta's mouth turned down at the corners, giving her round face a sour look.

"Thank God you and Marcus made it back. Never leave us again." Imani caught Nicole's free hand and squeezed it.

"What is up with you two? Today is beautiful, we've got happy customers again, and the weekend is only two days away. Life is just about perfect." Nicole grinned and walked toward her office.

"Sure. We've got a meeting. See you later," Imani said, her tone dry. She and Jacinta headed off.

"Maybe we can have lunch, ladies," Nicole called as she waved goodbye to them cheerily. The two women each mumbled an assent as they walked away.

"Hey, Cat. You look fresh as a Louisiana peach in picking season." Nicole scooped up a stack of mail and messages from the tray with her name on it.

"Look who's singing like the blue bird of happiness. No wonder, you didn't have to put up with Russell for a day," Cat grumbled.

"I've put up with him since I was born," Nicole wisecracked.

Cat's frown deepened. "You had parents to protect you. We were defenseless."

"Oh, come on. How bad could it have been?" Nicole headed into her office with Cat on her heels.

"Should I begin with the five memos he put out before lunchtime?" Cat let out a snort of disgust. "I thought I was the queen of nitpicking. And I don't need a lecture on how to answer the telephone properly."

"You should be used to him by now." Nicole turned on her

computer. "Anyway, I tried to make sure he couldn't be too much of a pimple on your butt."

"Very funny," Cat retorted and dropped into a chair. "You had to make things worse by letting him think he was in charge of something."

"Well, sorta kinda. We didn't get any 911 calls while we were in Lake Charles. So, I think y'all are exaggerating." Nicole settled into her leather chair and shuffled through the mail.

"The trip went very well, I take it."

"I actually felt like I knew what I was talking about, Cat. I think we can open offices in New Orleans and Lake Charles sooner than I thought." Nicole wore a feline smile of satisfaction. "Take that, all you Nicole skeptics."

"How wonderful. Just don't sick Russell on me again, or I can't be held responsible for the result. By the way, Mr. Phoung called twice. I put his message on top. You might want to call him first, considering."

"You're more priceless than rubies." Nicole dropped the stack of mail and punched in his phone number. She knew it by heart.

Mr. Phoung sounded as though he still felt leery of their services, but he did thank her for all the attention they'd given him. Nicole used her best diplomacy to mention his role in the security breaches. Mr. Phoung's tone softened considerably.

"Thank you, Mr. Phoung. We intend to earn and keep your trust." Nicole hung up the phone with a wide grin. "Life is perfect."

"Hello." Russell's latest flame, Aliyah Manning, stood in her door.

"Hi." Nicole rocked back in her chair and waited.

"I just happened to be passing by and thought we might have lunch," Aliyah said.

"I'm sorry, but I have plans." Nicole didn't have to think about her answer.

"Maybe you and Marcus could meet us, sort of a double date." Aliyah made the comment sound casual.

Nice try, sugar. "Marcus would have to make his own social commitment. I don't know his schedule," Nicole said mildly.

"Oh, I see." Aliyah arranged a silk oblong scarf across one shoulder. Her royal blue dress was impeccable and obviously expensive.

"Is there anything else I can do for you?" Nicole sat forward.

Aliyah didn't seem put off. "No, thank you," she replied with a polite smile. She opened a leather case containing a planner. "What about lunch next Wednesday? I'm free then."

Nicole suppressed a sigh of aggravation. This woman got the hint—she just had no intention of taking it. "What exactly do you do again, Aliyah?"

"I'm in freelance fashion marketing. Right now I'm between projects, thank goodness. I'll put us down for Wednesday at one." Aliyah's sugared manner was a thin cover for an iron will.

"Let me see." Nicole tapped a few keys as though checking her calendar. "Oops, can't do it. I'm booked. So exactly what do you market?"

"I've worked on projects for several hip-hop artists who have branched out into clothing, jewelry, and footwear lines." Aliyah took Nicole's question as an invitation to sit down. "The African-American and Latino communities love to style, you know."

"Must keep you busy," Nicole said. She gazed at Aliyah.

"Never too busy to get to know Russell's family. Russell and I have become very much a couple." Aliyah flashed her expensive dental work at Nicole.

"Is that right?"

"Between us girls, we're at the meet-the-relatives stage. At least that's what I think." Aliyah nodded to her. "With Russ's parents gone, I'll have to pass the test with his sister and aunts, I'm sure."

Nicole smiled. She'd pay to watch Jolene slice and dice Aliyah. Still, Nicole had a feeling Aliyah could probably hold her own. But she had too much work for such diversions, no matter how entertaining they might be.

"They're not all that bad." Nicole struggled not to laugh at the lie she'd just told. "Anyway, let me know how you make out."

"I was hoping you could give me some insight, maybe even a few tips. Being a woman in a man's world, you know what it's like to feel like an outsider." Aliyah nodded. "By the way, I really admire the way you've taken charge."

"Thanks. I didn't have much of a choice." Nicole had to admire Aliyah's technique. She slipped in the brownnosing with the right amount of subtlety.

"Choice or not, you've done a darn good job. Of course Russell isn't happy, but I'm sure you two can work things out." Aliyah beamed at her again, then stood. "Well, I've taken up enough of your time. I really hope we can be friends."

"Give me a call about lunch and we'll work something out." Nicole smiled back.

"I'd love that, Nicole. Bye-bye now." Aliyah turned to leave just as Marcus arrived.

"Nicole, I just talked to—" He broke off when Aliyah walked to him. "Oh, hi."

"Hello, Marcus. How are you today?" Aliyah nodded to him. "I was just on my way out."

"Don't rush off. All I wanted was to drop this off with

Nicole. Specs on the latest security system AlertCom is trying to sell us," he said to Nicole.

"Okay." Nicole took the binder from him.

She kept her tone professional. Yet she enjoyed watching
him move with fluid grace. The fabric of his light green shirt
and tan chinos molded to his muscular body. She wasn't the
only one looking, either. Aliyah couldn't resist giving his fine
masculine frame a quick once-over. As good as Aliyah was,
Nicole didn't miss the appreciative gleam in her eyes before
she shut it down. She'd just overstayed her welcome, Nicole
thought.

"Thanks. Bye, Aliyah," Nicole said.

"Bye again." She fluttered perfectly shaped and lacquered
dark pink fingernails in the air. Aliyah strolled out as though
in no hurry.

"Let me ask you a few questions before you go, Marcus."
Nicole gestured at him to close the door.

He looked puzzled, but he complied. "I've just got a few
minutes."

"Won't take long."

Nicole came up with what she thought was just enough de-
lay to allow Cat Woman time to get on the elevator. She ignored the worrisome thought that she was acting like a
jealous girlfriend. He leaned over her to read something she
pointed to, and her reservations were promptly forgotten. His
warm, spicy scent filled her senses and blocked out rational
reflection. She wanted to be close to him, not play games.
Which meant she was in serious danger of losing her heart.
Not exactly what she'd had in mind. Marcus had turned the
tables. And she liked it.

twelve

Marcus stared down at the dark hair a breath away from his cheek. Nicole was reading the technical description in the binder he'd brought in. He was reading her. Every inch of her excited him. There was no use denying it. Knowledge was power, however. Owning the attraction would help him build an effective defense. He had no intention of becoming her ghetto boy toy, one she'd discard when an acceptable breeding partner came on the scene. Despite knowing the reality, he wanted her. Despite having his choice of dates for the past two years, no woman had inspired anything close to a grand passion. Until now.

"This system is expensive. I don't see anything here that sells it to me. What's the advantage over, say, the standard security system? I see lots of fancy extras." Nicole flipped a page to a glossy color photo from the alarm company's sales catalogue.

Marcus breathed in the fruity fragrance from her hair when she moved her head. "Hmm."

"I have to admit, it is one grand set of bells and whistles," she said and turned another page. "Look at this set of upgrades. Voice recognition entry, a tie-in to software that protects a company's computer files."

"Right," he mumbled.

Nicole wore a slight frown. "Okay, so you disagree and want to push ahead. I'm still not sure."

Her full mouth was moist and coated with lipstick the color of burgundy wine. Marcus was suddenly very thirsty. "Okay."

She glanced up at him. "What's up with you today? Don't tell me you're having doubts about my emerging management style."

Marcus forced himself to move away and out of her direct line of fire. "Uh, no."

"Then what?"

Under scrutiny, he managed to pull it together. "Clients like Joe Daigre need those fancy extras. This is more suitable for big sites. We'd have to have our own response station to make it profitable."

"We've got a lot more planning before we get into monitoring. Let's concentrate on opening branch offices first." Nicole looked up at him.

"No problem." Marcus lifted a hand to rub his face, then thought better of it.

"You seem distracted." Nicole studied him closely. "Or maybe you're coming down with a cold or something. Feeling feverish?"

Fever was a good way to describe how he felt, he mused. He would have to find a remedy real soon. "I'm fine."

"You've been putting in a lot of long hours. Take a day or two off if you really need to, Marcus." Nicole's brown eyes danced with amusement. "Russell will be happy to help me run the place."

"You just cured me. I couldn't do that to you," Marcus joked.

Nicole's rich laugh flowed over him like warm sugar cane syrup. He gave up pretense and wiped beads of perspiration from his forehead. She was seriously messing with his mind. *Lord, help me.*

"I appreciate the thought." Nicole stood and walked to him. "I can put up with Russell in small doses. That's better than having you collapse from exhaustion."

Marcus was already in trouble. More distance was needed. He backed toward the door and looked at his wristwatch. "I'm okay. Really. Gotta get moving."

"Sure. We'll talk later?" Nicole followed him.

He kept going to maintain a safe space between them, if there was such a thing. "If I get through in time."

"Oh. You've got plans this evening?" Nicole kept coming at him.

"No, yes. I'm pretty sure I do. I think." Marcus wanted to kick himself in the butt. He sounded like a stumbling idiot.

"I get the feeling you're trying to avoid me." She pursed her full lips.

"Of course not," Marcus replied, still moving back.

"Okay. Call me on my cell phone and we'll meet for dinner, to discuss only business. Feeling safer?" Her dark eyes now had a devilish gleam.

He let out a rasping laugh from his suddenly dust-dry throat. "Funny. I'll call."

"Good." She grinned at him. "Bye, bye."

Marcus gave her a short wave, then made his getaway. He brushed past Aliyah without seeing her at first. Her voice stopped him.

"Hello again."

"Hi. I'm on my way out," Marcus said without thinking. "Sorry, but I'm running late."

"No problem. I'm leaving myself." She walked beside him

to the elevator. "I've been telling Russ what an asset you are to Summers Security."

"Really?" Marcus fiddled with his car keys. His mind was still on Nicole. Damn, he must be crazy to let a woman turn him inside out.

"Sure. He can't let his anger toward his daddy blind him to your value. The customers trust you." Aliyah brushed a hand through her shoulder-length copper hair.

Something in her tone got his attention. Marcus really looked at her for the first time. "Thanks."

"I know. You're wondering why I'm sticking up for you. Can we talk?" The elevator doors opened, and she stepped into the empty car.

Marcus followed her on and watched her punch the floor number to the parking level. "All right."

"I'm being practical. Nicole will get bored with her new toy, if the family doesn't toss her out first. He has a right to resent her. So do *you*." Aliyah tapped a long fingernail against his chest.

"Interesting assessment." Marcus felt cornered by a carnivore in designer clothing.

Aliyah appeared to interpret his observation as tacit agreement. A smile spread across her sharp features, giving her an even more predatory feline look. She nodded. "Once Nicole is gone the real brains can take over. Don't get me wrong—Russell is a sweetie, but he needs you to run this company."

The elevator came to a smooth stop and the doors opened. Marcus allowed her to get off first. "I'm surprised you're being so candid with me."

"Oh, you won't tell Nicole. I know you've got your own plans." Aliyah faced him.

What did she know that made her so confident? Marcus

gazed at her steadily. "How far do you and Shaun go back anyway?"

"We've got history. Just like you two. Listen, Marcus, we can help each other."

Marcus mused at how relaxed she seemed with him. Apparently her little chat with Shaun had taken care of any anxieties that they would blow her cover. "I don't think so," he replied.

She walked up close to him, ran her tongue over her lips, wetting them, and tilted her head up. "Think some more. You'll see I'm right," she murmured in a throaty tone.

Intrigued by her offer, Marcus decided to play along. He smiled. "I will?"

Aliyah's almond-shaped eyes flickered bright with satisfaction. She put a hand on his arm. "We'll talk more."

The elevator bell pinged and the doors opened. Nicole, Jacinta, and Imani were in animated conversation as they got off. Nicole started to laugh at something Jacinta said. Her smile froze, then melted away when she saw Marcus and Aliyah. Imani, standing right behind them, glanced at Nicole, then peered over her shoulder.

"Well, the parking garage seems to be the place to meet up." Nicole looked from Aliyah to Marcus. "I thought you were long gone to take care of business."

Marcus thought he saw a flash of anger in her pretty eyes, but it was gone in an instant. "I'm on my way. See y'all later."

"Yes, if you're not too busy," Nicole said in a dry tone.

She nodded to Aliyah and left with the two women in tow. Jacinta and Imani looked back with curiosity stamped on their faces. Aliyah laughed softly.

"Your boss is a bit possessive toward you. Oh well, such

is life. See you soon, Marcus." She sauntered off humming a tune.

Marcus let out a hiss of frustration. He took out his cell phone and dialed Shaun's mobile number as he walked toward his Acura. He muttered a curse word when Shaun's voice mail message came on. "Shaun, Marcus. Get in touch with me. I wanna talk to you."

"Dinner was delicious. We could share the bill. It was my idea after all." Nicole drank the last of her wine.

They sat in Pappadeaux's seafood restaurant. Marcus had barely been able to get down his shrimp Creole, so intent was he on controlling his reactions to her. Nicole could lift an eyebrow and start a fire. He should have made some excuse that he couldn't make dinner. He needed to keep her at arm's length. She smiled at him and his pulse rate skipped up. A few miles would be more like it, he thought. He looked away and pushed hard against her allure.

"Actually you could pay the entire thing, since it was your idea." Marcus cocked his head to one side.

"Smart-ass," she tossed back.

Her sassy attitude was like gasoline on the flames. He squirmed in his seat. "So, what was the business we were going to discuss?"

"I'm making you nervous?" Nicole waved at the passing waiter.

"More wine?" the young man said with a smile.

"No, bring me a diet cola. Thanks." Nicole turned back to Marcus when the waiter scurried off.

"Not nervous, just curious," Marcus replied. He drank more of his sweet tea.

"Okay, business it is." Nicole propped her elbows on the

table. "I'm worried about the Phoung incident. I know there's no indication we were at fault, but something about it just bothers me."

"Dayna tracked down the cigarettes and made two arrests. She thinks it was gang related."

"Okay, but still . . ." Nicole sighed. "I've got a bad feeling. Then the art gallery alarm goes off."

"Jesse and I have examined each incident. Stuff happens. Sometimes it happens in spells."

"Russell is using every little thing to build a case that I shouldn't be CEO. I can even feel Jolene's fine hand in some of his scheming. She's got a few more functioning brain cells than he does," Nicole retorted with a scowl.

"You're being paranoid, don't you think?"

"I know my family. We're a bit different from most. Everyone has a separate business, but they're all considered part of the Summers empire. Mama's folks are even more clannish." Nicole broke off when the waiter came back.

"Which explains why Mr. Summers wrote his will the way he did," Marcus said when the waiter left.

"You got it. For over a hundred years my family has made passing on the wealth a mission. Most African-American families haven't been able to hold onto land or keep a business going across generations."

"Seems almost an obsession." He really was curious now. Learning more about Nicole's family would help him understand her.

"Oh, yeah. It worked, too. If kids decided they wanted to start a different kind of business, the parents supported them. My great-great-grandfather even closed up his dry goods store when my great-grandfather became a doctor. They sold some of the first health insurance policies to African-Americans in the early nineteen hundreds."

"Forward thinkers." Marcus shook his head. He had to admire them. "Federated Insurers is huge today."

"My cousin Philip runs it. I come from a long line of overachievers. I've been mostly taking it easy."

"You finished college and grad school."

"Trust me, I found time to party. I took off a few months to rest after graduation. Then I got a job with one of my father's friends. Love those long business lunches." Nicole grinned.

"If you don't mind my saying . . ." Marcus looked at her before going on.

"Please." Nicole waved a hand.

"Mr. Summers had his quirks, but he was no fool. Your family knows that, too. He wouldn't have selected you if he didn't think you were up to the job. They also know Russell." Marcus raised an eyebrow at her.

Nicole laughed. "I love your gift of diplomacy. Yes, they know very well that Russell is a total screwup. Jolene doesn't want to bother with the dreary details of business, but she does want the money."

"Your uncle could have chosen anyone else. He picked you, and there must be more than one reason." Marcus turned this thought over in his mind for the first time. What potential had the crafty old rascal seen in her?

"Sure, he wanted revenge for all the times I kicked his shins as a kid. He dropped me right into a snake pit. Present company excluded," Nicole added when he looked at her sharply.

"It took time, but the employees came around." Marcus tapped out a beat with his fingertips and looked away.

"And have you?" she said in a soft tone and leaned forward.

Yeah. That's my problem. He risked gazing at her again. The muted lighting of the restaurant gave the brown skin of her bare arms a burnished look. Her silver bangle bracelets tinkled when she brushed a hand through her thick hair. *No fair*, he thought with an inward groan.

"I think we've established a good working relationship," he said.

"Oh please." Nicole titled her head back and laughed.

He clenched his back teeth and drummed his fingers faster. "What's so funny?"

"You." When he continued to stare at her without smiling, Nicole stopped laughing. She tried with limited success to assume a serious face. "Sorry, I didn't mean to be a—"

"Spoiled, pretty sorority girl used to teasing guys to get anything she wants?" he clipped.

Nicole batted her eyelashes at him and pursed her lips. "Who, me? I wouldn't dream of pulling such an act."

"Cut it out." Marcus squirmed even more, something he seemed to do a lot around her.

"Okay, bro. Let's get down to it then," she said in a lower voice. "You're attracted to me, but you don't like it."

"I never said . . ." Marcus avoided her penetrating gaze.

"So, you do like it." Nicole tilted her head to one side.

Marcus wondered at what point he'd totally lost control of this situation. Probably the first day Nicole strolled into his life with that brash attitude and smart aleck mouth. "Yeah, something like that," he murmured.

"So, let's consider the consequences of us hooking up." Nicole crossed her arms.

"How romantic." Marcus worked hard not to smile. Her naughty style thrilled him.

"Well, we have to use common sense. I'm under a giant magnifying glass. One might say I should concentrate on taking care of business—at the company, not with you."

Desire stabbed him like a knife that cut deep but felt good even as it drew blood. He rested one arm along the back of her chair without thinking. Her fragrance, something wild and spicy, curled into his nostrils. If he leaned only a millimeter toward her, his lips could brush her earlobe.

"Hmm," he hummed, unable to articulate much more for the moment.

"On the other hand, the will doesn't say anything about my love life. We're both single adults. In conclusion, our private life is nobody's damn business." Nicole turned to look at him, her face only a breath away from his. "Do you agree?"

"Technically you're right. But is it worth the uproar we both know it will cause? Your father won't approve for two reasons. One, we work together. Two, I'm not in your class." Marcus considered both points valid. Still he didn't pull back from the ledge he teetered on.

"I can draw the line between professional and personal. Not that I'm saying it will be a snap. As for not being in my class, I won't even dignify such a nineteenth-century concept with a serious answer."

Nicole's reply whispered toward him like a sweet-scented breeze. Against all common sense he leaned into it instead of away. "Then what are we going to do?"

"Pay the dinner bill and go back to the address," she said with a smile.

Nicole lifted a hand to get their waiter's attention. They argued over who would pay and Nicole won. Ten minutes after the waiter returned her gold card, they were driving in his Acura toward her house. She punched a button on his compact disc player, and Jill Scott's sinuous voice surged from the speakers. Soon Jill launched into her one-of-a-kind "tell-the-truth" explicit lyrics about love. Nicole hummed along.

"I know we're going to fit 'cause you've got Jill on the system."

Her throaty laugh instigated a tickle of lust that spread over him with hurricane force. Suddenly the trip to Nicole's house was taking much too long. Marcus shifted to a faster lane of traffic. He suppressed a moan of relief when the green exit sign they needed appeared. Nicole added to his torture by brushing a hand along his shoulder. He tried to concentrate.

"You're a devil wrapped in a satin tank top," Marcus said, his voice hoarse. His muscles ached from the effort to keep his hands on the steering wheel.

"Silk," she corrected with a small laugh.

Mercifully they arrived at her house a few minutes later. He pulled into the circular driveway. Nicole waited while he got out and opened the car door for her. She gave him a smile of reassurance as she walked past him to the tall, carved, double front doors. One tiny prick of doubt made him hesitate on the threshold. The moment passed at the speed of light. There was no way he would turn back now, not with the need to touch her thumping through him like a pleasant ache. Marcus followed her through the foyer and down a hallway to the den.

"You've done some redecorating." Marcus hadn't been in the house since the last company Christmas party, in fact.

"A bit," Nicole remarked over her shoulder. "Jolene raised such a fuss when I got the house, so I let her take some of the furniture. There was one old canopy bed upstairs that was a real monstrosity. The thing looked like something Dracula would swoop in at night to sleep in."

"Mr. Summers cherished those pieces. They were family heirlooms." Marcus settled on a butter-soft, honey brown leather sofa.

Nicole went behind a polished oak bar in one corner of the room. She retrieved two glasses and poured chilled white wine into them. Marcus enjoyed watching her movements. Her long tapered fingers wrapped around the fancy wine-glasses, their rose painted tips looked lovely against her café au lait skin. As she walked toward him, Marcus imagined them trailing up and down his back. Her impish half-smile hit him like a hot coal. The burn felt good. Nicole turned up the heat when she sat down next to him. She handed him one of the glasses and settled against the sofa.

"Jolene saw my 'surrender' as a victory, the one time my conscience forced me to fairness."

Marcus smiled as he savored the crisp taste of the chablis. "Was it?" He already knew the answer.

"Yeah, right," she tossed back with an impish grin. "Like I miss those grim dust-catchers. My housekeeper Rosaria danced for joy the day the movers took them out."

"I have to admit the place is brighter."

Marcus glanced around at the cool green paint on the walls topped by a soft eggshell white ceiling. New draperies, a light green leaf pattern that was almost abstract, had replaced the heavy dark emerald ones Mr. Summers had chosen.

"If you're wondering when I had the time, I didn't really. My mother did the legwork. I picked out colors and fabrics, and she hired the decorator." Nicole looked at the room with him. "The only time I let Mother take over my living space."

"She did a great job."

"True, but I don't want her to get any ideas. You might have noticed she can be autocratic."

"I only met her once, at the funeral. She seemed like a nice lady." Marcus remembered the stately woman with piercing greenish-brown eyes that seemed to miss little.

"What a diplomatic description," Nicole quipped and peered at him over her glass.

Marcus smiled. "I meant it actually. She was very gracious toward me."

"All the Summers women are fantastic at any social gathering, somber or happy. I'm the exception." Nicole's eyes narrowed, giving her a "bad-girl" expression.

Marcus studied her for a few moments. "Not as much as you think."

"Tell me more, Doctor Reed." Nicole crossed her legs.

He gazed at the shape of her thighs beneath the smooth linen-and-silk-blend white slacks. Marcus gave himself time to recover his breath so his words wouldn't tumble out incoherently. Nicole watched him with interest, as though gauging her effect.

"You attended the right high school, the right university, and belonged to the right sorority. Alpha Kappa Alpha, am I right?" Marcus remembered the snobbish young women he'd met in college.

Nicole nodded with a slight frown. "Correct up to a point."

"Your father got you a good job with his college buddy, a man from another old Creole family."

"You've made your point," Nicole broke in before he could go on. Music played softly as each grew quiet. They both seemed to consider their differences.

As little as six months ago Marcus would have laughed if anyone had suggested he'd be seriously attracted to such a woman. He'd dated women from the so-called better families. Several of them had been nice enough, but most had been picky and superficial. Shaun and he had gone on quite a few double dates in their efforts to trade up and out of the 'hood. Marcus had soon tired of being dissed by pretentious parents, but Shaun had had an uncanny ability to win favor. Perhaps his greater skill at deception had played a part. Whatever the reason, Marcus hadn't worried about it much. Concentrating on his career and portfolio had been his priority, not bagging a rich wife. Finding a mate had been very much on the back burner in his mind. Marcus had figured he would settle down with a pleasant middle-class woman from a moderately good family, a presentable wife with a professional job and ambitions in line with his own. At least that had been the plan. He glanced at Nicole. She drank from her glass with a faraway expression on her enticing face. Suddenly he felt bad about his description of her.

"Sorry. I bought into the stereotype. Not too cool."

"But accurate. I'm a hopeless Black American Princess. Yes, I own Prada shoes and at least one Gucci purse." Nicole sighed and put down her glass.

"What would your parents say about me? About us?" Marcus ventured.

"Daddy respects you a great deal. He'd have been just as happy if Uncle Hosea had made you CEO," she insisted.

"Nicole, be real."

She got up. "I need another glass of wine."

"Sorry again. I started this heavy discussion." Marcus followed her to the bar.

Nicole took his glass and poured until his half empty glass was full again. "Let's lighten the mood. This is just the first date."

"Is it?" he said quietly. Marcus placed his hand over hers as she handed him the glass. Nicole didn't pull away.

"Actually, you're right. If we're going to be more than colleagues—"

"Boss and subordinate," he corrected. "A big difference. A tricky situation."

"Then we need to have this talk. Your style, not mine." Nicole looked into his eyes steadily. "I'm used to just jumping into what I want. Call it the spoiled BAP in me."

"No, you're right. Why ruin the moment?" he murmured, gazing at her full lips. Wine still glistened on them.

"We'll have to consider the fallout sooner rather than later," she replied in a soft voice.

He pulled her to him until their noses touched. "But not tonight."

Giving in felt good. Marcus savored the first moment by gently rubbing his lips against hers. No warning voice or bell could sound loud enough in his head to stop his hands from roaming. The bare skin of her arms was supple beneath his fingers. He nipped at her mouth to taste an appetizer. Nicole sighed and leaned into him. She placed both palms on his chest. The sensation made him shudder. Her body molded to his like the perfect fit of a missing puzzle piece. Between asking in a whispered voice what she liked, Marcus deftly undressed her. With his eyes closed, he gasped with pleasure when she took off his shirt.

Nicole planted tiny kisses along his shoulders. Without pausing in her tender attention to his upper body, she took off his belt, unhooked his pants, and gave them a tug. Marcus stood back long enough to remove the rest of his clothing. With a sexy smile, Nicole did a little dance. She was dressed only in midnight blue high-cut satin panties and matching bra.

"I love this song," she said and grabbed the sound system remote.

Marcus watched in fascination as her hips swiveled to the bass bumping from the speakers. "Come over here."

She shook her head as she looped a finger beneath the front hook of her bra. "You come to me."

Before he took two steps, Nicole danced out of reach and up the staircase. "My bedroom is this way."

"Teaser," he called out as she ascended.

"Guilty."

She stood on the landing above. The bra came off, and she dropped it on the floor. Marcus was breathing heavily by the time he reached the top step, but not from climbing the stairs. Backing away, Nicole led him into a bedroom decorated in slate blue, green, and gold. One small lamp spread a soft yellow glow across the walls and furnishings. The thick comforter had been folded and placed on a hope chest at the foot of the bed. The sheets were turned back. Plush pillows were piled against the padded headboard. Music from the compact disc player below came from speakers set in the walls. His hand shook with the need to touch her flesh. Nicole pushed him further into arousal when she took off her panties. Marcus should have felt angry at what seemed like a setup, a calculated seduction. Instead he wanted her to win.

"You were expecting me," he said hoarsely.

Her playful smile melted into an expression of longing. "I wasn't sure. You're such a man of principle. I thought maybe you'd back out, keep it all business."

Marcus almost laughed at the notion. She'd been the subject of more than one heated daydream in the past four weeks. "Are you sure?"

Nicole blinked and placed her arms across her breast. "If you don't think we should . . ." Her voice faded. Anxiety clouded her dark eyes.

Suddenly what he wanted most was to please her. Marcus felt a surge of protectiveness he'd never experienced before. "Honey, I want you more than anything right now," he said.

She sank onto the bed. Marcus padded across the thick moss green carpet until he stood over her. Nicole wrapped her arms around his waist and pressed her cheek to his belly. He buried his fingers in her thick hair. They held each other that way for a time, each adjusting to their mutual decision. Then Nicole let go and lay back across the velvety, expensive cotton sheets.

Marcus lay beside her. They looked into each other's eyes as though searching for answers. In seconds they seemed to learn all they needed to know for the moment. He kissed her again as one hand cupped her right breast. With a sigh deep in his throat, Marcus stretched his body atop hers. Nicole enfolded him in a tight embrace. They caressed and kissed for a long time as though each wanted the foreplay to last forever. Her svelte form drove him to a tight arousal that bit into him. He nuzzled her lush breast, breathing in the tangy scent.

"Do you taste as good as you smell?" he whispered.

Marcus was sure he knew, but he fully intended to confirm his presumption. He licked both of her cocoa brown peaks. They tasted like honeyed chocolate candy. Nicole cried out when he traced a line of fire down her tummy with his tongue. Marcus paused. As though reading his thoughts, Nicole reached into the nightstand and took out a square foil. He put on the condom, then worked his way back up her body. After planting kisses over every inch of flesh he could reach, he gazed into her eyes.

"Baby," she breathed. Her fingers guided him inside her.

Both moaned low as their bodies settled into a rhythm of give and take. Slowly at first, they moved together. With each moment the sensation of being surrounded by her velvet heat pushed him to impossibly higher levels of delight. The measured beat of their lovemaking increased. Marcus experienced a sharp stab of hunger for more, and more. He pushed her to the limit, eager to be the source of her joy, wanting to make her scream only for him. Nicole whimpered in a voice of surrender.

"Look at me," he groaned.

Nicole panted as she gazed back at him. Her eyes widened and her body quivered, the tremors starting small, then taking over until she cried out. Marcus answered, though nothing he said made sense. Each thrust, faster and faster, took him into a yawning sexual pleasure so powerful he was sure he would pass out. He came, and the world went dark after a brilliant and blissful explosion. Slowly he saw small glimmers of light again.

"Nicole," he mumbled and went limp in her arms.

Marcus didn't know or care how much time passed. Being sheathed in her was the only place in the world for him right now. He stroked her hair and snuggled against her downy shoulder. As strange, frightening, and wonderful as it was, he felt whole. For the first time in his life he wasn't alone.

Nicole laughed. "Well, the next staff meeting should be interesting. Somehow we've got to get rid of this afterglow by the next business day."

"Hmm." He nestled even closer to her.

"Or maybe we should just let everyone know. Get it over with," Nicole said. She threaded her fingers in the tight curls on his head.

Marcus snapped out of his satiated stupor as reality reared its ugly head and bit him hard. She'd called him a man of principles. For weeks he'd carefully planted seeds of doubt about her ability in the minds of clients. He needed to tell her. *No*, a warning voice boomed inside his head. Saying "Baby, I stuck a knife in your back" was definitely not pillow talk.

"I don't think so, Nicole. Let's get used to what we have before we let the world in on it."

"Sure, honey. You're right of course."

Nicole smiled at him with tenderness. With a sigh of satisfaction, she closed her eyes and rested her head on his chest. While Nicole drifted off to sleep, he lay awake thinking of ways to undo the moves he'd already made to steal her business.

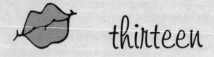 thirteen

Nicole smiled when she opened her front door. Her mother and sister, each dressed in casual elegance, had dropped by for Sunday brunch. "Good morning, dear family."

"Hi, brat." Helena winked at her.

Her mother gave Nicole a head-to-toe glance. Nicole must have passed inspection, since she made no comment. "Hello, baby. How are you?"

"I'm doing wonderful, thank you very much." Nicole spread her arms wide. "Welcome to my humble home."

"You look extremely pleased with yourself," her mother said. She might have been accusing Nicole of some crime. She accepted a kiss from Nicole on her cheek as though she were the queen mother.

"Mother, really. She isn't ten years old, you know." Helena rolled her eyes at Nicole when their mother marched through the foyer ahead of them.

"It's a mother's prerogative to keep an eye on her children. No matter how old they are." Analine's voice echoed back from the formal living room as she went through the arched entrance.

Helena put a hand on Nicole's arm. "She's got a bee up her you-know-what, so be careful. She and Daddy have been at it again."

"They're always having battles. I think they enjoy it." Nicole laughed.

"Why are you hanging back? Oh, you're talking about me. Well, when you're through, get me a glass of iced tea," their mother called out.

"Hello, Mrs. Summers. I'll get it for you," Rosaria answered from the hallway. "Hello, Miss Helena."

"Hi and bless you, Rosie." Helena blew her a kiss, then turned to Nicole. "Keep that smarmy expression off your face. Mother can smell a secret ten miles away."

"What makes you think I've got secrets?" Nicole sniffed.

Helena snorted. "I've been busting you since we were in nursery school."

"Damn! Okay, how's this?" Nicole passed a hand over her face and rearranged her expression.

"Much better. Let's go," Helena whispered.

They both smiled as they entered the spacious living room. Analine cocked an eyebrow at them to show she wasn't deceived. Still, she said no more, mainly because Rosaria came in pushing a glass-and-chrome serving table.

"Rosaria, you make the most delicious tea." Analine beamed at her. "Have you been home to Vera Cruz lately?"

"I go in three weeks. I can't wait to see the family." Rosaria's pretty round face lit up. "Thank you for asking, Mrs. Summers."

"A branch of our family, the Donatos, migrated to Vera Cruz around 1855. From St. Landry Parish. That's in Louisiana, Rosaria."

"Yes, you told me before."

"You've told us all," Nicole said under her breath. She

pressed her lips together when Analine sliced her with a sharp glance.

"Have a good trip home in case I don't see you before then." Analine beamed at her.

"Yes, ma'am."

Recognizing the cue to leave, Rosaria smiled back her gratitude, then left. The carved pecan wood doors came together with a soft bump. Their mother turned her attention back to them, the well-mannered smile now gone.

"So, Nicole. Tell me what you've been up to? Your father is pleased with your performance at Summers Security." Analine settled against the thick cushions of the embroidered settee.

Helena and Nicole retrieved glasses from the tray and sat in two wing back chairs across from her. They exchanged a glance, then sipped from their glasses to buy time.

"Well?" Analine prompted when neither spoke immediately.

"I talked to Francine a week ago. Jolene and Russell are still scheming. Watch your back, Nicole," Helena put in.

"Hosea did a poor job raising those two. Of course what can you expect? He was practically an old man when they were born." Analine pursed her lips in disapproval.

"Mother, that family gossip is over thirty years ago." Helena waved a hand.

Analine swept on. "He married a woman half his age, got her pregnant, and spoiled both children rotten. Then when they became problem children he blamed it all on her." She repeated Uncle Hosea's crime as though it had happened yesterday.

"No wonder the poor woman ran off with the mailman," Nicole said with a shrug.

"Insurance salesman," Analine corrected. "Her father tried to cut her off without a dime, but her grandfather wouldn't hear of it. Now those children can see Clarice without worrying Hosea will disinherit them."

"Interesting, but I want to know what kind of 'scheming' Russell and Jolene are doing," Nicole cut in before her mother could go on.

"Francine says they're so transparent it's hilarious, which doesn't make them harmless, Mother." Helena looked at Analine.

"Stanton and Lionel will keep them from interfering," Analine replied.

"The will does say that Nicole can be removed as CEO by a vote of the board. If she engages in questionable behavior that might harm the company or doesn't increase profits by at least eight percent in twelve months, the board is almost required to dump her." Helena chewed her bottom lip until her raisin lipstick was gone.

"We're expanding and signing up new customers. I could increase revenue by twice that amount. If I can show that we have signed contracts that will increase profits by eight percent or more, then the twelve-month deadline doesn't apply and I'm in." Nicole crossed her legs and lifted her tumbler.

"What are they up to? Not that it matters." Analine looked at Helena.

"Jolene is raising questions about Nicole's decisions and her behavior."

"Which brings us back to my earlier question. What have you done to give them ammunition, Nicole?" Analine raised a palm when Nicole started to speak. "I know you."

Nicole hissed with frustration. She had a wild itch to tell her mother exactly what she'd been up to with Marcus. After all, they were both adults, single, and fully within their rights to have an affair. To hell with the family, she thought fiercely. Not even control freak Uncle Hosea had considered that possibility when he'd drafted his insane last wishes. Yet she held back. There wouldn't just be her formidable mother to consider; the rest of the family would weigh in, too. Nicole needed to be in an unassailable position of strength first. She pushed down her gut reaction to challenge authority. Instead she took a deep cleansing breath and entered her persuasive zone, the mind-set she assumed in order to get what she wanted.

"So far Russell has been more a nuisance than a major problem. I came up with a new tactic—let him be in charge without giving him any authority. It's worked so far. The idiot." Nicole grimaced. "The good news is the staff has come around. We're working as a team."

"The Nicole magic wins again, eh?" Helena's mouth stretched into a thin smile. She darted an uneasy glance at Analine.

"Ultimately performance, not charisma, will satisfy the family," Analine said.

"Mother, nobody has worked harder than Nicole in the last few weeks. She and Marcus have done an effective job of making the transition smooth. Not only that, Nicole has put in long hours learning about the business from the ground up and—" Helena clamped off her speech when Analine glared at her.

"Don't lecture me," Analine clipped. "This is the first time Nicole has had to take on such significant responsibility. I want to make sure she understands."

"What she means is I've been leading a cushy life so far," Nicole said, her tone droll.

"You're very smart, Nicole."

"Gee thanks," Nicole muttered.

"Too smart for your own good sometimes," Analine continued.

"I knew more was coming." Nicole glanced at her sister, who shook her head in warning.

"Running a company requires that you learn to compromise. I hope you realize that by now. You can be difficult, stubborn, flighty, and demanding." Analine looked down her nose at Nicole.

"Hmm, I wonder where I got that demanding gene?" Nicole raised an eyebrow at her mother.

"You also have a smart mouth, Nicole Marie," her mother snapped.

"Don't faint, but I agree with you. I've been making an extra effort to curb my shortcomings."

Her mother wore a doubtful frown. "Really?"

"Yes. Russell has been really testing me, but so far I haven't broken. That's exactly what he wants me to do."

"Let's hope you can keep up the effort," her mother said dryly.

"Marcus has been a great help smoothing the waters when I've been stressed. He really has become my right hand," Nicole added. She planned to skillfully mention Marcus when talking to her parents from now on. That way their being a couple wouldn't be such a shock in the future.

"Then this challenge has been the best thing for you." Analine launched into a stream of advice.

Nicole smiled crookedly at her sister while their mother chattered on. She was quite content to let Analine assume credit for "setting her on the right path," as she no doubt would tell their relatives. Rosaria came back into the room.

"I've set the table in the sunroom, Miss Nicole."

"Thanks, Rosaria," Analine said as though she were in charge. She followed Rosaria out of the room. "I'm starving. This diet has been such a bore. I hope you've got more than fruit."

"Oh, yes, ma'am. I baked fresh croissants. They're still warm." Rosaria described her menu with enthusiasm.

Helena stood. She peered around the door before she looked back at Nicole and laughed. "You're dangerous, brat. I don't know of anybody that could have pulled that off on Mother, except maybe Daddy."

"I told the truth." Nicole lifted her nose in the air.

"Yeah, and that's even more scary." Helena's dark eyes narrowed until she looked like a younger version of their mother. "You're up to something for sure."

"Oh, don't you start." Nicole flipped a hand in the air. "Let's eat."

"Okay, but one more thing. A lot of people in our crowd think Russell was wronged. That includes some of our relatives." Helena looped her arm through Nicole's as they walked down the hall to the sunroom.

"I don't give a rat's behind what they think," Nicole retorted.

"You're sure there's nothing else that might blow up in your face?" Helena pressed.

"Stop it. You're sounding more like Mother the older you get," Nicole joked.

"You have a knack for doing things that create the most drama. Try to resist for at least another year. Okay?" Helena's hold on Nicole's arm tightened.

"On my honor as a girl scout." Nicole raised her right hand.

"They kicked you out of Troop K after that water balloon incident, only the last of a string of crimes."

"Will you let it go already?" Nicole laughed at her. "I told them you had nothing to do with it."

"Nicole," Helena said testily.

"Alright, alright. I'm on the path of respectability, I promise."

"Good. Russell may be a fumbler, but Jolene is one cunning witch. Pair her up with that jackal of a husband and they could do some damage. Francine and I will watch those two."

"Please don't worry. I know what I'm doing." Nicole smiled at her. Despite her words of assurance she decided to examine the will herself again. She would dissect every sentence just to be sure.

"Hey, Marcus." Shaun slapped him on the shoulder when he walked into the second-floor snack shop of the health club. Female heads swiveled when the smoothly muscled man in red and blue biking shorts and a white tank shirt passed.

Marcus shifted the sport bag to his left hand. He accepted a tall cup of mixed fruit smoothie from the woman behind the counter.

"You're late," Marcus said shortly.

"I'm a businessman even on Sunday, brother." Shaun turned his charm on the blond. "Got somethin' for me, sugar?"

"Always, Shaun," she said with a giggle.

They sat down at a small round table that faced a glass wall overlooking the interior of the health club. An athletic woman the color of cinnamon led about thirty people in a kick-boxing workout below.

"How's it going with that fine new boss of yours?" Shaun rubbed his hands together. He eyed the woman below.

"You should know. Aliyah is giving you the 411, right?" Marcus said evenly.

Shaun's attention snapped back to him. "What you talkin' 'bout?" he said, slipping back into the dialect from their Fifth Ward days.

"You know damn well what I'm talking about," Marcus replied. "She's coming on to me like she knows my business."

"Nah, brother!" Shaun visibly relaxed. He smiled and

spread his arms wide. "I wouldn't run my mouth to a woman."

Marcus stared at him. He considered Shaun's words and his body language for a few seconds. In Shaun's view women were a means to an end. Still, he needed to make a point. Marcus loved Shaun like a brother, but he also knew his flaws.

"You shouldn't be talking to anyone. Not some guy you think can help me or some woman you think has inside information. *No one*." Marcus stabbed a forefinger at Shaun's nose.

"Okay. You wanna be on your own, then you got it." Shaun affected an injured look. "We've always had each other's back is all I'm saying. I'm feeling sorta left out here lately."

"Who have you been talking to?" Marcus said, ignoring the pained expression.

"I know a dude who works for a dude who knows a dude in the security business. I didn't mention your name." Shaun abandoned his guilt trip for the moment. He leaned forward and lowered his voice. "You're highly thought of around this town. You can take as many Summers Security clients as you want."

"But you didn't mention my name." Marcus crossed his arms.

"No way. I asked about the top security firms. Being in insurance, I told him my clients can get rate reductions if they have good alarm systems or even on-site guards." Shaun warmed to the subject. "Summers Security is still considered tops, but only because of you. There's a lot of skepticism about Nicole."

"She's smart and learning fast," Marcus said. Shaun's eyebrows went up, a signal that Marcus had slipped. "Even if she does lack experience in security and management," he added with a shrug.

"Good intentions aren't enough in a competitive environment. She can't keep up. This dude says the security business is changing rapidly since this terrorist threat started." Shaun glanced around before continuing.

"Everybody is running to keep up with the latest technology. I was thinking we could add a few forensic people as contract employees. Folks with expertise on handwriting analysis, identity theft, and a forensic accountant." Marcus stared down at the bouncing and kicking group below.

"See? That's what I mean." Shaun pointed at him. "No way baby can beat you. Man, we can end up—"

Marcus glanced at him sharply. "What's with the 'we' stuff?"

"You provide the security and I'll specialize in insurance policies against terrorist acts. Hell, we both know most businesses won't be targeted. But *they* don't know it. What with the media scaring folks to death every day, selling security systems and insurance should be a breeze."

"Where does the money come from to pay claims?" Marcus squinted at him. When Shaun's grin widened he knew the answer.

"What claims? We bag the premiums, invest the money, and close up shop. Of course we hand them off to another company."

"Small or even medium-sized businesses can't afford expensive policies. The word *fraud* comes to mind. We'd be misleading them." Marcus waved a hand. "Forget it."

"Hey, think big."

"I'm thinking about possible jail time," Marcus shot back.

"We've been through tough times and we always survived. I think about those days. Remember Spiderman?" Shaun played his ace.

When they were fifteen years old, a gang member had targeted Marcus. Spiderman and Marcus had circled each other for days until a contrived confrontation had led to a showdown. Two days later shots had rung out as Marcus had walked down the street on an errand for his grandmother. Shaun had appeared out of an alley and yanked him to safety. Spiderman had been shot the next day. Paralyzed from the neck down, he'd ended up in a nursing facility at seventeen. Shaun hinted he'd "taken care of" the problem. Marcus didn't believe him. Spiderman had more dangerous enemies in their world. Still Shaun had saved his life. Though he recognized the manipulation, Marcus had a rush of guilt at the sharp tone he'd used with him.

"Like I could forget the thug who tried to take me out."

"Then you know I'd never put you in danger." Shaun clamped a large hand on his forearm and squeezed. "No way, no how, for nobody on this earth."

"I know," Marcus said finally.

In charge again, Shaun released his grip and sat back. His breezy smile returned. "Back to Aliyah. I let her think we're exchanging information. All the time she's telling me way more than I'm telling her."

Marcus had a picture of the two of them trying to outsmart each other. Despite Shaun's opinion, Marcus did not think Aliyah was so easily duped. "You better be careful. Not all women are dumb. And not all of them lose their common sense over what you've got," he added quietly.

"Can't prove it by me," Shaun quipped with a wink. "Ghetto girls or CEOs with advanced degrees, it doesn't matter. Combine the right sweet talk with good love and you got a fool for life."

Marcus gazed at his friend and saw a reflection of himself

to a degree. Though he hadn't been such a blatant user, Marcus had left behind women with barely a backward glance. He could brush off the most expert flirtation unless he wanted companionship, though he hadn't been able to brush off one particular set of alluring eyes.

"You'll meet your match one day," he mumbled, more to himself than to Shaun.

Shaun flashed a smile at a passing woman. "Say what?"

Marcus shook his head. "Nothing. I get the feeling Aliyah is after more than Russell. I'm wondering if you two have joined forces in some plot." He studied Shaun for signs of guilt.

"Not really. She thought I'd be able to give her some inside info since you and I are pals. I put her off." Shaun waved a hand as though the matter was trivial.

"Uh-huh. Well, she seems to think I'd be interested in jumping through hoops for her. I'm not," Marcus said pointedly.

"All I'm sayin' is this," Shaun replied, lapsing once more into his old speech pattern. His affable demeanor slipped away, and the hard street kid came back. "Aliyah's got skills when it comes to men."

"I'm not looking for a girlfriend, Shaun."

"I'm not talkin' about bling-bling in the bedroom. She can get weak-minded dudes to do almost anything. And our buddy Russell is the weakest I've seen. She's got his tongue hangin' out, brother. You make friends with her and she can get him to do just what you want with that company."

"No." Marcus shook his head hard.

"I know you've got your own plan to deal with Nicole. Once she's outta the way, you're still stuck with this Russell fool. Aliyah can convince him to sell out to you. Ain't that what you want?"

"Like you said, I've got my own plans. Those plans don't

include trusting Aliyah," Marcus said low and with intensity.

"She couldn't blow your cover without you blowing hers. Hey, lots of business arrangements are built on quid pro quo." Shaun lifted a shoulder as if his logic was obvious.

"I'm not sure I want to go through with my original plan anyway. Even if I did, I sure wouldn't include Aliyah." Marcus drank the last few ounces of his smoothie.

"You got some other brilliant move, huh? C'mon, let your boy in on it." Shaun's eyes sparkled with curiosity.

Marcus tapped his fingertips on the table for a few minutes. "Okay, I'm thinking maybe starting my own security company can wait. I gave Nicole's dad my word and—"

"Whoa, whoa. Back it up." Shaun waved both hands as though directing traffic. "What's with this 'I gave my word' nonsense?"

"I don't have to step on her for something the old man did. Her uncle promised to sell me the company, not her."

Shaun glanced around. The last couple seated at a table left. They were now alone. The counter girls were busy gossiping at the other end of the snack shop.

"Those people will walk all over you, man. They'll get rich off what you know and make sure you never become serious competition."

"Nicole's dad has already figured out I plan to be my own boss one day. They didn't get rich by being dumb, Shaun." Marcus smiled. "I kinda like the old dude and her uncle Lionel."

Shaun's eyes narrowed. "Nah, I'm not buying that line." He studied Marcus for a long moment. A smile spread across his face. "You plan to marry into the money and the business. Now that's the Marcus Reed I know."

"You don't understand."

Marcus remembered the fresh taste of Nicole. She was sweet and sharp, like the finest Creole hot sauce. Against all reason he wanted Nicole to show her family she could stand on her own.

"Damn, I can't believe this! You have lost your mind over a woman." Shaun's expression was a combination of dismay and disappointment.

"I revised my strategy, that's all. Look, just because we grew up ghetto doesn't mean we have to operate like thugs," Marcus said quietly.

"Thugs walk around dressed in gold chains, with gold teeth, acting stupid. Thugs end up dead or broke and in prison. I'm no thug!" Shaun leaned close to make his point.

They stared at each other for several tense moments. Marcus sighed. "I didn't mean it like that, man. I meant we didn't come this far to throw it all away trying to be slick."

Shaun took in a deep breath and let it out. "We're at each other because of some—" He broke off when Marcus frowned at him. "Okay, okay."

Both seemed to realize they were on the edge of doing damage to their friendship. They'd had disagreements before, yet somehow Marcus sensed this one could spiral into something serious.

"I'm just saying I've got a Plan B now, all right?" Marcus smiled to calm the suddenly stormy atmosphere between them. He punched Shaun's shoulder playfully. "Who knows which way it will go."

"Yeah, all right." Shaun wore a brief sulky face, then his expression opened up. "If you do get married, I'll be your best man. I'll be surrounded by rich desperate women."

"You must stay up nights thinking of ways to play folks." Marcus couldn't help but feel affection for his old friend. "And I didn't say anything about marriage," he added and pointed a finger at Shaun's nose.

"Don't be modest. I've got full confidence in you. You

learned your moves from the master." Shaun stuck his chest out.

Marcus laughed. "Let's go work up a sweat on the handball court."

Shaun grabbed his arm to stop him from walking away. "Serious again, Marcus. Old man Summers lied to you. She's one of them. Watch your back."

"I know what I'm doing," Marcus replied. "So, don't worry about me."

With a nod, Shaun let go of his arm. He seemed to let go of the subject as well. "I got ya, man."

They headed toward the handball courts trading good-natured insults about each other's athletic abilities. Beneath the banter Marcus could tell the undercurrent of their exchange still flowed. He knew Shaun well. Shaun would find another way to approach him about some kind of alliance. Hours later Marcus realized Shaun had not answered his question about how much he'd told Aliyah. Marcus also contemplated his response that he knew what he was doing when it came to Nicole. Did he? He was still trying to sort out the tangle of emotions she'd stirred to a boil. Despite what he'd told Shaun, there was no Plan B.

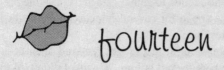

fourteen

Nicole stared at the report. Jesse wore a grim expression. Andre tapped an ink pen against his teeth until Jacinta pinched his arm. Imani stared ahead as though in a trance. Marcus walked into the conference room and shut the door with a hard thud. Russell alone wore a satisfied expression.

"This is the result of leniency with employees," Russell said. He gazed at Nicole with a smug curve to his upper lip.

Marcus sat down next to Nicole. He glanced at Russell. "I just got off the phone with Dayna. They haven't drawn any firm conclusions yet. And I don't see how inviting more staff input is related to a theft at one of our security sites."

"If your friend the detective has any brains, she'll be looking for connections. Summers Security is the common denominator." Russell looked around at the others as though letting his words sink in.

"He's right." Nicole heaved a sigh. "We have to face facts. Two incidents might be a coincidence. Now we have four in three months."

She clicked on the computer. A graph appeared on a

screen. Everyone swiveled around to stare at it. Nicole had assigned Andre and Jacinta to gather data and create the presentation. No one spoke for several minutes. They studied the color-coded results.

"One thing jumps out at me," Jesse ventured, then hesitated when the others looked at him. "Course I didn't go to college like y'all."

"You've got brains and experience. Go on," Marcus prompted.

"Well, take a look." Jesse pushed his chair back and went to the screen. "First thing is they started out in the high-crime neighborhoods. Which is why we didn't think nothing of it at first."

"We expect a certain level of shoplifting and petty theft," Marcus agreed.

"Sure. Everybody gets hit in those areas." Andre reached over and tapped a few keys. Another screen appeared. This one showed crime rates by neighborhoods.

Jacinta nodded. "But if you look at it farther back than two months, we've got a bigger pattern."

"Now they're hitting clients in the high-end neighborhoods. So?" Nicole frowned as she tried to sort through their logic.

Andre split the screen. "Another thing, the thefts were spaced out before two months ago."

Russell sat forward. "The fact is we've had a string of problems concentrated in the last two months."

"Why would the thefts and security lapses increase so fast?" Jacinta squinted at the figures. "Something changed."

"It sure did." Russell looked at Nicole.

"Let's do an *objective* analysis," Marcus shot back. He and Russell glared at each other.

Nicole put a hand on Marcus's arm. Russell lifted an eyebrow at the motion but said nothing. "Everybody just take a deep breath. Both points should be examined."

"Okay," Marcus replied. He turned from Russell. "What changed besides the fact that we got a new CEO?"

Imani leaned an elbow on the table. "Russell did most of the hiring until six months ago. Then Mr. Summers reorganized duties. Jesse started supervising and hiring security personnel."

"Yeah. Most of the guards Russell hired are still around," Andre put in.

"Don't try to turn this around on me!" Russell stood.

"If I've made any decisions that contributed to this predicament I'll be the first to own my responsibility," Nicole said.

Jesse cleared his throat. "Can I say something else?"

"Of course," Marcus said, cutting in while Russell's mouth was still open.

"I looked at the schedules. Tameka and five others volunteered more than anybody else to work overtime." Jesse opened a folder in front of him. "Here are the time sheets. I struggled to do one of those handy computer programs. I didn't get too far. Ended up doing it all by hand."

"Don't worry about it. Low tech can be just as good sometimes." Nicole got up and went to where he sat. She read where he pointed. "I'll be—"

"Yeah, they filled in at about half those sites," Jesse said. "With Mr. Summers getting so sick the last year things were kinda unsettled for a while." His voice trailed off.

"Right." Nicole knew Russell had created quite a bit of turmoil by fighting Marcus on everything.

"I still should have caught this trend." Marcus tapped a fist on the conference table's polished surface.

"Why would you?" Nicole said quickly. She strode to the screen and used a laser pointer. "Felony thefts in each of these areas have been stable."

"We've had news stories constantly on the crime rate inside Houston. One-third of our customers are still in the city." Andre sat back.

"Until two months ago our competitors had similar rates," Jacinta said.

"How do you know?" Nicole looked at her with surprise.

"I've got my own connections in the police department." Jacinta wore a brief grin, then got serious again. "Robbery division does their stats by businesses. All I had to do was look at who provided them with security."

"We make it a point to know the market share," Marcus said.

"Right," Jacinta replied.

"Which brings us back to two months ago," Russell insisted.

"I say we give Jesse's information to Detective Tyler," Andre said.

"Definitely. She can really look at them with a microscope." Marcus grimaced. "But I still feel like we'd better get an answer for ourselves."

"We're supposed to be leaders in private security, giving our customers more peace of mind than even the police," Nicole added.

"Because we're not spread so thin. They've got the entire city." Imani turned back to the graph on the screen.

"Let's start with another examination of those guards and their background checks, Jesse." Nicole pointed to the folder in front of him. "Then we'll interview our customers again about the thefts."

"Go back six months." Marcus glanced at Russell.

"Let me." Andre waved a hand in the air like an eager student. "I've got a program that will look for parallels and calculate probabilities."

"And just what do we tell our customers so that they don't get nervous? They're bound to wonder." Russell wore a sneer.

"We've already told them we're looking to improve security." Nicole ground her teeth in annoyance.

"I've been talking to them all about new technology," Andre added. "They're used to me asking a bunch of questions."

"Sounds good. End of the week I'll meet with Jesse and Andre for an update. Any major problems or developments, call me or Marcus immediately." Nicole nodded to signal the meeting was over.

The others bustled out, talking about their assignments. Russell held back and seemed about to say something more. Instead he merely gave Nicole a mean smile, saluted, and strolled out. Nicole and Marcus went to her office. She dropped into her leather chair. Every muscle in her body was wound tight from tension.

"What a day," she groaned and kneaded the back of her neck.

"I can promise it will get better." Marcus closed the door.

When he crossed the room and took over the massage, Nicole gradually relaxed all over. "Oh, yeah. Just what a woman needs, a man who keeps his promises."

He leaned forward and put his lips close to her ear. "I meant after we leave the office."

"How romantic. There's only one problem. We won't be leaving the office for a long time." Nicole wiggled with delight as his strong hands moved to her shoulders.

"When doesn't matter, baby. It will happen tonight."

Marcus continued to caress her arms. Soon he switched his attention to her sides. Nicole bent forward so that his hands could travel down her back. Suddenly the tailored navy blue jacket she wore over an emerald green satin tank top felt too restrictive. She allowed him to help her shrug out of it. The touch of his skin against the bare flesh of her upper arms brought on another round of sighs. He used his fingertips to gently rake her biceps. The pressure sent shivers down her spine.

"Keep going," she whispered, her head pressed against his midsection.

"Nicole, I think you ought to see this report and—" Cat froze with one foot in the air and stumbled as she entered the room unannounced.

Jacinta bumped into her. "Geez, Cat! Give me a signal next time. What's your problem anyway?" She was about to say more when she glanced at Marcus and Nicole. Her mouth flew open.

"I, I should have waited." Cat's words tumbled over each other.

"Yeah, we're leaving. In fact, we're gone. No, we never even came in. Right, Cat?" Jacinta blinked rapidly.

"Right." Cat pivoted and did a neat sprint out the door, leaving Jacinta alone.

"Bye." Jacinta performed her own sharp turn and vanished.

"The word is out." Nicole looked up at Marcus.

He glanced at the digital clock on her desk. "I'd say the office will know some version of the story in about one hour."

"I've got a dollar that says fifteen minutes," she tossed back.

"I trust the professionalism of our employees. They'll get started on those important assignments first. Then they'll take a coffee break and start talking," he replied dryly.

"What should we do?"

Marcus patted her arms, then walked to a nearby chair and

sat down. "Continue to run an efficient operation. Get back to work. I'm not feeling guilty. Are you?"

Nicole heard the real question. "No. But we should be more careful. I don't want a false issue to distract from the great work we're doing."

"Is it a false issue? You've got to be objective about every employee's job performance."

"You're doing a magnificent job. No question about that," Nicole said promptly.

Marcus let out a bass laugh that bounced off the oak paneling. Nicole drank in the rich sound as though it were cool chocolate milk flowing down her throat. She wanted to wrap herself around the essence of him. He shook his head and smiled at her with affection.

"Now that sounded *very* objective," he said after his laughter died away.

"It's true," she countered. "My family and a lot of other folks in the business think you walk on water." She grinned at him. "Even my father thought you could have made a fine CEO."

Marcus wore a thoughtful expression for a few seconds. He carefully placed the expensive pen back in the brass holder on her desk. "Except for one thing. I don't have the right pedigree."

"I'll make a promise."

"I'm listening," he said.

"If anyone, including my parents, is crazy enough to criticize you, I'll set them straight. They know better than to tangle with me." Nicole put both hands on her hips.

He stood with a rigid set to his handsome face. "I speak for myself. I earned my job with hard work and brains."

"I didn't mean—"

"So, don't think you're going to run interference between me and Daddy, all right?" Marcus said heatedly.

"I heard you. Now listen for a change." Nicole crossed her arms with a grimace.

"Sure. Just needed to be said."

"We should deal with any kind of reaction together. So, you might want to drop that defensive attitude with me." Nicole narrowed her eyes as she gazed at him.

Marcus rubbed his eyes. "Sorry, long day."

"From now on nobody but me gets to say nasty things about you," Nicole quipped.

His dark brows pulled together briefly, then relaxed. Marcus gave a tired laugh, then beckoned to her as he stood. "Okay."

Nicole walked to him. At first he didn't touch her. They stood so close that she could hear the soft whisper of his breath. She was eye level with his broad chest. Instead of looking up into his eyes immediately, she took in the shape of his muscles beneath the dress shirt. Nicole savored the delicious anticipation of waiting. Eyes closed, she enjoyed the scent of him. Obsession for Men mixed with his body chemistry to create a tantalizing result. Finally Marcus pressed his lips to her forehead tenderly.

"So, we've officially made up," Nicole whispered.

"This is part one of making up." Marcus put a hand under her chin, lifted her face, and kissed the tip of her nose. "Tonight?"

"Tonight," she replied.

The spell lifted for the moment, and they parted. Each seemed to know it was time to get back to business. Marcus smoothed down his tie. Nicole went back behind her desk.

"I'm happy with the office manager we hired in Lake

Charles. He's already hired support staff and has made progress setting up the computer system."

"Jesse was supposed to go this week to help him hire the first security guards. And Andre was going along to work with the computer contractor." Nicole sat down hard.

"I'll set them up to do a series of teleconferences for now. They can do the road trip next week maybe." Marcus glanced at her. "You agree?"

"Sounds good. We've got to get through this latest crisis. What are our customers saying?" Nicole frowned.

"Everyone is complaining about the crime rate, so no one has singled us out yet," he replied.

"*Yet* is the key word. I'm going to get with Jesse and we'll talk to those employees together."

"Okay, boss lady." Marcus headed for the door.

"What did I tell you about calling me boss lady?" Nicole snapped as she punched in Jesse's extension on her desk phone.

"Did I mention I have a problem with authority?" Marcus grinned at her from the door, then left.

"You didn't have to," she said as the door shut. Nicole laughed out loud.

"Your friend is being stubborn." Aliyah puffed on a cigarette. She crossed her legs, and the olive green short skirt hiked up her thigh another inch.

Shaun handed her a glass of brandy. "Because he didn't jump right into your bed."

They were in Shaun's town house. Expensively furnished and decorated in shades of blue and green, the living room had a spare elegance. Aliyah let out a stream of smoke, then took a gulp from her glass.

"You wanna slow down on that stuff. Does your rich boyfriend know his sweetie chain smokes and drinks like a fish? Not to mention getting high on weed."

Aliyah ground out the cigarette. "Russ likes a little recreational drug use. We've partied more than once."

"Likes a little wild thang, eh? I'll bet he doesn't know just how wild you can be," Shaun said. He reached over and raked his fingers on the skin of her thigh.

"Cut it out. I'm spoken for." Aliyah affected a prim look.

"Get real." Shaun drank from his glass.

"Anyway, a girl has to keep a few secrets. At least until after the wedding."

"Wedding?" Shaun's easy smile went rigid.

Aliyah smoothed a hand over her hair. "I've been looking at china patterns and dropping hints about which fancy neighborhood I want to live in."

"Baby wants nothing but the best." Shaun took his hand from her thigh. He put his glass down on the glass-and-chrome cocktail table.

Her expression hardened. "I'm tired of scrambling around on the ground like a squirrel looking for nuts. I want more."

"You're stupid if you think the Summers family is just going to welcome you with kisses and hugs."

"I don't give a flip what his bitchy sister or the rest of them think!" she snarled. "When he signs that marriage license I've got rights. I'll drop a couple of little Summers brats and wrap up my claim."

"I feel sorry for any kid with you as a mother." Shaun gave a scornful laugh.

"Can't be as bad as the two kids that have you as a daddy." Aliyah flinched when Shaun's eyes widened in anger.

"Don't screw with me, baby. You won't like how it turns out," Shaun said, his voice pitched low with fury.

"Ah, c'mon now. I was just playin' with ya. Look, I'm trying to get my own. I deserve it!" she protested.

Shaun picked up his glass of brandy again. "Whatever. But know this, bagging Russell better not mess with me getting paid."

"I'm not the one you oughta be worried about, Shaun. Marcus isn't being cool at all." Aliyah turned the focus from herself. "You told me he wouldn't work with you."

"I tossed the idea out to test the waters." He wore a thoughtful frown for several minutes.

"I don't get it. The insurance deal is a great idea." Aliyah stared at him.

"I might still work it. I just don't want him to know about you and me." Shaun went to the bar and poured himself more brandy.

"You can't trust him all of a sudden? He's supposed to be your boy from back in the day, bosom buddies, got each other's back to the end." Aliyah followed him. She held out her crystal tumbler so he could refill it.

"Yeah."

Shaun tipped the bottle and watched the amber liquid flow into her glass. He poured two fingers, then stopped. Aliyah scowled but said nothing as he put the bottle down. After several more minutes of silence, she fidgeted.

"Look, what are you gonna do about him?" Aliyah said.

"Find out from Russell what they're saying about the thefts. I'm thinking we'd better back off," Shaun replied.

"We're making a tidy profit finally!" she blurted out.

"Thought you were after the big prize, getting some serious Summers cash," Shaun teased.

"I've got expenses right now. Being a society girl from a prominent Black family in California takes money. I have to live in the right place and wear the right accessories." Aliyah tossed her hair aside to reveal fancy gold earrings.

"Well, you're gonna have to live on a budget until you march down the aisle with Russell," Shaun tossed back. Then he frowned again. "The next job is too far gone to stop. The buyer isn't somebody I can just cancel on."

"Who is it?" Aliyah asked in a casual tone. She darted a glance at him, then looked away.

"You don't need to know. You're sure Russell doesn't know how much info he's given away to you?"

Aliyah laughed. "No way. He's telling me the names and brands of their security systems. He thinks because he doesn't tell me codes or passwords it's okay."

"I see why his daddy didn't leave him the business," Shaun said with a grunt. "Be careful. Marcus is already suspicious."

"So what? He's going after Nicole." Aliyah shrugged.

"I think he's changing." Shaun became quiet again.

"You mean he's not going to raid their customers and open his own security company?" Aliyah sat down on the sofa again. She stretched out her long legs and studied them critically.

"I'm not sure what he's going to do. I don't think he is either." Shaun sat down in one of two large chairs that matched the sofa.

"Sounds like Marcus is trying to live right these days," Aliyah said carefully. "You're not going to tell him, are you? I mean, how those 'acquisitions' from his customers have helped his plan." She cast a calculating sideways glance at Shaun.

"Ruining confidence in Summers Security makes it easier for him to start his own business. I make money and he makes money. But I don't think he'll see the big picture," Shaun said more to himself than to answer Aliyah.

"Right. I'm sure your real purpose was to help your

buddy." Aliyah snickered and gulped more brandy.

Shaun seemed to snap out of his reverie. He wore an easy smile as his gaze traveled down her body. "I take care of my friends. Look at you. Baby girl is in designer everything right down to her toes."

"I did some of this on my own, Shaun." Aliyah bobbed her head, then snapped her fingers. "Not that I'm ungrateful for the way you look out for a sister."

"Then show me." Shaun slapped his thigh.

Aliyah put down her tumbler and walked over to him slowly. She sank onto his lap. "I love talking about money, especially how I'm going to get it."

"We're both going to get plenty, baby girl," he whispered. "Yes, we will."

fifteen

Nicole dressed in a sheer pink tunic blouse, hot pink bra, and white leggings. She tucked her hair behind her ears. Large silver hoop earrings dangled from her earlobes. "Whew! I'm glad this day is finally over."

She went into the den. After sorting through a stack of compact discs, she made ten selections and loaded the sound system. The lighting was soft, the music low, and the atmosphere just right after a tense day at the office. Rosaria had left long before Nicole had gotten home at nine o'clock. Nicole wondered how long she could keep the dinner warm before the pasta primavera was ruined. No doubt Marcus was still hard at work. Musical chimes sounded over the smooth voice of Eric Benet singing a love song. She went to the door with a smile and swung it open.

"Hey, baby. Dedication is fine, but the food is almost cold." Nicole broke off.

Jolene smirked. Dressed in a crisp white shirt and light blue denim jeans, she wore her hair pulled back in a full ponytail.

"I've eaten, but thanks for the warm welcome." She brushed past Nicole and into the foyer.

"Make yourself at home." Nicole pushed the door shut.

"I will, considering this house is rightfully mine," Jolene said over her shoulder. She kept going toward the den.

Nicole glanced at her wristwatch and followed her. "Is this catfight going to take long?"

Jolene was already at the bar pouring herself a glass of red wine. "I don't do catfights."

"Well, if you abuse my hospitality you will tonight," Nicole snapped.

Jolene glanced around the room. "Aunt Analine would be thrilled to hear you talk like that. Not my choice of color schemes, or furniture for that matter. And this artwork."

"Thanks for the home decorating commentary. If that's all, then good night." Nicole decided she wouldn't let Jolene get her angry—not an easy task.

"Expecting company?" Jolene swept Nicole with an appraising gaze. "The blouse is a little too revealing. The white satin leggings are cute, but way too tight. He might get the idea that you're easy or desperate, possibly both. Nice sandals, though."

"What do you want, Jolene?"

"To make your life simple, actually."

"You're just trying to be helpful. I'll write to the pope. You deserve sainthood." Nicole snorted.

"I'm going to ignore your usual rude behavior." Jolene wore a tolerant smile. She took a delicate sip of wine. "I realize you've been under a lot of stress lately."

"Not as much as you'd like to think." Nicole gave her a cool smile.

"You don't have to be brave with me, Nikki. Russell told

me about the thefts. Terrible." Jolene put on a pretentiou
concerned face.

"I'm touched by the depth of your compassion." Nicole
decided she needed a drink. She went to the bar and poured
herself a glass of merlot.

"Oh, but I am really worried. The family name is at stake
not to mention a lot of money. Summers Security is on the line
because of your, hmmm, lack of management experience."

"I'd like to finish this conversation before I reach
menopause, Jolene." Nicole went back to her chair.

"Take your act to some seedy nightclub. They could use
one more vulgar comedian," Jolene said in a tight voice.

"I'm not due for a career change just yet."

"Don't be so sure. Daddy's will clearly states that the family can remove you as CEO. They're not happy with the reports of staff misconduct and rampant thefts from the
customers." Jolene's oval face glowed with delighted spite.

"Reports being delivered on a regular basis by you and
Russell, I'm sure," Nicole said evenly.

"What are we supposed to do when they ask us how things
are going?" Jolene lifted a shoulder.

Nicole gave a sharp, cynical laugh. "Right."

"There have been thefts and employee problems in the two
short months you've been in charge. True or false?" Jolene
shook her head slowly. "Sad but true."

"We haven't anything that points to a serious systemic
problem in our operation. The police are investigating each
theft as a separate case," Nicole replied. "Bet you don't mention that in your conversations with the family."

"They have legitimate concerns about the operation of
Summers Security, Nicole. It reflects on you." Jolene finished
the last of her wine. Her smile had a distinct feline nastiness.

Nicole counted to ten until the red haze of fury cleared up

enough for her to see straight. She put her wineglass down. She walked over to Jolene, placed a hand under her elbow, and lifted her from the barstool.

"Thanks so much for stopping by to show your support and sympathy. It so happens I'm handling things quite nicely." She firmly guided Jolene toward the door leading to the hallway.

Jolene tried to jerk free but failed. "Stop digging those claws into my arm."

"In your next account be sure to mention that we haven't lost any clients. In fact, we just signed contracts with three new ones. The Lake Charles office is coming along nicely, and we're still number three of the top ten African-American businesses in the Southwest."

"You can't wiggle out of this fix, Nicole." Jolene skipped along as Nicole's pace picked up. She tried to dig her heels into the carpet but couldn't get a foothold.

"I've wiggled out of tougher places before." Nicole yanked her out onto the smooth hardwood floor of the hall.

Jolene managed to pull free. She faced Nicole, her face twisted with hostility. "Even Uncle Stanton will have to admit sooner or later you can't hack it. You're a selfish, egotistical fool to take the company and the employees down with you."

"Goodbye." Nicole waved to her.

"Wait a minute. I shouldn't have made those brutally honest observations about you. You're doing the best you can." Jolene adopted a tone of reason.

"Was that supposed to be an apology?" Nicole squinted at her.

"Let's put our childish antagonism aside. We can come up with a win-win solution," Jolene said with fervor.

Nicole titled her head to one side. "Go on."

"You resign with dignity and we'll make sure your contributions to the business are recognized by the board." Jolene nodded eagerly.

"You'd do that for me? I'm touched."

"Even better, you deserve a generous severance package." Jolene spread her arms, making her Maxx tote bag swing out. "Now you couldn't ask for a more equitable compromise."

"Hmmm." Nicole put one finger on her chin as though giving her offer consideration.

"I'm talking about a nice fat check and you can stay in the house. Well, another few months or so," Jolene added quickly.

"One question. If you're convinced I'm about to be tossed out anyway, why not just let it happen?" Nicole gazed at her.

"I'd hate to see the family torn apart in the process. This way we can save the company *and* keep peace," Jolene said.

"Your family sentiment is about as genuine as those acrylic nails you're wearing," Nicole retorted. "Out!"

"You're being stupid, Nicole."

"Our family likes cash more than sentiment. Summers Security is still profitable. I think they'll let me weather this storm." Nicole strode to the front door and opened it. "I'm not leaving the business or *my* house. See ya."

Marcus stood poised to ring the doorbell. He started at the sight of the two livid women, then recovered quickly. "Hello, Jolene."

Jolene's eyes widened, and her mouth curved up. "Hello, Marcus. You're putting in overtime, I guess." Her glance slid sideways to Nicole.

"Everyone is working hard these days," Marcus muttered. "Lots to do."

"I'm sure Uncle Stanton will be happy to know how diligent you're working." Jolene looked from Nicole to him and back again.

"Summers Security needs my attention. So, excuse us while we get busy." Nicole flashed a bold smile.

"Have a good evening. I'm sure you will." Jolene smirked at them one last time before she strolled down the brick walkway to her white Jaguar.

When Marcus stepped across the threshold, Nicole slammed the door. "Bitch!"

"Hey, calm down." Marcus put an arm around her waist.

"My family might start listening to her and Russell." Nicole huffed. "All my life I've been treated like a lightweight. Okay, so part of that is my fault. But these problems started before I took over and—"

"Honey, let it go." He turned her around and cupped her face with both large hands.

"I can't, Marcus, because she's right. This is a test of my ability to manage the company under tough conditions." Nicole pulled his hands from her face. "I've got to find out what's going on and deal with it."

"An empty stomach won't help your concentration. Let's eat," he said gently.

"Fine. Just don't treat me like an hysterical debutante." Nicole headed for the kitchen with Marcus close behind.

"I didn't mean to be patronizing. You seem to forget that you're not in this thing alone."

Nicole went to the large porcelain cooktop. She took the lid from a saucepan. "I'll bet the shrimp is mush by now. Damn it, I can't get anything right."

"Didn't you turn off the heat? Here, let me look." Marcus picked up a large ladle. He scooped sauce up and tasted a little. "Hmm, tasty."

"Of course I turned off the heat. Shrimp are delicate. They can't be overcooked. I guess you don't think I can learn to cook either. I followed the recipe exactly." Nicole snatched the ladle from his hands.

"This promises to be a relaxing evening," he quipped and crossed to the oak table set near a bay window.

Nicole found the remote control for the entertainment system. "Television or music while you wait?"

"Smooth jazz would help your mood." He raised an eyebrow at her.

"Fine," she clipped. Seconds later the sultry strains of a saxophone came from the speakers.

"Since you can't just forget whatever Jolene said before I got here, let's talk about it." Marcus stretched out his long legs encased in stone-washed jeans. He crossed powerful arms across his chest.

"Let me start water for another batch of pasta. This stuff is a lost cause."

Nicole dumped the colander of stiff fettuccini into the garbage can. She filled a large pasta pan with salted water and put it on the cooktop. Then she spread garlic butter on a split loaf of French bread.

"You don't act like a lady who can't cook." Marcus looked impressed.

"I never said I couldn't cook, just that I hate cooking. And cleaning and laundry."

"I get the message. Now let's talk."

"That fat butt no good—"

"Calmly," he broke in with both palms raised. "Rationally."

Nicole took a deep breath, let it out, and repeated the gesture twice more. She spoke in a controlled quiet tone. "Jolene, aka the stupid cow, had the gall to suggest I should resign for the good of the company. I told her in so many words that she could shove that suggestion up her lumpy rear end. See? Rational."

"Oh, yeah." Marcus shook his head slowly. "What a temper. I'm glad I got here on the tail end of that conversation. Never thought I'd be grateful for bad traffic."

"What really pisses me off is that I care! I had every intention of finding a way to dump Summers Security." Nicole leaned against the counter. "You want it?"

Marcus stared at her with his mouth open for several moments. "What did you just say?"

"I know, I know. You said to be realistic. Besides, the family wouldn't go for it. Uncle Hosea knew that." Nicole waved a hand in the air.

He drummed his fingers on the smooth wood surface of the table. "He did, huh?"

Nicole sat on the picnic-style bench of the table and rested her head on his shoulder. "I don't want to screw this up. Maybe things have come too easy for me and I don't know how to handle a real challenge." She closed her tired eyes.

"You dealt with Jolene pretty good," he teased. Marcus stroked her chin.

"Getting the best of Jolene in a fight is no contest. I've been doing that since I was two." Nicole sat up straight. "Maybe I should let it go like you said, I mean trying to run the business."

"This definitely isn't my idea of rational talk." Marcus replied.

"The will specifies that the board can remove me. I could ask them to vote on my termination. Why fight it?"

"I'll give you at least three good reasons. One, you have a chance to be among an elite group of female CEOs in a male-dominated industry."

"So a few guys think they're hot stuff. Nothing new." Nicole shook her head.

"Two, you told me how good it feels to succeed on your own. Now's your chance to prove something to yourself, way more important than proving you can do it to anyone else."

"I should've started small. Like manage a hot dog stand first." Nicole rubbed her temples with the tips of her fingers.

"At least you can still crack jokes," Marcus tossed back. "Third, you get to do numbers one and two while pissing Jolene off big time."

"All right, I'm beginning to feel your logic." Nicole wore a brief smile that faded. "Seriously, you should have been made CEO."

"I'd take the burden off those lovely shoulders if I could. But Mr. Summers followed tradition." Marcus gave her a quick squeeze. "Let's talk about it some other time."

"Hold on. My father thinks you're a cross between Hercules and Einstein when it comes to the business. He might support the idea." Nicole looked at him.

"Honey, tonight we're going to carve out time to just relax. No examining options or theories on crime conspiracies for a few hours." Marcus kissed her forehead. "We can start back up at nine o'clock in the morning."

"Deal. But we will talk about you being the boss man." Nicole pointed at him.

"If you insist. Now, where is the fabulous meal you promised?" He cocked an eyebrow at her.

Nicole jumped from her seat. "I didn't promise fabulous."

She put fettuccini in the now boiling pot of water. Twenty minutes later they laughed and joked over dinner. Nicole loved the cozy, intimate mood of eating in the alcove near the kitchen.

After dinner Marcus loaded the dishwasher while Nicole wiped off the stove and countertop. Then they went into the mini den just off the open kitchen. A wide sofa and chair upholstered in a plaid navy blue, dark red, and gold faced the massive oak cabinet. Doors that slid back on rollers revealed a wide-screen television. After a short debate they decided to listen to music. They cuddled on the sofa. Nestled in his arms, Nicole felt sheltered from the chaos swirling around her.

"This is the right way to end the day," she murmured. "A little wine, listening to D'Angelo sing his heart out, and you. Not necessarily in that order."

"I was about to say," he joked. "I'm going easy on the wine. I've gotta drive, you know."

"Drink up, mister. You'll be here for hours." Nicole rubbed the soft cotton fabric of his striped knit shirt.

"Then I'll need a clear head." Marcus grinned.

"You're safe with me." Nicole laughed.

"Am I?" he whispered. "I've been wondering about that since the day you put a Louisiana hoodoo spell on me."

"No magic. Once we got over that first week of you being a sexist pig who didn't think I had the brains of a tick—"

"I had an attitude for about a minute," he broke in. "Forgive me?"

Nicole looked up into his toasted almond–colored eyes. She traced the line of his jaw, then the oval shape of his full mouth. "Forgive what?"

She nibbled at his lower lip, delighting in the warm, moist, first contact. Marcus tightened his embrace. Their tongues teased and tasted until both sighed. Nicole made the first move by tugging his shirt out of his jeans. She ran her hands under the shirt and rubbed his chest.

"Bedroom," he mumbled, still kissing her as he lifted her blouse.

"No, here. Now."

In a red heat, she fumbled with the side zipper of her pants. Marcus moaned as he pulled the blouse over her head. He groped the single front fastener of her lacy pink bra until it popped open. Nicole shivered when his tongue licked each nipple in turn. They completely undressed each other between feverish kisses.

"Be right back." Nicole kissed him hard. He held on when she tried to pull away. "I've got to get a—"

"I'm armed and ready." Marcus only had to reach out to where his jeans lay tossed across the sofa back. He retrieved a foil square from the back pocket.

"Boy scout. I like it," Nicole murmured.

She took it from him. Looking into his eyes, she used both hands to unroll the thin latex over his erection. Marcus breathed hard as he watched her caress him. Nicole then pushed him back onto the sofa in a sitting position. She mounted him and began a gentle rocking motion as she licked his earlobe. He tenderly cupped her breasts in his hands. Her restrained rhythm gave way as she ground her hips faster against him. Deep inside a small pinpoint of craving spread over her body. She twisted and rocked frantically to satisfy the overpowering hunger that tore into her body and soul. Distantly she heard her voice and his answering cry a few moments later. Marcus dug his fingers into her hips and lifted them both as he came. Slippery with perspiration, Nicole cradled his soft wooly curls as he buried his face against her breasts.

"Baby." His voice was low and hoarse. Marcus groaned when they both went limp.

She combed his hair with her fingers. "Scandalous. You seduced me in the den."

"Your idea," he panted. "Good one, too."

"Catch your breath and then we'll take this party to the bedroom." Nicole rubbed her cheek on the top of his head.

"Woman, are you trying to kill me?" He lifted his face to look at her.

Nicole threw her head back and laughed. "I only meant we could have dessert in bed. I've got fresh Louisiana strawberries and whipped cream."

"Hmm, whipped cream. I'm getting an inspiration." Marcus wore a wicked grin.

"Don't blame me for how you feel in the morning."

"I'll be ready for the world tomorrow," Marcus said. He wrapped both arms around her waist.

"Me, too. Not even Russell will get to me. I've got you." She touched her fingertips to his face.

"We'll make it, baby. No matter what they throw at us," he said softly.

"You and me."

He nodded. "Me and you."

Shaun crossed his arms. "I heard you wrong. Say again?"

"You got it right," Marcus replied.

The two men gazed at each other. Standing face-to-face in Shaun's living room, neither heard the driving thump of hip-hop music in the background coming from the FM radio station.

"Romancing the rich girl is one thing. Now you gonna let them use you." Shaun shook his head slowly.

"Nobody is using me." Marcus strolled to Shaun's kitchen and got a can of root beer.

"Nicole is using you. She needs your brains to hold onto the business *you* should have gotten. She even admitted it." Shaun followed him.

Marcus waved a hand and went back into the living room with Shaun on his heels. He sat down in a large easy chair. "Drop it."

Shaun pulled a hand over his face. "Damn! You're in love."

"I'm touched that you're happy for me," Marcus retorted.

"You're headed for a big letdown. Something told me she was real trouble. But I didn't think my boy would fall for it." Shaun dropped into the chair facing Marcus.

"I make my own choices. She's not just another woman." Marcus stared down at the soda can he held.

"Summers Security should be yours. Wake up!" Shaun said loudly as though Marcus were in a trance.

"I'm not going to punish Nicole because the old man lied to me."

"Fine. You got the hearts and flowers thing going. If you trust her so much, then tell Nicole what her uncle promised. See what she does." Shaun gazed at him with a skeptical expression.

Marcus looked away. "No, I can't do that right now."

"Uh-huh. You've got doubts." Shaun jabbed a forefinger at him.

"That's not it," Marcus replied too quickly. He frowned. "I want to wait for the right time. I don't see why she needs to know. What difference does it make?"

"Keeping your options open and your guard up. Now that's the first thing you've said that makes sense. She doesn't need to know if you end up running the business anyway."

"I'm not playing her." Marcus raked his fingers over his hair. "I want something I never knew I could have, something I didn't think existed."

"What are you talking about?" Shaun blinked at him in bafflement.

"Somebody I can really be with." Marcus grappled for a way to explain. Shaun's befuddled stare boring into him didn't help.

"Huh?"

"We don't have to talk sometimes. See what I mean?" Marcus tried again.

Shaun's eyes lit up with lustful comprehension. "Oh, yeah. I've had those kinda nights. All that blah-blah-blah ain't necessary."

"I'm not talking about just sex." Marcus blew out a breath in exasperation.

"Hey, done right it's never *just* sex, my brother," Shaun said with a leer.

Marcus gave up. "Look, I'm not going after Summers Security or Nicole. We've got something real."

"Something real," Shaun repeated in a flat tone.

"That's it." Marcus took a deep gulp of root beer.

"I see. All right." Shaun tapped the arm of his chair for a few minutes as silence stretched between them. "I wasn't going to say anything, but . . ." His voice trailed off.

"Say anything about what?"

"I've had some financial setbacks lately. Don't let all this fool you," he added when Marcus glanced around the room.

"How bad?"

Shaun sighed. "Bad. To tell you the truth, I was counting on that insurance thing I told you about. Plus, I figured you could help me out in other ways. Strictly legit."

"Your insurance idea was barely on the right side of legit, Shaun." Marcus put the empty soda can down.

"Hey, I'm willing to revise my business plan." Shaun slid to the edge of his seat. "Just hear me out. You're not sure about Nicole and or her kinfolks."

"I never said—"

"C'mon, this is me you're talking to. What do you think her daddy will say when he finds out about you two?" Shaun's eyes narrowed.

"He might not be too thrilled at first." Marcus tapped a fist on his knee.

"Remember when you tried to date those bourgie girls in

college? You were too dark and too poor. We both know what his reaction will be."

"I don't need a trip down memory lane, all right? I'll handle my own business," Marcus snapped. Shaun's words hit too close to a sensitive spot. He wasn't sure Nicole would stand up to family pressure or generations of tradition.

"Just think about it is all I'm saying," Shaun pressed. "You know I don't ask for help unless things get tight. We've always had each other's back, even when we couldn't count on family. Don't forget that."

"I want to help you out, man." Marcus rubbed his chin.

After a few moments Shaun's expression turned bitter. "To hell with it. I shouldn't have to be beggin' you, *brother*."

"C'mon, don't trip. I'm not trying to leave you out." Marcus spread his hands out in a gesture of conciliation.

"Yeah."

"You've got skills. I know at least three people with big companies that could use somebody with your brains," Marcus said. "I know, you like being your own boss. Look at it this way, you could make money, get on your feet, and start again. What about it?"

"I'll get back to you," Shaun said dully.

"It's not the perfect solution, but you have options a lotta brothers don't have. You're one helluva salesman." Marcus forced a light tone.

"Must not be. I didn't sell you," Shaun said with a tight smile.

"I know you too well," Marcus teased. Still, the tension between them hung heavy in the air. He stood. "I gotta bounce outta here, man. Early day tomorrow."

"Uh-huh." Shaun didn't get up.

"I'll call you, okay?" Marcus gazed at him.

"Sure. Later."

"Right." Marcus hesitated. Yet there was nothing more he could think to say. "Bye."

"Bye."

Marcus left without looking back. He didn't need to, because he could feel Shaun's gaze like a laser beam. Well into the night he tried to reconcile the pull of his old life with what he wanted now.

Sixteen

Nicole gazed through the car windows at a world she'd only seen in movies or read about in the newspaper. Marcus drove them through Bloody Fifth, the grim nickname for the Fifth Ward in Houston because of the high murder rate. An oppressive summer breeze that didn't cool or refresh stirred a few pieces of paper in a vacant lot. Late-model cars with speakers booming so loud that their frames shook cruised by or were parked on the curb. Groups of fierce-looking young men, some with bare chests, stood on a street corner. All wore tattoos on their arms. Nicole checked to make sure the doors to the Durango were locked.

"Why are you showing me this?" she said, still looking around uneasily.

"I want you to see where I came from," he replied. He turned a corner.

"The Fifth Ward isn't you anymore." Nicole glanced at the poised, handsome profile dressed in a Brooks Brothers gray pinstriped suit.

"The Fifth Ward will always be a part of who I am. If

you're going to be with me then you have to know that."
Marcus nodded toward a teenager with an angry scowl at no
one in particular. "Look at him and you see me thirteen
years ago."

"Ready to fight the world. The same spirit that led you out
of here." Nicole placed a hand on his thigh.

He slowed the Durango until it rolled to a stop, then he
pointed to a row house with faded and peeling brown paint.
"This is where I lived. Mama moved us around a lot. We
lived there the longest, six years."

A small child with thick braided hair sat on the front steps,
grinning and waved at them. Nicole waved back with a smile
then turned to him. "Us?"

Marcus gazed at the house for several minutes before he
spoke. His expression was unreadable behind the dark sunglasses. "I have three brothers."

"They still live in the neighborhood?" Nicole looked for
some resemblance in the features of men walking by.

"You're right. I don't know why I brought you. Let's get
out of here." He wheeled the vehicle away from the curb and
into traffic.

Nicole waited a good fifteen minutes before she spoke.
"You wanted me to know, so tell me about your family," she
said quietly.

"My oldest brother is dead. Darius was killed in a gang
fight back in ninety-four. LeLand is serving a life sentence.
He got revenge. My youngest brother, Dondre, lives with his
dad's parents. I don't see him much, but I hear he's doing
well. He graduated from high school this year."

"And your mother?" Nicole watched him wince.

"She's around," was all he would say.

Nicole decided not to press the issue. Marcus didn't seem
ready to offer more at the moment. She realized suddenly

what it had taken for him to show her the Fifth Ward. Marcus had opened up a painful part of himself. More than anything she wanted to be worthy of this gift of his trust. Just when she was sure the touchy subject was closed, he cleared his throat.

"My mother didn't raise us. Her mother did. Mama had a lot of problems. With alcohol and men," he added after a long pause.

"How awful for all of you." Nicole waited patiently. Marcus seemed to struggle with how to go on.

"Yeah. Well, anyway, my older brothers kinda raised themselves on the streets. Grandma took us in when I was still young enough to listen at least some of the time. It was too late for them, I guess. She couldn't handle all of us, so my baby brother went with his father's folks." Marcus spoke in a strained voice, as though pushing each word out.

"Grandmamma Pearl did a great job, considering she was almost sixty when we moved in on her. She put a lot of love and hard work into us. I didn't always appreciate it." Marcus was silent for five minutes. "She died six years ago."

"I'm so sorry, Marcus." Nicole put a hand on his shoulder.

"I try to honor her in my own way these days," he said softly. They rode in silence for several miles.

"Thanks," she said.

"Instead of taking you to a cozy café for lunch I brought you to a high-crime area. Your father would have my head if he found out."

Nicole looked back as they drove toward the freeway entrance ramp. She thought of the young men who seemed primed to strike out with violence any second.

"I'm not talking about this road trip, unique as it is. Not that I need to repeat the experience," she said.

He laughed with genuine humor. "Don't worry, babe."

"You took a risk bringing me to that other world and telling me about your family."

"If you can't hang, then I want to know sooner, not later." Marcus glanced at her, then ahead. "And then there's your parents."

"They're not as judgmental or narrow-minded as you might think."

"Uh-huh. How many dudes from the Fifth Ward have you dated?"

"Hmm, one so far." She patted his thigh.

"So, I'm the test case. Great," he deadpanned. "Sure you want to go through with the ordeal?"

Nicole leaned over and kissed his cheek. "Yes, I'm sure."

"Okay, but I have some advice. Tell your mother I don't have a trust fund soon. That way she won't faint when she asks about my assets at our first family dinner." Marcus grinned.

"Mother would never ask crude questions about money over dinner. She prefers to delicately extract information like a skillful surgeon. You won't even feel the incisions," Nicole wisecracked.

His expression turned serious. "Let's put off that scene for a while."

"No problem. We'll spend time on us first," Nicole replied with a nod.

"You agreed real fast. Sounds like you're not eager for Mom and Dad to find out."

"Was that suggestion some kind of test for me?" Nicole gazed at him steadily.

Marcus pulled into the parking garage for their office building. "No. Guess I'm being too sensitive."

"It's okay. Anyway, you're right." Nicole heaved a sigh. "More family drama is what I really don't need right now."

"I know, baby. Here I'm making things worse." Marcus

parked in the space reserved for Summers Security. He turned to her. "Tell you what, I'll take care of Russell."

"Russell isn't going to listen to you. Wake up from that dream." Nicole snapped her fingers in front of his face.

Marcus caught her hand and kissed the back of it. "He will listen to the right approach."

"Such as?"

"My secret weapon. Trust me." Marcus winked at her.

"In other words, you just thought up the idea and still have to figure out what to say. Right?" Nicole looked at him over her sunglasses.

"Something like that," Marcus said with a mischievous grin. "Have a little faith. I've made a lot of tough sells in my time."

"Good luck, hon." Nicole tilted her head to one side. "You've got a devious side, Mr. Reed."

"I'll take that as a compliment."

Nicole clenched and unclenched her hands beneath the conference table. Her father and Uncle Lionel wore twin grim expressions. She wondered when Marcus would come back from lunch, and she glanced at her wristwatch once more.

"Let's start. Marcus can catch up when he comes in," Uncle Lionel rumbled.

"Right. Nikki, I can't hold back the barbarians at the gates forever. How close are you to clearing up this mess?" Stanton folded his hands on the conference table's polished surface.

"You shouldn't listen to Russell." Nicole couldn't quite keep the impatience from her voice.

"I'll be damned. I used to pat your pigtails, missy. Let me tell you—" He stopped when Stanton put a hand on his arm.

"We don't have time to bicker," Stanton said to Uncle Lionel. "These thefts give your cousins the ammunition they need," her father said to Nicole in an unruffled tone.

Nicole flexed her fingers to release tension. "Of course. I've already told you the police are investigating. I spoke with Detective Dayna Tyler today after you called. She's still working several leads."

"Do any of them lead back to Summers Security?" Uncle Lionel said bluntly.

"We might have to weed out some problem children. Nothing definite," Nicole added quickly when their frowns deepened. "Just some coincidences that smell bad."

"For instance?" her father asked.

"Several guards seemed to work the sites with thefts. These same employees have a history of disciplinary problems." Nicole rubbed her neck. "I've spent the last few days reading personnel files."

"Have Detective Tyler check them out," Uncle Lionel said.

"She has. They don't have criminal records, thank goodness. It's their employment histories that are shady." Nicole grimaced. "Russell was responsible for background checks back when these folks were hired. Bet he didn't tell the family that, did he?"

Uncle Lionel snorted with disgust. "Of course he didn't. We can definitely let Cousin Hilton and the others know."

"Not so fast, Lionel. I don't want this to turn into a family grudge match with Nicole and Russell trading accusations. He might not see it, but neither one of them will win." Stanton glanced at Nicole.

She smiled at him tiredly. "Don't worry, Daddy. I could have started my own whisper campaign if I'd wanted to. I've got enough evidence of his screw ups around here. But I didn't for the same reason you just gave."

Her father nodded approval. "Smart girl."

"Woman," she said.

"Corrected," Stanton replied with a grin.

"In the meantime, Russell and his bratty older sister are stirring up trouble. I'm tired of getting phone calls from my tedious kinfolks," Uncle Lionel complained.

"Obviously your suggestion that I give Russell more authority didn't appease him." Nicole shook her head. "He wants the company."

"It was a long shot anyway." Stanton shrugged and sat back in the leather chair.

"Jolene would never let him back down even if he were inclined to, which he definitely isn't," Uncle Lionel added.

"The bottom line is we've identified the problem employees. Jesse has paired them with reliable staff. They won't be working alone," Nicole said.

"Good." Uncle Lionel's expression lightened for the first time.

"The bad news is two of the clients who have had thefts are coming up for contract renewal." Nicole sighed. She rubbed her tight neck muscles.

"Not good. With the thefts still fresh on their minds, they might blame Summers Security." Uncle Lionel frowned again.

"Right," Nicole admitted. "Marcus and I have been holding their hands, so to speak. It might pay off. Mr. Phoung is so testy about the subject of who is to blame. He's even been checking around with our other customers."

"And?" Uncle Lionel said.

"So far we've been able to convince them not to dump us for another company. Marcus has done a fantastic job of damage control." Nicole lifted a shoulder.

"You two have become a real team, eh?" Uncle Lionel glanced sideways at her father.

"We got over that first week, thank goodness. Except for Russell we all work together very well." Nicole smiled. "I'm doing much better at being a diplomatic executive."

"In fact y'all have gotten very *close*, we understand." Uncle Lionel's thick black eyebrows formed a V shape.

Stanton shifted in his seat as he stared down at the table's mirror surface. "Nicole, your personal life is your own, obviously."

"Obviously." Nicole swore silently. Jolene had been talking about more than her performance as CEO.

"Under normal circumstances I wouldn't say anything, but—"

"The conditions under which you took over this company are anything but normal, young lady," Uncle Lionel jumped in. "You've got to be scrupulous in your behavior."

"Meaning?" Nicole clipped.

"This place is in enough turmoil without adding a steamy office romance with your employee. I thought you had more common sense." Uncle Lionel rapped the leather-covered arm of his chair.

"You know how much we respect Marcus. As vice president he's proven his worth repeatedly. But . . ." Stanton looked at his brother.

"Any kind of relationship with this man is not only bad for business, he's totally unsuitable. Your father might be reluctant to tell you the truth, but I'm not." Uncle Lionel crossed his arms.

"By unsuitable you mean he's not rich and he doesn't come from a family you approve of."

Nicole couldn't pretend she was surprised. She knew the

unspoken views of her older family members. Members of the old Creole families carefully orchestrated their children's social circles from kindergarten to college. Few of the younger generation bucked tradition.

"I'm sure Marcus is a fine young man, Nicole. But now is not the time to experiment." Her father gazed at her steadily.

"Marcus isn't a school project, Daddy. Whatever our relationship, and by the way it's nobody's business, this company has not been affected. It never will be."

"Nicole—"

"Do you have any more questions about business?" Nicole stared at them hard in turn.

"You're being way too stubborn. The rest of the family won't be so nice." Uncle Lionel scowled at her.

"I know you, Nicole. Don't rebel for the sake of it. This is too important." Stanton spoke in a fast, intense manner.

Nicole stood. "Uncle Hosea left me this company for better or worse."

"We're trying to help you to hold on to what you've got," Uncle Lionel said.

"I appreciate it, though in this case you're a little misguided," she said crisply. "Marcus and I are careful about how we behave in front of the employees."

"Not what I heard," Uncle Lionel muttered.

"Stop listening to coffee break gossip," Nicole barked. She placed her hands palm down on the conference table. "The subject is permanently closed."

Marcus came in. "Sorry I'm late. I got caught in traffic." He glanced at the two men, then gazed at Nicole. "Everything okay?"

Nicole continue to glare at her father and uncle. "Yes."

Tense silence followed for several seconds before Stanton cleared his throat. He stuck out his hand. "Hello, Marcus."

"Good afternoon. What did I miss?" Marcus shook Stanton's hand. He nodded to Uncle Lionel, who nodded back.

Jesse peered around the door. "S'cuse me, but we got more trouble. Robbery at the LaSalle Jewelry Store. The manager got hurt."

"When?" Marcus said.

"Around nine o'clock last night. The manager was getting ready to leave with the day's receipts when they hit. They got away with loose diamonds, a shipment of Colombian emeralds that came in two days ago, and some of the more expensive pieces." Jesse spoke in a rush. "An employee found him this morning."

"Found him?" Nicole's heart thumped at the way Jesse shook his head.

"They took him to the hospital, but he's got massive head injuries," Jesse replied. "He's in a coma."

"So, he can't tell the police anything. Damn!" Marcus rubbed his forehead.

Dayna Tyler strode in seconds later. "Afternoon everybody. Sorry to interrupt. Marcus, we need to talk."

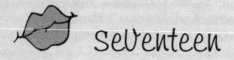 seventeen

Nicole walked around the conference table. "Hello, Detective Tyler. We can talk right here."

The statuesque detective paused, then gave a curt nod toward Stanton and Uncle Lionel. "Introduce us."

"Mr. Stanton Summers and Mr. Lionel Summers. They are very much involved in what happens to Summers Security," Marcus said. He glanced from Dayna to Nicole. He needed to head off a battle of wills. Instead he seemed to have fanned the flames.

Though she didn't say anything, Nicole's heated glance sent him a clear message. She looked at Dayna. "My father and uncle most certainly can hear whatever you have to say."

"Fine with me. While we're at it, let's call the media, because they'll love this story," Dayna shot back. She stared hard at Nicole. "You've got a theft ring operating right under your nose."

"What!" Stanton blurted out.

"Oh crap!" Uncle Lionel clapped a hand to his forehead.

"I said Nicole would destroy all my father and I built. No one would listen." Russell stood in the open conference room door. He crossed his arms and glared at Nicole.

"There's gotta be some kinda mistake." Jesse shook his head. "Can't be. We got problems, but—"

Cat pushed the door shut with a bang. Russell jumped clear to avoid getting his rear end snapped. "I'll get sodas for everybody. Denise will help." She hurried over to Nicole and whispered to her.

"Immediately, Cat. Thanks," Nicole replied. Cat left through the side door leading to Nicole's office. "Have a seat, Detective Tyler."

Dayna sat down. She wore a stylish short-sleeved denim jacket with a white T-shirt beneath it and dark denim slacks. She rolled her shoulders as much to get comfortable as to relax. Marcus caught a glimpse of a black shoulder strap before she pulled the jacket closed again.

"Thanks. Sorry to be so abrupt. It's been a bad day. A detective from the robbery division is interviewing your staff right now," she said. "We're working together because this seems connected to the burglaries at the Phoung business."

"You walked in and started interrogating my employees without telling me?" Nicole said.

"To say we're investigating a serious crime isn't a cliché from some cop show on television. Time is critical. I was going to tell Marcus," Dayna said calmly.

"I'm CEO," Nicole clipped back.

"I wasn't sure who these gentlemen were and if you'd want me to speak freely in front of them." Dayna gazed at her steadily.

"Quite reasonable. Nicole, wouldn't you agree?" Nicole's father gave her a pointed look.

"Of course," Nicole said after a few moments. She sighed. "My day hasn't exactly been fun so far either. I apologize for being touchy."

"You've got reason." Dayna's harsh manner eased as she visibly relaxed.

"You can understand our reaction. A security company has to inspire complete trust in our procedures and employees," Marcus said.

"Humph! You can kiss trust goodbye then," Russell retorted. "I'll have a hard time getting us back on track after *this*."

"You're not in the CEO chair yet, Russ. Nothing guarantees you ever will be," Uncle Lionel growled at him.

"I wonder what it will take before you people wake up!" Russell hit the table with his fist.

"Enough!" Stanton stood up as his basso voice boomed. Everyone blinked in shock.

Dayna even sat up straight as though at attention. "Damn, sounds like our commander," she said in an undertone.

Marcus strode over to stand beside Nicole's father. "Mr. Summers is right. Now isn't the time or place to hash out such issues."

"Tell us what you've found out, Detective Tyler." Stanton sat down again, but not before he sent an icy warning look around at everyone.

"Yes, sir." Dayna slipped a small pad from a jacket pocket. "Store manager Glenn Howard was ambushed as he closed the shop. The last employee left a few minutes before nine. She says Howard was on his way out then. The shop closed at six. They usually left by seven-thirty. Because of a shipment and payroll they had to stay later than usual. There was no forced entry. We think one of two things happened. Someone

Howard knew came to the door, he let them in, and was beaten. Or they caught him still in the door and forced him to disarm the alarm."

A tall white man came in and beckoned to Dayna. "Excuse me."

"This is Detective Bates." Dayna got up and went to him. They spoke in a low tone for several minutes.

"I don't like this one bit." Nicole eyed the two police officers.

Marcus exchanged a glance with Russell, who sneered back. Nicole's father and uncle talked low with their heads together. Marcus moved closer to Nicole protectively. Dayna nodded once to something Bates said, and they parted. Bates left again.

"Your employee Tameka Grant was arrested two hours ago trying to sell a diamond pendant stolen from LaSalle Jewelry last night," Dayna said.

"Oh God," Jesse muttered and covered his eyes.

"The lady has incredibly bad luck. She got caught in an entirely different sting. The robbery division set up a fake storefront to buy stolen merchandise. Apparently Tameka got impatient and decided to cash in fast." Dayna wore a tight expression.

"She worked in David Phoung's stores. I knew there was a good reason I didn't like her," Nicole said.

"Tameka isn't a one-woman crime wave, folks. We've got more going on here." Dayna looked at Marcus. "I'm real sorry, but get ready for a long day with us underfoot. We're going to need office space."

"No problem," Marcus said.

"We'll need employee files. We'd like to get in touch with as many people as possible," Dayna added.

"My secretary will make the arrangements," Nicole said. She hit the speaker button on the phone at her elbow and gave instructions to Cat.

While she spoke, Marcus pulled Dayna aside. "You have a sense of how bad this looks?"

"For you guys? Bad," Dayna said quietly. "I'm talking gang connections, Marcus. I can't say more right now."

"Cat is showing Detective Bates to our file room. Might as well use it, since it's big enough and the employee records are already there. You'll have a phone, fax machine, and copier close at hand, too."

"Perfect." Dayna put both hands on her waist. "Listen, I know this is a real rough ride for you folks. Best thing we can do is wrap it up fast so you can get back to business."

Russell grimaced. "What's left of it."

"I'll check in with you later," Dayna said to Marcus and walked out.

"I'm gonna talk to the owner, Hector LaSalle," Jesse said as he stood. "Better check out the security system soon."

"Get back fast in case the detectives need you," Nicole replied.

"Okay." Jesse strode off.

"Well." Uncle Lionel drummed his fingers on the conference table.

"We'd better start working on our disaster plan, Nicole." Stanton wore a grave expression.

"Exactly," Uncle Lionel agreed. He hunched his shoulders and sat forward. "First, can we keep the fact that our employee is a suspect quiet?"

"Depends. Let's check the newspapers and watch the television." Nicole called Cat again with instructions to bring in newspapers. Then she opened a cabinet containing a television and video equipment.

"Maybe Dayna can help us out. I'll ask her." Feeling jumpy, Marcus got up and paced while he thought. "Our customers are bound to hear about it."

"You better do something and quick," Uncle Lionel grumbled.

"I agree." Nicole turned to Marcus. "We've identified the employees who have given us the most problems. Once they finish talking to the police we can either suspend them immediately or terminate the worst offenders."

"Jesse wanted to work with several of them. We're talking about people who need their jobs." Marcus rubbed his jaw. "Jesse and I know how valuable a second chance can be."

"Forget that bleeding heart stuff!" Uncle Lionel cut in before Nicole could reply. "Those people are stealing your clients blind and are well on their way to destroying this company."

"Now you see the quality of decision making around here, Uncle Lionel," Russell put in.

Marcus struggled against a tide of rage. He looked at Uncle Lionel. "*If* more than one employee is involved, the planning started long before Nicole came."

"Good point," Russell said promptly with a nasty smile. "While you were the boss courtesy of my senile father."

Nicole's eyes flashed fire. "You were in charge of hiring and background checks, Russell."

"Everyone knows I was never given the authority I should have had once Dad hired Marcus. Don't try to shift this off your boyfriend."

Nicole leaned across the table with a forefinger pointed at Russell's chest. "Keep talking and you'll find my foot up your—"

"She even helped pay for baby-sitters so the thieves could be free to commit robberies. Nice going, cousin." Russell's lip curled with scorn.

"You're pathetic." Nicole glared back at him.

"Stop it!" Stanton roared. "Obviously this kind of conflict distracted you both."

"Along with other things," Uncle Lionel mumbled and glanced from Nicole to Marcus.

Stanton looked at Nicole with a taut frown. "You wanted to be in charge with no interference. Fine. Put together a plan to deal with this situation and be ready to present it to us in two days."

Nicole didn't flinch as she returned her father's gaze. "I will."

Stanton turned to Russell. "Don't have too much fun gloating. If this company fails, a chunk of your income goes with it. You should have worked harder to help Nicole."

"Me? You can't possibly try to blame me." Russell's mouth flapped open.

"Yes, I can. And so will the family. Lionel and I will start forming a board right now." Stanton looked at them. "We'll use the conference room."

Marcus cleared his throat. "We'll get started, too. Come on, Nicole and Russell. Let's meet in my office."

"At least one of you sees the value of working together." Uncle Lionel pulled the phone toward him and picked up the receiver. "Better not use the speaker for these calls," he muttered.

"You didn't see fit to let me in on things before now. Now you want me to share the blame. No way." Russell started to leave.

"You will cooperate with them or I'll make damn sure your behavior in this crisis is discussed at the board meeting." Stanton's voice cracked like a whip.

Russell's café au lait skin went pale. "Yes, sir," he mumbled.

"And Russell," Stanton barked louder.

"Yes, Uncle Stanton?"

"I mean cooperate in the sense of offering constructive input. We don't have time to deal with tantrums." Stanton shot a warning glance at Nicole. "Are we all on the same page?"

"Yes." Nicole clamped her lips together, turned, and strode through the side door to her office.

Marcus motioned for Russell to go ahead of him. Russell kept his expression blank as he followed Nicole.

After Marcus closed the door no one spoke for several minutes. Nicole stood with her back to them, gazing out the window. Russell sat down in a chair that put the most distance between him and Nicole's desk. He crossed his arms. With a sigh, Marcus decided he had to break the impasse.

"We need to find a way to work together. Now is the perfect time," Marcus said. Neither responded. "Well?"

"Jesse and I went over the records of several suspect employees. We have grounds for termination. Maybe Russell could pair up with him and have those exit interviews," Nicole said finally.

"I should never have been cut out of the process," Russell complained.

"Let me remind you why," Nicole snapped as she spun around.

"Nikki, don't," Marcus said low.

Russell glanced from him to Nicole. "Yes, *Nikki*. We're supposed to cooperate."

"Nicole's suggestion is a good one. She wants you to play a critical role. I thought that's what you wanted." Marcus glared at him.

"Could have happened sooner," Russell mumbled. Then he squared his shoulders. "I'll get with Jesse."

"Why don't you call him now? He's in the process of rounding up those people." Marcus gestured toward the phone on Nicole's desk.

Russell seemed about to argue, then thought better of it. "Fine."

"Nicole, let's sit down," Marcus said in a calm tone. He felt like a grade school assistant principal dealing with squabbling students.

"Yeah, right," she replied.

Nicole marched over to the round table in a corner of her spacious office. She sat down hard in one of five leather chairs arranged around it. With a sigh he followed her.

"Listen, your father is right. This isn't the time to fight each other," Marcus said quietly.

Nicole tapped a fist on the arm of her chair for several seconds. Finally she nodded assent. "So, let's start working on mission impossible. No way will we keep our customers from hearing rumors of some kind. My question is, do we confess everything and risk losing customers or do we try to filter information?"

"We can't tell customers anything that might compromise the police investigation. Otherwise I say we should be as open as possible."

"I don't know." Nicole shook her head. "Admitting we hired thieves to guard their valuables won't inspire confidence."

"Let's ask Imani, since she's the marketing expert," Marcus said.

"Now we're looking for ways to spin the bad news. Geez, what a mess." Nicole squeezed her eyes shut.

"The truth is there is no good way to talk about a breakdown in our system. I'm suggesting we find the least bad way to present it." He waved to get Russell's attention. "Call Imani and ask her to come in."

"I'd thought of getting her input," Russell said in an aside as he continued talking to Jesse.

"Wonderful," she muttered and massaged her temples, but she stopped when she saw Russell glance at her.

Marcus felt a flush of pride in her grace under fire. He gazed at Nicole as she sat straighter and lifted her chin. The cobalt blue jacket and matching skirt made her honey skin look even more delectable. Even taking care of business she stirred a fire in him. Suddenly Marcus wanted to take Nicole into his arms and comfort her. Russell's voice reminded him that he could not.

"Of course I know that, Jesse," Russell said, biting off the syllables in irritation. He hung up and punched the keypad. Moments later he was talking to Imani in an officious tone.

"The Russell Summers art of alienating people. That's what I have to put up with." Nicole looked at her cousin with a sour expression.

"I feel the same pain. Remember I've been here with him longer than you." Marcus leaned closer to her as he spoke.

Nicole's taut frown eased somewhat when she looked at Marcus. "Reason enough for you to earn a high salary," she deadpanned.

Russell came toward them with a purposeful stride. "Jesse says the first employee will be here in an hour."

Marcus nodded. "Good. Might as well get it over with. We were just discussing how to inform our customers."

"Inform them? That's suicide. I say we keep quiet except to answer questions if they call," Russell said.

"If we let rumors run wild and keep silent, they'll think we have something to hide. Trust me, speculation can be even more damaging than telling them as much as possible," Nicole replied.

Marcus silently gave her points for her composed response. "Nicole is right. Keeping secrets will only make them trust us even less. We've got to take the initiative."

Imani came in. "I caught the tail end of your comment, but you're absolutely correct. We can't let them hear it from our competitors."

"Or worse, hear it on the evening news," Nicole added.

"Maybe Imani has a point," Russell admitted grudgingly. "I took communications classes in college. I could write out a script for Nicole. She'll need to be coached on handling the media."

"Having a speech that sounds like a script is exactly what we don't want," Imani said quickly. She sat down at the table and turned on her PDA. "Marcus and Nicole, you're seen as leaders of this company. Be yourselves and be truthful, up to a point."

"Marcus. It's always him," Russell muttered under his breath.

"Yes, Marcus," Imani cut in before Nicole could speak. "Like it or not, Russell, Marcus has tremendous credibility. Nicole is still considered inexperienced."

"They're wondering if I can handle the company, let alone this disaster." Nicole nervously tapped the arm of her chair with one fist again.

"Since you said it, yes." Imani nodded. "Now is the time to show them you can. Let's show them how we respond to a breach in our own system."

"Tell them we've tightened our internal security, that precautions in today's world must evolve, and we're prepared to be ahead of trends," Nicole said.

Imani grinned in approval. "Good. Criminals stay up late thinking of ways around security systems. We're staying up even later."

"Sounds like an ad campaign," Marcus said.

"I agree. Let's develop print ads and develop a television thirty-second spot." Nicole leaned toward Imani.

"Damn, boss, that's a great idea. You're a quick study." Imani attached a keyboard to her PDA and entered notes.

"When should we start calling our clients, Marcus?" Nicole looked at him.

Jacinta stuck her head in the door. "Heads up, people. A pal of mine that works at the newspaper says the LaSalle robbery will be in the *Chronicle* tomorrow. He also says the manager has taken a turn for the worse."

Marcus looked at Nicole. "Tomorrow?"

"Yeah," she said and rubbed her temples again.

"Gotta run." Jacinta disappeared.

"Me, too. I'll work on these ads." Imani detached the keyboard and stood.

"Keep the costs down." Russell frowned at her. "I mean, we could be losing business. I think we need to economize."

"Russell—" Nicole's eyes narrowed to slits.

"He's got a good point to a degree," Marcus jumped in to head off another battle. "No need to give the board more to complain about."

"I can do the graphics and write the copy. That will save us money. Andre can help me do a simple video ad using our digital equipment and computer." Imani looked at Nicole.

"Print space and television airtime are both expensive," Russell put in.

"I can still save money depending on which channels we choose and the time of day the commercials are shown," Imani said to him.

"Do a budget and we'll look at it." Nicole turned to Russell. "How's that?"

"Those ads could bring us more business. Something we'll need if customers dump us," Marcus put in.

"I'm willing to listen after we look at the figures," Russell replied.

"Thanks." Nicole pursed her lips as though restraining more words.

"I can have the total in one hour." Imani left.

"I'd better get with Jesse to make sure he's prepared. Leave a message with my secretary if you need me again." Russell strode out with a determined expression.

"You did very well," Marcus murmured to Nicole. He put a hand on her arm and kneaded her rigid muscles.

"Remind me again why I want this job." Nicole squeezed her eyes shut.

"To show the world you can handle a challenge, which you're doing," he added firmly.

"I'm in over my head. I know it, my family knows it, and pretty soon the world will know it." Nicole's bottom lip trembled.

"We're going to get through this together. Even Russell is trying to be helpful." When Nicole let out a snort, Marcus grinned at her. "In his own unique way."

Nicole tried to smile and failed. Her eyes glittered with unshed tears. "I love you for trying, but it's no good. I'm not CEO material. My family was right."

Marcus felt a rush of heat. "Say that again."

"My family never thought I could take on such a big job and they were right. I—"

"No, the first thing you said about love." Marcus put his arms around her.

She rested her head on his shoulder. "You're the only person who believes in me. I love you for it," she whispered.

"And for other reasons, I hope." Marcus kissed her forehead.

"Lots of them." Nicole relaxed in his embrace.

"Same here," he replied.

Marcus kissed her nose, then her mouth. Nicole moaned softly as her lips parted. For one intense moment they took comfort in each other. More than physical, the emotional connection hit him with such force that he felt dazed by the blow. Seconds later they pulled away from each other with effort. Nicole stroked his cheek once, then tugged at her jacket and glanced around.

"Last thing I need is for Daddy or Uncle Lionel to catch me kissing you during business hours." Nicole went to her desk. She took a cosmetic mirror from her desk drawer and stared critically at her lipstick.

"Have they said anything about us?" Marcus grabbed a tissue from a nearby dispenser and dabbed at his own mouth.

Nicole went into her private rest room. When she came out her lipstick was perfect again. She brushed off her jacket and skirt before sitting at her desk.

"The usual, office romances are a bad thing, I'm not giving the company my full attention blah, blah, blah." Nicole fluttered a hand as though brushing away their criticisms.

"I'm sure they mentioned how different we are, our backgrounds I mean." Marcus studied her.

"To tell you the truth I stopped listening two seconds into their spiel. I let them know that my personal life is my own. End of story." Nicole smoothed her hair in place.

"Not hardly, Nicole." Marcus was about to say more when Nicole's father and uncle came in from the conference room.

"We'll have our first meeting next Thursday. Couldn't get everybody together any sooner." Uncle Lionel looked less than pleased.

"Just as well. Maybe we'll have some positive developments by then," Marcus replied. The two men looked from Marcus to Nicole with stern expressions.

Marcus walked over and stood beside Nicole. "I'm sure we will," he said in a definite tone.

"Humph!" Uncle Lionel said as he left.

"I hope so," Stanton said and followed Uncle Lionel out.

Nicole looked up at Marcus. "Have you lost your mind? No way will we have 'positive developments' a week from now."

Marcus wondered just what had gotten into him. Still, he placed a hand on her shoulder. "Be optimistic. Dayna could crack the case by then. We could keep the fallout with our customers to a minimum and bounce right back."

"Uh-huh. All that will happen by next week, along with a snowstorm in hell." Nicole shook her head.

Marcus touched her cheek. "I happen to think anything is possible these days," he said softly.

Nicole grasped his hand tightly, then let go. "Okay, you've got me convinced. Now clear out of my office so I can concentrate on something other than your fine body."

"Yes, ma'am. We've got a long day ahead of us. I'd feel a lot better knowing you're at the end of it."

She gazed at him with a sigh. "Oh, yes. Your apartment?"

"It's a date."

He planted a quick kiss on the top of her head, then went to his office. Staff scurried around like mice on special missions. The phones rang nonstop. Marcus calmed two agitated secretaries, smoothed out a dispute between two employees, and checked in with Dayna on the way. Even as turmoil swirled around him, Marcus felt joy deep down. Nicole loved him.

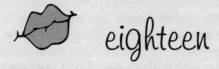 eighteen

"Loose ends drive me nuts." Dayna twisted an ink pen as she frowned.

"Like we get all the loose ends tied up even when we solve a case," Detective Bates replied with a shake of his head.

"I know. I should be used to it by now, but I'm not, damn it. I want to know who done it and why." Dayna shuffled papers on the desk before her.

"Which makes you a good cop," Marcus put in.

"Hmm." Dayna seemed to have tuned out everything.

He'd sat quietly waiting for the two detectives to explain why they'd called him in. Even though it was seven o'clock at night, the office still buzzed with activity. Marcus hadn't spoken to Nicole since leaving her office five hours ago. Yet he burned with the anticipation of having her in his arms soon. If only he could give Nicole some good news.

"Learn anything useful yet?" Marcus tried to read upside down and failed.

"Can't tell you. Everyone is a suspect." Dayna looked up

at him, her dark brows drawn together. "Including Ms. In-Charge."

"Nicole is the least likely suspect. She doesn't need to steal because her daddy's got big money. Her mama comes from money."

"My grandmother used to sing a favorite old blues song called 'God Bless the Child That's Got It's Own.'" Dayna sat back with a guarded cop expression.

"Come on," Marcus said with a grunt.

"Maybe Daddy wouldn't come across with the cash for some reason. Say they think she hooked up with Mr. Wrong." Dayna lifted a shoulder.

"Okay, now you're in my business. Is this the cop talking?" Marcus squinted at her.

Irritation flashed across her face. "I'm trained to examine human motivations."

"Yeah." Marcus continued to stare at her.

Dayna blinked first by looking away. "All right, smart-mouthed rich girls tick me off in a special way. Guess I'm just pissed. I missed the signs when I got the Phoung case."

Marcus switched gears to get information. "Signs?"

"I shouldn't have been so quick to dismiss this place as being the connection. Now Robbery is gonna get the glory." She tossed a sheaf of papers aside in a gesture of self-disgust.

"You're going to be a big part of the investigation. Maybe you'll move over to Robbery on your way to that big promotion you deserve." Marcus hunched forward, ready to move into his own set of questions.

"Real smooth, but don't get your hopes up. I can't give you any information," Dayna said before he could speak.

"I need to know if any of our employees look dirty, Dayna. Our company is on the line."

"You've heard the phrase innocent until proven guilty, I'm

sure. We're following up on all leads," she intoned as though speaking at a press conference.

"Which tells me nothing," Marcus said with a frown.

"Now you get it," Dayna wisecracked.

"So funny," Marcus grumbled and sat against the back of the chair. "I'm about to lose six years of hard work, and you give me Comedy Central."

"Okay, you help me and I'll help you." Dayna crossed her arms.

"How?"

"Tell me more about Nicole. I hear she's a spoiled party girl who is only serious about the next shopping trip. How does she end up running a successful business? Who were her pals before she started working here?"

"Nicole is intelligent and her late Uncle Hosea saw skills her own parents didn't see. As for her friends, from what I gather they're all pretty much like her. You know the profile, old money and old family names." Marcus shook his head. "Not fertile ground for the America's Most Wanted list."

"Humph, you'd be surprised. Mummy and Daddy cut off the funds and suddenly you've got classy thieves. Toss in a drug problem and stealing comes easy."

"Not Nicole," Marcus said in a tight voice.

"She got into some trouble seven years ago. Seems our princess got wasted and took a swing at somebody." Dayna tilted her head to one side.

"Seven years ago she did something stupid. We all did at one time or another," Marcus replied. "Nicole paid a small fine for public disturbance."

"No signs she's drinking too much or got some shady friends hanging around?" Dayna frowned. "I'm assuming you'd tell me if she did."

"No to both questions and maybe I would, maybe I wouldn't," Marcus shot back.

"You're not objective. I wonder if you could see the warning signals," Dayna replied.

"No, I'm not," Marcus said evenly. "But that doesn't have anything to do with the facts. You won't find a trail that leads to her."

Dayna wore a crooked smile after a few seconds of gazing back at him. "Just testing the waters. Sure wish I had a guy sticking up for me with such passion."

Marcus relaxed. "You will one of these days."

She held up a palm. "Don't tell me some guy will be lucky to have me, blazy-blah."

"Okay, even though it's true." Marcus grinned at her. His smile faded when a thought occurred to him. "Who told you about Nicole's little run-in with the law in Louisiana?"

"Guess."

"Russell. I should string him up." Marcus clenched his hands into fists.

"He doesn't like his cousin at all. He's not that wild about you either." Dayna laughed. "Don't worry, I saw through him fast."

Marcus waved a hand. "Russell swings from being a minor nuisance to a major pain. He and his father didn't get along. Mr. Summers may have been unfair toward him for years, but Russell didn't help."

"So I heard. Could be he's taking revenge against his father and Nicole." Dayna rocked her chair back and forth. "Now there's a possibility. If he can't have the company, no one can."

"Russell couldn't plan a one-float parade, let alone a slick criminal operation." Marcus gave a short, humorless laugh. "Not that I wouldn't love to see his aristocratic ass in jail."

Dayna grinned. "Yeah."

"Your turn. I know you can't tell me a lot, but give me something." Marcus leaned forward.

"We pulled up the arrest record of Tameka Grant. Three years ago she had a charge of harboring a fugitive. It was dropped. The people we're looking at have some shifty acquaintances." Dayna waved a legal-sized sheet of paper.

"Can I see that?" Marcus nodded at the sheet. Dayna handed it to him. He scanned the faxed copy. "Two years before she was hired here."

"Yeah. Recognize any of her buddies?" Dayna handed him three more sheets.

He scanned them. A name stirred a memory. "Olandon D'Jarrod Jackson," he mumbled.

Marcus blinked hard. Shaun's cousin had literally been their partner in crime on more than one occasion, except Olandon had progressed to more serious offenses. Marcus had finished college and Shaun had earned an associate degree, just barely. Olandon had been studying his chosen profession in various jails and prisons for the past twelve years.

"Somebody you know?" Dayna stared at the list as though trying to see what held his interest.

His old habit of protecting a partner from the 'hood kicked in. "Nah, just thinking out loud. Can I get a copy of these?"

"Why?"

"Nicole has to know. She is my boss," Marcus added when Dayna started to object.

Dayna continued to gaze at him a beat longer. "All right. I can print out another one. Just don't tell that idiot Russell. He's got an itch to be the hero. He wants to be the boss bad."

"Oh, yeah," Marcus said, his thoughts on the list of names he held.

"You don't seem too worried. He's got plenty of ammunition against Nicole." Dayna tapped a finger on a stack of reports detailing the thefts.

"We'll see what the board thinks." Marcus frowned as he carefully folded the sheets of paper.

"Are you gonna tell me?"

Marcus glanced up to find himself the subject of Dayna's piercing scrutiny. Marcus forced his facial muscles to relax. "You know it all, Detective. I've got a super-sized mess on my hands. I don't think the board will seriously consider putting Russell in charge of anything more than office supplies. That doesn't mean Nicole won't have problems."

"Interesting dilemma. If they decide you should be CEO, there could be real trouble in love land." Dayna pursed her lips. Her expression almost suggested she'd welcome such a development.

Marcus stood. "They could fire us both. I've been working here longer than Nicole."

"Russell is at least smart enough to know he needs you. If Summers Security is the center, then someone has done a good camouflage job."

"Until Tameka slipped." He slapped the folded reports against the palm of one hand.

"Solid police work and stupid criminals, a combination that warms my heart," Dayna wisecracked. "Remember, don't tell Russell. Knowing him, he'd tell some of the employees before we have a chance to follow up."

"Gotcha. Thanks, Dayna."

Marcus left the small office she'd turned into her interview room. He forgot about Russell in seconds. Instead he turned over the issue of how to approach Shaun. They hadn't spoken in almost two weeks. Looking back over their last conversation, Marcus felt bad about the clumsy way he'd handled it. Shaun's ego had been bruised. Still, deep down Marcus realized that the distance between them was growing by the day. Despite what Shaun believed, Nicole was not the reason. They both wanted the fine life they'd dreamed of as ghetto kids. Unlike Shaun, Marcus drifted away from the old methods of getting there.

"I just hope this dude's name popping up is a mad coincidence," Marcus whispered to himself.

Nicole stepped out of the shower and wrapped the oversized terry cloth around her. Steam fogged the mirrors. Humming along with a tune coming from the radio, she walked to the front section of her master bathroom. Marcus watched her from where he sat in the wide Jacuzzi-styled bathtub. Jets sent swirls of hot water over his muscular body.

"You really should have joined me in here." He sighed and rested his head on the cushioned ledge.

"Not for me. I prefer having pulsating streams of water pound my troubles away."

Nicole sat down and let the towel fall. She poured creamy lotion into her hand, then massaged it into her skin. The honey almond scent soothed her jangled nerves even more. Marcus splashed around in the tub. None of the nasty details of the day had followed them into this sanctuary. Suddenly Marcus was standing behind her. He picked up the ceramic bottle of lotion.

"Let me help."

He poured lotion across the length of her shoulders, then spread both his large hands flat and made circular motions down her back. Nicole closed her eyes to better savor the sensation. When he reached around to gently knead her biceps, Nicole moaned with pleasure.

"You're better than my aunt Jacquelyn's hideously expensive New Orleans masseuse." Nicole squirmed at the tingle of sexual hunger growing in her pelvis.

"I minored in kinesiology, even took a few acupressure courses." Marcus kneaded her biceps as he spoke in a soft voice.

"I'm not sure what that is, but I like it. I feel tranquil and energized at the same time," she murmured. Her body went limp from his tender attention.

"That's the point, to bring the body back into balance," he replied.

"Umm-hum." Nicole rested her head against his belly. "Balance is a good thing."

Marcus laughed deep in his throat. He bent forward and nuzzled her neck just behind one ear. Nicole turned around until she faced him, still seated. She planted delicate kisses across the flat, firm flesh of his stomach, then down, teasing him until he cried out. His fingers combed through her hair.

Nicole looked up at him, totally relishing the sight of his tall physique. Tiny beads of moisture made his toasted brown skin glisten. He gazed into her eyes with his lips slightly parted. His breath hissed like steam. The effect drove her to want him so much it was an ache between her thighs. She drew back and spread the thick wide terry towel on the floor. Marcus knelt on it, bringing her down with him. When she lay down, he stretched his powerful body on top of hers.

"I love you, baby," Marcus whispered.

"I love you back." Nicole wrapped herself around him.

Their lovemaking was slow, deliberate, and delicious. Every movement seemed choreographed, yet perfectly natural. His rhythmic thrusts drove Nicole wild, then eased her back from the edge. After what seemed like a forever of mind-bending bliss, Nicole took control. She pushed against his strapping body until he got the message and flipped onto his back. Once on top she rode him hard and didn't stop until they came together.

"Wow," Marcus panted.

Nicole lifted her hips, then lay atop him as though he were a firm mattress. She whimpered when he stroked her buttocks. "I'm so balanced my head is spinning," she gasped.

"Me, too. I think the phone is ringing." Marcus didn't move.

"Hmmm." Nicole didn't move either.

"Baby," he whispered in her ear. "Too much is going on right now. Better answer it."

"I'm not ready to leave paradise," Nicole mumbled with her eyes closed.

"Neither am I, but we've got alligators snapping at our butts." Marcus gave her buttock a playful swat to emphasize his point.

"Damn! You've got to be Mr. Practical at this very minute?" Nicole extricated her arms and legs from his and got up. She padded to the phone before the answering service could cut in on the sixth ring. "Hello. Yeah, Russell. No, you're not interrupting us. Cut the opening monologue and tell me why you called."

As she listened to his report, Marcus padded in wearing the robe she'd bought for him. He sat down on the edge of her queen-sized bed. Nicole rolled her eyes at him to signal she was fed up with her cousin.

"Okay, I'll call Jesse and see what he thinks. I'm not questioning your word, but—"

"Tact," Marcus whispered.

"Fine, fine. I'll talk to you both tomorrow." Nicole tossed the cordless phone onto the bed. It bounced once and landed on the thick carpet.

Marcus retrieved it and put it back in the charger cradle. "Cool down."

She stomped one foot and let out a loud growl of frustration. "Lucky for him his neck isn't within reach right about now."

"What did he say?" Marcus reclined on the pile of pillows on the bed. He patted the sheet next to him.

"They interviewed staff after your pal got through with them. Several were shaking in their shoes and confessed to doing stuff we didn't know about, hadn't even suspected." Nicole lay down beside him and took a deep breath to steady her nerves.

"Like what?"

"Nothing criminal, just lying on their time sheets and covering for each other. Bad enough, since the company paid overtime as a result." Nicole shifted to snuggle closer into the crook of his arm.

"If it goes back far enough, we could be talking big money." Marcus combed his finger through her hair. He frowned in thought.

"I'm going to meet with them and get the details. At least Russell didn't jump the gun and fire anybody."

"See? Even Russell can use good judgment in a crisis," Marcus replied.

"Please! Jesse had to tell him." Nicole propped herself on an elbow. "You mentioned alligators. Well, I feel like I'm surrounded by them. There's Russell, our customers, the police, and my family. I can't take much more."

"Yes, you can. *We* can." Marcus enfolded her in a protective embrace.

"I don't want them to take it out on you," Nicole said.

"Your family can't throw anything at me I can't handle."

"Don't let those fancy manners fool you."

"If fighting your family bothers you that much, then give in. Quit. You'll be free to shop in the middle of the day and party all night again."

Nicole gazed at him through slits. "Be very careful, Reed."

He shrugged. "I'm just saying. You made a good showing for a few weeks. Nobody can say you didn't try."

"I'm not going to ride off into the sunset to the nearest mall," Nicole snapped.

His full mouth curved up at the corners. "Just checking."

She poked his side with a finger. "You're so obvious. Okay, no more whining. Tomorrow I'll deal with it like a grown-up."

"With me close by," he added. "You can whine to me anytime, baby. No one is going to hurt you unless they go through me first."

"Let's try to forget again. For a few more hours at least."

Nicole rested her head on his chest as he caressed her back with his long fingers. She closed her eyes, and Marcus kissed her eyelids. The rest of the night he did a fine job of keeping the shadows away.

nineteen

Marcus hesitated, then pushed the button. Chimes played a tune inside Shaun's town house. Moments later the door swung open. Shaun leaned against it and stared at him. His gaze seemed to dare Marcus to come in. Ignoring the attitude, Marcus walked past him into the living room.

"What's up?" Marcus glanced around. Two long-stemmed goblets of amber liquor were on the cocktail table.

"Just kickin' back enjoying my solitude." Shaun shoved the door closed.

"Uh-huh." Marcus nodded to the glasses.

"I don't do dishes that often." Shaun picked up both goblets and took them into the kitchen. He came back immediately. "Okay, now you tell me what's up."

"You must have heard about all the stuff going down at Summers Security." Marcus sat on the sofa.

Shaun stood over him. "Nah, I'm too busy with my own thang, if you know what I mean."

Marcus bit off a comment about Aliyah keeping him up to

date. No need to make their conversation tougher than it had to be just yet. "Right, right. One of our customers was robbed, a jewelry store. The manager was badly beaten."

"Damn, that's too bad. Crime is out of hand." Shaun cocked his head to one side and waited.

"Yeah. So, how've you been doing?" Marcus propped an ankle across his knee.

"Pretty good. Look at me forgetting my manners. I'll get us something refreshingly cold."

Marcus said nothing as Shaun went to the kitchen again. He came back carrying two bottles of imported beer and a bowl of corn chips. Shaun wore an easy smile.

"Like I said, I've got no complaints." Shaun handed Marcus one of the bottles. He put the bowl on the cocktail table. "Sounds like you've got troubles," he said casually.

"The police are looking into crimes committed against our clients in the last two years." Marcus got a handful of chips and ate them.

"Hell, Houston has crime everywhere. The thugs make sure of that, man." Shaun let out a gruff laugh. "Your girlfriend is getting a real shock, huh?"

"Nicole has led a totally different life, for sure." Marcus took a sip of beer.

"She might as well learn now. How else is she going to understand the risks of the security business?" Shaun stretched out his long legs.

"I hate to see her getting all kinds of pressure. She really has tried hard to be a good CEO." Marcus stared down at the dark green bottle he rolled between his palms.

"Okay, so she gets credit for effort. It's your call, but I still don't see why you sweatin' her problem. You got played once." Shaun glanced at him.

"Nicole needs me and I'm going to be there for her. I was angry at first about the way things went down, but not anymore."

"Sweet happy ever after." The scorn in Shaun's voice leaked out.

Marcus looked up at him. "Something like that."

"Be a country club member and hang with the upper crust, you mean."

"I don't give a damn about being in the Who's Who club, Shaun. I want a reason to look over my shoulder."

Shaun's eyes glittered with anger. "You talkin' to me?"

"If the shoe fits, then wear it good," Marcus shot back.

"Oh, so now we're coming to the real reason you stopped by. This isn't a friendly visit to hang with your boy. Wait, I forgot we're not boys anymore." Shaun glared at him.

"I've got different goals. Don't make this some kinda test of our friendship." Marcus leaned forward and thumped the bottle down on the cocktail table.

"A test. Guess you're right. When your friends need you and you don't step up, then you get a failing grade," Shaun replied.

"How about respect for a friend's right to choose his own path?" Marcus gazed back at him.

Shaun sprang from his seat and jabbed a finger at Marcus. "Don't give me that talk show crap! Two months ago you were itching to put a knife into the heart of Summers Security. Now you're looking down your nose at me."

"You're crazy." Marcus stared up at him.

"Don't even try it. I blew it off when you started kissin' the old man's ass. Just knew my partner had a plan." Shaun gave a snort of disgust. He spun around with a twisted smile. "Yeah, right."

"True, my first instinct was to get payback ghetto style. Then I thought it over. My grandmother always said don't live down to expectations just because you grew up in the Fifth Ward." Marcus stood to face his accusations.

"Don't play me, man! Nicole is your ticket to respectability. You wanna leave behind all your baggage, your crazy mama, your jailbird daddy, and *me*." Shaun slapped a palm to his chest.

"You're going too far, Shaun." Marcus clenched both hands tight.

"Think you can snap your fingers and be one of them? Nicole will dump you fast even if she doesn't find out the whole truth. And don't try to tell me you've spilled it all," Shaun spat.

"I have to say you hid it well, man." Marcus tried to feel anger, but sadness filled him.

"You started changing when old man Summers filled your head. Driving around like you own the damn world. I asked you to come in business with me and you turned up your nose."

"What are you talking about? That insurance scam wouldn't have worked."

"It didn't just start with Nicole and you know it. A year ago I could have closed a big contract to consult with one of your customers. What did you say?"

"So, I'm supposed to let you use me? I don't think so. The friendship test goes two ways. Instead of carrying a grudge you could have understood where I wanted to be in life."

"Uh-huh," Shaun grunted. "Look where ass kissin' and loyalty got you. Good thing I've got some *real* friends on the hook."

They stared at each other for at least sixty seconds. Neither heard the steady thudding bass of hip-hop music coming from the speakers of Shaun's sound system. Marcus heard a click-clack in his head as pieces fell into place.

"Like Olandon?" he asked in a hushed voice.

"I've got lots of friends, man. Forget it. You're trippin' these days." Shaun turned away.

"Tell me about the business deals with your real friends. Another thing, I didn't mention a theft ring operating out of Summers Security." Marcus stood very still as he stared at Shaun.

"Why else would you mention the police being at your office all day?" Shaun snatched his bottle of beer off the table and took a long pull from it.

"I didn't."

"Then Aliyah must have said something. I don't know and don't care." Shaun went to a stack of compact discs on a shelf. He shuffled them, studying each one. "Look, I was having a quiet evening. Take that drama out when you leave."

"Thought you didn't see much of Aliyah." Marcus took two steps closer to him.

Shaun faced him again. "Don't come in my house challenging me. Time to go."

"All right. Tell ya girl Aliyah I said hello." Marcus jerked a thumb in the direction of Shaun's bedroom down the hall.

Shaun nodded to the front door. "When you're ready to be real again, gimme a call."

Marcus slammed the door hard as he left. "Damn! You messed up."

Not that he'd expected Shaun to tell him anything. Marcus drove home trying to figure out at what point he and his only close friend had become enemies. Shaun's accusations that he'd sold out buzzed around in his head like angry yellow jackets. More than once Marcus started to turn his car around and go make things right with Shaun. Or at least give it a try. Still, not even guilt could banish the troublesome feeling that Olandon's name on the list of suspects was no coincidence.

She forced herself to go on with the staff meeting even though her heart wasn't in it. Nicole issued instructions and made decisions. She even managed a short pep talk before the staff left. Once the door to her office closed, Nicole slumped in her chair and closed her eyes. She opened them again at the sound of a male voice outside her door. Cat came in a few minutes later.

"UPS just delivered the new Dell server," Cat said. "Andre is all excited. You'd think Santa just delivered his Christmas toys."

"At least somebody is happy." Nicole stared out the window again.

Cat dropped a stack of mail into Nicole's in basket. "Hey, he's got this new neat program to help catch hackers. I'm thinking maybe I could start helping him. I took computer courses at the community college."

"Uh-huh."

"I like the idea of turning the tables on those little chumps." Cat leaned over her. "You heard me?"

"Yes." Nicole couldn't work up interest in anything at the moment.

"Snap to it, boss lady. We've got work to do." Cat turned Nicole's chair around until she faced the desk.

"I'm taking a break." Nicole tried to swivel back, but Cat stopped her.

"Break over. I wanna see that smart aleck lady that tells everybody where they can go and what they can kiss." Cat crossed her arms.

"My mother would say good riddance to her." Nicole's

eyes felt gritty and dry. She squeezed them shut. Too little sleep.

Cat sat on the edge of Nicole's desk. "You want to quit?"

Nicole let the question roll around in her mind for a while. Quit, she mused. She tried on the notion and found it didn't fit.

"No, I'm not going to quit."

"That's what I'm talkin' about." Cat slapped her hands together and grinned.

"Here, you can send these off."

Nicole handed Cat a stack of letters she'd signed. She sorted through mail left unread for several days. Together they cleared Nicole's desk. Cat helped Nicole prioritize the phone calls she needed to return.

"Sorry to just drop in." Kelli Caldwell peered around the half open door. "I was in the neighborhood."

"Hi, Ms. Caldwell. I'll get y'all something to drink," Cat said.

"I've got sodas in the refrigerator, Cat. Thanks anyway." Nicole waved her friend in. "Good to see a friendly face."

Kelli sat down and waited until the door closed behind Cat. She gazed at Nicole with a critical eye. "How are you?"

"Getting better. Don't tell me, everyone has already written my obituary in this business." Nicole raised an eyebrow.

"A few," Kelli admitted.

"Well, like the old saying goes, I'll go down fighting." Nicole tried for a smile and didn't make it.

"Lost any contracts yet?" Kelli crossed her legs.

Nicole sprang from her chair to relieve nervous energy. She walked to the window then back to her desk. "Two that were up for renewal. We're not in trouble yet. If he weren't already dead, I'd strangle Uncle Hosea."

"He must have known you could run this company."

"No, this is his revenge for all the times I kicked his shins as a kid," Nicole retorted.

"So, you're going to kick him again by making it work," Kelli teased.

Nicole paused. "What?"

"Come on, you like the idea of giving folks the finger, in a manner of speaking." Kelli fussed over a wrinkle in her red skirt. "I wouldn't try it literally, though. Bad for business."

Nicole dropped into her chair again. "I need to run this company for my own reasons, not to show my parents or even Uncle Hosea. And not to impress Marcus," she murmured.

Kelli glanced up at her sharply. "I agree, since you mentioned it. Listen, I've been debating whether to tell you something. I hate repeating gossip, but . . ." Her voice trailed off as she fidgeted.

"Yes, Marcus and I are lovers. Is that what you're getting at?" Nicole tilted her head to one side.

"Oh, crap!" Kelli chewed the red lipstick from her bottom lip.

"I haven't let it affect the business." Nicole knew her family wouldn't buy the argument.

"Rumors are circulating that Hosea had promised to sell out to Marcus. When Hosea died and left Summers Security to you . . . well, some people are saying Marcus might have orchestrated these problems as payback." Kelli grimaced as though the words hurt as they came out.

Nicole stared at her for several seconds, then laughed. "I can't get angry because that's just downright stupid. Marcus has as much to lose by destroying Summers Security."

"I hear he's been quietly recruiting customers."

"Even if I thought Marcus would stab me in the back,

which I don't, it still doesn't make sense." Nicole got up and paced again.

"Tell you the truth, I don't believe the rumors," Kelli said.

"Thank you," said Nicole.

"Course he could be taking advantage of an opportunity that happens to fit his plans." Kelli dipped her head to one side as though ducking when Nicole shot a heated glance her way. "Or not," she muttered.

"I don't believe it for one minute."

"Then ask him."

"I will."

"Let me know what he says. You might not be objective." Kelli pointed a forefinger at her.

"I have a highly developed sense of smell when it comes to bull," Nicole snapped. She sat down hard.

Kelli held up both palms. "Okay, okay. Change of subject. I had a similar series of unfortunate events when I started out."

"A crime wave started by your own employees?" Nicole clenched her teeth.

"My niche is a bit different, true."

"For sure," Nicole said. Kelli's firm specialized in body-guards for celebrities and special events such as music concerts.

"One of my guys had a hot affair with the wife of a famous NFL tight end—who shall remain nameless," Kelli added quickly when Nicole leaned forward eagerly.

"Aw c'mon, a little dirt will take my mind off my own troubles," Nicole urged.

"The point is I had to clean up my good name. Well, the name of my company anyway."

"Easy. One affair with a client's wife is nothing." Nicole waved away her example as trivial.

"Oh yeah? They conspired to steal money and paintings

from the husband's equally wealthy celebrity pals. Got away with six burglaries, too."

"Building up their nest egg so they could be together." Nicole was interested now.

"Uh-huh. Her hubby was no dumb jock, had a solid prenuptial agreement. If the Mrs. left him she got zip. Except for the felony thing I'd have been sympathetic. Her husband was an arrogant jerk."

"I had one of those," Nicole retorted.

Kelli laughed. "Anyway, I helped the cops clean up nice and neat. The customers who knew got called first with a complete report. Honesty is the best policy."

"I agree. I've been open with the clients who have called so far. Painful, but the best way." Nicole winced just thinking about some of her conversations.

"Folks might still bail out on contracts, but you'll have a better rep than if you lie. Not good for a security firm." Kelli stood. "I see you're ahead of me."

"Yes, Marcus and I—" Nicole broke off when she thought of him. Maybe that mysterious smile hid something sinister.

"I'd say you need to have a little talk with the man. If only to prove the gossip is wrong," Kelli said.

"Yeah." Nicole tapped her Mont Blanc pen on the edge of her desk.

Kelli's digital cell phone made a chirping sound. She read the number and made a call. "Hi, Moesha. It's me." Her expression turned harsh as she listened. "I'll be back in fifteen minutes."

"No, you won't. Your office is at least twenty-five minutes away in good traffic. We both know Houston doesn't have good traffic," Nicole joked.

"Trust me, I'm going to get there fast. One of my customers was robbed two weeks ago. Your police officers think it's connected." Kelli sprang from her chair.

"Dayna is not *my* police officer. And what are you talking about?" Nicole stood and walked around her desk.

"Girlfriend, seems your larceny bug is contagious." Kelli pursed her lips.

"I don't understand."

"Several of your part-timers also work for us."

Nicole blinked at her hard. "Damn."

"Damn is right. How widespread is this thing, anyway? Better go." Kelli swung her purse over one shoulder and strode out.

"Call me. I don't care how late it is," Nicole yelled after her.

"Okay," Kelli shouted back without breaking her stride.

Russell stepped aside to avoid a collision as he stepped into Nicole's office. "Geez, Kelli! You're moving like something is on fire," he said.

"I hope not," she replied, and kept going.

"What's going on with her?" Russell nodded in the direction Kelli had gone.

"Something urgent came up at her office." Nicole decided not to give him any more ammunition than he already had. "I'm really busy getting ready for the board meeting, Russell."

"I'll bet. As it happens, so am I."

"Then why are you here?" Nicole sat at her desk and sorted through her notes.

"Give it up. Marcus is considering supporting me. He implied as much in so many words," he added when Nicole glowered at him.

"Bull."

"I'll overlook that crude outburst. You're under tremendous stress. Bye." Russell smirked at her for a few seconds before he walked out.

"The next person who comes in here will suffer, I swear!"

Nicole got up and slammed her door shut. After ten minutes of fuming, she punched Marcus's four-digit office extension. After four rings his voice mail came on. His smooth baritone voice stirred hot images. She shoved them aside and left a curt message.

Aliyah crossed her legs and gazed at him. Marcus had to admire her nerve. She didn't even twitch when he laid out his accusation. He ignored the muted buzz of his desk phone.

"I don't have a clue what you're talking about." Aliyah's slick smile dared him to prove otherwise.

"Sure you do. You've been talking to Shaun."

"I hadn't seen him for months before we bumped into each other out in the hall that day." She spoke with the ease of someone comfortable with lying.

"Shaun is probably coaching you on how to skin Russell of everything he owns. I know my old buddy. Maybe Shaun even set it up for you to meet Russell." Marcus didn't have all the angles figured just yet. By the cunning light in her eyes, Aliyah could tell as much.

"I know a lot of prominent people. I met Russ at a charity brunch. I'm big on giving to the poor, you know." Aliyah brushed back her hair. "I'm sure you know I'm from the 'hood, too."

"Shaun mentioned it."

"Which is why we should stick together." Aliyah nodded as though her argument spoke for itself. "Look, we're all after the same thing. We're out of the ghetto and we don't want to go back."

"Yeah, but we've got different means of moving up." Marcus stared at her steadily.

"Not so different. I notice you and Nicole have gotten tight." Aliyah raised her perfectly shaped auburn eyebrows.

"I plan to have my own, not marry it." Marcus gave her a wry smile.

"I feel ya. Go your own way." Aliyah lifted a shoulder.

"I'm being real." Marcus didn't really care if she believed him or not. In fact, it was better if she didn't.

"I'm gonna be honest with you, all right?"

"All right." Marcus doubted Aliyah had the capacity, but he assumed a listening position. He would cull through her mixture of lies and half-truths later.

"I did pump Shaun for information on Russell when I found out he knew you. He held out. You know how Shaun is."

"Yeah, I know how Shaun is," Marcus said in a dry tone.

Aliyah went on as though she hadn't noticed his cynical response. She smiled. "I let him think he was being slick. Actually he told me enough to work with. I'm that good."

"Russell isn't exactly a challenge," Marcus replied.

"True, but his sister is a real bitch and he listens to her." Aliyah's lips curved down in a resentful expression.

"Might be hard to change years of habit. Jolene knows how to handle her little brother." Marcus was careful to keep his voice casual.

"So do I." Aliyah stood and walked around the desk until she stood before Marcus. "I'm carrying a concealed weapon."

He gazed up at her. Aliyah was pretty, he had to admit. The apple green sleeveless knit tank dress molded to her curves. If a man wasn't paying close attention to the ravenous gleam in her light brown eyes, he'd get sucked in. Russell Summers would be just the type Aliyah would target—rich and clueless. Even better, he was used to being controlled by iron-willed women. Marcus needed to keep Aliyah talking.

"I'll bet," he answered with the hint of a smile.

She nudged his chair until it swiveled around so that he faced her. Then she placed a hand on each of his shoulders. "You and me could clean up. There's no reason we can't have it all. Shaun thinks he's hot stuff. He's gonna slip up soon."

"Slip up how?" Marcus tensed, though he kept his cool outward pose.

"Just a gut feeling. I mean if Shaun is so shrewd, why isn't he rich by now? Now, you're a smart one. You're working from the inside out and getting paid a big salary in the process."

"Shaun has a different approach to getting ahead is all."

"Bet you didn't know he makes fun of you. Says you're a chump working for chumps." Aliyah eased down onto his lap and hooked an arm around his neck.

"Is that right?" Marcus let his expression tighten.

She nodded slowly as she leaned her face close to his. "But we can show him how it's done," she murmured.

Marcus had had his fill of her. Far from being alluring, he found Aliyah contemptible. He'd grown up around predators. Designer clothes and expensive cologne couldn't disguise what she was.

"We've had this conversation. I'm not looking for a partner." Marcus pushed her from his lap and stood.

Aliyah's eyes only gleamed brighter. "Hard core. You've still got enough ghetto in you to make life interesting."

"Work on your technique. I'm not Russell." Still holding her arm, he pulled her toward the door. It swung open before he'd taken two steps.

"You've been back in the office for over an hour, so answer your damn phone," Nicole said. She came to a halt and stared at his hand on Aliyah's arm.

Russell pushed past Nicole from behind. He blinked rapidly when he saw Aliyah. "Honey, what are you doing in here?"

She smiled at Nicole before letting her gaze slide to Russell. "Baby, you know I'm still not used to this place. I took a wrong turn. Marcus was nice enough to tolerate the intrusion."

Marcus managed to force a smile. "I was about to show her a shortcut to Russell's office."

"Yes, I was going to surprise you, baby." Aliyah strolled over to Russell.

"Surprise," Nicole said in a glacial tone. She crossed her arms and looked at Marcus.

twenty

Aliyah leaned close to Russell. "I think they need to talk," she whispered.

"Definitely. Goodbye." Nicole spat without looking at either of them.

"Wait for me outside, Aliyah," Russell said.

"But baby—"

"This is business. I won't be long." Russell led her out and came back. "The board knows everything, including your attempt to put the blame on me. It won't work. I've given them a report of the decisive actions I've taken."

"Such as?" Marcus turned from Nicole's hostile scrutiny to look at him.

"I have fired staff and hired replacements already. Jesse had his hands full with other things. I'm going to contact my college roommate in the attorney general's office. He might help speed up criminal background checks." Russell lifted his chin.

"The attorney general's office doesn't have anything to do with background checks," Marcus replied.

"He knows people. That's how business is done at a certain

level, Marcus." Russell gave him a brief, dismissive glance before he looked at Nicole. "Marcus doesn't have connections and you don't have ability. I'd say my chances are good."

"Don't redecorate my office just yet," Nicole answered.

Russell ignored her and looked at Marcus again. "Stay away from Aliyah."

"Aliyah wandered into my office. I suggest you keep an eye on how often your girlfriend gets 'lost,'" Marcus snapped, the words flying out like steel-tipped darts.

Judging from the loss of color in his tan face, Russell got the message. "Just wait until I'm in charge." He marched off.

"What an ass!" Marcus went to his door and slammed it. He faced Nicole and waited.

A good sixty seconds went by before she spoke. "I have a question."

"Yes, Aliyah made a play for me. I refused the offer." Marcus folded his arms across his chest.

"Okay, not that I was all that interested." Nicole's nostrils quivered.

"Uh-huh."

Marcus let his expression communicate how little he believed her. Then he waited for the follow-up questions. Women always had them when it came to another woman. What she said next hit him like a punch in the gut.

"Were you planning to steal clients from this company and start your own business?"

Nicole stood very still. Her lovely brown eyes burned with suspicion and anger. Walking in on that scene with Aliyah had surely added gasoline to a raging fire. Marcus let his arms fall to his sides.

"What—" He walked to his desk. Marcus could feel her gaze boring into his back.

"Did those few seconds give you time to come up with an answer I might believe?" Nicole did not move.

"I told your father I was considering other options," Marcus hedged.

"We were talking about other job offers, damn it. This company opened doors for you that you couldn't have gone through otherwise." Nicole walked toward him as she spoke.

"Right. I had the great privilege of being saved from the gutter by the magnanimous Summers clan." Marcus glared at her.

"I didn't mean it that way," Nicole shot back.

"Yes, you did. I worked twelve-hour days, took his crap for two years, and earned every penny in my paycheck. Sure I was grateful when he made me vice president. But let's get this straight, I had it coming and more."

"So, you decided to stab him in the back for not stepping aside and handing you the keys to the company." Nicole's mouth curved into a sneer.

"Mr. Summers told me he would sell me the business. I go to his funeral and out comes this video will. He lied, had me work like a dog knowing all the time he had no intention of honoring our agreement."

"Why didn't you tell us?" Nicole gazed at him through narrowed eyes, as though she could discern his veracity by doing so.

"I didn't have anything in writing. Your family has a reputation for being ruthless. You people weren't at your best at the funeral."

"Yeah, well . . ."

"I'm sure your family would have wanted me out of here. Who needs a resentful employee hanging around? Especially one with access to sensitive company data. I was going to leave on my terms." Marcus met her gaze without flinching.

"I see. Guess you've got a chance now."

"What are you talking about?"

"I was dumb enough to be flattered that you seemed to accept me as CEO. You made such a show of deferring to me in front of our biggest customers. Deniability. You can walk away and tell everyone I made the mistakes." Nicole's eyes flashed again.

"That's not true, Nicole. I didn't count on loving you." Marcus started toward her, but the antagonism in her expression stopped him.

"Oh, right. I guess this is where I melt into your strong arms and beg you to swear your love is true."

"Trust would be nice," he said quietly.

"Cuts both ways, doesn't it? After we got closer, made love—" Nicole looked away.

"I didn't think it mattered anymore. We were a team. I felt ownership working side by side with you. I'm not lying to you." Marcus spread his arms out.

"I don't know." Nicole pinched the bridge of her nose.

After a cautious sounding knock, Shelly opened the door. She glanced from Nicole to Marcus. "Uh, I hate to interrupt."

"What's up, Shelly?" Marcus answered when Nicole didn't respond.

"That guy with the commission is on line four. I don't think it's good news," Shelly mumbled, then made a hasty exit.

Marcus ground his teeth as he picked up the telephone receiver. Shelly was right. As he listened to the director's assistant, his stomach muscles tightened.

"Yes, of course. Fifteen working days." Marcus hung up the phone. "Mr. Phoung and three of our clients filed a complaint. We have to answer in writing."

Shelly came in again. She handed Marcus a long envelope. "This certified letter was just delivered."

"From the commission?" Nicole stared at him with a dismal expression.

Marcus nodded and opened it. "The allegation is that we didn't follow licensing regulations in hiring or supervising staff."

"I guess Russell is right. When my family hears our license is at risk—" Nicole closed her eyes. "Damn!"

"I'll get y'all some coffee." Shelly tiptoed out and eased the door shut as she left.

"I'll call our attorney. Maybe when Russell hired some of the staff the regs were less stringent." Marcus frowned and read the letter again.

"What does it matter? We should have done thorough background checks annually. No, we can't spin our way out of this fix." Nicole dropped into a chair.

"Let's not jump to conclusions." Marcus punched the buttons on his phone. "Jesse, come to my office."

Nicole's shapely eyebrows bunched together. "What are you doing?"

"I want to check something out."

Jesse knocked once and came in. He nodded at Nicole. "Afternoon. I hear we got another problem."

"Yeah. How many of the employees had criminal records?" Marcus got right to the point.

"Two had misdemeanor summons, no convictions. Russell didn't do a great job of screening them, but these folks weren't major gang bangers. Just less than squeaky clean backgrounds." Jesse shrugged when Nicole let out a groan.

"Then we have a good defense against this complaint. Well, maybe good is too strong a word," Marcus said when Jesse and Nicole looked skeptical.

"Please! I've been studying those regs. As a licensed security agency we can be held accountable for the misconduct of our employees," Nicole said.

"But what if they lied to us? The law says we have to make reasonable legal efforts to check them out." Jesse glanced from Nicole to Marcus.

Nicole stood. "Call the lawyer, Marcus. We're definitely going to need him."

"I'll be in my office. Got three more folks to hire. Just hope their fingerprint checks come back clean. The problem is not all of the police departments report to them. These dudes could have been arrested in some little town or other. How would we know?" Jesse started for the door.

"Stop!" Nicole shouted.

Jesse jumped, and his eyes popped wide. "What'd I do?"

"He's right. The database on convictions is only as good as the reporting." Nicole turned to Marcus eagerly. "Let's run their names now. If nothing comes up, then we're covered."

Jesse nodded slowly. "I'll run searches on the Department of Public Safety Crime Records Service."

"Good. Get back to me." Marcus waved at Jesse as though to speed him on his way. When the door bumped shut and they were alone again, he looked at Nicole. "You've done one helluva job studying the law and this business."

"Thanks." Nicole didn't look at him. "I'm going back to my office."

"Wait."

She paused as though gathering strength, then turned to face him. Marcus stuck his hands in his pants pockets, unsure of what to say now that he had her attention. Nicole gazed at him for only a moment before she looked away. He cleared his throat.

"Don't walk out without telling me something. Yell, curse, make smart-ass comments about my ghetto childhood. Anything." Marcus spoke in a low, urgent tone.

Nicole gave a sardonic laugh. "First time I've been invited to verbally abuse someone." More silence.

"I screwed up. Okay?"

"Yes, you did."

"Tell me how to make it right." Marcus stood close to her. He rested his forehead against hers. His hopes rose when she didn't push him away.

Nicole gazed into his eyes for a few seconds, then moved away. "Let me get back to you on that one. I need time to think."

"Sure. Just one more thing, make it tonight. Please." Marcus watched her expression with a knot of anxiety in his chest. She nodded, and he was able to breathe again.

Do you believe him?

Nicole frowned at the oncoming traffic as she drove. The question her sister had posed kept bouncing around in her head. She'd called Helena for advice the way she had since childhood. Helena was not only wise but she also wouldn't consider social status in judging Marcus. Not that Nicole was at all sure about herself in that regard. She was, after all, a product of her mother's upbringing. Analine Darensbourg Summers was a social snob, though she'd hotly deny it. So was her father, and he admitted it. Was she a chip off the old block?

She took a deep breath, hoping more oxygen would clear her head. The apartment building where Marcus lived loomed ahead, and she still didn't have an answer. Nicole parked, walked to his front door, and rang the bell.

When Marcus answered, her heart beat faster. He stood tall even in flat brown leather sandals. He wore a tan pullover knit shirt and khaki chinos. The colors blended with his smooth skin, which was the color of roasted pecans.

"Glad you came." He stepped aside to let her in.

"Hi." Nicole tingled all over when her shoulder brushed his broad chest as she walked by and into the living room.

"I've got your favorite." Marcus smiled and pointed to two tall mugs of root beer, a bowl of tortilla chips, and another bowl of salsa.

"Thanks for remembering."

Nicole deliberately sat down in a chair. She held onto her small straw purse. She glanced around as though seeing the room for the first time. Light green and red lights danced on the controls of his sound system, a swirl of patterns in time to the music that played softly. A rich female voice she couldn't identify sang a ballad. Marcus sat close by on the sofa. He seemed content to wait on her.

"We both had another long day," she said.

"Yes."

"Jesse told me about the background checks. Nothing came up on those employees. Of course five of them had been fired from other jobs. Two had been suspected of stealing from their employers," Nicole said. "Why didn't we know about it though?"

"I talked to Russell before I left the office. He didn't check the references. He just accepted the letters as authentic on two of them. The others were recommended because their former bosses didn't want to be sued." Marcus tapped one foot, as though impatient.

"Why would they be sued?"

"They were laid off supposedly because the places where

they worked had to cut cost, not because they could prove the thefts."

"So, instead of going through the trouble of confronting them, they took an easy out."

"Happens all the time. Folks are lawsuit crazy these days. Anyway, Russell got defensive, and the day ended on its usual low note." Marcus lifted a shoulder.

"Well, the board should realize Russell hasn't developed brain cells in the last few weeks," Nicole joked.

"Slamming him isn't the best strategy, Nicole. I'd say concentrate on what you're doing right. Let them see the contrast."

"Yeah. I better read up on anger management in the next week." Nicole gave a short laugh.

"You can practice right now," Marcus said quietly. "You're still angry with me, right?"

"Some people might say you were using me." Nicole watched him for a reaction.

Marcus continued to gaze at her. "I'm only interested in what you say."

"You're either a very smooth operator or telling the truth," she replied.

Nicole's heart wanted to believe the latter. Her head warned against being deceived again. She had a flashback to her ex-husband.

"I'm not him," Marcus said as though he'd looked right into her thoughts.

"I grew up knowing exactly which fork to use, which colleges my parents would pay for, and which friends I should choose. My ex was from the right family. The only thing he cared about was that I was from the right family, too." Nicole twisted the leather handle of her purse between her fingers. "I was a fancy designer handbag with nothing important inside."

"You could have had anything you wanted." Marcus shook his head. "Hard to understand why you were unhappy. Man, I hated being poor."

"One day I asked myself, 'What are you really worth?' I didn't have an answer." Nicole looked at him.

"Oh, baby," Marcus murmured.

"You can only blame your parents for so long, you know. But it was fun while it lasted," Nicole said with a humorless smile.

"I had a teacher in high school, Mrs. Estevens. One day I was in trouble again, can't remember what I'd done, to tell you the truth. When I started yelling about my mother being a drunk and my missing-in-action thug father, know what she said? 'So what, Marcus. What are *you* gonna do?' " He shook his head slowly. "I thought about that for a long time."

"You have to decide who and what you're going to be in spite of everything."

"Right." Marcus wore a thoughtful expression.

"After I got over the shock, I started seeing Summers Security as my chance to be more than a useless ornament. I don't want to be a means to somebody's end." Nicole stared at him.

"You're not, at least where I'm concerned," he said.

His voice came to her softly, a gentle vibration that made her heart hum in response. Marcus held out a hand in invitation. Nicole left the chair to obey. Realizing she still held her purse, Nicole gazed at it. She could still leave, her warning voice said. Just get your car keys and go, it urged. Take time to think. Yet she needed the solid feel of his arms around her chasing away years of loneliness, especially now. Nicole needed to feel part of him, needed the reassurance of this man who had become her friend and lover. *So much for you,*

Nicole said to her cautious alter ego. With a flip of one wrist, the purse landed on the chair behind her.

Nicole settled on the sofa and into the arch of his strong right arm. "Think we can make the whole world go away for a little while?"

"I'm going to give it my best shot," he whispered.

His full mouth tugged up at one corner in a half-smile that was both seductive and secretive, as though he held a surprise. Nicole shivered, eager to get whatever prize he offered.

"It's late and we're short on time. The phone could ring at any minute. Your pager might go off," he spoke close to her ear and nipped her lobe.

"True." Nicole closed her eyes as he reached down her blouse and cupped a breast.

He looked into her eyes as he unhooked the front clasp of her bra. "Don't make me wait."

A stab of hunger bit into her. "No."

Like a video in fast-forward they undressed rapidly, kissing each other hard over each inch of flesh as it was exposed. Their foreplay lasted sixty seconds at most. Naked and driven by a yawning need, Nicole straddled his lap without taking her mouth from his. Her tongue pushed through his lips in a demand for satisfaction. Marcus moaned and gripped her thighs as he penetrated her. Or rather Nicole swallowed him with a guttural whimper in the back of her throat. She wanted to be the taker. He gave in willingly.

Nicole rocked and rolled her pelvis. She lifted her body and then plunged down as waves of desire crashed over her. Marcus buried his face between her breasts and growled with pleasure.

"Please," he begged.

"Baby," was all she could whisper in reply.

Nicole could hardly breathe. And she came. Clouds split

and her mind cleared of everything as she fought for every inch of him, every drop of the joy he offered. Marcus came seconds later with a grunt that threatened to become a roar, except that his mouth was still pressed against hers. Nicole shuddered as a smaller orgasm took over. Suddenly they were both still. Gradually she heard the music from his compact disc player again.

"Baby, it's all about you." His eyes still closed, Marcus shook his head. He planted a tender kiss on the tip of her nipple.

Nicole sank onto the sofa. She exhaled when Marcus pulled her down to stretch out beside him on the wide cushions. He shifted until she was neatly tucked, spoon-fashion, with her back nestled against him.

"About us. I'm not into being the self-absorbed Black American Princess you called me."

"I never—"

"Not to my face." Nicole smiled at the expression she imagined he wore.

"Okay, maybe once," he confessed with a chuckle.

"I knew it."

Nicole closed her eyes and drifted into a glow she'd never had with another lover. She savored the circle of his arms around her waist. A thumping rhythm came from the sound system speakers. They lay together, wrapped in the music and each other. After a long moment Marcus nuzzled the back of her neck.

"Baby, things might get worse before they get better," he whispered.

"Shhh, you're messing with our moment," she mumbled, already half asleep. "I'm ready to take it on. I've got a secret weapon this time." His reply was to tighten his embrace.

* * *

Marcus rapped hard on the door. He'd stood outside Shaun's condo for fifteen minutes pressing the white button. Then Marcus pulled the cell phone from the holster clipped to his belt. He dialed Shaun's number. A recording announced that the number was disconnected.

"Come on, Shaun. Open up," Marcus shouted.

"He ain't there," a deep voice rumbled.

Marcus spun around to face a man of about sixty with iron gray hair. "Excuse me?"

The man shifted an empty metal garbage can from his left hand to his right. He adjusted the silver metal eyeglasses that had slipped down his nose. "I said he's gone. Moved out three days ago. Had six months left on his lease. Gonna mess up his credit rating."

"Moved," Marcus repeated and stared through the window.

Only then did he really look through a part in the curtains. Shaun's fancy leather sofa, love seat, and chair were gone. So was everything else, it seemed.

"Yep. Always did think he was slick looking. Told my wife, too. I said, 'Bet he's a criminal or something.' Real smooth talker, like my grandmamma used to say."

"He was in sales," Marcus replied. He'd grown accustomed to defending Shaun as a reflex.

"Same difference in my opinion. Always hookin' folks into paying more than they intended for stuff they don't need. Can't trust nobody these—"

"You live close by?" Marcus broke in to stop his rambling.

"One door down," the man answered and pointed ahead. "Bud Wilson is my name. First name Budweiser. My daddy was a drinking man." Bud laughed.

"Nice to meet you." Marcus stared through the curtains again.

"I manage the place to earn a little extra. My pension

doesn't go far these days. No-good corporate crooks ruined the stock market and—"

"Did anyone else come looking for him in the last few days?" Marcus cut in again.

Bud's friendly expression turned to one of suspicion. His eyes narrowed. "Depends. Who are you?"

"I'm an old friend. I've been over here quite a few times." Marcus took off his sunglasses and stuck out a hand. "Marcus Reed."

"Hmm." Bud scanned Marcus's face as though he were in a police lineup. "Yeah, come to think of it I did see you around here a few times. Hope your friend hasn't gotten himself in trouble."

"Me, too. I've been calling him for the last three days."

"Call his mama or daddy," Bud said. His eyes crinkled again in appraisal. "Since you're an old friend."

"His mother is dead. His father isn't reliable. He hasn't been there for Shaun in years." Marcus shook his head.

Bud's eyes twinkled with interest. "Had a rough childhood, huh? Damn shame for a man to walk away from his responsibilities. Too bad."

"Yeah. We got into scrapes back in the day. But we went to college and both got jobs. Moved out of the Fifth Ward. I just hope Shaun hasn't slipped back into old habits." Marcus adopted the same chatty tone Bud had earlier.

"Son, you can't change another man. All you can do is be a friend and show him the way." Bud's voice dipped low in a fatherly fashion.

"Yes, sir. I still can't help but worry about him, though." Marcus had no trouble sounding sincere, even though he was trying to finesse information from Bud.

"Listen, a couple of rough-looking dudes have been over

there. They didn't look happy when I told them the condo was empty. Whatever your friend has gotten into is bad. You better be careful."

Marcus decided not to press for more. Besides, he doubted Bud could tell him more anyway. "Thanks, Mr. Wilson. If you see or hear from Shaun, call me." He handed Bud one of his business cards.

"Summers Security," Bud read. "I saw an article way back in the *Chronicle*. Black man built that company from the ground up."

"Hosea Summers. He was considered a pioneer. He died a few months ago."

"Vice President of Operations," Bud read again. "Good to see a young man come from hard times and make good."

"Thanks."

Marcus smiled distractedly as he glanced back at the condo. He pondered asking Bud to let him look inside. If he knew Shaun, the place would be so clean even a forensics crew would have trouble finding anything.

"I've been telling the owners we need better security." Bud nodded with vigor and waved the card.

"Yes, sir. You have them give us a call."

"Sure will," Bud replied and slipped the card in his pants pocket.

"One more thing, have you seen a woman come by lately? She's tall with dark reddish hair, wears expensive clothes and drives a red BMW."

"Her." Bud grinned. "My wife Carrie calls her 'Miss Thang.' Not that she was the only woman over there. Yeah, come to think of it, she came by a few nights before he took off."

"Thanks again, Mr. Wilson. Don't forget to call me if—"

"Right, right. You be sure and remember what I said. Be

careful. You might need to let him go his way and you go yours." Bud started off when a handsome older woman stuck her head out a door and called to him.

Marcus waved back, then stared at what used to be Shaun's front door. "I can't do that, Bud."

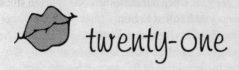 twenty-one

The board members left the conference room with sober expressions. Nicole stared hard at her father. Marcus wanted to hold her hand but knew better. Stanton Summers smoothed down his silk paisley tie. Lionel Summers cleared his throat and shot a meaningful look at his brother.

"I'm going to ride back with Ethel and James, Stan." Uncle Lionel stood.

"Right. I'll stay and talk to Nicole for a while."

Marcus rose. "Goodbye, Mr. Summers."

"Stay," Nicole said.

Her father's brows bunched together. "It would be better if we—"

"No, it wouldn't," she clipped.

For once Uncle Lionel didn't intervene to correct what he perceived as impudence. Instead he cleared his throat again and left the room. Nicole and her father continued to gaze at each other.

"I'm okay with letting y'all talk alone," Marcus said quietly.

"You need to hear what I'm about to say," Nicole replied without taking her gaze from her father's face.

"Nicole, honey, you know we're only interested in the survival of Summers Security," Stanton began.

"With the exception of Marcus, no one else can easily step in and run things in the middle of this mess," Nicole asserted. "Not even my smart, competent brother."

"And he doesn't want to. Terrell made that perfectly clear. I think you two must have prepared for this meeting." Stanton drummed his thick fingers on the wood surface.

"Of course we did. I'm glad we cleared the air," Nicole said.

Marcus gazed at her with pride. Nicole had surprised her relatives by being calm and in charge. Once they'd gotten over their shock, the real work had begun. She'd endured two hours of being grilled, challenged, and thinly insulted by Russell and his supporters. Through it all Nicole had maintained a cool poise.

Stanton studied her for several minutes. He gave a curt nod, as though he'd reached a decision. "All right, keep going. Let's see if you can hold it together."

"I will." Nicole stood as a signal the meeting was over.

Marcus blinked hard and glanced at her formidable father. Stanton rose with the shadow of a smile on his broad face. He seemed to accept the dismissal.

"I'll be in touch," Stanton said. "Nicole, I like this new you."

Nicole shook her head. "Not new, Daddy. I'm just directing my energy in a different direction."

Stanton kissed Nicole on the forehead. "That's my girl. Goodbye, young man," he said over his shoulder.

"Goodbye, sir." Marcus still wasn't accepted, Stanton's tone seemed to say.

"Daddy, one more thing. Marcus is important in my life. You need to understand just how important."

"I believe I do. I'll call you soon," Stanton said in a restrained tone. He walked out without looking at Marcus.

"I don't think the subject of our relationship is closed," Marcus murmured.

"They'll get used to it." Nicole stared at the door as though she could still see her father.

"If you say so." Marcus doubted they would, but he let it go. "You did a wonderful job today." He smiled at her.

Nicole dropped into a leather chair. "God, but I'm glad it's over." She rubbed her eyes.

"Russell is very frustrated. He was so sure the board would fire you." Marcus sat on the edge of the conference table next to her. "He'll try again."

"He can't do anything." Nicole rested her head against the dark red leather.

"Yeah, you're probably right. Are you okay?" Marcus brushed a tendril of her hair back in place.

"I will be one of these days. Just not today."

"Go home early tonight, baby."

"You mean at ten o'clock instead of midnight?" she joked.

"No, if the staff works late, so will I."

"They don't have to deal with your family. Honey, please. You're exhausted."

"I must look really awful." Nicole patted her cheeks.

"You're the most beautiful woman in the world on your worst day," he said with passion and meant every word.

"Good answer," she said with a tired grin. Then she used the arms of her chair to push herself up. "Now it's back to work."

"Okay, just one more thing." Marcus caught her hand before she could leave. "I love you."

Nicole pressed a palm to his left cheek and gazed into his eyes. "I love you, too."

Cat bustled in with Andre and Imani close behind. "Sorry, Nicole, but we've got to talk about this invoice."

"Yeah, but can we get to her first?" Imani squeezed past Cat. "Just take a look at my draft outline. It will only take fifteen minutes. I've got to get the producer working on our television spot today."

"Me next," Andre put in.

"Now wait a minute!" Cat protested. Her plump cheeks puffed out with irritation.

Nicole's worn-out expression disappeared. She raised a hand in the air. "No fighting, kids. Let's head to my office. Andre, I read your report. I already made notes."

"Great! I can get moving on the next project. I've got two clients on a new firewall for their servers," Andre chattered as he followed Nicole through the side door into her office.

"Stand in line, sonny," Imani muttered and yanked him back.

Marcus had to smile at their antics. He went back to his office. Shelly sat at her desk shuffling papers. "I'm back with all my fingers and toes," he joked.

"I didn't hear shouting, so the meeting must have gone fairly well." Shelly handed him a stack of incoming mail.

"Actually the board members weren't all that bad." Marcus looked through the letters.

"I meant Nicole." Shelly grinned at him.

"You would have been proud of her. Not once did she lose her cool." Marcus winked at her.

"I know Russell tried." Shelly leaned across her desk and dropped her voice. "His secretary says Russell has been on the phone with his sister every day for the last two weeks. Plotting."

"No surprise. The good news is it didn't work." Marcus started to say more when he saw Shaun's name on a pink message sheet. "When did he call?"

"Who?" Shelly stretched her neck to look at the message he waved.

"Shaun Jackson. You didn't put a time on here." Marcus spun around and strode into his office.

Shelly followed him. "Sorry, but the phones went crazy around here. Which reminds me, and I sure hate to tell you. A reporter named Tamara Collins called from Channel Thirteen."

"I'll deal with that later. Better yet, let Imani handle it." Marcus itched to call Shaun.

"She might find one of our disgruntled employees." Shelly pursed her lips.

"I've got to make some calls. Take messages for me and don't let anyone in." Marcus walked her to the door.

"Mr. Sullivan from the commission is supposed to come by and—"

"Take him to Nicole if I'm on the phone."

Marcus closed the door behind her as she walked out. He punched in the number and let it ring a long time. Finally Shaun answered. When the cheery voice requested that he leave a message, Marcus swore. Unable to concentrate, Marcus sat staring at his phone for fifteen minutes. When it rang, Marcus somehow knew it would be Shaun.

"Yeah, Shelly. Put him on." Marcus gripped the receiver. "Where the hell are you?"

"Hello, Detective Tyler." Nicole extended a hand to her.

"Hi. Thanks for seeing me on short notice. Is Marcus around?" Dayna shook her hand and sat down.

"His secretary says he's on an important phone call. I'm

sure he'll come in when he's through." Nicole sat down at her desk. "I hope you're bringing good news."

"I'll let you decide. Maybe we should just wait for Marcus." Dayna wore a tense expression.

Nicole felt a knot of unease as she looked at her. "I'll catch him up when he shows. What have you found out so far?"

Dayna seemed about to resist, then let out a gust of air. "Okay. You already know Tameka Grant was arrested for possession of stolen goods. At first she was all mouth, talking a lot of trash about her lawyer and police harassment, blah, blah, blah. We hear it a dozen times a week."

Nicole nodded. "I had the pleasure of listening to her my first week. Another client had a theft."

"Right, Mr. Phoung. We traced some of his goods to one of Tameka's brothers. Set up a food wholesale business with stolen merchandise. But there was no violence involved. The thieves would either steal a truck or get jobs as drivers and disappear with the goods."

"Getting jobs in order to set up thefts is part of their operation," Nicole said.

Dayna smiled. "You caught on to that one fast. You're right. These folks aren't your average street thugs. They've done some thinking and pretty impressive planning."

"Such as?" Nicole rocked back in her chair.

"Like I said, some of the gang get jobs. The ones that do don't have arrest records, or if they do, no convictions. But they also have friends, relatives, or girlfriends get jobs, too."

"They don't lie on the applications and their names aren't in arrest records. Clever." Nicole shook her head.

"If the jobs require drug screens, they get pals who don't use. We think they've infiltrated one of the labs to doctor drug tests." Dayna flipped open her notepad. "Hope you haven't used Advanced Tech Labs."

"I'll check." Nicole wrote down the name.

"Several other security firms do, which is why I asked. Bad stuff going down. They've got quite a criminal enterprise."

"I can't see Tameka being the brains behind such an organized scheme." Nicole tapped her ink pen against the yellow legal pad she'd written on.

"Nah, she's middle management at best. I haven't put together the whole picture. And my bosses are skeptical." Dayna's scowl deepened.

"I know a little bit about not being taken seriously," Nicole retorted.

Dayna glanced up from her notes. "Right, right. About my attitude earlier—"

"Forget about it." Nicole waved away Dayna's apology. "Tell me what you think is going on."

"This is all theory." Dayna got up and paced for several seconds.

Nicole reined in her impatience. Obviously Dayna needed to gather her thoughts. "Sure, I understand."

Dayna stopped pacing. "I think one of the local gangs has diversified. There's a lot of money in drugs, cocaine, especially. But it's a bloody business."

"I see." Nicole didn't see at all. Still, she knew to keep her mouth shut.

"Say members of this gang in the Fifth Ward, for example, decide to get into stuff with a better survival rate. So, they sell their drug trade to another gang and set up white-collar types of crimes."

"You mean . . . Wow."

"Wow is exactly what I said when it hit me. This gang is

looking toward the future." Dayna sat down again.

Nicole tried to work through the intricacies mentally. "But they would need lots of connections. I mean, the police aren't dummies."

"Glad somebody noticed," Dayna quipped.

Nicole grinned at Dayna briefly, then frowned again. "Our clients work with local precincts to coordinate crime watches and connect their alarms to police stations."

"One procedure I tried to implement has gone exactly nowhere," Dayna complained. "I wanted to use a grid to plot out certain classes of crime, even developed a computer program model. The bosses put it on hold."

"Lack of vision."

"Nope. They'll just wait a few months, then present it as their idea," Dayna said with a sour face.

"Ouch."

"Yeah, well." Dayna shrugged it off. "Anyway, it might not have worked. These crimes didn't fit a neat pattern anyway."

"You're thinking of ways to modify the model." Nicole's respect for her grew.

"Any kind of organized effort leaves traces of the pattern. In this case it's what was missing that counted." Dayna squinted.

"The stolen goods didn't show up on the street immediately, for one thing. Another thing, the usual suspects didn't pop up on the radar screen," Nicole said.

"You're no dummy at this yourself."

Nicole blushed. "Thanks. So, the pattern fooled some smart people. Including Marcus. When we first realized we had a problem, he was upset about missing the signs."

Dayna's expression tightened again. "Speaking of Marcus, why don't we check on how much longer he might be?"

Nicole noticed a subtle change in Dayna's tone. She punched his number, and Shelly answered. "Gone where?

Yes, as soon as he comes back. Marcus had to leave."

"Oh." Dayna didn't appear pleased. "I really need to touch base with him."

"You've got this funny look on your face. What's up?"

"I interviewed Tameka. She got kinda quiet when I mentioned several names. One of them is related to Shaun Jackson." Dayna shifted in her seat.

"Marcus's pal from the old neighborhood Shaun Jackson?"

"Yeah." Dayna frowned.

"That's a common name." Nicole watched her closely.

"True, but it's him. This guy is Jackson's cousin, and he's not very nice. He's got arrests for assault, armed robbery, and possession with intent. His record goes back ten years, and that's just in adult court."

"They came from a rough area of the city. So?"

"So . . ." Dayna's voice faded off as her frown deepened.

"Come on, tell me," Nicole prompted.

"It just so happens Jackson's cousin has been spotted hanging around with even nastier dudes. Which is really saying something." She paused to glance at the door as if wishing Marcus would appear.

"He's not coming. What is this about?" Nicole felt the hairs on her arms stand up.

Dayna looked at Nicole again. "There is another investigation. Jackson and his cousin have been spotted together."

"Another investigation," Nicole repeated. She sat very still now and watched every nuance of body language the detective displayed.

"Yeah, not of them and not connected to the thefts from your customers. I can't say more than that."

"But the two investigations might connect," Nicole said.

"I don't have any evidence of it at this point," Dayna

replied, lapsing into what sounded like police press conference spin.

"Uh-huh." Nicole chewed on what little Dayna had revealed. An ugly thought hit her. "You can't suspect Marcus is involved!"

"I need to ask him some questions is all. Don't trip." Dayna raised a palm.

Nicole studied her for several minutes. Dayna had known Marcus long before she'd met Nicole. Then Nicole remembered the vibes between them, the clear signs that Dayna and Marcus had dated once.

"You wanted to talk with Marcus before anyone else had to know. Including me."

"His buddy Shaun isn't exactly clean. Nothing proven, you understand," Dayna replied carefully.

"Like hanging around with criminals." Nicole didn't like the picture forming. She could tell Dayna wasn't thrilled with it either.

"Right. Jackson could be using his relationship with Marcus to get information," Dayna offered. She lifted a shoulder.

"We both know Marcus isn't stupid enough to be used," Nicole replied with a grimace.

The words that formed in her mouth left a sour taste behind. She couldn't bring herself to voice the suspicion implied by Dayna's silence. Neither could Dayna apparently, so they merely looked at each other for a few more minutes.

"Shaun Jackson isn't stupid either. In fact, he's very smart," Dayna said finally. "He's known Marcus longer than either of us. A bond that goes back to hard times on the street can be real strong."

"No," Nicole said firmly.

Dayna gestured to Nicole's phone. "Can I call Marcus's secretary?"

Though puzzled by the request, Nicole nodded her assent. She turned the phone around and pushed it to the edge of her desk. "Extension 202."

Dayna dialed the number. "Hi, Shelly. This is Detective Tyler. I was going to call Marcus, but it's not urgent. If he left to visit a customer I won't disturb him. I see. Thanks, bye." She hung up the phone. "He talked to Shaun Jackson before he left, so Shelly thinks maybe they're having a late lunch."

"Marcus could have his own suspicions. He might be going to confront Shaun for all we know," Nicole said in his defense before Dayna could say more.

"Possible," was Dayna's terse and less than convincing reply.

Nicole thought about the Marcus she knew, the man who had held her in his arms. She couldn't have mistaken the caring in his touch.

"There is a reasonable explanation. Marcus can't be held accountable for shady stuff his friend gets caught up in."

Dayna nodded. "I thought of the same thing. But I wasn't sure you'd see it that way."

"So why did you tell me about Shaun, his cousin, and the rest?" Nicole stared at her hard.

"I'm not real sure. Maybe I was hoping you could give me solid reasons Marcus couldn't be involved." Dayna looked at her steadily.

"Or evidence that he might be. Unless you'd prefer to think I'm in a scheme to rob my own customers," Nicole said.

"Personal feelings aside, I'm a cop. I'll follow whatever trail has the most signs pointing to a likely suspect." Dayna let out a noisy sigh. "I can't help myself."

Nicole nodded her understanding. "Now what?"

"I'll call Marcus and set up a meeting to ask my questions." Dayna stood and walked to the door.

"I'll page you when he gets back. I intend to be present." Nicole didn't flinch when Dayna spun around with a flinty expression.

"Fine."

Nicole sucked in air and let it out slowly. The pounding behind her eyes began to build up even more. She tried to ignore it as she dialed Marcus's mobile number.

Marcus circled the block three times before he spotted Shaun, who had appeared in the short three minutes it had taken Marcus to circle back. Shaun strolled along and puffed on a blunt cigar. Though his pace seemed leisurely, his eyes scanned his surroundings. Marcus turned into the lot of an office building. He found an empty space, parked, and walked quickly down the sidewalk toward Shaun.

Shaun's usually jaunty grin stretched his wide mouth tight. The glitter in his eyes wasn't good-humored, either. "Hey, dude."

"What the hell is up with you, Shaun?" Marcus blurted out when he got within a few feet of him.

Shaun nodded to the east of where they stood. "There's a little sandwich shop down the way. I'm hungry. Let's go." He started off.

Marcus fell in step beside him. "I want to know what's going on."

"Don't we all," Shaun replied and kept walking.

Ten minutes later they were seated across from each other, both with their hands folded atop a bright yellow table. Shaun had a tall plastic cup of strawberry soda. Marcus refused his offer to be treated. They sat in a corner away from the only other two customers having a late lunch.

"Well?" Marcus frowned at him.

"Can't decide on the ham and cheese po'boy or the roast beef. Gotta be careful. I haven't had a chance to work out in the last week or so." Shaun patted his flat abs.

"Forget the menu and start talking," Marcus grumbled, careful to keep his tone low.

"I'm having a few problems. Nothing I can't handle." Shaun lifted a shoulder.

"Handle as in skip out on your condo lease and drop out of sight. Exactly who is after you for money?" Marcus leaned forward as he spoke.

"Don't trip, man. I'm gonna bounce for a few days then come back strong. I'll pay everybody, eventually." Shaun waved a hand. "That's not why I called you, though."

"This thing with Olandon—"

"I'm through with that chump. I've given him too many chances. Whatever he's gotten himself into this time is his problem." Shaun's mouth twisted in a sneer.

"He's implicated in the thefts of our customers. I find that real strange." Marcus stared at Shaun.

"Look, man, I admit to maybe going too far to help family. But that's it."

"Really?"

"Yes." Shaun returned his gaze without blinking for several moments.

"So, tell me exactly why you disappeared," Marcus said finally.

"I owe some business partners, ran short on cash. I didn't want to leave town without letting you know." Shaun sipped through the straw.

"What?" Marcus blurted loudly. When the servers behind the counter glanced at them, he tried to appear relaxed.

"You need to chill, man." Shaun looked around. "I've got some business interests that should pay off soon. First I gotta take a short trip."

Marcus shook his head slowly. "I sure as hell hope you're not doing something really stupid."

"When have you known me to be stupid?" Shaun grinned.

"First time for everything." Marcus continued to stare at him with a taut frown.

Shaun sighed. "Okay, since you just have to get in my business. I bought some cheap goods in Hong Kong that I've had in storage. Remember I went on that trip six months ago?"

"Yeah." Marcus nodded. "Another one of your ideas to make a killing in the import business."

"Right. Well, my partner bailed. I finally tracked him down and found where he'd stored the goods. I had to use a little firm persuasion." Shaun tapped a fist into the palm of his hand.

"You did what?" Marcus said, this time careful to speak softly.

"He'll be fine once they take the cast off," Shaun quipped. Then he grew serious again. "I've got a market for the stuff, and then my money problems will be solved."

Marcus weighed his explanation. He couldn't find holes in the story. Yet he knew Shaun too well. "Olandon fits in there somewhere."

"I hired that fool to help me move the stuff. He never showed. I keep trying to save his sorry ass only because my grandmother asked me to. Not anymore." Shaun shook his head hard.

"Shaun, don't cover for him. If you know anything about his involvement in these thefts, tell me now," Marcus pressed.

"I swear, Marcus. I might bend the law until it almost

breaks, but none of that gangsta stuff." Shaun clamped a hand over Marcus's wrist. "You know me."

Marcus studied his intense expression. Neither spoke for several minutes as Marcus considered his explanation. Shaun had his faults, but sneaking into stores after hours to steal wasn't his style; at least not since their teen years in the Fifth Ward. Still, Marcus could not ignore the gut feeling that Shaun was being Shaun. His account might be the outer layer concealing the core truth.

"Yes, Shaun. I do know you. I hope all you're into is debt because of a bad but *legal* import deal."

Shaun wore a crooked grin. "You're not even gonna stick it to the Summers fat cats. Where is the dude I know and love?"

"Shaun, listen to me. My pal Dayna—"

"That hot lady detective? You havin' way too much fun without me." Shaun laughed and sipped more soda.

"Dayna will probably connect Olandon to you. I need to know if there is any reason he could pull you down with him," Marcus said with vehemence.

"Everything is cool with me." Shaun shoved a set of keys toward him. "I left my Escalade at your place. All my worldly goods are in there, sold most of the other stuff. I'll call you."

Marcus looked at the keys, then at Shaun. "You haven't told me everything."

"We've got a lot of friendship between us, and trust. I always thought we'd have trust. Yeah, we've had our moments. But when it comes down to it I'm there for you and you've been there for me."

Seconds ticked away as Marcus studied Shaun. Finally he nodded. "You need to be careful who you hang out with, man."

"Tell me about it. Two days tops and I'll take my junk off your hands. I'll treat you to steak at Brennan's." Shaun's facial muscles relaxed into his trademark easy smile that had charmed so many. He rose and looked down at Marcus.

"You owe me steak and lobster for all this drama." Marcus stood.

Shaun laughed and waved goodbye. He took time to flirt with one of the servers behind the counter before he left. Marcus couldn't help but smile with affection as he followed him. With one last grin, Shaun walked quickly down the street. Marcus watched him cross to a pay parking lot and get into a white Ford Focus with a rental license tag.

Marcus went back to his car. He checked for digital messages on his mobile phone. Nicole had left her number and added 911 after it. She picked up on the first ring.

"I'm sorry. I got tied up and—" he started to explain, then stopped. Nicole's near frenzied voice blasted through in a stream of words. He listened, and his stomach twisted.

"Slow down, Nicole. Did you say murder?"

twenty-two

Nicole willed her hands to loosen their tight grip on the arms of her chair. She felt surrounded by the full force of the police department. Dayna sat across from her, her face unreadable. The newcomer, a short husky man the color of milk chocolate, seemed to be considering whether or not Nicole was a suspect. Homicide detective Larry Holmes wore an expression of infinite patience, as though used to waiting out confessions. His partner, Frank O'Connor, watched her every move. All four sat around the round table of the seating area in Nicole's office. Determined not to be the first to blink, Nicole clenched her teeth to keep from talking. Detective Holmes cleared his throat at last. He looked more like a high school principal, with his gold wire-framed eyeglasses and starched white shirt.

"How well did you know the victim?" Holmes blinked at her through the lens.

"We met a few times. She dated my cousin." Nicole thought of the ashen color of Russell's face when she'd seen him last night. "Naturally he's devastated."

"Dated," Holmes repeated and paused. "How serious were they? Engaged?"

"Russell seemed very much in love. They hadn't announced an engagement." Nicole shifted in her seat.

"You said *he* seemed very much in love. Maybe you don't think she felt the same."

Nicole took her time answering. "Like I said, I only met her a couple of times. Mostly I heard Russell talking about her."

"But you didn't say 'They seemed very much in love,' " Holmes persisted.

"The few times I saw them together she was very affectionate." Nicole felt a flash of anxiety at the look he gave her.

"Your cousin is at home," Holmes murmured. He rubbed his chin as he looked out the window of her office.

"Yes." Nicole bit back the urge to remind him she'd already said Russell had gone home.

"I'll interview him later," he said as though talking to himself. Then he glanced at Nicole. "What do you know about Ms. Manning?"

"Only what Russell told me, that she came from a prominent family in California. I think he said San Jose, or maybe it was Sacramento. She worked in fashion marketing. I don't know where."

"None of which is true," Dayna said.

"Aliyah Manning grew up in a New Orleans housing project. Her family moved to the Fifth Ward in Houston when she was thirteen. She had three children by the time she was eighteen, all being raised by relatives. She has a history of arrests for passing bad checks, receiving stolen things, and felony theft." Holmes rattled off the account.

"Busy girl." Nicole's mind raced as she digested the information.

"You think your cousin might have found out?" O'Connor squinted at Nicole.

Nicole glanced at Dayna for a cue. She didn't get one. Dayna kept her expression blank. "I don't think so. They were still tight the last time I talked to him."

"I see." Holmes seemed to consider whether or not he believed her. "What about these thefts?"

Nicole started at the sudden shift. "What?"

"Your customers have had problems. One of them thinks your employees are involved." Holmes glanced at Dayna.

"Yeah. Tameka Grant, for one," Dayna said.

"We haven't found any kind of widespread conspiracy, if that's what you mean. And what does this have to do with Aliyah?" Nicole asked. The three detectives exchanged glances.

"Ms. Manning knew Shaun Jackson," Holmes said.

"Okay." Nicole waited.

"One of our suspects in the LaSalle Jewelry Store robbery is related to Jackson," Dayna said. "Olandon Jackson."

"Did Mr. Reed know Ms. Manning?" Holmes asked the question in an offhand manner.

"Aliyah came to the office several times to see Russell. Marcus knew her in the sense that they'd met that way." Nicole glanced at Dayna again. Still no cue.

"I see." Holmes waited again.

"What is all this about?" Nicole said.

"Just seems like a lot of strange coincidences," O'Connor replied. "Burglaries that progress to an armed robbery and now a murder. They all link back to Summers Security some kinda way."

"Are you suggesting that Marcus, Russell, and I are suspects?" Nicole looked at each detective in turn.

"We're just trying to figure out what it all means, Ms. Benoit." Holmes wore the expression of a kindly uncle.

"Right." Nicole didn't feel reassured at all. Her temper started to simmer.

"So, you don't know this Olandon Jackson who happens to be the cousin of your vice president's best friend?" Holmes spoke in a level tone. One bushy eyebrow lifted as he gazed at her.

"No," Nicole said in a calm voice. "I don't know the second cousin twice removed of my secretary's hairdresser either."

Dayna sucked air. "Funny."

"Lady, this isn't a joke," O'Connor put in. He started to go on, but Holmes lifted a palm.

"I like your sense of humor," Holmes nodded, though he didn't smile.

"Thanks." Nicole worked hard to ignore the jittery feeling of having three top cops pissed at her. *Put the safety lock on your big mouth.*

"This particular cousin is on a list of suspects, not to mention his criminal history." Holmes went back to looking pensive for several more seconds. "Where did you say Mr. Reed is right now?"

"On his way back from a meeting," Nicole replied.

"Hmm. Tameka Grant has interesting things to say about his friend Shaun." Holmes looked at her expectantly.

"I see." Nicole folded her hands in her lap. She pretended not to notice Dayna's muttered curse word or O'Connor's glower.

Holmes appeared undisturbed by her response. He nodded again. "Yes, indeed. She thinks he's somehow involved. A strange coincidence."

"She thinks. She's never seen Shaun or talked to him." Nicole tilted her head to one side.

"No, she hasn't," Holmes admitted. His half-smile appeared apologetic.

"Interesting. Guilt by association." Nicole crossed her legs.

"We're fleshing out all the twists and turns." Holmes spread his hands out.

"Good. That's what we're hoping for here at Summers Security." Nicole smiled back at him.

"I would think so, since your business depends on trust," Holmes replied. "I'm sure your clients want to know you're fully cooperating with us."

"We've told them so." Nicole brushed nonexistent lint from her navy blue skirt.

"Shaun Jackson has a few skeletons in his closet," O'Connor blurted out.

"He and Marcus grew up in the Fifth Ward. I know about it." Nicole glanced at him briefly, then looked at Holmes again.

"Did you know that Mr. Jackson has been accused of fraud in several telemarketing schemes?" Holmes said in a quiet voice.

"Accused, not convicted?" Nicole asked.

"He's slippery," O'Connor said.

Nicole looked at Dayna. "What do you think? You've known Marcus for awhile."

Dayna looked at her colleagues before she answered. "Nobody here is suggesting Marcus is dirty. There's just no evidence. Right now we're looking at a jumble of facts. We need to see what fits and what to throw out."

Nicole had the feeling she'd made that point to them before. "Of course."

O'Connor's cell phone played a musical tune. He unhooked it from his belt, stood, and answered. He left the room still talking low. "Yeah, what is it?"

"You don't know Shaun Jackson well." Holmes repeated what Nicole had already told him twice.

She pushed down irritation. "I've only met him a few times."

"Larry, come over here a minute." O'Connor beckoned from the open door.

"Excuse me." Holmes strode out.

When they were alone Nicole turned to Dayna. "What the hell is wrong with you accusing Marcus?"

"I didn't accuse him," Dayna snapped back as she glanced over her shoulder toward the door. "But this crap with Shaun stinks. He's been slippin' and slidin' around the law for a long time."

"You really think Marcus helps him scam people?" Nicole glared at her.

"No, I don't. But Marcus is extremely loyal to the guy. They've got ties strong as blood." Dayna bit her lower lip.

Nicole started to protest, then paused. Marcus had few ties that had lasted, even fewer people he had been able to count on over the years. Could he let a sense of loyalty lead him to protect his friend and betray Summers Security? Then she remembered the talks they'd had about the company's future while holding each other close. She couldn't be that big a fool or Marcus that good an actor.

"No. Marcus might try to save Shaun, but he wouldn't be his accomplice. Not even by shielding him."

"I hope you're right. He—" Dayna broke off when the two detectives came back in.

O'Connor stood with his legs apart and both hands on his hips, suit coat pushed back. "More pieces are falling into place by the minute."

Dayna glanced from him to Holmes with a frown. "What?"

"That meeting Mr. Reed had was with Shaun Jackson," Holmes said.

"Oh sh—" Dayna clamped her lips together to cut off the expletive.

Nicole fought the dizzy dip the floor beneath her seemed to take. She breathed in and let it out slowly. Seconds ticked by as the three detectives stared at her. Finally Nicole stood.

"If that's all, I need to get back to work," she said, amazed her voice sounded steady.

O'Connor opened his mouth, but Holmes cut him off with a sharp glance. He reached into his jacket, took out his card, and dropped it on the table.

"Have Mr. Reed call me. Soon," Holmes said.

"I'll tell him." Nicole didn't touch the card or look at it.

"Goodbye." Holmes walked out of her office.

O'Connor followed him, after casting a solemn glance at Nicole for effect. Dayna stayed behind for a second, seemed about to speak, then followed the two men out. Nicole dropped into her seat.

"What are you up to, Marcus?" she muttered.

Cat entered Nicole's office without knocking. "He's back."

Nicole sprang from her chair and strode past her. Seconds later she arrived at Marcus's office. "No calls, no interruptions," she instructed his wide-eyed secretary.

"Yes, ma'am," Shelly replied promptly.

Marcus had his back to her but spun around when she slammed the door. "Nicole, what the hell is going on?"

"Excuse me, but that's my line," she snapped. "Start with your buddy Shaun, aka the sleazeball con man."

"What did the police say?" Marcus rubbed his chin with one hand.

She studied him through narrowed eyes for several seconds. Guilt stamped his face, giving him a shifty look she'd never noticed before. "You're prepared to cover for him."

Marcus took his hand away from his face. His eyes sparked fire. "Let me explain something about Shaun and me, okay? I met him on an empty lot when I was nine years old. Three boys twice my age and size were beating the hell out of me. Here comes this lanky kid swinging his fist like a crazy man, and he saves my ass. Since then he's had my back. You don't know anything about the obstacles we faced."

Nicole walked closer to him. "Don't hide behind the fact that you grew up poor. Poverty doesn't excuse robbery or murder."

He blinked as though each word she spoke slapped him hard across the face. Marcus exhaled like a man who had been holding his breath too long. He sat down hard in the executive chair behind his desk. "I need you to understand, that's all."

"Then give me some answers. Shaun knew Aliyah. Was she part of the thefts from our customers? Did Shaun know about them, too? Was he in on it with his cousin and—"

"I don't know." Marcus rubbed his forehead and frowned. "I just don't know. Shaun says he didn't know anything about what Olandon was up to, that he tried to help him stay out of trouble. Look, Shaun has his faults."

"Yeah, that's one way of putting it," Nicole retorted. "The police call his faults larceny and felony theft by deception."

"Stop it." Marcus jabbed a forefinger at her. "Shaun comes close to the line. Okay, he's crossed it more than a few times."

"This is your defense of him? Please!" Nicole threw up both hands.

"But," Marcus shouted, "slick talking somebody out of

money? Sure, that's Shaun. Setting up a questionable invest-ment scheme? He's right there. But he's not into robbery and he sure as hell isn't into murder."

"Tell me something. How close have you two been in, say, the last couple of years? You know all his friends and what they're into, Marcus?" Nicole walked to his desk and leaned on it with both palms flat. "Because if you answer yes, then—"

"What? I'm a criminal, too?" Marcus stared at her hard. "All us ghetto boys are the same underneath. Sure we can get cleaned up. But deep down we're gangstas dressed real nice. Is that what you're saying?"

"The police don't believe in all these coincidences. Nei-ther do I. Aliyah lied about her background." Nicole gasped when Marcus looked away. "You knew."

"Not at first."

Nicole's eyes narrowed. "She and Shaun were lovers?"

"A long time ago. Shaun swore to me it was over. He didn't stay with one woman for long," Marcus replied.

"Another admirable character trait. What does he say about the murder?"

"I don't think he knows."

"Oh come on!" Nicole slammed her hand on the wooden surface of his desk.

"He didn't mention it when we talked today!" Marcus yelled back at her. "Shaun would have said something."

"The police must be following him, or you," Nicole added, and frowned. The thought struck her suddenly. "Damn, I should have known."

Marcus looked up at her sharply. "What?"

"You knew Aliyah, too. You wanted to take over, but Uncle Hosea went back on his verbal promise—"

"Hold on, Nicole." Marcus stood.

"Kelli told me you were putting out the word about starting your own security company." Nicole backed away from him. A horrible picture formed in her head, awful images flashing like a camera snapping pictures.

"Honey, listen to me." Marcus came around the desk with his arms outstretched.

Nicole felt a sting at another image that popped into her head—Aliyah smiling seductively as she stood close to Marcus.

Marcus must have seen something in Nicole's eyes. He shook his head and walked toward her. He stopped when she held up both hands as a shield.

"Maybe the plan got away from you. Did your pals Shaun and Aliyah get greedy? Aliyah grew up in your old neighborhood, too. Maybe Shaun wasn't the one she was sleeping with." Nicole swallowed hard.

"You know that's not true," Marcus said quietly.

"I have no idea what's true and what's not these days." Nicole opened the door.

Russell shoved her aside. "Him! He killed her. I saw the way you looked at her. When Aliyah wouldn't give in you killed her!"

Andre rushed in and grabbed Russell's arms. "Come on, man. This is not a good idea. The cops are here and—"

"Good. They can arrest Marcus!" Russell pushed Andre hard until he hit the wall.

Cat hurried in and shut the door. "They're coming down the hall right now."

"I'm ready for them. What about you two?" Russell glared at Nicole and Marcus.

Nicole planted one palm on Russell's chest and shoved him down into a chair. She put her face close to his. "Shut up and listen. You're a suspect, too. Aliyah lied to you. Maybe you found out she was screwing around behind your back. She was a ghetto girl out to get your money and maybe she even used you to set up those thefts."

She spat out the theory in a rush. Seconds later they heard Shelly's voice outside trying to stall Detective Holmes. Everyone froze. A hard knock made them all jump at the same time.

"They can't possible think I—" Russell blinked rapidly. A single drop of sweat rolled down his face. He whimpered when a harder series of knocks sounded.

"Mr. Reed, we really need to talk," Detective Holmes said through the door. "Let's do this easy. I wouldn't want my officers to damage this nice solid wood door."

"Everybody listen to me," Nicole said low. "We're in this with Marcus whether we like it or not." She turned to him. "And I sure as hell don't like it, but right now I don't have a choice."

"Nicole—" Marcus started forward.

Nicole cut him off when she opened the office door. Detective Holmes came in with Dayna and two uniformed officers. Dayna stared at Marcus as if sending him a silent message. Holmes glanced around until his gaze settled on Marcus.

"Good morning," Holmes said.

"Hello, Detective Holmes. What can we do for you?" Nicole stepped between them.

"I need to have a little chat with Mr. Reed here." Holmes nodded toward Marcus.

"Fine." Nicole managed what she hoped was an easy smile. She turned to Russell, Cat, and Andre. "Excuse us, please."

"I'm staying right here to correct any lies you two tell." Russell crossed his arms.

"Leave," Nicole said through clenched teeth.

Holmes turned abruptly to face Russell. "You'll have a chance to give your statement very soon. Right after these officers search your office."

"What?" Nicole and Russell said in unison.

"Actually we're going to search the entire office. Won't take long. One of our detectives is on your computer system," Holmes continued calmly as though discussing a routine detail. "Andre Allen?"

"Sir," Andre croaked and blinked hard.

"You'll need to assist Detective O'Connor. He's already at one of your computers in the conference room, I believe. Thank you," Holmes added.

"Like we have a choice," Nicole said in a tight voice.

"Oh, speaking of which." Holmes took out a long white envelope. "Warrant to search the premises."

"For what?" Nicole took the envelope without opening it.

"Evidence, of course," he replied in a distracted tone.

Holmes nodded to the officers, who left with Andre. Then he glanced around the room as though conducting his own visual search. He walked around the desk and looked out the window. Nicole beckoned to Cat, who hurried to her side.

"Call our lawyer. Fax him this and explain what's going on," Nicole said to her. Cat nodded and slipped from the room quietly.

"All in order," Holmes said over his shoulder.

"I'm sure it is." Nicole joined him at the window. She followed the direction of his gaze. "Ready to start?"

Holmes sighed as though in no rush. "Nice. Summers Security has been very successful. Hosea Summers was quite a character."

Nicole felt like a character in a vintage mystery movie. "He had his way of doing things."

"Like leaving his business to a niece instead of his own son." Holmes faced them.

Russell took the bait. "My father was an old, sick man who was unduly influenced by her parents."

"I thought you wanted to question Marcus," Nicole said, ignoring her irate cousin.

"Based on his reputation, Mr. Summers didn't sound like the kind of man who could be manipulated. He thought a lot of Mr. Reed, gave him a lot of authority." Holmes looked at Marcus.

"My father could be spiteful and irrational," Russell grumbled. He shot a heated look at Marcus.

"Must have been a huge disappointment when Mr. Summers left the business to Ms. Benoit," Holmes said.

"His will won't stand up. My father was seriously ill, probably not mentally competent and—"

"I was talking to Mr. Reed," Holmes broke in.

"It was his company. He had a right to leave it to whomever he chose." Marcus appeared unruffled.

"You had an agreement, though. Mr. Summers promised that he would sell you his interest in the company. He lied to you, obviously." Holmes walked over to stand directly in front of Marcus.

"He changed his mind, yes. I accepted it," Marcus said carefully.

"I don't think you did, not that easily. You made it clear to several of your biggest clients that you would go out on your own soon. So, if Summers Security suffered, you would benefit." Holmes cocked his large head to one side.

"Starting my own business isn't a crime. People do it every day. Raiding my employer's client list may not be considered ethical, but it's not against the law," Marcus said with a lift of one shoulder.

"No, it's not." Holmes shot a quick glance at Nicole, then back at Marcus.

"You were planning to stab me in the back. No wonder you acted funny when I talked about us being partners." Russell scowled at him, then looked at Holmes. "More evidence he was behind those crimes."

"Seems you had all kinds of options." Nicole stared at Marcus, anger bubbling in her stomach like acid.

"I never once considered working for Russell. And as disappointed as I was that Mr. Summers went back on his word, I didn't plot to ruin Summers Security." Marcus spoke in an even tone.

Nicole had to admire his composure under such pressure. Of course he was cool as ice. Look at how well he'd deceived her. She turned away from him to the view outside his window.

"How well did you know Aliyah Manning?" Holmes asked.

"I only met her once or twice. Yes, I know she and Shaun had been involved at one time," Marcus replied.

"When did you find out?" Holmes walked around the room picking up objects from the desk. Then he peered at the flat-screen computer monitor.

"A few weeks ago. Shaun told me after we saw Aliyah and Russell here."

"So, you knew she wasn't from a prominent family with money. You had to suspect she was up to something," Holmes said.

"Wait a minute. Aliyah and I loved each other," Russell protested. "She was probably embarrassed about her background. But that doesn't mean she was a criminal."

"Aliyah Manning had an arrest record, Mr. Summers. She

was scamming elderly men with money by the time she was in her late teens. I'm sorry to put that news so bluntly." Holmes watched Russell over the wire rim of his eyeglasses.

"I don't believe it," Russell said stubbornly.

"You think these charges were all a mistake," Holmes said in a dry tone. "Or maybe you found out she was lying."

"It wouldn't have mattered. I loved her." Russell lifted his chin.

"Hmm." Holmes appeared skeptical but said no more for several minutes. A slender white man with blond hair, dressed in a steel gray suit, came in without knocking. "Detective Ferris is our computer expert."

Ferris nodded a greeting to them all, then turned to Holmes. "I finished up."

"Good. You and Frank can interview Mr. Summers." Holmes pointed to Russell.

"Your office should be fine." Ferris opened the door and waited.

"I don't have anything to hide," Russell said.

Still, his indignant expression faltered. He rubbed his mouth with a shaky hand. Ferris glanced at Holmes briefly, then followed Russell through the door. Holmes held the door open and looked at Nicole. He didn't speak, simply waited for her to leave. Nicole tried not to look at Marcus before walking out, but she couldn't help it. Cat and Shelly stood outside. Both wore frightened expressions.

"What did that detective say?" Cat whispered.

"Marcus isn't in trouble, is he?" Shelly twisted her hands together. Both women looked over their shoulders at the same time.

"Holmes asked a lot of questions, and I don't know how much trouble Marcus is in right now."

Nicole was about to say more when one of the officers walked by. She went to her office with Cat and Shelly right behind her.

"The lawyer said the warrant is good," Cat said once the door closed.

"There's no such thing as a good search warrant," Shelly muttered.

"You know what I mean. Anyway, they've been looking at personnel files again. Andre says they accessed the database. What in the world could they be looking for?" Cat stared at Nicole.

"I have a feeling we'll find out real soon," Nicole murmured. She paced for a time, then sat down.

"The phones are ringing like crazy. Go back to your office, Shelly. We can't hide out all day." Cat gestured for her to leave.

Shelly stood. "Marcus didn't do anything wrong, Nicole. I'm positive."

Nicole wanted to be just as sure. She couldn't bring herself to agree, because doubt chewed at her. All she could do was nod. Shelly left, and Cat waited a few seconds before she spoke.

"What now? I know you're not going to just sit around waiting for the other shoe to fall," Cat said.

"In spite of everything, we do still have a business to run. What's going to be left of it, anyway, once the news gets out." Nicole sat down at her desk. "I'm not going down without a fight."

"Mr. Hosea would say the same thing. You've got his genes, all right," Cat quipped.

"Please, I'm trying not to be depressed. Don't make things worse," Nicole shot back.

Nicole looked at her desk. She didn't make an attempt to deal with any of the paperwork or go through the pile of telephone messages. Her thoughts skittered around, making concentrating on anything but Marcus and his interview with Holmes impossible. She finally decided to give in.

"Anything on my desk a fire that needed to be put out yesterday?" She waved a hand at the neat stacks Cat had made.

"Imani and Andre could handle some of it, I think." Cat started sorting through the messages.

"Good. Make a list."

Nicole gave Cat instructions. Then she called Andre, Imani, and other employees. After making several telephone calls she pushed aside business as usual. She signed onto one of three information databases she'd subscribed to, and she started her own investigation.

twenty-three

The nightmare continued the next day. Nicole sat in her office at eight in the morning. Most of the staff had not yet arrived, but Nicole and Cat had gotten a head start on a long list of chores. Still, she couldn't ignore Tuesday's edition of the Houston *Chronicle*. Aliyah's murder had made it to the front page.

Cat peered over Nicole's shoulder at the headline. "What a horrible way to die."

"There's a good way?"

"Yeah, peacefully in your sleep at a ripe old age; not beaten to death, strangled, and tossed into a bayou." Cat shivered.

Nicole read the newspaper article about Aliyah's murder for the fifth time. She shook her head. A nameless reporter had summed up Aliyah's life in so few words. Twenty-six years in four short paragraphs.

"Mr. Daigre from Lake Charles called again," Cat said.

"I'll call him," Nicole answered in a distracted tone.

"I might be out of bounds, but . . ." Cat's voice faded.

Nicole looked up from the newspaper. "I'm listening."

"The cops are more likely to suspect Marcus. He's the one from the 'hood, and Shaun is his pal." Cat frowned. "It doesn't look good."

"No," Nicole said in a short tone.

In the last twenty-four hours she'd ridden the emotional equivalent of a monster roller coaster. Marcus had withdrawn from her. His code of street silence had driven a wedge between them. Nicole had begun to wonder just how much he knew about what Shaun had been doing. Busy trying to salvage their remaining contracts and deal with employees, Nicole had had only scant time to wonder why he hadn't sought her out to explain. He had to know questions were eating away at her. Cat's voice broke through the swirl of suspicions nibbling away at her trust in him.

"Ahem, like I was saying," Cat began again. Her eyes sparkled with zeal. She dropped the papers she held onto Nicole's desk. "I think we should figure out who killed Aliyah. Or at least give the police a more likely suspect."

"Us?" Nicole tilted her chair back and rocked gently.

"We've got the tools at our fingertips. Don't tell me you haven't started some investigating of this stuff."

"Yes, I have. Only to find out more background information on Aliyah," Nicole admitted.

"And?"

"I didn't learn much more than what Detective Holmes told us. She had expensive taste and liked to spend other people's money." Nicole grunted. "Shaun Jackson had a few close calls with the police, mostly white-collar stuff. Aliyah did work with him at least twice in the last three years in telemarketing scams."

"Any connection between her and Marcus? I know it had to be on your mind," Cat said when Nicole squinted at her.

"None that I could find." Nicole couldn't shake the image of Aliyah standing close to Marcus as though sharing a secret.

"She wasn't his type." Cat shook her head slowly.

"How long does it take to really know someone?" Nicole murmured, asking herself the question rather than asking Cat.

"She probably shook her groove thang at him, but Marcus prefers substance, not empty flash."

"Watch it! I've been called empty flash in my time," Nicole tossed back.

"You might like a good party, but you've got brains, principles, and family loyalty. Why else would you put up with Russell's crap?"

"Uncle Hosea's will wouldn't let me fire him," Nicole retorted. "Firing Russell was the least of what I've wanted to do to him in the last month or so."

"I didn't say you were perfect," Cat joked.

Nicole gave a short, humorless laugh, then frowned. She swiveled her chair around to the window. Fluffy white clouds hung against a bright blue background. The peaceful scene didn't do anything to calm the jitters in her stomach.

"I just wish Marcus would talk to me," Nicole grumbled.

"Maybe he doesn't want you to be in danger. He could be on the trail of the killer and—"

"You've been watching too many old action movies. I'm not Foxy Brown, and Marcus isn't Shaft." Nicole turned her chair around again.

"I'm just saying we should find out the truth," Cat said with a nod.

"You mean we should track down the maniac who cracked Aliyah's skull and let him know we're onto him. Right?" Nicole crossed her arms.

Cat put a hand to her throat. "Uh, when you put it like that it doesn't sound like such a great idea."

"Damn right it doesn't sound like a good idea," Nicole said. "Let the police handle it."

"They are pointing a finger at Marcus. We should do something," Cat protested.

"They're considering Russell as a suspect, too. And me, as a matter of fact." Nicole felt a chill.

"More reason to take action," Cat said. "Okay, so maybe we won't look for the murderer. But we can help Marcus."

Nicole stared past Cat without seeing anything. "Except he's not talking."

"Then make him talk." Cat stood and planted both hands on her hips. "Shelly says he came in a half hour ago."

"Right." Nicole didn't move.

Cat picked up her phone and tapped the keypads. "Marcus, Nicole for you." She stuck the receiver in Nicole's face.

After mouthing a silent curse word, Nicole snatched the receiver from her hand. "Guess it's time for that talk now. I'm on my way. Happy?" she said to Cat after hanging up.

"I'll be happy when this whole mess is over and none of us land in prison." Cat picked up her stack of work again.

"Hold that thought," Nicole muttered and left. Shelly nodded to her when she arrived outside Marcus's office. "No calls or interruptions."

"You got it," Shelly replied.

Nicole paused to prepare. *Tact and composure.* She opened the door, mentally reciting the words like a mantra. Marcus stood in front of his desk, arms folded and a stiff expression on his handsome face.

"Hi." He swept a hand out toward the chairs.

"Hello." Nicole stood in spite of his invitation.

"I know. You don't believe me."

His blunt statement brought her up short. "Well, you could help by telling me what your friend Shaun has been up to lately."

"Shaun isn't involved in the burglaries, much less a murder," Marcus said in a firm tone.

"You know this for a fact?" Nicole paced in a small circle in front of him.

"I know Shaun."

"So, you've been with him every moment of the day for the past few days? I'm not even asking about the past six months when the burglaries increased." Nicole stopped to face him.

"You know the answer," he replied with an edge in his tone.

"I suppose it's simply an incredible coincidence that Shaun's cousin is connected to the thefts, the robbery at LaSalle's Jewelry, and that Aliyah is Shaun's old girlfriend." Nicole paced again.

"You forgot to mention Shaun and I being friends."

"I was getting to it, trust me," Nicole snapped. She sucked in a deep breath and let it out when his eyes narrowed. "Look, whatever he's done, at least tell me. That way we can deal with it together."

"Don't worry. Shaun is having money problems. He swore to me that he didn't have any idea what Olandon was doing or know anything about Aliyah."

"You've talked to him in the past day? The police want to question him. Marcus, if they find out—"

"Shaun is going to call them," he said.

Nicole whirled around and put both fists on her hips. "Oh, come on! I'll bet your pal is headed to a country that doesn't have an extradition agreement with the U.S."

"Drop the drama, all right?" Marcus leaned against his desk. "Shaun isn't going anywhere. He doesn't have the money, and Shaun likes to travel first class."

"Shaun has plenty of cash somewhere for just such an emergency. And he's left you holding the bag. Wake up!"

"You're wrong. I talked to him this morning." Marcus pressed his lips together.

Nicole walked over to him until they were inches apart. "Where is he?"

"He's in town. Most likely he'll consult his attorney and get in touch with the police." Marcus let his arms fall to his sides. "Everything is going to be okay."

"Aliyah worked for Shaun not so long ago. But I think you knew that." Nicole stared at him hard.

Marcus frowned. "Look, you don't know about police harassment on your side of the tracks. They can build a case around you so that you look guilty. He needs time to get his defense lined up."

"He shouldn't need that much time if he's innocent," Nicole shot back. "Detective Holmes said—"

"I don't care what that so-called brother says," Marcus hissed.

"The man isn't a traitor because he catches criminals. Black on Black crime is a fact of life. Thugs who steal what we've worked hard to get should be locked up," Nicole said, her voice raised.

"Most of your relatives don't work for anything. They sit on their fat assets all day. People like Shaun have to scuffle for a decent share of the pie. I'm not defending her, but Tameka came from the same place we did. Being poor can push people to the limit." Marcus gazed off, as though looking back to his own rocky childhood.

"Lots of kids grew up poor. Guess what? They went to school and got good jobs, not so they could scam their employers either," Nicole said.

He squinted at her. "You're talking about me?"

Nicole sat in the nearest chair with a sigh. "You shouldn't be surprised I've got questions. The police are telling me about drugs and armed robbery. I feel like I'm trapped in a gangsta rap movie."

"So, we're all alike."

"I didn't say that."

"Sure you did," Marcus clipped.

"I thought you'd grown out of that life. Stop making excuses for those people. I meant Tameka, Shaun, and Aliyah," she added when his dark eyebrows pulled together. "They're from that thug life culture. You know exactly what I mean."

"Yeah, I'm afraid I do." Marcus looked at her with his mouth turned down at the edges.

"Don't give me that self-righteous attitude," Nicole said defensively. "You wondered about Shaun or else you wouldn't have disappeared to track him down."

"You're right. But I listened to him. I didn't let accusations change the way I feel about Shaun. Because of our friendship I chose to stand by him," Marcus said evenly.

Nicole stood and faced him. "Or maybe you've chosen to believe what you want to, in spite of the facts."

"The system's version of the facts?" Marcus gave a short, grim laugh. "Even bourgie Black folks get stopped by the police just because, Nicole. You people kid yourselves that your money, family names, and connections mean something. You live in your insulated world and think you're so damn special."

"We have to deal with our share of barriers," Nicole replied heatedly. "We don't commit felonies in response."

"No, you drink too much, shop, and when that doesn't work you play at being hardworking business folks."

They stared at each other in silence for several minutes. "The truth of what you think about me finally comes out," she said.

"I was just thinking the same thing." He gazed back at her.

Nicole searched his expression. "Let's stop before we say too much. We're both stressed out and more than a little wired. Space and time is what we need."

"I agree." Marcus went to his desk and sat down. He tapped the keyboard of his desktop computer.

"What are you doing?" Nicole frowned at him.

"You'll have my resignation in two minutes. I'll keep it simple." He continued to type.

She strode over and pushed his hands away from the keys. "Don't be ridiculous."

"No sense in putting it off. Your father and uncle should be asking for this any minute now. Besides, you don't trust me either." Marcus started typing again.

"I questioned your judgment when it came to Shaun, but—"

"I was going out on my own and made it clear to several of our biggest clients. Those clients would have followed me. My best friend is being implicated in a robbery and a murder. You know your father and uncle. What are they thinking?"

"I'll deal with them. You could make it easier if you'd just . . ." Nicole heaved a sigh.

"Kick Shaun to the curb? I won't do it." Marcus shook his head and went back to typing.

"I'm going to toss that thing out a window in a minute." Nicole picked up the keyboard. "Stop making your big statement for a second and let me think."

"Okay. Next question. Do you believe in me?" Marcus said quietly. He grabbed her wrist in a tight grip.

"I know you didn't intentionally help Shaun do anything wrong. I mean, you're taking this loyalty thing too far. And you should have been honest with me. Even you have to admit it looks bad. I . . ." Nicole's voice faded as his facial muscles pulled tight.

"Thanks for the strong vote of confidence. I'll mail the resignation." Marcus stood.

Nicole blocked his path and put both hands against his broad chest. "Things are coming at me so fast I can't see straight. Slow down."

"Maybe I need space even more than you do, Nicole." Marcus carefully removed her hands.

"I don't have the energy for a fight with you. Go home, cool off, and call me tonight. Try my cell phone first. I could be here real late." Nicole pressed a palm to her forehead.

"Uh-huh." Marcus went around her to the door.

"Marcus," Nicole called when his hand twisted the handle to open it. He turned slowly. "You'll call me?"

He opened the door. "I don't see the point."

Nicole's heart tightened into a fist as she watched the back of his suit coat moving away from her. He didn't look back, not even when she called his name a second time. Shelly watched him walk by, then came to the open door.

"Is Marcus okay?"

"Sure, he's fine. We're all on edge. He's just going to take a break." Nicole spun around so that her back was to Shelly. She wiped a stray tear that almost escaped down her cheek.

"How are you doing? It's been one hell of a twenty-four hours," Shelly said in a caring tone.

"Fine." Nicole faced her again. She stood erect, hoping she looked more in control than she felt. "I'm going back to my office."

"Right. I'll tell Cat to put on a fresh pot of coffee. We're going to have another long day." Shelly wore a maternal expression on her young face.

Nicole could only nod. She couldn't trust herself not to

break down. Instead she strode off. Russell came out of his office seconds after she passed his door.

"Can I have a word with you?" Russell's face looked pale and pinched.

"I can't deal with much more today. If you've got complaints, accusations, or your usual insults, save them for the family. You usually do," she added in an undertone.

"No, no. We need to be on the same team. Come in," Russell said quickly. He gestured to her.

"The same team," Nicole repeated. She hesitated a moment before turning back and going into his office.

"Hello, Nicole." Her father waved her in. Uncle Lionel sat in one of three leather chairs.

"Hi, Daddy. How are you, Uncle Lionel?" Nicole went on guard, feeling outflanked by the three men.

"Been a helluva lot better." He rubbed his neck and grimaced.

"Sit down, Nikki. We've got some serious talking to do." Stanton patted the back of a chair.

Nicole didn't move. "I'm listening."

Stanton adopted a stern father scowl. "Don't be stubborn, young woman. Sit down," he ordered.

"Let's not play the control game, Daddy. My patience has been stretched to the limit today. Now what's up?"

"We certainly agree that you've been through a lot in the past few days. Which is why I think, well, the entire board, actually . . ." Stanton put an arm around her shoulder. "Take a few days off, a week even."

"A month," Uncle Lionel added. "Nobody can say you didn't give it a try."

Nicole shook her head. "The employees need to see me going strong or they'll lose it. Hold it, are you giving me a choice?"

Stanton and Uncle Lionel exchanged a glance. Her father patted her. "Honey, you did a really fine job, considering."

"You can't fire me. The will—" Nicole swallowed hard. She wanted to get angry, but all she could feel was despair. First Marcus walked away and now this.

"You're bleeding money like crazy," Uncle Lionel said. "Your clients don't trust you, not to mention Marcus having ties to a crook. Damn it, girl, we shouldn't have to tell you any of this."

"My father made the mistake of putting his trust in an outsider, and so did you." Russell wore a self-important, serious face. "Uncle Lionel and Uncle Stanton agree with me."

"Do they really?" Nicole glanced from her uncle to her father. She didn't know whether to cry or curse a blue streak.

"I'm afraid the decision has been made, Nikki," her father said gently. "As executor of the will, Uncle Hosea's attorney has appointed me interim CEO until the next board meeting."

"Like hell." Nicole could feel anger taking control.

"Now, Nicole," her father warned and puckered his lips in censure.

"Your sister Helena will pitch in, too. Thank God she can take time off from her company," Uncle Lionel added. "You should be grateful we're taking this monkey off your back, young lady. As I recall, you screamed like an angry kitten at having your party life interrupted."

"Under the circumstances, a change in management makes sense. I know our clients well," Russell said as he smoothed down his Ralph Lauren silk tie. "In fact, I've already made a few calls. Two clients decided not to cancel their contracts this morning."

"Really? We'll discuss the details with you after we're through with Nicole." Uncle Lionel blinked at Russell in frank surprise.

"Now we need to know how much the media knows. If they connect the thefts with this girl's murder—" Stanton broke off when Russell flinched. "Sorry, son. I know you cared a great deal for her."

"Yes, terrible thing no matter what she did," Uncle Lionel rumbled in a subdued voice.

Russell sighed. "Thank you for the concern. I'm still trying to wrap my mind around it all. She left me with happy memories in spite of, well, you know. I expressed my condolences to her family."

"Very appropriate, Russell." Stanton nodded.

Russell wore a troubled frown. A respectful silence fell for a few moments. All three men looked down at the floor with somber expressions, like pallbearers at a funeral. Then Russell cleared his throat.

"Difficult as it might be, I'll have to carry on. I offered some modifications in the contracts. You could call them concessions that persuaded those two clients to stick with us. I also have a list of changes in hiring and staff supervision we can discuss." Russell became the dignified, but determined-to-press-on, businessman.

"Excellent start." Stanton smiled at him briefly. His smile faded as he turned to Nicole. "Nikki, I'll stop by your house this evening. Why don't you go to your favorite spa and treat yourself. Use the company credit card."

"Goody! Can I have a double scoop ice cream cone, too, Daddy?" Nicole said, and batted her eyelashes. "That should make up for being insulted, fired, and humiliated in front of the entire city."

"Now, Nicole, don't make a scene," Stanton warned with a stern look.

Nicole stood. "Wait until the next board meeting. I'll give you a scene. What's more, I did a damn good job. I'm not going to go quietly."

"You'll make things worse. I think we should all do what's best for the family and Summers Security." Russell affected an empathetic air. "Not that I don't sympathize with what you're feeling. I've been there."

Nicole gazed at him for several seconds. "You bounced back from grief very well."

The façade vanished and Russell glared at her. "I had my new secretary move all the important files from your desk and into my office."

"You did what?" Nicole spluttered and took a step toward him with balled fists.

Stanton stepped between them. "That's enough, Nicole. We'll talk after you've calmed down."

They stared at each other. Nicole saw the determination in her father's eyes. Stanton would not back down. The other two men seemed to hold their breath as tension filled the room. Finally Nicole shook free of her father's firm grasp and strode from the room. As she walked by employees, conversation ceased. Cat met her halfway to her office.

"I'm sorry, Nicole. Russell's latest secretary barged into your office while I was at the coffee shop downstairs. I came in just as she was leaving. Told me, 'Mr. Summers gave me instructions.' Honey, she didn't know how close she came to going from blond to bald." Cat marched after Nicole, fuming. "I hope you give him a very public whipping on this one, boss lady."

Nicole went to the closet and found a large Neiman Marcus shopping bag. "Don't worry about it, Cat. Besides, I'm not the 'boss lady' anymore."

"What? You can't quit. I know things are rough right now, but—"

"I've been kicked out. My father and uncle just told me." Nicole's throat tightened. She pressed her lips together as she cleared her desk.

Cat watched her in stunned misery. "But Mr. Hosea's will put you in charge."

"On certain conditions. In spite of my woofing and growling, there's not a whole lot I can do about it. And I'm not sure I want to try."

Nicole thought of Marcus standing tall beside her. She hadn't realized just how much strength she'd drawn from him. Maybe too much. He'd put his old ties ahead of her. Deep inside Nicole had to wonder just how far he'd go to help Shaun. His defense of Shaun hadn't helped ease her mind.

"Well, I'm going to let them know how I feel." Cat wore a fierce expression.

Nicole dropped one last item in the bag she was packing. "Thanks, but this is my fight."

"It's not fair!"

"Actually, in their shoes I'd probably make the same decision." Nicole shrugged.

"What will you do?"

"I'm going to make one huge effort to see the good side of this entire situation." Nicole forced a smile and tried to feel it. "I can sleep late again. I'll get to watch those action-packed court TV shows during the day."

Cat wasn't fooled. She crossed her arms. "Get over this pity party act and get mad."

"I've been working fourteen-hour days for the past five

weeks, Cat. I'm too drained to wrestle with anything more than my fuzzy slippers and favorite sloppy T-shirt. Now if you'll excuse me, there's a gallon of pecan praline ice cream with my name on it."

"Sure, let them all say, We knew she couldn't deal with the big stuff," Cat wheedled.

"Frankly, I don't give a crap what *they* say. And I see right through you. Very obvious." Nicole winked at her. "Bye, girl. In case I didn't mention it, you're the greatest. I appreciate everything you did for me."

Cat's expression softened. "Hey, I had to earn that paycheck and feed parakeets. The employees are behind you. They know Mr. Hosea made the right choice when he left you in charge."

Nicole gave her a quick, fierce hug. "That's the highest compliment I've ever gotten. Call everyone into the conference room. I owe it to them to say goodbye."

"Sure." Cat brushed a tear from her cheek as she turned and walked away.

When Cat buzzed her ten minutes later, Nicole steeled herself to give one last brave performance. She'd be able to break down later, she mused. Nicole headed down the hallway feeling empty. In one twenty-four-hour period she'd lost way too much.

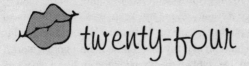 twenty-four

"That's tough about Nicole. Black folks like her look at us and see ghetto thug life. Nothing else. Hey, might as well find out who's really on your side." Shaun spread his arms out wide.

Marcus nodded slowly and took a pull from the bottle of beer in his hand. They sat in a hotel room in Katy, Texas, a small town on the outskirts of Houston. He'd left the office and Nicole earlier that day. As if he'd known, Shaun had called him moments after Marcus had driven off. Three hours later Marcus had followed his instructions, taking great care that he wasn't followed this time.

The large-screen television played in the background. Wesley Snipes, dressed in tight black leather pants and vest, silently kicked butt in some futuristic thriller movie. Neither man paid much attention to the screen. Shaun paced with a cell phone in one hand. In contrast to Shaun, Marcus felt numb, lethargic even.

"You know what?" Shaun pointed the phone at him.

"Huh." Marcus barely mustered interest enough to respond. Even so his grunt wasn't a question.

"The police tryin' to set me up. Yeah, that's what this is all about. They couldn't get me on those other bogus cases, so this is payback. They can kiss my ass, 'cause it ain't gonna work," Shaun snarled. He stabbed the phone in the air like a weapon.

"Uh-huh." Marcus tried once more not to think about Nicole. His effort didn't work any more than it had for the past twenty hours.

"I'm faster than they can keep up."

Shaun let out a rasping laugh of contempt. He flipped open the slim digital phone and dialed a number. With his back turned to Marcus, he moved to the other side of the room to talk. Marcus barely noticed he was gone. He ran through his list of options. They all included Nicole in some way. Should he call her? Hell no, he reminded himself. If he did, what should he say? Nicole looked at him the same way other upper-class Black folks had through the years. Seeing the question and mistrust in her beautiful eyes had cut deep. Anger mixed with grief drove his mood swings. One moment he seethed with thoughts of showing the entire Summers clan. Just as quickly he'd sink into a hole so dark he couldn't see the point of doing anything but having another beer. Speaking of which. Marcus put the empty bottle down on the table with a thump. Shaun strode over and put a fresh bottle of a fancy imported brand next to it. He continued talking into the cell phone. Marcus grabbed the frosty dark green glass. He glanced around the room without paying attention to the décor.

"What am I doing here?"

"We're hanging together like we did back in the day." Shaun slapped his shoulder, then someone on the phone grabbed his attention again. "What? Hell, don't give me that weak-ass excuse!"

Marcus hadn't even realized he'd spoken aloud. He drank more beer and turned up the sound on the television. Without thinking, he channel hopped. His finger paused on the local news. A female Latino reporter stood outside the police station.

"Yes, Dan. What started out as an investigation into a single robbery has widened, with some surprising results. Summers Security, one of the largest African-American-owned businesses in the Southwest, seems to be at the center of a crime wave. Sources tell us that the recent murder of Aliyah Manning may even be linked. Suspicions of gang involvement have some in the department concerned. Earlier we spoke to Stanton Summers, acting CEO of Summers Security."

A taped interview of Nicole's father appeared. Marcus recognized the lobby of Summers Security. Stanton stood in front of a wall with the picture of Hosea Summers in the center. He wore a stern expression.

"Certainly we're cooperating fully with the police department. Our staff has been instrumental in providing key information."

The reporter made a concerted effort to pry more details out of Stanton, but he sidestepped her questions. He even managed to do a fair job of spinning the situation to help the image of Summers Security.

"We've investigated all levels of staff. Those with questionable ties have been terminated." Stanton gave a curt nod.

"Does that mean that your employees are suspects in the murder and the thefts?" the reporter shot back as she pushed the microphone at him.

"No former or current employee has been charged.

Thank you." Stanton marched off before she could ask more questions.

The station switched back to the news set. "Dan, we have learned from police that they have several leads and expect to make arrests soon. Marietta Sanchez reporting."

"They throwing you to the wolves, bro. Damn, your lady cut you out cold!" Shaun stood behind him, still holding the phone to his ear.

Marcus changed the station. "I didn't hear anything about me."

"Call you later. Right." Shaun hit the button and dropped the phone into the chest pocket of his Fubu shirt. "Look, I know it hurts, but you gotta face facts. She's hanging you out there, man."

Marcus wanted to argue back. Unconsciously, he touched his silent cell phone. Nicole should have reached out, his pride told him. In his old world a man didn't chase down a woman or beg her to support him. Shaun seemed to read his mind.

"She hasn't called. Now what does that tell you? She's listening to her daddy, that's what," Shaun said before Marcus could respond. "I'm not going down for murder just because I was born in the ghetto."

"Yeah." Marcus pressed the channel button on the remote harder than necessary.

"First time something happens she can't be found. I know it's rough, but hell, there it is."

Marcus wanted to change the subject from Nicole. "What pisses me off is how those employees pulled a fast one."

"You know, people gonna steal. It's human nature, right? If you don't pay folks enough, they pay themselves. Listen, they don't have anything on us and they know it." Shaun broke off when the hip-hop tune of his cell phone played.

When Shaun moved away again, Marcus got up to stretch

his legs. He walked to the small bar, then back again. Nicole pushed her way into his head. Memories of the way she smelled right out of the shower sent a shiver down his back. Marcus closed his eyes and could see her padding toward him across the lush carpet of her bedroom. He thought of the last evening they'd spent together. Lying in bed bedside him, she'd rested her head on his bare chest. Her thick, cashmere-soft hair smelled of flowers from the shampoo she'd used. He forced his eyes open to stop the images.

"Hey, you all right?" Shaun put his arm across Marcus's shoulder.

"Yeah, I'm okay." Marcus put his empty beer bottle on the counter.

Shaun went to the small refrigerator and got two more. "Man, we need to get this stuff off our minds and have us a party up in here."

Marcus shook his head and waved away his offer of more to drink. "I'm going home."

"You can't leave. They're probably sitting outside your place waiting to swoop." Shaun put one of the beers back and popped the cap on another one.

"I don't care. Like you said, they don't have anything on me. And they won't get anything 'cause there is nothing to get. The police can question me all they want to."

Marcus was drained, but not because of the investigation. There was nowhere he could go that he wouldn't drag his longing for Nicole with him.

"Right, right." Shaun sat on one of the three bar stools. "What else did y'all know about the thefts?"

"We didn't notice anything unusual just looking at critical incidents. That's what we called them."

"Oh?" Shaun drank more beer.

"After Tameka was arrested the pattern started to show."

Marcus frowned and glanced at Shaun. "We both know Olandon's old territory. You could find out who he's been hanging with."

"Maybe. I mean we haven't been tight in a while. Except for me trying to straighten him out," Shaun added quickly.

"Try anyway. We need to do something." Marcus rubbed his face hard.

"I'll see what I find out on the street." Shaun's right knee bounced as though it contained all his pent-up energy.

"Find out whatever you can."

"Sure. I don't want you on the hook for something Olandon did." Shaun stood up like a man unable to keep still for long. He took out his phone and checked his pager messages.

"Who would want to kill Aliyah? She wasn't into anything heavy." Marcus looked at Shaun.

"Who knows?" Shaun bit a fingernail, then took his hand down. "She had a taste for bad boys. Could be one of them caught her with another guy."

"Maybe I'll find out more when the police question me. Yesterday they 'invited' me to help them investigate."

"To hell with them. Don't go." Shaun scowled. "Nah, don't fall into that trap."

"Other than the fact that I don't have anything to hide, running from the police will make things look worse for me. In fact, you should talk to them yourself." Marcus knew what Shaun's reaction would be.

"I'm not exactly Mr. Clean like you. I've got to get my stuff together before I go. I'm gonna walk in with my lawyer."

"Yeah, well, just tell them what you know about Aliyah."

"Some jealous lover got hold of the woman. Aliyah jumped from dude to dude," Shaun said.

"Seems like the police would have tracked him down by now. Besides, she put all her energy into Russell and his big bankbook." Marcus shook his head. "The way she was beaten means somebody was really mad at the lady."

"Sounds like a love thang gone wrong to me. Russell dude must be pretty shook up."

"I hear he's consoling himself by lobbying to be the next CEO." Marcus twisted and turned what he knew, trying to discover answers.

"He's fired a bunch of people. Guess he's searched that data you were talking about," Shaun said.

"More than likely they'll turn up something. You know, if it was an organized theft ring using our employees, whoever came up with the idea was smart. They recruited people who didn't have criminal records, like they thought it all out. You know?" Marcus glanced at Shaun.

"But why would law-abiding citizens agree? That's a wild theory, brother." Shaun lifted a shoulder.

"Like you said, hard times can push people to the limit. If I know Nicole, she's digging right now. I just don't see her giving up easily."

"You think?" Shaun tapped the cell phone against his jaw and frowned.

"When Nicole is angry she does something about it. She really was into that job. Not for the power or prestige."

"Her family must not think so. Her daddy is acting CEO now." Shaun waved a hand toward the television, as though Stanton were still on the screen.

"Nicole won't roll over. When she makes up her mind to do something, watch out," Marcus said. He imagined Nicole's lovely burnt almond eyes flashing with anger and determination.

"Uh-huh, just like she made up her mind about *you*." Shaun pointed to him.

"Right," Marcus said quietly.

He let out a long, slow breath. He sat down on the sofa in front of the television again. Shaun's phone rang and he muttered into it.

Nicole walked off the elevator at Summers Security. No matter what her father and the rest of the family said, she still felt part of the company. Imani rounded a corner and broke into a wide grin when she saw Nicole.

"I'm glad to see you. What do you think?" Imani showed her a catalogue of high-tech security products.

"The voice and fingerprint recognition systems. Looks good. So, my father and Russell are moving forward with going after big corporate accounts."

Imani nodded. "They're riding on the work you and Marcus did. We all know it."

"Thanks." Nicole gave her a grateful smile. "I've been watching the news. I see your brains behind the smart way y'all have been dealing with the bad publicity. Good work."

"Thanks back at ya, boss lady." Imani gave her arm a squeeze.

"Better not let Russell hear you. I'm not in charge of anything around here." Nicole walked with Imani beside her.

"You should be," Imani replied. "Not that I don't respect your daddy, but you and Marcus had a real feel for this business."

Nicole felt a sharp, stinging sensation at the mention of his name. She didn't want to go down that path. Not after three nights of no sleep and regrets. "So, how is it working with Russell these days?"

Imani let out a tortured groan. "I now believe in purgatory."

"Bad, huh?" Nicole smiled at the way Imani screwed up her face.

"Your dad is trying not to show it, but he knows Russell is

a management disaster waiting to happen." Imani glanced around and dropped her voice low. "A classic example, Russell ordered six thousand dollars' worth of palm pilots for the security guards."

Nicole laughed out loud. "What for?"

"To keep them on schedule. Six have disappeared already. Seems he had Jesse distribute them too fast. Some of the fired employees suspected in the thefts got units." Imani raised a hand. "I know what you're thinking. Remember this is Russell we're talking about."

"Daddy must have breathed fire for days." Nicole tried not to look as pleased as she felt.

"Honey, we all kept a low profile for a week. I—" Imani broke off when Russell appeared.

"Hello, Nicole." Russell turned to Imani before Nicole could answer him. "I'm sure you've got the rough outline for marketing our new services."

"Mr. Summers is looking it over," Imani said in a cool tone.

"I was supposed to get the first look," Russell said.

"Mr. Summers asked for the proposal, and I gave it to him. You could go ask him to give it back." Imani raised an eyebrow.

Russell's jaw muscles worked for several minutes. He turned away from Imani. "I thought you'd cleared out the office."

"I'm holding up well. Thanks for asking." Nicole brushed past him.

He followed her. "Uncle Stanton is busy. Next time call for an appointment."

"Hi, Cat." Nicole ignored Russell's attempt to get her attention.

Cat bounced from her chair with a wide grin. "Hey, boss lady." She hugged Nicole.

"You have a stack of work to finish and we're on a tight schedule," Russell said to Cat.

"I'm caught up," Cat replied, her smile now stretched thin. "So, tell me what you've been up to."

"Resting, working out at the club, and shopping. You know, a strict therapeutic routine. Is my father in?"

"I'll let him know you're here." Cat reached for the phone on her desk.

"We've got meetings with three clients today, proposals to upgrade their systems to complete, and an overseas call to make." Russell motioned to Cat not to dial. "Maybe you can call him later."

"Okay," Nicole said with a half-smile. She went around him, knocked on the door, and went in.

Russell came in behind her. He marched over to stand next to Stanton, who was seated behind the desk. "As usual, Nicole assumes it's all about her."

"Nicole has been barging into my office since she was in diapers. Why should today be any different?" Stanton rose and walked to her with his arms out.

"Hello, Daddy." Nicole accepted his peck on the cheek. She gave him a chilly smile.

"Hi, Nikki. You look wonderfully relaxed and beautiful as usual." Stanton shot a glance at Russell.

Nicole noticed the subtle signal but pretended she'd missed it. "Thanks. I stopped by to talk—privately."

"Sure, baby. I've got at least a good twenty minutes to spare." Stanton waved to the seating area. He shook his head when Russell headed for a chair.

"But I—" Russell broke off when he looked at Stanton's frown. "I'll be back for the meeting shortly."

When the door closed, Stanton smoothed down his ivory dress shirt. After Nicole was seated he pulled a chair close to her and sat down. "I'm so glad to see you, honey. You should have returned my calls."

"I needed time alone to think." Nicole gazed at him. Stanton nodded with a wise paternal expression that seemed to say he understood all.

"Of course, of course. It wasn't only my decision either. Not that I'm trying to back out of my role. I did agree that—"

"I know," Nicole broke in. "I won't lie and say I can see your point. For once I didn't live down to everyone's expectations. You should have given me more support."

"Now, baby, let's not get into a scene. You can really be a handful when your temper is—"

"Don't worry, I'm not going to throw a fit. Let's stick to facts. You've seen the contracts, the work I did while I was here." Nicole gazed at him with her head tilted to one side.

"Yes, I must say you accomplished quite a bit. But you were overwhelmed when these thefts started. I also think your judgment of Marcus was, er, clouded." Stanton's dark eyebrows pulled together.

"Uncle Hosea had confidence in him," Nicole replied.

"I guess he fooled us all. Considering his upbringing, well, we shouldn't be surprised." Stanton patted her arm. "I'm just sorry he hurt you. Still, it could have been worse. Better that you found out before you two got more serious."

Nicole repressed an urge to let him know just how serious they'd gotten. "I didn't mean to imply that I believe—"

"It's okay, honey. He wasn't simply a poor boy who pulled himself up by his bootstraps. Did you know he had an arrest record as a juvenile?" Stanton frowned in distaste. "His father is in prison."

"Marcus never lied to me about his background." Nicole felt distaste as well, but not for the same reason.

Stanton grunted. "He left out the part about having criminals as best friends. I'm just glad you finally saw through him."

"What are you talking about?" Nicole glanced at him sharply.

"Russell told me you confronted him. Getting his resignation was very appropriate under the circumstances."

"I didn't ask him to resign, Daddy." Nicole winced at the flashback of that day.

Stanton seemed not to hear her. He looked at his watch. "So, what did you need to tell me, baby?"

Nicole ground her teeth in frustration for several seconds. "You don't listen very well, at least not to me."

"Now, Nikki, you know I love you." Stanton put on his best patient father expression.

"I'm talking business now," she tossed back crisply.

Her father's indulgent demeanor slipped a notch. "Okay, business it is."

"The board meets in one week. I plan to attend and get my job back." Nicole stood.

"Wait a minute, young lady. I thought we'd settled this issue." Stanton rose to tower over her with a scowl.

"I'm sure you did. I've already spoken to Aunt Maida. I'm on the agenda." Nicole met his fierce gaze without cringing.

His nostrils flared, his eyes glazed over in anger, but he appeared to rein in his fury. They stared at each other for a few seconds more. Finally Stanton gave a sharp nod.

"Fair enough. I won't treat you like a little girl," he warned.

"I won't act like one. See you in one week."

Nicole walked out. She held up until she was alone in her car. Only then did she let out a shaky sigh. Now all she had to do was perform a miracle.

* * *

The police station fit every cop-show stereotype she'd seen, Nicole mused. An array of rough characters milled around as though waiting to be interrogated. She squirmed in her seat as a beefy man plopped down next to her on the bench. He gave her a full body exam through narrowed eyes. Nicole inched away from him and kept a firm grip on her leather purse.

"Come here often?" the man said, leaning closer with a grin at his joke.

"No, and we've never met before." Nicole shot a stony look his way, then turned from him.

"Humph, you psychic 'cause that was my next question." The man laughed. "I'm Chuck."

"Okay." Nicole mentally swore at Detective Holmes for making her wait.

Chuck tapped his foot and hummed a tune for several minutes. "You live in the city or what?"

"I'm busy thinking important thoughts, Chuck," Nicole replied.

"So it's like that, huh? All right. Just tryin' to pass the time." Chuck took a bag of peanuts out of his shirt pocket and began eating his way through them.

Nicole heaved a sigh of relief. At least she was surrounded by police officers. Now if Detective Holmes would put down his donuts and get her interview done, the day would improve.

Suddenly Marcus strolled through the door. Nicole felt a stab of excitement. At first he didn't see her and took a step toward the waiting area, then he halted. He seemed to recover after a split second. Still, he scanned the room as if deciding how far to sit from her. Nicole stared at him in irritation.

"Don't worry, lady. I ain't gonna let him bother you," Chuck said.

"I guess that's your job today," Nicole murmured with a scowl.

Chuck annoyed her even more by laughing out loud. "You got one great sense of humor, honey."

"Calling me 'honey' is not the way to be my new friend." Nicole studied Marcus intently.

"Touchy today. Ain't my fault they caught ya." Chuck laughed harder. "Just playin' around. I can look at you and tell you're no crook."

"Gee thanks. Now leave me alone," Nicole said firmly. Her voice must have carried, because several people looked at them, including Marcus.

"'Scuse me, Your Highness."

Marcus walked over and sat down in a chair next to her. "Hi."

"Hello." Nicole willed the tension from her shoulders.

"Detective Holmes called you, too?" Marcus looked ahead as he spoke.

"Yes. How have you been?" Nicole made it sound like a polite question only. She wasn't going to beg him for scraps of attention. Still, she wanted to know what he was thinking and feeling.

"Considering the situation, I'm okay. What about you?" Marcus glanced at her, then away.

"Aside from this little disaster, I'm doing just great," Nicole said, trying to make it a joke. She was afraid the quiver in her voice spoiled the attempt.

"Sorry," was all he said.

"Me, too. I—"

Detective O'Connor strode toward them. "Good afternoon. I got held up," he said to Nicole. Then he turned to Marcus. "You're early."

"Not by much. Guess you didn't want us talking to each other." Marcus's mild expression didn't change.

Before O'Connor could reply, Detective Holmes walked out. Holmes wore an almost friendly expression, unlike his brusque partner. Nicole seethed with anger at all men, including Chuck, who watched them and munched peanuts like he was at the movies.

"Hello and thanks for coming on such short notice. Ms. Benoit, come with me. Detective O'Connor will talk with Mr. Reed." Holmes swept his arm out like a head waiter seating guests.

"No problem. Hanging out with criminals at a police station is more fun than a trip to the mall." Nicole walked ahead of Holmes.

"I promise this won't take long," Holmes said without losing his affable expression.

Nicole watched O'Connor lead Marcus down a different hallway. Her irritation gave way to uneasiness. She'd never been inside a police station before, much less questioned in one. Holmes took her to a small room with a square table in the center of it. Four metal chairs were arranged around the table. One wall had a mirror set into it. She wondered if anyone would be watching.

"Please." Holmes waved at a chair. He waited until Nicole had sat down, then sat across from her. Seconds later O'Connor joined them. "Now let's go over a few things."

"You became acting CEO about two months ago, right?" O'Connor took out a blank notepad sheet. He acted as though he hadn't heard the same facts at least ten times.

Nicole bit off an acid reply, deciding it was wise to act as though she hadn't told them the same facts at least ten times. "Yes. My great-uncle basically left instructions that I become CEO and run his business."

"Summers Security, Inc.," O'Connor said.

"Summers Security, LLC," she corrected, sure he knew the

company's corporate status better than she did. Nicole drummed her fingers, then forced them to be still. "Have you found out any *new* information?"

Holmes rested both elbows on the table. "We're looking into a few interesting things. Aliyah Manning seems to have made some enemies."

"I didn't think a good friend killed her." Nicole pressed her lips together when O'Connor glared at her.

"Possibly someone she thought of as a friend, or at least someone she didn't think was a threat," Holmes answered with no trace of annoyance.

"She and your cousin, Russell, wanted you out of the business," O'Connor put in.

"Detective, her ambitions didn't bother me. You really think I'd kill her for being a wannabe?" Nicole felt fear in spite of her composed façade.

"Maybe she helped set up the thefts to make you look bad. Your cousin was extremely bitter that he didn't get the company." O'Connor stared at her hard, as though expecting an admission.

"That's a very thin theory," she said with a frown.

"Sometimes theories lead to evidence," O'Connor replied.

"You have anything more?" Nicole clenched her fists beneath the table.

"Marcus Reed and you have a romantic relationship. He was seen talking to Ms. Manning in what's been described as an intimate fashion." Holmes blinked behind the wire-rimmed eyeglasses.

"So, now I'm a jealous woman scorned and looking for revenge? I've been patient, but now—" Nicole stood.

"Mr. Reed had ambitions as well. He expected to run Summers Security. Then you came on the scene. He might have formed an alliance with his friend Shaun Jackson and Aliyah." Holmes lifted a shoulder.

"You'd be understandably furious," O'Connor added, picking up the narrative. "He's lying to you about his feelings and trying to ruin your business."

"No," Nicole blurted out.

O'Connor went on as though she hadn't spoken. "Reed's affair with Aliyah Manning added insult to injury. How long did it take you to find out?"

"You're wrong. I don't believe it." Nicole hated hearing the detective coldly put her worst fear into words.

"Where were you on June seventeenth, Ms. Benoit?"

Holmes posed the question in a mild tone, as though murder weren't involved. He gazed at her with a sympathetic expression on his broad face. His avuncular approach invited her to confide in him. Nicole glanced from him to his partner. O'Connor's eyes gleamed as though he wanted to pounce. Her heart beat double time.

"I know this is a cliché from an old mystery movie, but I was at home. I wasn't alone, though. I was with Marcus." Nicole sat quite still while the two men digested her answer.

"Neat. He's your alibi and you're his." O'Connor grunted.

"We need to have the truth, Ms. Benoit," Holmes said.

"You have it." Nicole steadied her breathing in an attempt to slow her heart rate. *Think!* The men seemed content to stare at her in silence. The muted sound of ringing telephones and footsteps put her nerves on edge. Nicole felt as though all activity in the police station was aimed at proving her guilt. She willed herself not to panic.

"Well?" O'Connor cocked one eyebrow at her.

"Well what?" Nicole played for more time.

"I wouldn't protect him if I were you," he replied. "Reed hasn't earned this kind of loyalty, ma'am."

Nicole mentally grabbed pieces of information that seemed to fly toward her at the speed of light. *Think!* Then it struck her.

"Am I trying to frame him or save him?" Nicole stared at O'Connor.

"We're following solid leads, Ms. Benoit. Believe me, Mr. Reed figures in somewhere and we're going to find the trail," Holmes said.

Nicole wasn't impressed. She stood and looped her purse strap over one shoulder. "You're just flinging out theories like a handful of darts hoping one or two hit the target. You people have more work to do on this case, like gathering reliable evidence. I suggest you get to it. Thieves and murderers are ahead of you."

"Not for long," Holmes replied.

"I'd be happy to help you in this investigation. Call me when you have *real* questions to ask. Goodbye."

Nicole walked out. Her legs felt weak despite her show of bravado. She expected uniforms to converge on her and push her back into the room. Instead she made it out the front door and into the sunshine. Nicole gasped with relief and took in several deep breaths. She jumped at the deep voice over her shoulder.

"Did you believe them about me?" Marcus asked.

"I'm having a bad enough day as it is. Adding heart failure to the list won't help." Nicole pressed the heel of one hand to her forehead. Pain from a budding migraine thumped behind her eyes.

"Today wasn't fun for me either. Not that my week was any better. I'm unemployed and under suspicion." Marcus put on his sunglasses.

"Yeah, well, you walked out on your job. As for being under suspicion, you brought that on yourself as well. You're protecting Shaun. I have to ask myself why." Nicole glared at him.

"I'm standing by a friend. Something you obviously don't think is important," Marcus snapped back.

"Because you knew what he and Aliyah had planned?" she replied angrily.

"Okay, you answered my question. Just so you'll know, I blew them off when O'Connor suggested you had a motive to kill Aliyah. There was nothing going on between her and I."

"Whatever." Nicole looked away and brushed back her hair with the flip of a hand.

"Yeah, whatever."

"You need to—"

Nicole turned to face Marcus, but he was gone. All she saw was his broad back as he strode across the parking lot. She wanted to shout at him to come back. Instead she watched him walk toward his Acura. Somehow Nicole felt she'd made a mistake. As she headed for her car, two men in a dark green Ford Explorer stared at Marcus as they drove by. One of them was Shaun.

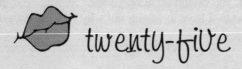 twenty-five

"**Y**ou're sure it was him?" Kelli Caldwell crossed her long legs.

"Yes." Nicole dropped down onto Kelli's russet sofa. "By the way, thanks for returning my calls." The rest of the women from their networking group were avoiding her. Not that she could blame them, given the circumstances.

Kelli waved a hand. "Don't give me props just yet. I thought about running in the opposite direction. But I know what being stuck with no support feels like."

"I still think you're wonderful," Nicole replied with feeling. "Right now I don't want to talk to my own family."

"They shouldn't have dumped you. Far as I'm concerned you were a helluva CEO. Kick ass at the board meeting." Kelli lifted her mug of beer in salute.

"If you know any magic spells, put 'em in action. I'm gonna need all the help I can get."

"Give them the facts. If they don't accept it, then the decision had nothing to do with your skills. Believe it," Kelli said.

Nicole managed a smile. "Thanks."

"You're welcome. So, Marcus is the real issue. Right?"

"Partly. I have a track record of being less than responsible, too. But to be honest, our affair really set them off. Especially my parents." Nicole groaned. "I can just hear my mother. 'Stanton, Nicole has lost what little common sense she got from *my* side of the family.'"

"Sounds like my mama. I feel for you, girl." Kelli shook her head slowly and sipped more beer. "Shaun Jackson has nerve hanging around a police station. The question is why?"

"I don't want to believe Marcus is involved with Shaun in something shady, but . . ." Nicole sighed. Marcus was acting guilty. *Guilty and stubborn.*

"I don't know the guy, but Shaun Jackson must be cocky to take such a chance. I don't think Marcus knew he was cruising around the block either," Kelli said.

"He could have followed Marcus. They might have agreed that if things got tough, Shaun would show up and they'd bail each other out with the same story." Nicole chewed her lower lip.

"Oh, please. I thought I was suspicious. This guy is a scumbag and Marcus just can't see it. You should tell Marcus his pal was there."

"Marcus won't listen to me," Nicole muttered. "Not after our last two encounters."

"Oh?"

"He's being a real chump! Anybody can see Shaun would be happy to let Marcus take a fall for him."

"He loves the guy like a brother." Kelli lifted a shoulder.

Nicole rubbed her eyes. "Yeah, yeah."

"Marcus wouldn't just kick his brother to the curb. That's the kind of guy he is. Strong, silent types are intense when they care about someone," Kelli said.

"Marcus hasn't had a lot of relationships he could count on in his life. He's going to go down for Shaun."

Kelli leaned forward and tapped Nicole's knee hard. "He might unless somebody can get through to him."

"I pretty much accused him of being either a crook or a fool. I'm not the somebody." Nicole stared at the wall in misery.

"Okay. Let him twist in the wind while you go shopping."

"Cut it out." Nicole frowned at her.

"In fact, your family might be impressed you tossed him aside. Could get you back in as CEO," Kelli went on in a mild tone.

"You know damn well I don't care what they think. If I want to be with Marcus, then—" Nicole broke off when Kelli pursed her lips to suppress a smirk. "How very transparent."

"Worked though."

"No, it didn't. I'm not going to find Marcus and cry out that I've been such a fool," Nicole said.

"Why not?" Kelli dodged when Nicole threw a small accent pillow at her head.

"Two minutes ago you thought I was the greatest thing since the microchip." Nicole squinted at her.

Kelli shrugged with a rueful grin. "I'm fickle. But that's all I'm going to say."

"I'm sorry for being so ungrateful. You're more supportive than anyone right now." Nicole reached out and patted Kelli's arm.

"I'm not paying attention to half of what you say." Kelli stood and walked to the wet bar. "Have another beer."

"No, I'm going home to get what little sleep I can."

Nicole gave a short, bitter laugh. Tonight would likely be no different from the last three or four nights. She'd wind up sitting in front of the television staring at it and thinking about Marcus. Kelli gave her one last pep talk, and a hug, and she extracted a promise that Nicole would call on her anytime. Nicole got into her Honda CRV and headed for the very empty house. She thought about how cozy it had felt only a week ago when Marcus had held her close. He'd filled every space inside her as well.

"Guess I better start rehearsing my 'I've been a fool' speech," Nicole said and took the nearest exit on the interstate highway.

Marcus threw the cordless phone down. "Damn!"

He'd been trying to call Shaun all day. Finally he'd gotten the message that Shaun's cell phone was off. His apartment closed in on him like a jail cell. Marcus felt cut off. Shaun seemed to have gone underground, he couldn't talk to anyone at Summers Security, and Nicole was gone from his life. A sharp stab of loss made him forget about Shaun. The way she'd looked at him at the police station had hurt the most. In her eyes he was just another ghetto rat. Maybe she was right. Fifth Ward life seemed to follow him no matter where he went. He swore again. When the phone rang, he scooped it up.

"Yeah," he snarled into the phone.

Marcus let out a string of curses after he heard a click. When the doorbell rang minutes later, he was at the boiling point. He twisted the locks open and yanked on the door.

"You better have a damn good excuse for all this sh—" Marcus blinked rapidly. Instead of a six-foot-three-inch target, he stared down into a pair of lovely but scared almond brown eyes.

"I could come back later when you're in a better mood," Nicole stammered.

Anticipated pleasure sent a surge of electricity up his spine. In five seconds he noticed the thick hair that framed her face, inhaled the enticing citrus scent of her perfume, and hungered to touch her mink-soft skin. Be realistic, he told himself. Still his hopes skyrocketed. After all, she'd come to him. In spite of his desire, Marcus affected an impassive expression.

"I won't be in a better mood any time soon. Might as well come in." He swung the door wide.

"Gee, thanks for the gracious invitation," she murmured. Nicole glanced at him cautiously before she came forward.

Marcus braced against another jolt when Nicole paused and faced him. She stood close to him for only a second before she walked past him into the living room. He tried to collect himself as he closed the door.

"I definitely didn't expect to see you here. Your father would probably freak." Marcus went to his sound system.

"Probably. But since they already fired me, what do I have to lose?" she wisecracked.

"Yeah. So I'm a safe playmate these days," Marcus replied over his shoulder. He switched off the rich soulful tones of a love ballad.

"Not if you count being a possible murder suspect, or at the very least an accessory."

Marcus spun around to stare at her. Nicole gazed back at him with her arms folded. "Is that what you believe?"

She let her arms fall. "Hell no. Maybe you planned to stab me in the back at one point, but I don't see you beating Aliyah to death."

"Thanks. I'm only a petty criminal." Marcus tried to keep perspective. Her words weren't exactly a declaration of love.

"Not so minor. You had a pretty slick plan in place." Nicole glanced around the room. "I've had a long night. At least invite me to sit down, even amaze me by offering some refreshments."

Marcus swung right along with the change in direction.

He went to the kitchen. "Sorry. Soft drink or something stronger? I've got snacks, or maybe I could whip up some hot hors d'oeuvres for the lady."

"I could go for some of those cocktail sausages or maybe Swedish meatballs." Nicole let her shoulder purse slide down and drop onto the sofa. "Second thought, peanuts and root beer will do me."

"Good, 'cause that's all you're gonna get," Marcus answered with a scowl. He tried willing his body not to tingle every time she spoke. Nicole was the only woman that could get him hot by being a smart-ass.

"Hey, I'll compromise." Nicole sat on the barstool at the counter that faced his kitchen. She watched him, both elbows propped on the ceramic tile surface.

"Really? Does that mean you'll 'settle' for somebody like me? A guy with no fancy family name or connections?" Marcus ripped the top from a can of mixed nuts as he spoke.

"I'm just talking about snacks, Marcus," she said in a muted tone.   •

He put the can down and looked at her. "Answer the question."

"Okay. You tell me if you can handle my fancy family background and connections."

They stared at each other for a long time. Her question was a fair one. He would have to lose his attitude toward Black folks he considered terminally "bourgie." Marcus turned away. Grateful for the time it bought him, Marcus played host. He poured nuts, chips, and onion dip into a set of bowls. After placing everything on a tray, he went back to the living room. Nicole hopped off the barstool. Each sat in one of the chairs that matched his sofa. Marcus poured the root beer with care. He sensed Nicole gazing at him. She accepted the mug from him. Both avoided looking into each other's eyes, as though afraid of finding painful answers. Minutes ticked by in tense silence.

"You're pretty good," she said.

"Are you talking about snacks now?"

Nicole put down the mug. "I was, but since you mentioned it . . ."

Marcus couldn't risk looking at her. Instead he studied the foam that topped his root beer. "We never really had a chance. Your family is just one part of the equation. You and I tried."

"If you say we can always be friends, I swear—"

"No," he said quickly.

Nicole banged her mug down on the glass cocktail table and stood. "Wonderful. I drove over here in the middle of the night to get dumped. Where the hell did I put my purse?"

Marcus caught her bare arm before she could pick up the black leather bag. The heat from her skin went right to his heart. "Nicole," he whispered.

"A friend suggested I admit to being a fool. I think we're both guilty."

She kissed him and he let her. His sensible voice, the one that told him they were too far apart, faded fast. Nicole caressed his hips and thighs with both hands as though determined to keep that voice away. The phone rang a number of times before he looked at the caller ID box. Instead of a number, the word "Unknown" flashed.

"I need to answer that," Marcus said.

"No, you don't. Shaun is going to jail, and he wants to take you with him." Nicole's hold on him tightened.

"You ever been down, Nicole? I mean, really down low with nobody and nothing? I won't assume he's guilty." Marcus grabbed the phone on the fifth ring before his voice mail could answer.

Nicole let go of him and walked away. Marcus watched her even as he listened to Shaun's rapid-fire speech. She sat down on the sofa. The soft light in her eyes had faded. Her expression changed to one of suspicion. They were back to square one.

"I don't know if—" Marcus turned away from Nicole. He walked into the kitchen. "Look, you're making things worse. Damn it, Shaun! What? Okay." He hit the button, ending the call.

Nicole stared at him without speaking for several beats. Then she stood and grabbed her purse. "You've made your choice."

"I'm not going to let either of you force me to choose. That's emotional blackmail." Marcus dropped the phone onto the base, making it rattle.

"When you kept secrets from me about Shaun's involvement you sure as hell did make a choice." Nicole pointed at him.

"He's not involved," Marcus shot back vehemently. "Shaun didn't know that his cousin had hooked up with Tameka. Olandon is a true thug."

Nicole started to counter his argument, then paused. She let out a slow breath. "All right. Believe whatever you want to. But something is up with him, Marcus, and you're running away from the truth."

"That's your prejudice talking. Shaun may be ghetto underneath the silk blend suit, but that doesn't mean he's a crook." Marcus sighed.

"Here we go with the 'you can't understand.' Well, don't even try it!" Nicole strode over to him and grabbed both his arms. "What price are you willing to pay—give up on us?"

Marcus gazed into her eyes. He saw the end of loneliness, a world he didn't believe existed. Nicole wore an almost desperate expression. Still, she wanted him to abandon a friend. With all Shaun's faults, Marcus couldn't see making her understand his world. Even if Shaun had made mistakes, he couldn't leave him behind. Not without trying to help.

"I can't walk away when Shaun needs me the most. He didn't leave me when things got rough. Please, Nicole. Trust me," Marcus said in a strained voice. His throat tightened with grief when she let go of him a second time.

"He followed you to the police station," Nicole said.

"What?" Marcus lost focus at the sudden turn.

"That's right. When you were being questioned by the cops, your good pal didn't step up."

Marcus rubbed his forehead, as though the motion would help him comprehend. "You must have made a mistake. Shaun intends to stay miles away from the police."

"How admirable, considering your ass is on the line," Nicole retorted. "Let's examine his motives. Shaun's got balls from what I've seen of him. So, he follows to see if you're cooperating. Or maybe he hoped you'd get arrested."

"No way. Shaun has always taken chances. He likes the rush of . . ." Marcus frowned.

"Yeah, he likes to boogie on the edge. Shaun also has expensive habits like luxury cars, designer clothes, and flashy women. Like Aliyah. Put those two together and—"

"Hold up, Nicole." Marcus backed away from her as he tried to sort through his thoughts.

"What are the odds Aliyah would hook up with Russell? Oh, right, another coincidence." Nicole advanced on him.

Marcus didn't want to hear what she was saying. "You're wrong about him."

"I'll admit it, Marcus. I'm a typical Black American Princess. More of my parents' attitudes have rubbed off on me than I ever thought," Nicole said.

Marcus ached inside. She seemed further from him than ever. "You're also caring, warm, and the sweetest taste I've ever had on my tongue."

She bit her lower lip. They stood apart, staring at each other for a long moment. Finally she moved toward him. "Is that your roundabout, strong-silent-type way of saying you love me?"

"Yes," Marcus whispered.

Nicole caressed his cheek, and he closed his eyes to savor her touch. Her mouth pressed against his, insistent that he respond. He gave in willingly, eager to feel the matchless sensation of blending his body and soul with hers. Forever went by in only a minute. When the kiss ended, he felt stunned.

"Don't walk away from me. Not now, not ever," she murmured.

"Sticking by Shaun isn't walking away from you, baby." Marcus lovingly traced the outline of her delectable mouth. "It's just something I've gotta do."

She pushed his hand away with a frustrated groan. "I'm a class-conscious pampered brat, but I'm not stupid. Why was he circling the police station that day?" Nicole's voice cracked with the effort to convince him.

"I don't know, but I have to give him a chance to explain," he replied with as much intensity.

"Then we'll ask him together."

"Hell no," Marcus said promptly. "You're going home to that nice, safe development with the private security patrols."

"Uh-uh. If you trust him so much, then we can both have a chat with your good buddy. Let's get going." Nicole pursed her pretty, full lips, giving her an obstinate look.

"Don't be a little idiot, Nicole."

"Oh, so now you want me to be a pampered bourgie girl." Nicole put both hands on her hips.

"I love who you are, baby. Attitude and all," he said in a gentle tone. "Don't change. I may be a little defensive at times about where I came from, but be patient with me."

Nicole's expression softened. "Deal. I may slip into my upper-class clueless bag every now and then. So, you be patient with me."

"Deal. Now go home." Marcus pushed her toward the door.

Nicole tried to dig her heels into the carpet. "Forget it. The police put me on the hot seat, too, you know."

Marcus easily lifted her up. "Which is why you're going home. Period, don't even waste your breath," he said when she started to argue again.

"But I—"

"If you're right about Shaun, then I could walk into any kind of situation. Another excellent reason *you're not going*," Marcus said firmly.

"You do think he's involved in all this." Nicole wore a worried frown.

"No, I don't. But who knows what his thug cousin has set up? Now go."

"I'm going to wait one hour. If you don't call me, I'll call your cell phone." She pointed a forefinger at his nose.

"Fine, bye-bye." Marcus gave her a quick kiss on the forehead.

Nicole wrapped both arms around him and held on. "I'll see you later," she whispered with her eyes squeezed shut as though it were a fervent prayer.

"Yes, baby. You will see me later."

Marcus rubbed her back to comfort her. Then he gently forced her to let go. Nicole caressed his face with her fingertips before she walked out the door. His phone rang again, and he picked it up.

"Yeah, Shaun," he said, knowing who it was by instinct.

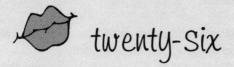 twenty-six

"It's all a lie." Shaun paced the concrete floor stained with large oil patches.

Five men stood around them. Marcus recognized two from their old neighborhood. The others were strangers. Shaun had given him directions to an abandoned auto repair shop on Lyons in the Fifth Ward.

"What I know is your cousin pops up on the Most Wanted list connected to thefts from my company. Then I find out Aliyah is still doing you while she's playing Russell Summers. Fix it up for me, Shaun." Marcus ignored the five pairs of hostile, paranoid eyes trained on him. The whole scene gave him a bad feeling.

Shaun strode over to stand inches from his face. "What you tryin' to say?"

Marcus had thought hard on the drive over. His trip had been more than just a series of turns onto familiar streets. He'd traveled back to his past. Much as he'd hated it, he'd started to examine Shaun's character and behavior over the last ten years.

"I remember you used to run with Olandon. In fact, you used to be his brains."

"Oh yeah?"

"Yeah. I don't think Olandon could have come up with such an intricate scenario," Marcus said quietly.

Shaun stared at him for several seconds. His intimidating frown melted into a hard smile. He took out a slim cigar, lit it, and blew out a thin stream of smoke. "I'm gonna take that as a compliment. Relax, all right? You ain't in this."

"You put me in this," Marcus replied with a steely edge to his voice.

"Come on. The most you'll lose is that cushy job." Shaun glanced at Marcus from head to toe. "With your degree and fancy connections, you'll land on your feet. Nicole will hook you up."

Marcus felt a sharp stab of disappointment between his shoulder blades. "That's a piss-poor way of apologizing for sticking a knife in my back. How'd you do it? I never told you sensitive information about our clients."

"Computers are amazing. I'd visit you at that impressive office you had. I'd sit there waiting while Mr. Big Time finished up some important work. You never noticed me watching those keystrokes when you typed in your password, did ya? Guess you didn't think I was on that level." Shaun's eyes flashed resentment. Then he smiled again and stepped back from Marcus.

"It wasn't like that," Marcus said, shocked to see the hostility that flared in a brief moment. How had he missed it?

Shaun went on as though Marcus hadn't spoken. "Russell helped me out by going through all those secretaries. I dated three and got a little more information each time. None of 'em stayed long enough to get suspicious about me. Lucky break. Besides, ladies really like me. It's a gift."

"How did Aliyah fit in?" Marcus glanced around. Two of the men now blocked the door Marcus had entered.

"Every once in a while I'd hook up with Aliyah. She liked it rough, and I believe in givin' a woman what she wants, at least in that department." Shaun let out a guttural-sounding laugh. "Anyway, she had what they call social ambitions. She did a fairly good job of cleaning herself up. You know, a fake story about where she grew up and her prominent family. Thanks to you, I told her where she should hang out to meet Russell."

"He was a perfect sucker."

"Yeah," Shaun said with a broad grin.

Marcus shook his head. "You spent three years planning this?"

"Hey, like your grandmother used to tell us—do it right or don't do it at all. Summers Security got bigger and better, thanks to you. I decided to go along for the ride." Shaun waved the hand that held his cigar.

"I trusted you." Marcus looked at someone he didn't know after all.

"Once you started hanging with the elite you forgot about me." Shaun slapped a large palm on his chest.

"Come on, Shaun."

"All my business ideas were beneath the great Marcus Reed with his picture in *Black Enterprise* magazine."

Marcus pushed away the pain. His anger crystallized into a thin, blistering laser beam aimed at Shaun. "You smiled in my face and used me."

"I won't lie and say it wasn't personal." Shaun's face twisted with animosity.

Despite the agony of knowing the truth about Shaun's feelings for him, Marcus had to know everything. "So, what did Aliyah do to you, Shaun?"

Shaun stared at him for several minutes. He puffed on the

cigar and walked in a circle. "I don't like people messing up my plans. Bitch gets uppity with me. Where's the gratitude?"

"So you killed her." A cold sense of desolation spread through Marcus as he watched Shaun shrug. "What are you going to do with me now? I mean, you can't just let me walk out of here."

"No proof, bro." Shaun shrugged again. The ghost of his brotherhood for Marcus appeared in his light brown eyes. "I was hoping you'd be down."

"No way, Shaun."

The five men moved toward Marcus at the same time. Shaun lifted one hand, and they stopped. "Look, man. I'm into serious debt with some dangerous dudes, but it's worth the risk. I'm talking millions, international-type business arrangements."

"Meaning drugs or guns, probably both." Marcus glanced at the men. They all had the look of organized gangstas into big cash. They wore real gold chains and expensive clothes.

"I ain't no street dealer, brother! This is me, Shaun." He tossed the cigar on the concrete floor. "Look, a few of my boys got stupid and lifted small stuff. I let 'em slide. You know, a perk, so to speak. I was into the computer systems linked up to government sites."

"You talk too damn much," a short, burly man to Shaun's left barked.

Shaun shot a heated glance at the man. "Marcus is in, fool. Some of his clients have federal security clearance."

"He already said he ain't interested. He don't walk outta here. The deal is off."

Shaun looked back at Marcus. "See, now you gotta go with me. C'mon, man. Don't be dumb."

"Right, I should let you use me some more."

Marcus had nothing left to lose. He punched Shaun and dashed toward a window. Two of the men caught him and pinned his arms before he could break the glass. A fourth man punched Marcus in the stomach, causing him to double over. The men snapped him back. Pain ripped through him until Marcus saw white flashes. He groaned. Shaun recovered his footing and rubbed the reddish spot on his face.

"I gave you one last chance, brother. It's outta my hands."

The door to the garage exploded open. "Don't move, Shaun. You ain't my friend, okay?"

Dayna held her Glock pistol with both hands. Five uniformed police officers stood on either side behind her, their weapons drawn.

Marcus glanced at one of the men holding him. "Get off me," he managed to pant, despite the throbbing in his midsection. They lifted their arms in surrender.

"You brought the police? You wrong, man." Shaun stared at Marcus with a malevolent scowl when an officer led him away. "My lawyer will have me out soon. I'll see you later, Marcus," he yelled over his shoulder.

Dayna studied Marcus for a few seconds, then lowered her gun. "I was hoping you weren't gonna be dumb enough to meet up with him."

Marcus tried to stand straight, winced, and decided walking bent over wasn't so bad. "I was hoping you weren't dumb enough to lose me with all the turns I made."

"Right, like you knew I was behind you," she said with a snort. She slipped the gun into her shoulder holster.

"Dark blue Chevrolet Lumina with a dent in the side." Marcus wheezed slowly to get air and avoid more agony.

"C'mon, smart-ass. We need lots of answers." Dayna nodded for him to walk ahead of her.

"I'll be glad to come to your party, Detective. I've just got one phone call to make." Marcus was careful to show her the slim cell phone before reaching for it.

Her eyes narrowed. "Your lawyer?"

"My lady."

Nicole and her father stared at each other across the boardroom of Summers Security, LLC. Stanton glanced away when one of the board members approached. He wore a tight expression. Nicole suppressed a sigh. For once she wanted them to act more like a family than a corporation. Apparently she wanted too much. Russell stood ten feet away, resisting another cousin's attempt to mollify him. Jolene left his side and approached Nicole.

"You'll screw up again," she murmured through the smile she wore for show.

"Maybe. But on my worst day you can't touch me," Nicole replied in a low voice with an equally fake smile.

"Bitch." Jolene glared at Nicole. She rearranged her features into a smile again when another relative approached. "Aunt Philly, I didn't get a chance to say hello at the AKA charity ball last month."

With a sigh of disgust, Nicole walked away. She was at least glad this hellish board meeting was over. Now if only she could think of a civil, yet effective, way of clearing them all out of here. Her father extricated himself from one of his elderly aunts and headed over to her.

"Here we go," she muttered.

"Relax, I'm right behind you."

Her irritation melted at the sound of the deep baritone. Nicole glanced up into Marcus's rich, chocolate brown eyes. "Thank goodness. Otherwise there might have been bloodshed in here."

Marcus smiled. "That kind of behavior is expected of us ghetto rats."

"These high-class folks can be just as cold-blooded," she said in a quick undertone before her father arrived.

"Hello, Marcus. I want you to know I have the greatest respect for your ability. What I did was to protect Nicole and the company," Stanton said and stuck out his hand.

Nicole raised an eyebrow. "Protect me, huh?"

"Yes, Nikki. I certainly hope you don't hold a grudge. You have to admit the situation didn't look good. You're my little girl, but business is business."

"The unique Summers perspective." Nicole gazed at him for a few moments, then smiled. "I needed the rest before I took over again, I suppose."

Stanton threw back his head and laughed loudly. Russell and Jolene glanced at them sharply with twin frowns. Other relatives smiled with relief.

"Damn if you didn't come in swinging just the way I would have, Nikki. You kicked my butt. Never got such a whipping before," Stanton said.

"Think of it this way, Daddy. Getting spanked builds character." Nicole beamed at him.

"What the—" Stanton burst out laughing again. He stopped long enough to plant a kiss on her cheek before walking off again. "She's going to take this place over the top," he announced to those nearby.

"Can we have a moment?" Marcus pointed toward her office.

Nicole nodded and led the way. Once the door closed, she turned right into his arms. "People will talk."

"I don't think they have much left to say at this point," Marcus replied, and kissed her.

After one hard knock Russell swung open the door. "The future of Summers Security in the hands of a former juvenile delinquent and an amateur."

"I wanted to discuss your future with the company. Might as well do it now, since you seem so eager to see me." Nicole gestured for him to enter.

"I can't be fired."

"I could with effort, but I won't have to. You're going to resign." Nicole glanced at Marcus.

"You're crazy if you think I'd make things easy for you!" Russell said.

"No, you're going to make it easy for yourself." Nicole walked to Russell and adjusted his Yves Saint Laurent silk tie.

He brushed her hands away. "What are you talking about?"

"You're more devious than I gave you credit for. You knew Aliyah was using you. As long as it made Marcus and then me look bad, you didn't care. Plus you got her and wild sex as a bonus." Nicole made a circle around him, then went to her desk.

"You really *are* crazy." Russell gave a short laugh.

"The police don't think so. Aliyah decided to blow off Shaun." Nicole leaned against her desk.

"Except Aliyah didn't realize Shaun was on the hook with some major league criminals," Marcus put in. "He couldn't afford to have his access cut off to all those computer networks. Aliyah thought they were stealing liquor, cigarettes, jewelry, stuff like that."

"Shaun didn't tell her everything," Nicole said.

"You let her think she was fooling you. The loss wasn't that big. You figured once Nicole and I were out, you could put a stop to her little scheme." Marcus studied Russell with his head to one side.

"Interesting the way you two fire each other's imagination." Russell put a hand in the pocket of his pants. "You should write a script for one of those cheap made-for-TV movies."

"You let her get inside information on our customers. By the way, I had Andre do a forensic sweep of your computer. The only real way to destroy data on a hard drive is to chop the darn thing up with an axe," Nicole said with a smile.

Russell's smirk wilted. "Anyone could have used my desktop."

"Nice try, but you've got a real sophisticated encrypted password set up. Not so hard for a whiz like Andre, though," Marcus replied.

"You used an online payment service to hire an out-of-state private investigator. That's how you found out Aliyah was lying. Once Marcus and I uncovered the extent of the thefts, you had to stop her."

"You found out about her and Shaun, right?" Marcus stood with both arms loose at his sides.

"Then to add insult to injury, Aliyah decided to blackmail you. You got over her death real fast for a guy so deeply in love," Nicole countered. "Either way, you killed her."

"You're living in a dream world, Nicole. Marcus was all over her that day in his office. He and his best friend Shaun were in on the thefts. I wouldn't be surprised if they were sharing Aliyah," Russell snarled.

A series of booming knocks on the door made them all jump. Detectives Holmes and O'Connor came in without waiting for an answer. Holmes glanced at Nicole, Marcus, and, finally, Russell.

"You've got some explaining to do, Mr. Summers," Holmes said.

"Nicole is trying to protect Marcus, and he wants to bail out his pal!"

Nicole's father came in from the conference room. "What is going on in here?"

Uncle Lionel scowled over his shoulder. "Oh, crap! The police again."

"Uncle Stanton, Nicole has lost her mind. She's trying to save her lover boy by pointing the police at me," Russell said as he spread out his arms. "Well, it won't work."

"Here's a search warrant that includes your car. A spray of luminol shows traces of blood." Holmes slapped the warrant into one of Russell's outstretched hands.

"I want my lawyer. Now!" Russell shouted.

"Sure. We follow the rules, pal." O'Connor snapped a handcuff on Russell's other hand and pushed him out the door. Holmes gave them all a curt nod and followed.

"Somebody better tell me what the hell just happened," Stanton thundered. "Nicole?"

"Shaun Jackson beat up Aliyah in a rage, but he didn't kill her. Russell finished her off. Marcus was right all along," Nicole said, and looked at him.

Marcus shook his head. "Not really. Shaun isn't the man I thought he was."

"I'm so sorry, babe." Nicole looped her arm through one of his.

"You're telling me Russell killed that girl?" Stanton's mouth went slack with horror. "Oh, God. This is going to be a PR nightmare."

"How the hell are we going to spin a murder?" Uncle Lionel clapped a palm to his forehead.

"Maybe we should think about what pushed Russell to be so callous," Nicole said in a steely voice. "This family has some soul-searching to do, if you ask me."

"Nicole figured this whole thing out. Incredible deductive reasoning, Nikki."

"You mean inductive reasoning, Stan," Uncle Lionel corrected. He snapped his fingers. "Our brilliant young CEO tracks down the breach in security and solves a murder. She didn't stop even when the answers led to her own family. Could it work?"

"We don't have a choice, Lionel," Stanton said with a deep sigh. "You've got another big hurdle, Nikki. But we're behind you." He and her uncle strode out, talking over strategy.

"So much for soul-searching," Nicole quipped. She turned to Marcus. "I don't see how a security company can survive this series of disasters."

"We'll have to reinvent ourselves if necessary. Actually, your Uncle Lionel's approach isn't bad at all." Marcus put his arms around her waist.

"What?" Nicole gaped at him.

"Listen, you did one helluva detecting job. Big corporations pay reformed thieves and computer crackers to help them design security procedures. Summers Security could do the same." Marcus grinned at her horrified expression.

"Oh, no, you're starting to think like them." Nicole rested her forehead against his chest.

"Some of that upper-class cunning was bound to rub off on me. You body slammed poor Russell the way a real player from the 'hood might have."

Nicole gazed up at him with a soft smile. "Some ghetto smarts was bound to rub off on me."

"Not a bad combination." He lovingly brushed a tendril of hair from her cheek.

"Not a bad combination at all." Nicole kissed him long and hard.

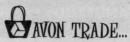